DARK HORSE

DARK
HORSE

Doug Richardson

AVON BOOKS  NEW YORK

AVON BOOKS
A division of
The Hearst Corporation
1350 Avenue of the Americas
New York, New York 10019

Copyright © 1997 by Doug Richardson
Interior design by Rhea Braunstein
Visit our website at **http://AvonBooks.com**
ISBN: 0-380-97314-6

Library of Congress Cataloging in Publication Data:

Richardson, Doug, 1959–
   Dark horse / Doug Richardson.—1st ed.
      p.   cm.
I. Title.
PS3568.I31743D37   1997   96-25521
813'.54—dc20   CIP

First Avon Books Printing: February 1997

AVON TRADEMARK REG. U.S. PAT. OFF. AND IN OTHER COUNTRIES, MARCA
REGISTRADA, HECHO EN U.S.A.

Printed in the U.S.A.

FIRST EDITION

QPM   10   9   8   7   6   5   4   3   2   1

for Karen

ACKNOWLEDGMENTS

I'm grateful to those who, without their grace,
wit, wisdom, friendship, and encouragement,
this book would never have been written.

Karen Adams, Lou Aronica, George Woods Baker,
Sharon Bernhardt, Bill Carrick, Rae Corbett, Jim Crabbe, Gary Cramer,
Zachary Feuer, Carrie Feron, Lucas Foster, Mark Frost,
Leonard Goldberg, Robert Gottlieb, Marge Herring, James David Hinton,
Wendy Japhet, Michael Lynton, Ron Mardigian, David O'Connor,
Dennis Palumbo, Gary Ross, Stephanie Ross, William Saracino, Jr.,
Tom Schulman, Mike Simpson, Cathy Tarr, Allison Thomas,
Alan Wertheimer, Harley Williams,

and, of course, my wife.

PART

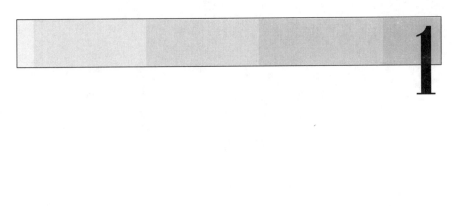

1

The recipe was simple.

A burlap sack, twenty-five feet of nylon rope, and a cash purchase of four live rabbits from the local livestock supply. With the ingredients assembled, the animals' throats were slit, the twitching carcasses dumped into the burlap sack, and the rope used to securely tie the sack closed.

Rabbit stew, thought the cook.

He climbed into his saddle. Small and slender, he was barely a wisp on the nag's back. He checked his watch and patiently waited for the dogs to come.

And come, they did. Right after sunset, on time and howling like the devil. There would be two of them. Both hounds, leading the old man on his Tuesday hunt. They would pick up the smell of the dead rabbits, key on the scent, and set a new heading.

Sure as shit, the old man would follow.

The rider spurred his rented horse and cut a path through the woods, dragging the burlap sack behind him in a snakelike pattern. Not too complicated, though. He didn't want to confuse the dogs. Just the old man. And the sooner, the better, he figured. It would be dark soon. That meant the polls would be closing back in Texas. The rider would want to make phone calls and hear the good news.

But there was work left to do.

As the burlap sack bumped and tumbled along the wooded floor, dragged behind the ever-quickening horse, it marked leaves and dead-wood with the deadly rabbit perfume. The dogs would soon lock on and give chase.

The game would begin.

Those damn bitches were too far ahead!

The old man cursed the coming darkness. Night was falling on the familiar woods, and the old man was too fat and too drunk to kick the horse into a full-on chase. He'd surely fall. The tree branches were too low to duck at any kind of speed.

But the damn dogs. Without a tight rein, they'd be sure to run all the way to the next county and tree some poor house cat. The old man urged the animal on past a trot into a canter, turned the horse too sharply, and scraped a tree trunk. The bark took some skin off his arm. It didn't hurt too badly, though. The alcohol had certain medicinal effects, taking away the pain and the lousy memories along with it. Had he knocked back any more of the hard stuff that after-noon, the old man was certain he himself would never find his way back home, let alone the poor dogs, who, as smart as he'd sometimes brag them to be, turned dumb once they'd locked on to an animal's scent.

Dumb-ass hounds.

As the howling grew more distant, worry set in. The pale blue of day had vanished underneath a thickening blanket of branches. In the woods it may as well have been night. Trees became shadows. Brush, a fog to be navigated. The old man knew about fog. Had grown up with it in a Gulf-side city far from where he was at that moment. He'd learned to negotiate the fog along with the local politics, becoming a force so great, some likened it to a hurricane. And though the roots had come undone long ago, transplanted onto a horse farm next to that Virginia wood, back home the name "Hurricane" had stuck.

Primary Tuesday. The good people of that Texas Gulf-side city would cast their votes for the old barnstormer, just as they'd done for the past twenty years. Didn't matter a lick that he wasn't even inside state lines. He was the incumbent. And he was unbeatable.

Instead of prepping for the usual electoral bows, the old man was drunk, lost, and chasing a couple of dumb-ass hounds who wouldn't know a fox from a squirrel . . .

. . . from a burlap sack full of dead rabbits.

The old man heaved. He could feel his lunch coming up with the day's booze. The horse returned to a trot. She didn't like the darkness or the trees. She was a thoroughbred, reared and trained in Kentucky for open fields of turf and wildflowers. Hardly the breeding for Virginia foxhunts. But this wasn't so much a foxhunt as it was a *dog hunt*. And the dogs were winning.

Branches stung the old man's face. *Enough already*. He reined the animal to a halt, took off his Stetson, which was, other than himself, his singular holdover from his home state, and lent his ear to the woods. Listening would tell which way his dogs had run. At first it was dead quiet, save for the pounding of his leaded heart and the horse working the bit. What followed was a rustle of leaves as the wind carried over the trees. Then, fainter than that, the dogs. The familiar yowling came from his left. The horse knew as much and turned forty degrees toward the sound. The old man listened once more and thought maybe they were circling back. On the chase. A fox, maybe. After all, squirrels hide in trees. Rabbits in holes. And foxes run.

Bearing some sixty degrees even farther ahead of the dogs, the old man dug his heels back into the thoroughbred and charged ahead into the darkness. Louder were the dogs. Still moving left. Faster, too. He could hear them like a slow-moving truck across an intersection, tracking from right to left. The old man dropped his head under a low-hanging branch. As quick as a prizefighter, he thought. The alcohol was wearing down under the onslaught of adrenaline. Blurred vision turned into a tunnel effect. *Aw, to hell with the darkness,* the old man snarled. *We're huntin'.*

Yahoo.

George "Hurricane" Hammond fit well into the saddle, his hefty frame resting on a back strong enough for two men. And if any fellah were to ask the old man when he'd begun his day's drinking, Hurricane would have quickly resurrected a story about his daddy, his fifteenth birthday, and a Mexican whore from San Antonio. The story never failed to produce a laugh from the listener, but in fact it demonstrated his usual and practiced sleight of hand in the art of changing-the-damn-subject.

The drinking? That was a problem and the old man knew it— figured he would eventually die from it. Give it up, though? Never. It religiously stopped the pain from the loneliness life had served Hurricane some twenty years back when he'd lost his one and only wife, Renatta, to leukemia. If the truth were told, *that's* when he had started drinking. He hadn't really stopped since. And it kept him from nothing. Not working. Not raising the roof at public functions. And certainly not from his Tuesday evening foxhunts.

A typical day for the Texas congressman, whether at the Virginia farm, Washington, D.C., or on his home-state terra firma, would begin with delegating assignments to his various aides and assistants. The earlier the start, the faster the work, the speedier the finish, the sooner he could drink. If The House was in session, he'd hit the floor juiced, greasing the opposition with rehearsed homilies and C-SPAN-savvy sound bites.

"Prep me, prop me, and point me at the camera," he'd tell his staff. "And don't gimme no guff about the booze. It makes me loose. It makes me happy. And it makes for better Goddamn government."

And the *boozing* usually began at lunch.

One administrative assistant described Hurricane's style as "100 proof politics," named for the alcohol content one would normally expect in the famed congressman's blood. The *real* day would start with a Bloody Mary lunch with a willing lobbyist, followed by an afternoon in the corner booths of a variety of Washington lounges. Then there were always the nightly cocktail receptions and black-tie dinners. Thereafter, bed and the hope of a dreamless sleep. The next day would begin at 5:30 A.M.

One hundred proof. Yahoo.

But on Election Tuesday in Texas, the bottle nipping had started earlier than usual. By late afternoon—despite the warmth that his old friend and campaign manager, Marshall Lambeer, had brought to the party—Hurricane's warm alcoholic glow had turned malicious.

The polls for the Texas primary would soon close. The incumbent congressman was expected to carry eighty-plus percent of the Republican majority. So popular was Hurricane that he didn't even need to be there to take home the prize nomination. He was an arrogant bastard, all right. And with good reason.

The old man couldn't see the dogs, but he could hear them racing ahead in an utterly untrained pursuit. He found a patch of clearing and the last bit of blue sky overhead. He looked up, but everything swirled. The booze was fighting back. The adrenaline was in retreat. Yet the dogs howled ahead. *It must be a fox,* thought Hurricane. It was too fast. The dogs too sure of their course. After all, they had their instincts, as Hurricane had his. Heels digging in again, he galloped the horse across the clearing, plunging into wooded darkness again.

"That's far enough!" he growled when he found the howling had turned silent.

At first he thought they'd gotten away from him again. But the familiar sound wasn't distant. It was nonexistent. The woods were quiet again. Just darkness and trees and the strange sound of sweat clogging the old man's ear.

"Goddamn it-all."

Hurricane cleared out the goo in his ear canal and gave the mare a good kick, and she shifted into an easy trot.

"The little shits!"

Silence meant one thing: They'd actually caught the damn fox. And now they were somewhere nearby, devouring it like packed carnivores. *Regressive beasts,* he thought. They should know better.

Squeals punctured the wooded silence, and it wasn't a hound's normal yowl. One of the dogs was in pain, wailing for help in the not-so-far distance. Panicked, the old man wheeled the horse toward the mournful cry and, without so much as a second thought, brought a long rein down across the mare's flank. The horse got the message and sprang into a sudden gallop, almost leaving the old man in the dirt.

A horse trail switched back and forth through the trees, requiring a speeding rider to lean with every turn. But the alcohol surging in the old man's bloodstream placed a numbing vise on his motor memory. To regain his balance he reached for the saddle horn and found none. It was an English saddle. Hurricane hadn't ridden western since last year's annual Fourth of July parade down the famous Strand of his hometown, Cathedral Island. English was the tack of Virginia, and hell if that wasn't what Hurricane wanted. English horses and English saddles. That's what the upper-crusters rode. Then so would he. But damn it if right now he didn't want a western horn on which to hang his overbloated body.

Another hanging branch raked the congressman's puffy face as the horse cut another turn in the path, homing on the lamenting dog. The trail had become a tunnel, ever constricting underneath sprawling oaks and willows. He wanted to call for help, but his stomach had once again turned and clotted his throat with his lunch of salami and cheese. *It was the last vodka,* thought Hurricane, *that was cutting his reflexes.* He damned Marshall for letting him drink it. His arms were stiff across his chest as he hunched over the animal's neck, feeling the cropped mane stabbing his forehead with every surge.

Help me.

The reins had long slipped from his grip. The two leather straps dangled dangerously from the horse's bit, knotted together at the ends. The mane left little for him to hang on to except the horse's neck, leaving others to wonder if maybe that was what caused the accident.

The old man plunged his weight onto the mare's neck, forcing the poor beast to dip her head until one of those galloping, out-stretched hooves caught in the knotted reins. The animal hurtled to the earth, and Hurricane followed.

How the old man crawled from the wreckage of his accident was beyond his recollection. Consciousness returned only after he'd managed to prop himself up against a nearby oak. The mist that was his vision lifted with barely enough detail to make out his poor, twisted mount. Neck broken, but still alive. Her nostrils flaring, clearing leaves with each heavy exhalation.

Nor could Hurricane move. His neck was stiff. Blindly feeling down along his left leg, he came upon a protruding bone. His femur, decided the old man. The cotton of his trousers felt wet, warm, and sticky with blood. But feeling was nil.

The Goddamn vodka.

He laughed at his own dumb self, then coughed blood. And though ribs had obviously pierced his lungs, hell, he seemed alive and fit enough to survive until somebody found him. Or at least until the alcohol in his bloodstream held the inevitable pain at bay. After that, the old man didn't want to think about it. If he didn't talk, he could breathe. He tied his belt just above his thigh-high injury for an adequate tourniquet. That would do until dawn, when his staff would arrive, discover he was missing, and send out a search party.

Until then, he reasoned to let his eyes close and conserve his energy. He tried to let his thoughts drift away from the woods and all the way to Texas. The polls would soon be closed. After which he would be declared the winner of the Republican nomination. The winner of the Democratic primary, some poor, nameless nobody, would rejoice in his meager victory.

The TV and newspapers would tout the opposition candidate as a *dark horse*. They always did. Every two damn years. A new face. A new challenge.

Followed by a landslide defeat.

But those media folks would give the candidate free publicity. Pictures, newspaper articles, and on-camera interviews galore. The candidate would get a brief feeling of confidence. Power even. Then the *real campaign* would begin. The Hurricane Hammond political machine would gas up and slowly roll over the enemy, crushing the poor bastard's hope of political ascension forever.

Hurricane, you arrogant old fart.

If he'd only gone to Texas, put in his obligatory campaign-day appearances, maybe he wouldn't have gotten drunk. Or gone hunting. Maybe he wouldn't have been paralyzed there against that damn tree, looking out over the darkness and his dying damn horse.

Serves me right.

The old man laughed and spit up more blood. That one hurt. So he made a pact with himself not to think amusing thoughts. Try to sleep, maybe. Morning will come soon enough. Then the rescue. A short hospital stay. Notes of health and encouragement. Gifts of fine scotch and vodka from all those loving lobbyists. Recuperation. And eventually a good-luck call from the President of the United States himself. Then back to business.

The old man forced his eyes closed. That's when he heard the hounds again. Closing fast. His eyes snapped open and peered against the blackness, finding a light swirling at the edge of his periphery. Painfully he swiveled his neck to the right. He instantly recognized the beam of a flashlight tracing the floor of the wood. He caught glimpses of his dogs, leashed, and tugging along a man.

Those dumb hounds! But maybe not so dumb after all, the old man thought. They were coming for him, bringing help at the end of their leads. A little man with a flashlight.

The rider.

The hounds yodeled as they closed the gap, getting good sniffs off their master's scent and happy to be reunited. The rider, though, yanked on those leashes and, twenty yards from the old man, tied the dogs to another tree. The dogs grew louder.

"Hush up," said the rider. "I want your boss to hear me." The dogs didn't understand the command. Nor did the rider seem to care. With the flashlight held at his side, he approached as a shadow. "You okay, old man?"

Hurricane didn't speak, fearing another hacking fit accompanied by blood and sharp pains. He was saved. He simply shook his head weakly.

"Gonna live, huh?" said the rider.

He nodded this time.

"I'll hand ya this. You ride pretty good for a drunk old fucker." The rider knelt. "Figured you for a tumble a good thirty minutes ago. Those hounds of yours are plumb tuckered."

The old man didn't understand. The words were a jumble of sound and garble. The alcohol, maybe? Or even the clots in his ears? When would this little savior call for help? Did he have a cell phone? Everyone nowadays had a cell phone. Why hadn't he called 911?

"I need to go to the hospital," choked Hurricane. As expected, the hacking followed. The worst pain yet.

"Sure you need a hospital. Need more than that, I reckon," said the rider, his face still nothing more than a shadow. "Betcha wish you was in Texas."

Texas?

Hurricane recognized the accent, instantly wondering what other luckless Texan would be found in a Virginia wood after nightfall. Was it fate? Chance? But hell, a savior's a savior, no matter the flavor of a man's voice.

"Need help," gasped the old man.

"I know, I know. First things first. Can you move?" The old man shook his head. Nodding in affirmation, the rider dug the flashlight into the dirt, directing the beam into Hurricane's face. "Well, whaddayou know? It's Hurricane Hammond in the flesh. Son of a gun!" But the surprise in the little man's voice sounded disingenuous. Hurricane recognized bull when he heard it.

Never bullshit a bullshitter.

The rider put on a pair of rubber gloves, then reached into his back pocket and removed what looked like a wallet or a small purse. A zipper sound followed. The old man couldn't see the movements, but hoped the savior had some kind of emergency medical training. Military, even. After all, the shadowy figure sported the short crop of most of the military men he had known and supported with congressional votes over the past decades. Hurricane was red, white, and blue—all the way to his marrow.

Then came the syringe. Its needle gleamed when it caught the flashlight's beam and startled the old man. "Oh, don't be scared. Just a little something to help you along," echoed the rider's words between the drumbeats of Hurricane's heart. And as if to distract, he spoke in the practiced tone of a nurse with a nervous patient. "So who'd you vote for today? Absentee, I'll betcha."

"Me," he whispered.

"Yeah. Me too," said the little man, gently touching a bloody scrape around the old man's neck. "What about that guy Mitch Dutton? Know him? He's gonna get the Democratic nod."

Mitch Dutton. That's the fellah's name. He'll surely be the challenger in

November. This year's dark horse. Marshall's spoken well of him. Too bad he'll spend the race as designated loser.

"Now look up this way," said the little man, raising his left hand for Hurricane to follow. "This shouldn't hurt at all."

With that, the syringe plunged into the old man's bulging vein, followed by a volley of air that sucked back into the old man's heart.

"Betcha wanna know who killed ya," whispered the rider, picking up the flashlight and shining it into his own eyes. Otherworldly. Cobalt blue.

The old man's heart gulped with air, losing the prime as the ventricles grasped for liquid. The hiccup turned into an instant heart attack. He wheezed for some air, his arms flailing.

The rider withdrew, syringe in hand, and remotely observed the final moments of the great man's life. The cardiac arrest was instant and killed quickly. Hurricane's eyeballs glazed and rolled back and his body contorted in one last painful convulsion. Yet all the rider cared to consider was whether or not he'd been seen. If, in that brief moment, the old man had actually gotten a good look at his killer, peered into the eyes and seen the man who'd finally beat him. Or if he'd felt the power of his prolonged incumbency diminish along with life itself.

Heady stuff, thought the rider.

2

"I accept your nomination," muttered the candidate back to the TV. Shallow breath. A classic sign of nerves.

It was shortly after 9:00 P.M. when Cathedral City's Channel 9 first reported the news. Mitch Dutton, local attorney and community activist, would be the Democratic nominee for the thirty-first congressional district of Texas. As he sat at the edge of the hotel bed, remote control in hand, watching the returns, Mitch could hardly come to grips with it himself. He'd made the first, all-important stride toward public office.

Congressional nominee Mitch Dutton.

Putting the evident jitters in check, he continued to rehearse the all-important crowd pleaser of a line. "I accept your nomination . . . I accept your . . . I accept *your* nomination," he practiced.

The room was dark, save for the bathroom light left on from his shower. Once again, with the remote in hand, Mitch started switching channels. All the news programs had their own snazzy sets and special election graphics. And he could see that all the reporters spewed the same kind of newsspeak—a kind of surface-to-air rationale—A Much Ado About the Very Obvious: Mitch Dutton was the nominee. He'd beaten a crowded field of local politicos and hopeful opportunists with a modicum of skill, luck, honesty, and looks, and maybe he'd said a good thing or two in the process that the voters had taken in earnest—something for the people.

After all, he was their candidate. Every pundit and TV twinkie seemed to say so. As did some of the print media. Mitch Dutton. The People's Candidate. Ready to do battle with the Republican nominee and House incumbent of twenty-eight years, George "Hurricane" Hammond. The Great Wall of Will. Not a single Democratic challenger had pulled more than forty percent of the popular vote against him since the latter end of the sixties. The challenge would be impossible. Nobody expected Mitch could really win. Except, maybe, for the candidate himself. Hurricane was unbeatable.

"I'm going to do it my way," Mitch had persisted in God-knows-how-many interviews. "How will I beat the incumbent? I'm going to define the debate. I'm going to bring new ideas to issues that matter to our community, as well as America."

As if the media really cared. All they could see was the matchup, which they would play up as the fight of the decade, sell the commercial time, then toss off Mitch's expected loss in some matter-of-fact, nobody-really-thought-he-could-beat-old-Hurricane eulogy.

"I'm here to show that a man with character can win," he continued, talking back to the TV, as if to see if the words would convince himself, let alone the thousand or so supporters who were waiting downstairs. He continued without his note cards, "I'm here to show that campaign promises are not meant to be broken. But kept as a public trust. And that in the months ahead, instead of lowering the level of discourse, we can rise, each and every one of us, to this occasion with the responsibility of new ideas and embrace a better, more prosperous—"

"Ten minutes, Mitch," interrupted the familiar voice from the other side of the door, breaking his train of thought. They were all out there. His whole staff, waiting for him throughout the rest of the suite. At his request, they'd left him alone to gather his thoughts. "Mitch. Still breathing?"

"Ten minutes," repeated the candidate, "and I'm breathing just fine."

Ten minutes and he'd be making the speech of his life. Live on all local channels, telling the good people of Cathedral why an unknown local lawyer deserved to occupy a seat on Capitol Hill. It would be a rally to arms against the evils of incumbency. He turned back to the TV. Surfing the channels for one last time. Yes sir, no doubt, in ten minutes or so he'd be on every one of those channels, throwing down the gauntlet. The fight would be on.

"Hey, Mitch!" rang the voice again. "Fitz says you got about twenty hands to shake before you go on."

"Be right there," he assured, still staring at the television. It was then that he noted a trace of sweat running from his temple to his cheek. The fire in his belly was leaking through his calm veneer. He called back, "Is my wife out there?"

"Gina's holding her hand in the bathroom." The voice at the door belonged to Murray Levy, law associate and the Dutton campaign's resident twenty-something. A buttoned-down boy who was Generation X's answer to tomorrow's political mover. Mitch thought he was a good kid with a good heart. Just what his campaign called for.

"Is she sick?" Mitch asked through the door. "You know, she's got no stomach for this stuff." He knew his wife about as well as any husband of more than ten years could. Running for office wasn't her idea. He knew she'd secretly hoped he'd lose so all this would end. Now she'd have to look forward to five months of more of the same. *Possibly even worse,* he thought. Campaigns had a tendency to get a little nasty, but George Hammond's campaigns could get downright dirty. He hoped his wife would survive it.

"She's a little shaky," Murray called back. "Gina gave her a shot of Cuervo, so I figure she'll be okeydokey by show time."

Five minutes. He switched off the TV, slipped back into his shoes, and pulled on his jacket. Facing the mirror, he saw a fit man closing on forty years. Slender. Six feet. Handsome enough. Traces of his father with his thick, blondish hair and brown-sugar eyes. Boyish dimples when he smiled, aptly named Mr. Proctor and Mr. Gamble by a college roommate seeking a career in advertising. Mitch was campaign material, all right. And he knew that in the right circumstances he could sell soap, salvation, or even ice to an Eskimo. A possible liability? He sometimes wondered if the package looked better than the actual product.

"I'm here to say that a man with character can win," said Mitch back to the man in the mirror.

With closer inspection, and only minutes before show time, he found himself examining his two physical defects. One, a broken nose from an errant grounder while playing high school baseball. The other was the scar just under his chin where a boat hook had grazed him at fifteen. Took just that many stitches, too. Fifteen, he recalled. The light surgery took just enough skin and hair follicles to make it impossible for the candidate to cover it up with a beard. Hair just wouldn't grow over the scar. So it remained a character mark. Toughened his look, Connie sometimes said. Made him less of a Ken doll.

"You look too damn serious," complained the candidate. "Lighten up. Smile at the cameras."

Because you're not supposed to win, Mitchell.

"Gotta go, Mitch," called out Murray from the other side of the door, "before Fitz has a coronary."

"Just one minute."

Losing. Or losing gracefully. That would be a hard pill for him to swallow. He'd never lost a damn thing in his life. And when losing was a possibility, he simply wouldn't play. The campaign game, though. That wasn't about winning or losing. It was about stepping in the ring and throwing a few punches just to get your name on the next fight card. Hammond was a heavyweight *and* a champion. He would surely whip Dutton's ass. Everybody said so.

Everybody but Mitch.

Tonight, though, he was still a winner. Pristine and untarnished. His record intact. Undefeated: 1 and 0. And tomorrow? Well, anything could happen in a campaign. He might get lucky. The incumbent could stumble. Or even better, Mitch might just surprise everyone and pull out the upset of the decade with a brilliant campaign. Because beyond the good looks and camera-ready posture, Mitch had *a plan.*

Candidate Mitch Dutton would take the high ground, riding it all the way to Congress.

"Mitch, please!" urged Murray, smart enough to stay on his side of that door.

"Coming," he answered, hardly moving from the mirror.

It was the candidate's opinion that the not-so-honorable George Hammond had long since forgotten what the high ground looked like, let alone the coast of Texas. And though Mitch respected the incumbent, he'd come in recent years to see the congressman take the public trust for granted, preferring to remain ensconced on his Virginia horse farm.

But the old man was dead.

Mitch didn't know. Hell, nobody knew. Or would know for a good while.

The high ground. That's all that counted.

With that credo in mind, and resolved to win, he straightened his tie and checked his breast pocket for his note cards. They were all there, neatly stacked and ordered for his speech. It was show time.

The ballroom at the Cathedral Island Hilton was big enough for most functions. Weddings. Meetings. And the occasional soiree. The windowless hall was jam-packed with political revelers and, as many would later note, a large contingent of that same twenty-something crowd that Murray Levy was a part of. The obvious attraction being Mitch Dutton. To them, *their* candidate was *different.* He understood them. At least he played it that way. They were all dressed in the requisite political collage of red, white, and blue. Mitchell Dutton's name glued to just about every surface. That, too, was Murray's job. The sniping, an act normally reserved for vandals and graffiti artists. A political snipe tries to plaster the landscape with placards and bumper stickers. In this case, it was wall to wall with MITCHELL DUTTON: A CHANGE IS COMING, there for the cameras, TV, and others. Not a single lens could possibly escape the message.

It was all money well spent, figured Fitz Kolatch, Mitch's rotund, bearded campaign manager and resident Master of Spin. As he waited upon the dais, spiked legs performing a balancing act, he glanced at his watch from time to time, poring over the amassing crowd of young folk brandishing *all those blessed signs.* Money hadn't been easy in this race. Beg for it, spend it, and beg for it again. But now, with the nomination, the party would be kicking into the kitty. So what's overdoing it on the sniping going to hurt? It looks good on camera and Mitch'll sure get a charge when he sees all these cheering folks waving his name in the air.

"Where the hell is he?" barked Fitz into the walkie-talkie.

The radio crackled back with Murray's voice. "Candidate's en route."

"En route from where?" he snapped. "The can?" He'd told the news stations they'd have his candidate for ten o'clock straight up. "And where the hell's Gina with the missus? Goddamn it if a woman can't go to the ladies' room without it turning into major fucking surgery!"

Foregoing his trademarked Doc Martens for his first wingtips, Murray appeared at Fitz's side in time to soothe the oncoming tirade to a muffled rant. Fitz had started the campaign loathing Murray, seeing him as a latent boy toy, representing the godless generation of slackers and crack heads. Yet in recent months, he had come to admire the young man's tireless spirit. Murray was a new kind of political gonzo.

"Mrs. Dutton's hooked up with Mitch in the kitchen," answered Murray, no need for the radio this time. "He's getting some honey 'n' tea for his throat. They should be right out."

As if on cue, Fitz spun, snapping his fingers at the riser filled with TV cameras. A blaze of light ignited the dais. A band kicked into a timeworn, patriotic tune as if it were a fresh arrangement, and the young crowd revved itself into a preconcert frenzy.

As she threaded a path through the hotel kitchen, Connie Dutton squeezed her husband's hand. The roar of the crowd echoed even in there, enough, it would seem, to shake the hanging pots and pans. To make things worse, the tequila hadn't relaxed her; if anything, it had put an uncomfortable buzz in her head. Life as she knew it was changing—even spinning, she might say. At thirty-four, she was five years younger than Mitch, a gulf that sometimes felt like ten—like a child who'd been held back two grades, always trying to catch up and never, ever allowed sit with the grown-ups.

"Nervous?" she asked him, hoping for an answer that would ease her own apprehension.

"What do you think?" he confirmed for her, noticing her hair as if for the first time. Short. Black. Easy. "What did you do to your hair?"

"I cut it."

"Damn right you did."

"You like it?"

"I'm not worried about me."

Mitch was running for Congress, and tonight he was halfway there. Congress meant Washington. And Washington meant they would have to leave the small, sunny Texas Island. A thought Connie could hardly bear. With no real, nineties kind of job to hold her in South Texas other than caring for the house and gardens, she would have no excuse but to follow him or separate.

And now he was worried about the haircut.

So there she was, playing catch-up once again. Hanging on to his hand for dear life as they eased toward the Hilton ballroom and the deafening crowd. Deathly afraid that her comfortable life was about to be upturned—if elected, Mitch would be taking a pay cut as a House member—and ashamed that such petty thoughts had even come to matter, she was beginning to wonder if they'd be able to afford to keep the Flower Hill manor. The competition of conscience ricocheted about in her head. The alcohol had made her dizzy. Then she nearly tripped on a torn rug seam leading into the ballroom.

"Are you gonna be okay with this?" He caught her, giving her a moment to catch her breath and balance.

"I'm fine. Thank you." She relished the ever-so-brief attention. "Maybe I'm getting too old for heels."

"Not this old heel." He kissed her with that one. It was his corn-ball one-liners that she'd grown to love. Delivered, she thought, with the slightest hint of insincerity as if to remind her that he still knew from where he came. "A hick with a heart," he'd say at some of his early stumps. It had worked too, but that was before Fitz had got ahold of him and slicked Connie's husband into a walking, talking Icon of Change.

People they'd never met, she would add to her list of friends—contributors, political wannabes. And here they were, patting her on the back, offering sincere congratulations for a campaign she'd had nothing to do with. "You must be so proud!" came one woman's voice. "You're married to a star!" whispered another. Connie was just trying to keep on her feet.

"Ladies and gentlemen," the voice boomed over the sound system. "I give you the next congressman from South County . . ." The roar was so loud, Mitch didn't even hear his name. Hanging tightly on to each other and blinded by the glare of TV lights and flash units, the couple eased into the swarm of well-wishers and glad-handers. He did his best to shake as many hands as he could while on his way up to the stage, knowing that once he'd spoken, he'd want to make like Elvis and leave the damn building.

Jesus. Not Elvis.

The self-imposed reference wasn't lost on the candidate. He was becoming a celebrity. Celebrity was a good thing. It was power. It could be used for the common good, giving his *ideas* a voice.

Waiting with outstretched hands, as Mitch climbed to the dais, were the usual suspects. As in Ike Matsuo of the Asian League with a congratulatory grip and words of encouragement. "Go get 'em, killer!" Kristel Keener, who organized all the coffee chats and precinct walks. Mark Bingham from the law firm. Candice Guttenberg of the Trial Association, a woman in desperate need of a personality change. There were Mike Menken and Holly Wiseman from the local ACLU. The local Democratic party chair, Elton Burnett, slapping the nominee's back. To win, he would have to be all things to each of these people. Fine. But he wondered if he'd be able to keep anything for himself, let alone have something left over for his marriage.

Stepping onto the dais, Mitch and Connie turned to the crowd. And just when they thought the room couldn't get louder, it turned deafening. Totally. Connie nervously said to Mitch, "I can't believe this." But he only saw her lips move. So he answered with a kiss. After which the room got even louder.

Levitated for all to see and cheer, there was their candidate and his wife. Hands held and raised like prizefighters in victory.

"Keep it to five," Fitz whispered in his ear after the roar subsided. "Any longer and the TV's gonna start talking over with all that commentary crap."

"Gotcha."

"One step back, three quarters to the right," Fitz reminded Connie. By now, she'd learned to obey Fitz when she had no other option. It was better than showing her actual contempt. So she made that one step back, three quarters to the right. That would keep her on camera should the TV want to start on a two-shot. Yet it would give them something to "push into" just in case they wanted to go close on Mitch as he got rolling in his speech.

A chant raised the room. "MITCH, MITCH, MITCH, MITCH . . ." This took the candidate by surprise as the room rocked with his name, reaching for another crescendo. It was a powerful rush that he was none too quick to kill.

"Get to it, Mitchell," Fitz snorted over the din. "Free TV is free TV."

When the hounds found their way back to the farmhouse was anybody's guess. A live-in horse hand returned from a softball game and dinner around 10:30 P.M. and fed the poor beasts their singular meal of the day before turning in himself. He'd assumed the old man had drunk himself to sleep early and had simply forgotten the chore.

It wasn't until Wednesday morning that an alarm was sounded. Congressional campaign aide Mary Riverton showed up for her usual 8:00 A.M. meeting with an armful of daily legislative details. When she discovered the congressman missing, she first called Hammond's campaign manager, Marshall Lambeer, who immediately dropped the previous night's election figures and instructed her to call the police.

Hurricane's hounds led them all to the body.

The black-and-white forensic photographs seemed to spell out all there was to know. The mare was found twisted clear around, her head pinned underneath her own shoulder. A few yards away, Hurricane was propped up on the nearest tree trunk. To all who observed, he had obviously crawled from the wreckage of his tumble like so many drunk drivers after they've destroyed mini-vans loaded with families.

The autopsy would venture that cardiac arrhythmia had turned Hurricane's racing muscle into a quivering stutter, the first pains probably numbed by the vodka. When death finally arrived, it seemed to have come as an excruciating shock. By the twisted look on the old man's face, he'd had a chance to look at death straight on and in all its bloody horror.

The coroner called it an accident.

History would record it as Hurricane's last tumble. He'd taken so many in his stellar career, physically and politically, always to rise and dust himself off to climb up those Capitol steps one more time. No longer, though. This final defeat would send a resounding shock wave across the Beltway, and hats flying into the thick Cathedral air.

Standing back from the body while the coroners figured out how to carry it from the woods to the road, the aging Marshall Lambeer, Hurricane's longtime friend and aide, couldn't help but blame himself. If he'd only pressed the old man harder, shoveled the bastard onto a late afternoon flight to Houston, boozed and all, and driven him to Cathedral for a victory salute. Just as they'd done so many times before. Then, by Wednesday morning he'd have slept it off and been left with little more than a hangover.

The future, once again, would have been bright.

But the old man was dead. Marshall was unemployed. And nothing, ever again, would be the same.

Fitz Kolatch could barely contain his glee. While showering, he'd heard the good news over radio KDRL, Cathedral's one and only *All News Station*. Bursting from a ghetto blaster taking up half the bathroom countertop, the news was more an early morning blowing of "Taps" than a trumpeting of the tragic accident. George "Hurricane" Hammond was dead. Fitz toweled his way from the bathroom to grab the nearest telephone, leaving all vanity behind. He had to call one man, Charlie Brewer in D.C. He'd be able to confirm the radio report. The campaign manager's heart pounded as the phone rang at the other end. "C'mon, c'mon, c'mon," he prodded. Last ring, he decided, when finally Brewer picked up.

"Hello?" He knew Brewer's voice cold. Brewer was the wonk of wonks. He was also a lightning rod on the pulse of D.C.

"Charlie, it's Fitz—"

"Say no more, Kolatch. Hurricane's dead. Looks like your horse race just turned into a sure bet. So double congrats. Or should I say, condolences. I'm sure the old man's death has got you all sad and gooey-eyed." Suffice it to say, Brewer knew Fitz.

"This is confirmed?" urged Fitz, tugging on his size XL Jockeys. "I don't wanna go getting my candidate's hopes up."

"He was drunk, fell off his horsey, and had a heart attack. The *Post*'s already rolling on it. Anything else?"

"No . . . That'll do me."

"What's your candidate's name? Looks like we'll be seeing him out this way come January."

"Dutton. Mitch Dutton. He's the real thing."

"They all are, Fitz."

When Fitz hung up, and before dialing his next number, he could be seen by the ritual morning swimmers doing a nearly-naked jig in front of his condo's big window overlooking the pool. His flab-flaked body shaking effortlessly to silent Irish strings.

The phone calls continued as he drove to the campaign office in his leased BMW, a success-draped sedan colored black with a tan leather interior and a self-defining vanity plate.

ISPIN4U

The idea was that the darkened Euro-car was supposed to be a symbol of prosperity. Much like the Burberrys suits and Rolex watch. It *looked* prosperous, but the reality was that the expense was a serious burden for a campaign manager on a ten-year losing streak. And the car, always seeming to need another tune-up, was a payment he didn't need. Still, it was bait for the candidates who wanted a winner on their side. A bet of political craps that was looking like it was finally going to pay off. Big time.

During his short drive, he worked the cellular phone and surfed the AM radio dial. Every sound bite about old Hurricane's tragedy gave the man tingles of success.

Four years earlier Fitz had first met Mitchell Dutton. He was in

Dallas on a party swing through the West that had finished in Texas. Mitch, a corporate attorney from Cathedral Island, had shone bright in the eyes of one talent scout, namely Fitz Kolatch. Young, articulate, attractive, with a sense of purpose. Plus a singular quality difficult to define, but certain in the eyes of the beholder. Mitchell would call it belief of self.

Fitz called it destiny. All the boy needed was a little convincing.

Four years, it took Fitz. Mitch was happy in his law practice. The work suited him and left him time for his pet projects: pro bono work and the South Coast Education Committee, which he chaired, as well as his constitutional interests. As much as he might've fancied what a House seat would afford him, what it took to get there wasn't appealing in the least. Campaigns ran dirty. No matter where they started, they always seemed to end up in the mud.

A judgeship. That's where Mitch had his sights. He fancied the idea of spending the rest of his career in the cradle of the bench. Maybe do some teaching. Write a book, even. Fitz convinced him that the political gambit could be the means to that very same end. But the convincing took time.

Fitz kept at him. Phone calls and target polling and plane tickets galore. At one point the party gave up and stopped footing the bill. Fitz was left with his own piggy bank to swing the potential candidate. And if that wasn't risky enough, he knew that even if Mitch decided to throw his hat into the political ring, he certainly bore no legal obligation to retain Fitz Kolatch as his campaign manager.

In the end, though, despite a myriad of other options Mitch had picked Fitz. Not because he thought he would lead him to the winners' circle. Mitch wasn't expected to win his first one. He knew that. Most contenders' second or third runs brewed success. No. Mitch liked Fitz because he felt he could exert a measure of control over the show runner. Mitch had insisted that he would run a clean campaign. Issues only. No negative attacks on anything but Hammond's voting record. The Dutton campaign would be about *ideas*.

Fitz agreed. He was thinking bigger anyway. Lose the Hammond race. But in the process, get some solid backing and roll up some serious numbers. Name identification was the key. Then two years hence? A U.S. Senate bid. One of the two state seats would be empty and the race would be wide open. Jack Kennedy had done as much and as quick. That's when Mitch would shine brightest. Statewide. Big media. Without Hurricane Hammond as an opponent.

And once again Fitz would be flavor of the moment.

But the rules had changed. It looked like Fitz's ship was heading ashore sooner than he'd planned. If only he could find Mitch to give him the happy news.

"Call every Goddamn number until you find him," he railed. "Then patch me through on the cellular!"

It took nearly an hour to find the candidate. Not that this was so unusual. He had a habit of sneaking off without telling a soul, a behavior Connie had complained about for years. So had his law partners. He would simply up and excuse himself. Vanish. Later explaining he'd needed time to think. That morning following the primary, Mitch had wanted to think about the rest of his life.

Then he heard the news.

The first thing he said at the news of George Hammond's death was, *"Oh my God."* The ramifications of the tragedy were not yet obvious to him, proving that the politics of opportunity weren't necessarily instinctive to the candidate.

"We've got to talk about what this means to us. And fast," said Fitz over the phone. "I'm thinking about that hotel over in Abby."

"The Beacon Hotel," answered Mitch, still in shock. "Why all the way out there?"

"I'll explain later. Let's meet there at noon."

"Wait . . ."

"Wait for what?" asked Fitz.

"I should call the Hammond family."

"Good idea. But first things first. The Beacon Hotel, Mitch. Please?"

Mitch hung up last, then asked his secretary to shut the door of his law office. He glanced briefly at his call sheet. Connie, Fay Lindsay, Fitz, his uncle Jasper, his father, Fitz, Fitz. He didn't return a single call. The news of Hammond's death winded him. Not unlike the day when John Lennon was shot or when the space shuttle exploded. It was as if at the actual moment the news was delivered, the air went dead. His muscles went limp and his body felt weak. George Hammond was more than celebrity. More than congressman. He was a presence during three quarters of Mitch Dutton's life. Old Hurricane was the local icon on whom the sun rose and set. He was everybody's favorite uncle. He was fabric and family.

For the moment, political gains and possibilities would remain in the opportunistic hands of Fitz Kolatch.

3

"**H**e's dead and I'm sorry about it," Mitch spoke as he entered the Beacon Hotel Saloon. More like a hunting lodge, he thought. Stuffed animal heads on the wall. Sawdust on the floor. Thick, varnished tabletops. He'd been standing there a good thirty seconds before anybody had noticed. His core campaign staff was already raising booze-filled glasses in jubilation.

Fitz turned to him, with a toast. " 'Death slew not him, but he made death his ladder to the skies,' " he quoted. "So forgive us for toasting the old fucker on his newest venture in space travel." With that, he guzzled a glassful of Chivas.

Mitch crossed the room and found a seat at the bar. "Anything you want, *Congressman*. On the house," spoke Kevin the barkeep.

"I'm *not* a congressman and I want a Perrier," he shot back.

Fitz approached with a swagger in his walk. "I take it you didn't like my quotation?"

"Chaucer." He was only guessing. English lit wasn't his forte. But he recalled Chaucer as being something of a morbid-minded poet.

"Spenser," answered Rene Craven, from behind Mitch. The Mississippi in her gave the singular-sounding *Spen-suh* a defined swing of sex. At least that's the way he heard it. When he turned to face her, he was instantly struck. As if it were the first time he'd ever looked at her. Rene had that quality. Long, sandy hair, curls, slightly mussed in the humidity. One long leg stretched out from underneath an Armani skirt, the other bent and tucked under her perch on the stool, high heel dangling from her toes. That and her dark, untanned skin with a fixed nose that betrayed her family's long-lost Hebrew heritage.

Swamp Jews, she'd say of her family.

"Spenser," he repeated to her. "I shoulda known Fitz couldn't pick his own quotations."

"So whaddayou think we pay her for?" answered Fitz.

Mitch returned to Rene, trying to ignore her striking looks. It was easy to look at her. Too much so, Mitch would often think. Rene was detached, yet clearly available. She gave to him, but never seemed in need. She was drawn to him, yet smart enough to know that he'd burn her like the dickens should she get too close. He was married. Principled. And she respected him. None of which kept her from being a first-class tease. Mitch liked that most about her. "It's a lousy way to sum up a man's life in public service. Tell me we're not using it."

"It's up to you. I think it's poetic. But Fitz thinks it's not down-home enough for all you dogs of Arkansas."

Dogs of Arkansas.

Fitz claimed it was a term of affection he'd long ago given to anybody whose coastline faces south. Local populations with the combined intelligence of homeless dogs who always seemed to run in powerful packs, voting in solid, yet ignorant blocks. Mitch allowed him his silly, idiosyncratic notions of southerners and especially forgave him for the Arkansas comparison, though in certain parts of Texas, guns would be drawn over less. As long as Fitz saved such representations from public consumption, Mitch would turn a deaf ear. Fitz was a Yankee and in need of forgiveness.

"I grew up with George Hammond," Mitch began with a crisp caveat. "Me along with everybody else around here. And when I say I'm sorry he's dead, I mean it."

"Like the man but not his politics." Fitz was musing on the theme. "I like it. It could work. Rene?"

"It's real. Some of the press would snipe, but who's going to respond?" Rene leaned over her legal pad and began jotting down notes.

"The opposition has no response because—*there is no longer any opposition!*" Fitz roared, clearly on a roll.

"You wanna dance on Hurricane's grave, Fitz, well, be my guest," Mitch snapped, his patience worn thin. "Just wait until the election's over and your Yankee ass is back in New York."

Fitz saw he'd gone too far. He stepped over to a nearby table and pulled out a chair for the candidate. "Murray, grab a couple more chairs. Mr. Candidate? This one's for you."

"I'm comfortable right here, Fitz. What's on your mind?" He didn't move an inch from the barstool until Rene slipped off her perch with her arm around him.

"You're going to want to sit," she eased. She had him by the elbow, drawing him over to the table.

They were an effective tag team, Rene and Fitz. Good cop and bad cop. Bombshell and bombast. Together they could manipulate their candidate. Against one of them, Mitch could always hold his ground, but against both . . .

"Okay, all joking aside, let's get real for a minute," said Fitz as he found his own seat. "Let's look at what's what."

Mitch fired a look over to Rene. She nodded her approval, although Fitz had yet to speak. "Just listen to him."

Fitz continued, "George Hammond is dead. That's a fact of life that cannot be changed. Your chances of being elected to Congress have increased tenfold."

"I can't believe that," he interrupted. "The Republican Central Committee will name a candidate in Hurricane's place. Probably Alan Middleton or Jaime Hernandez. Both of them are strong—"

"Shakespeare McCann." Fitz dropped the name flat on the table.

"Who?" Mitch asked.

"I'll say it again." This time he said it real slow, making sure Mitch heard each and every syllable. *"Shake-speare Mc-Cann."*

"What is this, some kind of joke? Who's Shakespeare . . ." Mitch still didn't catch the last name. Rene would fill in the blank.

"McCann. Just give it a little listen," she said. "You might even be amused. Murray?"

"Okay. Shakespeare McCann, born 1951. Where? Nobody knows. He was Hammond's lone opposition in the primary," began Murray, flipping through his notes. "Now, we all know that every major incumbent, Hurricane included, always has some extreme voice of dissent that throws his hat in the ring."

Mitch interrupted. "I've never heard of this guy."

"You and just about everybody else. *Including* the state Republican Committee," chimed Fitz.

"So how can they run him?" asked Mitch. "They'd be crazy to go with an unknown."

"Remember, we're in Texas," answered Fitz, handing off again to Murray. "So listen and learn."

Murray tabled his Zima cooler. "Now, Texas election rules are clear on this. In circumstances resulting in death, impairment, or withdrawal of a primary victor, the candidate's party shall nominate one of its own instead."

Mitch insisted, once again, "That's what I just said."

"It goes on," Murray continued, "and I quote: 'In such cases where the second-place finisher garners a minimum fifteen percent of the electorate, the second-place candidate shall be *automatically nominated* and his or her name executed onto the November ballot.' "

"That can't be constitutional," insisted Mitch.

"It is. It's local election law. Written in 1911, I'm sure, with a pen in one hand and a six-gun in the other," said Murray.

"Shakespeare McCann." Fitz completed the picture, his hands framing the name in the air. "This lone nut took fifteen points off the one and only Hurricane Hammond."

"How could he? A total unknown," was all Mitch could think to ask.

"That's where it gets *really* good." Murray grinned. The boy wonder was a wonk through and through. "I talked to some people who talked to some people. Turns out this guy owns some kind of print and photography business."

"A photographer?" asked Mitch. None of it was making sense. Fifteen points off of Hurricane's primary bid?

"Step up to the plate, Murray," barked Fitz.

Murray cleared his throat. "I called a friend of mine who works with the State Elections Commission. You know how we all have to send Xerox copies of every contribution we get? The checks, you know?"

"Tell him who *Shakespeare McCann's* supporters are," laughed Fitz. He just loved saying that damned name.

"Nobodies. The elderly. Giving him five dollars here. Ten there. Personal checks, some even postdated."

"Poor white Baptist trash," volunteered Rene. "Same folks who give money to the 'Old Time Gospel Hour' because they're promised Salvation Vacations."

"My friend faxed me some of the canceled checks," continued Murray. "They all got those little Christian fish in the corners."

"You making fun of Christians?" warned Mitch. "They vote in solid blocks. And they *believe* in something."

"No. It's just that they appear to be McCann's target group," answered Murray. "Anyway, I made a call. You know. To one of those names on the checks. Five-dollar contributor named Suzy Summers. Know what she told me?"

"I'm all ears," said Mitch, still waiting for the other shoe to drop.

Fitz took over. "This woman is fifty-five, living on her dead husband's disability. She's got three girls, all married with kids. She tells Murray she'd never heard of Shakespeare McCann until she gets a phone call selling *portrait plans.* She was interested, so an hour or so later this guy Shakespeare came knockin' on her door to deliver her the coupon. He explains the deal. Family pictures. You know, a buy-three, get-one-free kind of deal? Anyway, this lady's got grandchildren, and who wouldn't want more pictures of their little grandkids? She pays him the money. Then at some later time, he takes the pictures for the contracted price and, upon sending the family photos, *includes his pitch as a candidate for congressional office.*"

"Can you believe it?" added Rene. "He's just kissin' babies like any other old-time political hack. Just this time, he's doing it through pictures from the post office."

"You're kidding me," was Mitchell's cautious response. "It sounds like something born from a boiler-room scam."

"But it's not. It's legal," interjected Fitz. "He buys a list of likely voters. The hard-core, elderly, Christian right. Sells them a good product, but leaves them with his political pitch on the doorstep. It's just *targeting.*"

"I made some more calls. Same story. And like Fitz says, all legal," reported Murray. "All the good folks said is how great their babies looked in the pictures. And what good sense McCann made when he sat down to talk with them."

"A baby photographer," Mitch said with wonder.

"Here's what I figure," said Fitz, digging in. "Republican primary, big-time incumbent means low voter turnout. Thirty-five, forty percent tops. So you crunch the numbers. Six hundred thousand in the district's population base. Two hundred thousand registered voters. Little more than a hundred thousand Republicans. Low turnout means only thirty or so thousand actually turn out to vote.

"So this Shakespeare guy," he went on, "buys a Republican voter analysis of South County. The real conservative Bible Belters. The ones who always vote no matter what the Tuesday. He targets the elderly with grandchildren. Sells them the plan. Takes the pictures. The way those numbers work out, that's barely five thousand votes, and it gets him fifteen points off of Hammond. Who woulda guessed that would be enough to put a fellah in the November slot?"

"Five thousand votes," repeated Murray. "*I* could get five thousand votes."

"Makes sense," said Mitch, the pragmatist's tone taking over. "But that's for just your fifteen percent. Do you think he actually was crazy enough to think he'd do better than half the vote to carry the primary?"

"Like I said. He's a Looney Tune," pointed out Fitz.

"And lucky," reminded Rene.

Fitz finished, "Probably believes in Elvis and O.J. conspiracies. And now he's your only opposition."

It was sinking in. Mitch sat in wonder, looking back at the three faces before him for confirmation that this was indeed some kind of prank.

Fitz gleefully guffawed. "Just think about those Republican horses' asses up in Dallas and the bricks they're shitting cuzza the news."

"They'll challenge it. Recount the votes," said Mitch.

"Let 'em," said Fitz. "It'll take a month at least. Meanwhile, the ACLU takes this Shakespeare guy's case. Sues and probably wins. That's another month that we're out there, running the race our way and without credible opposition."

Murray added, "Their hands'll be tied. Nothing they can do when it comes down to it. They'll have to run this nobody."

Finally Mitch added his own guess. "Ten'll getcha a hundred that when it's all said and done, the Republicans crap out on the poor SOB. Don't give him a dime." Suddenly he was thinking like a candidate. "No point in chasing good money after bad. They're no dummies. After all, they're Hammond's cronies, handpicked by the old man himself."

"That's the ticket," said Fitz, jacking the last shot of Chivas into his mouth. He pounded on the table and called for another round. "Reload!"

Mitch thought to remind the bartender. "Perrier."

"Aw, have a real drink, *Congressman*," goaded Fitz. "Here's to you!"

The words slapped Mitch in the face. It was premature. It didn't ring true at all.

Congressman . . .

4

The Mitchell Dutton for Congress campaign office was on the Island in a grungy northside section underneath the span that crossed over to Cathedral City. It was out of the way and cheap. A campaign hellhole designed to be abused by volunteers. But it did include a helicopter landing zone on a rooftop that offered great views of the mainland, especially when necessitated by a TV press conference.

"It is with great sadness that I join the Hammond family in mourning the loss of a great politician and patriarch. No doubt about it, he was a great man and a father figure to this community. I will miss him," said Mitch to the press, already halfway through his prepared statement.

At rear of the media pack stood Hollice Waters. Bored already with the eulogy, he nudged a young TV info-babe, ready for her first round of election politics. "So would you vote for him?"

"In a heartbeat."

"Would you sleep with him?"

"He's married."

"Never stops Mitch."

"No way. He's a Boy Scout." But the young woman had swallowed—hook, line, and sinker. "You think?"

"Woman on his campaign staff. A real Southern Delight. But you didn't hear it from me."

Then she thought about it and came back with "You think his wife knows?"

Hollice answered with a trademark shrug. He didn't know shit, let alone have any factual support for his theory. If words were power, Hollice was deadly. If he'd wanted, he could sink a new candidate like Mitch. He'd simply laid the pipe and primed the pump with little more than a whisper of hearsay. All somebody had to do was turn the valve and the flood of rumor would begin. He wasn't concerned about whether it was true. He'd heard a little talk and that's all he was doing. Talking. There surely wasn't a fact at issue yet, or enough to print that would hang the candidate on the horns of his own character. That would come, he figured. It always did.

"Obviously we had our differences," Mitch continued on with his statement. "And it was because of those differences that I chose to run against him, thus challenging his congressional seat. But to speak any more of politics, or to answer questions concerning the race on this sad day, would only exploit what should be a day of mourning. We've lost one of our own. And today we should be remembering him. Thank you very much."

Despite Mitchell's subtle urging that the press put their political questions on the back burner out of respect for the deceased incumbent, they clamored for more. Having laid the seed of rumor at the rear of the media pack, Hollice pushed forward, ready to snag Mitch with another barbed hook.

"So, Mitch, what do you think of your new challenger, Shakespeare McCann?"

"I've never met the man," said Mitch. "So I must assume he's a decent human being and a worthy opponent."

"Okay, so how's it feel to be front-runner then?"

Hell, thought Mitch. *There hasn't even been a poll yet and I'm the front-runner.*

"Please!" he urged the throng of TV and flash cameras, shouting beyond Hollice but making sure the writer knew the statement was directed at him. "Today belongs to the Hammond family! I'm asking you to have some respect!" With that, he shoved his way from the rooftop location and back into his campaign office. He'd meant what he'd said, too. He'd had enough speculation of what would be. He needed to put his thoughts together.

Holed up in his office, he ignored the Hammond eulogies on the

TV. Instead he returned phone calls, then headed for the door shortly before dusk. He'd nearly made it to his car when Rene stopped him. "You did well today."

"Better than Old Hurricane, I'm sure."

"I meant with the press. We weren't expecting you to answer any questions."

"Only the one. But Hollice is an old pal," he answered. "And when in doubt, tell the truth. It's easier to remember," he continued. "At least, that's what my old man used to say."

Mitch's old man. Quentin Donovan Dutton. Immigrant, gentleman farmer, shrimp boat entrepreneur, and a not-so-loving father. But from time to time he'd left his son with a little wisdom. Little road maps Mitch would sometimes dig up to find his way through the darkness. That evening Mitch had returned every call but one. Quentin Dutton's.

"Going home?" asked Rene.

"Going home," he answered. "It was supposed to be my day off. Nobody was supposed to find me."

"Break time's over. It's hard work from here to November."

"You keep telling me." He was trying to ease his way out the back door. Rene, though, was hard to leave—no matter how much a man might love his wife. She was that beguiling.

"But I can see now that you're up to it." She smiled. "You're the kind of man that can go all the way."

It was a certain tease that wasn't lost on the candidate. It was her way, though. The way she dealt with men. Some women can't help it. And most men can't help but think to follow suit. Every instinct told him to lean in and kiss her good night. Even if it was just a polite, gentleman's kiss to the cheek. Instead, he gestured toward the car. "Home is as far as I'm going."

By most standards the commute home was short. But there were no thoroughfares on the Island. All the streets were tight, and stop-lights were plentiful. The turbo on the Volvo wouldn't get a chance to kick in until he made the right turn off of Broughton Drive onto the long, sloping drive that wound its way up to the stately hilltop where each house was afforded a view and a lion's share of sweet Gulf breezes.

Mitch pulled up to the old Victorian around seven. For a brief moment he gazed up at the mansion and wondered if he'd miss it should he go to Washington. It was home to him, that's for sure. But it wasn't his. It was Connie's. And it would always be hers.

Key in the door, he entered the house from the kitchen, dearly hoping his nostrils would discover the happy leftovers Connie was used to leaving. But it was early yet. So instead of cooked food and the sweet smells left to linger, the air was stale with the smell of burning cannabis. Gina. He knew she was there. Marijuana was her usual calling card.

"If it's not my wife the pothead and her friend Gina," he said with disgust. It was as much reserve as he could muster.

"Well, look who's here. The star of the five-o'clock funeral hour." They'd obviously had a good laugh watching the TV. And Gina had a way of making Mitch feel unwelcome, even in his own home. "They said on the news you're a shoo-in to be congressman. The wife and I thought we'd celebrate." She passed the roach back to Connie.

"Sweetheart?" Mitch kissed his wife, who stuck her tongue in his mouth and giggled.

"Oh, don't gimme that look. You know grass makes me horny." Connie giggled again. She was stoned, no two ways about it. The comment was more for Gina's sake than Mitch's.

He blamed Gina for this.

Dos Amigas. That's what they called themselves. Instead of a clan of women surrounding her, Connie had Gina Sweet. A trust-funder with unlimited time for her adopted sister.

They'd met back in their sorority days at SMU up in Dallas. Gina was always a candy-eyed miss with a nose for trouble and the name to get away with it. A self-diagnosed neurotic with what she liked to call a Traumatic Expectations disorder, she was always deathly afraid her parents would up and die on her. Tragically so. And when they didn't, it was no surprise that she latched on to young Connie Hamilton, a scholarship student who'd lost her own parents in a boating accident years earlier. The two friends had ended up rooming together during their last two years before the traditional postgraduation split. During that time they'd smoked enough pot to resurrect the *Hindenburg.*

"Just promise me you won't smoke outside the house," Mitch gently warned. He didn't want to tangle with it now. It wasn't the time. Plus Gina was there.

"That's okay. We didn't *inhale.*" Gina burst with laughter, making about as sophisticated a political reference as she could. Connie joined in the laughter. He tried to ignore them.

"Is there anything to eat?"

"Frozen pasta in the freezer," snapped Connie.

Mitch gave up, starting for the stairs. "On second thought, I'm not hungry. I'm going to go upstairs and get some work done. Make sure the seeds go down the sewer and not the garbage cans."

"I should go up, too. He's usually not home this early. I should be thrilled, right?" Connie said, straightening up and trying back on the disguise of the good wife. She called after Mitch, "I think Rosa washed your clothes. They're on the bed in the guest suite."

Gina tried to rope Connie into staying. "Leave him be. He's just being Mr. Political Party Pooper."

"C'mon, G. We've barely talked since election night. He *needs* me."

Gina. Sweet-tooth Gina. Sweet-assed Gina. Gina the Sweet. Gina the Sweater Gal. Mitch had heard all the nicknames and, in most respects, figured they were accurate. The SMU days were one long party for Gina Sweet, interrupted only by the occasional schoolbook or exam. Gina lived to be the *first*. In the sorority, she was the *first* to do cocaine. The *first* to make it in the house mother's bed. The *first* to do it with two guys at once—or at least *consenting* to, she'd later say. And the *first* to have an abortion. She'd had the procedure in the afternoon in time for a mixer that night. Her roommate, Connie, was a wreck over the incident and skipped the party. Instead, she went to the campus chapel and prayed for her friend.

It was later in their senior year that Connie herself had gotten pregnant by a psychology professor. Then it was Gina's turn to play the Good Mother. She drove Connie to the clinic for the abortion. It was Gina who paid for it. Connie would wonder every so often if something had gone wrong in the termination procedure that would later explain her difficulty conceiving and taking a pregnancy to full term. And while arrogant doctors scoffed at Connie's theory, Gina was always there to hold her hand, just as she had after Connie's abortion.

Dos Amigas.

Upstairs, as Mitch ditched his suit for something more comfortable, the day replayed itself in Technicolor. It had been long and difficult, preceded by a week of aggressive campaigning as the underdog candidate. No longer, though. The old man was dead and Mitch was in first position. Hurrah. Then why wasn't he celebrating?

Instead, he switched on the TV for some background company, then found some peace of mind in a briefcase full of memos and notes messengered over from his law practice. Salivating at the prospect of having "Congressman" on their firm's letterhead, Mitch's partners had picked up most of the slack when the campaign kicked into high gear. But Mitch missed what he called "real work." The kind that paid the bills on those Flower Hill mortgages left him by Connie's frivolous parents.

The old master suite stretched over nearly a third of the upper floor, the pine floors dented with over a hundred years of wear, waxed weekly to an antique sheen. Persian rugs flanking her parents' old four-poster that Connie had reconfigured for a king-sized mattress. Enlarged windows for maximum breezes. Irish pine furniture. All of it Connie's. The house was the memory of her parents.

He heard the pipes whooshing below, a sure sign that Connie was flushing the evidence of contraband. Minutes later she appeared, carrying a tray of cheese, crackers, and microwaved chicken wings. "I'll bet you didn't eat lunch."

"Not much," he said, hoping she wouldn't make him feel guilty for killing her party. "You didn't have to do this."

"No matter. It's the least I can do for the front-runner."

"So you saw the news?"

"I did. It's sad about Hurricane," she said, changing the subject ever so slightly. The front-runner thing scared her. It meant leaving home. Something she didn't want to face right away. She'd rather just seek some affection. "I liked what you said."

"On the news?"

"About Hurricane. Did you mean it?"

"Of course I did."

"Gina said it sounded like bullshit."

"Gina wouldn't know shit from a shaman."

"I know. She's got a mouth when she's stoned."

"When she's stoned?"

"Let's not start with Gina. I thought we could eat. Maybe play Scrabble." She bit into a cracker and passed the rest to Mitch, stepping into his arms to let him take hold of her. He proved up to the task, carrying on the embrace until all thoughts of the day dissolved into the sweet sweat of her skin. He brought his lips to hers and kissed her.

"You're taking advantage of me cuz I'm stoned," she giggled.

It'd been weeks since they'd made love. Not their longest stretch, by any means. But long enough so interest was higher than normal, as was the politics of intercourse. It had begun some three years back when Connie had decided the household needed a baby. *They* needed a baby. Age was creeping up on her, as were fears of infertility. She'd never used birth control with Mitch and had never been pregnant since that one time in college.

He was fine with the prospect and game to try. But trying was one thing. Performing was something else. After two difficult years, lovemaking was no longer spontaneous. Rapture and romance were reduced to timetables set by Connie's schizophrenic ovulations. Medical science was in charge of each and every sexual sojourn. But Mother Nature came up a winner every time. It left her crying each month when her cycle returned. And Mitch cold. So they swept their failure under the bed and stopped talking about the subject altogether. All that was left were *moments.*

She switched off the lights, stripped naked, and settled next to Mitch, barely making a dent in the bed. She was small, fit, barely a hundred pounds. Green eyes. And ears that never quite grew into her face. The short haircut was brave. He gave her that.

Her skin glowed milky white in the mixture of moonlight and ambient light from the streetlamps well below the windows. So pale and tracked with fine blue veins was she that she'd long feared it was unattractive to Mitch. Hardly the bronze of a South Coast beach babe. So daylight was damned in favor of a darkened bedroom. It turned everything monochrome and romantic.

But to Mitch, her skin was perfect and somehow untouchable. Porcelain, easily bruised. After the sex, he silently retired to the shower to wash the sweat off. By the time he'd returned and toweled dry, she'd switched the TV back on. They watched the finish of a prime-time news show placidly and without any conversation until he'd fallen asleep by eleven.

At 12:22 A.M. the telephone rang. Mitch woke with his heart pounding, then checked the clock and cursed. Then again, he could simply reach over and turn off the ringer and let the machine pick up the call, but his curiosity would get the better of him and he'd have to check, trekking all the way downstairs to retrieve the message. It could be Fitz. Or worse, something about his father. He let the phone ring twice again before answering, barely croaking out, "Hello?"

"Mitch Dutton?" asked the voice.

"Speaking," he answered by rote.

"*Candidate* Mitch Dutton?"

"Who is this?"

"It's George Hammond."

"Who?" He thought he'd heard wrong.

"George Alexander Hammond. But you can call me Hurricane."

Mitch had heard Hammond speak about a zillion times. It wasn't him, even if he were alive. "Is this some kind of joke?"

"I don't hear you laughing."

"Listen, pal. I don't know how you got my number—"

"Not yet, I don't."

He heard the *click-clack* of a hang-up. Just before which there was some kind of external cue. A background sound of a truck rushing past. A phone booth, he decided. Some drunken prankster with Mitch Dutton's home phone number and a quarter left over from his nightly bender.

"Who was that?" Connie called out from the bathroom.

"Hang-up," he groaned. He placed the phone back into the cradle, then reached over to pop open the window. A breeze drew into the room and billowed the curtains.

A truck roaring past a telephone booth.

Connie returned to bed, pushing the covers aside and snuggling close to Mitch, her arms wrapped about his waist. This was her favorite time. Late night. When they were both awake and he was hers alone. They would lie nose to nose and talk. She could feel his breath with every word he spoke. She would keep him awake for as long as she could, knowing that once he fell asleep she would lie awake and feel so darn lonely.

"So you're going to be a congressman after all," she said, trying her best to sound proud.

"Nothing's certain," he cautioned.

"But on the news—"

"The news means nothing. I've got a new challenger. Who knows? He could be good."

"They said his name. What was it?"

"Shakespeare McCann, I believe."

"That's not a name. That's a used-car salesman," she joked.

He laughed.

Then she got serious. "You weren't supposed to win."

"Nobody runs to lose, Connie."

"Hammond was unbeatable."

"What can I say? The rules change. People die. Hell, forty-year-old men get heart attacks. I could die tomorrow."

She put her finger to his lips. "Don't say it. Please don't."

"How about we just go to sleep." He rolled to his side and she spooned him, curving her body to fit into his. Her hand tracing the lines of his chest to his belly button, then slipping inside his shorts.

"Wanna try again?"

He knew what she meant. She was still high. They'd smoked plenty of grass in years past. It was her call to his wild, when sharing a single joint they'd get high and screw for hours. Always in the dark. So he let her fondle him until he could no longer lie still, whereupon he rolled back to face her before crawling between her legs. She guided him in, leaving his hands free to cup her face and bring his mouth to her ear, whispering, "I love you, Connie."

The words she so desperately needed to hear.

All in all, though, it soon turned into the same old mechanical act. Robotic and passionless, filled with too many insipid memories of fruitless copulations followed by dreams of unborn babies.

Just to keep the soured act going, Mitch closed his eyes and thought about Rene Craven.

5

In the week following George Hammond's death, the Dutton campaign office was flooded with calls curious about Cathedral's new front-runner. Fitz, hooked up to a telephone headset like an air traffic controller, stood at room center and passed need-to-know information off to various volunteers. Line one: *Dallas Evening Report* wanting a candidate's statement and a picture. Line two: The League of Women Voters, wondering if, instead of a debate, there could be a series of lectures by the candidate. Line three: a local printer wanting payment on that extra run of bumper stickers. "We're good for it," Fitz told him, "but then again, you could call it a campaign contribution to your next congressman. You didn't know? Dutton's a shoo-in. He's also probusiness."

A whorehouse aeons earlier, the campaign's building had withstood a century or so of hurricanes and ocean salt. In 1983 Hurricane Alicia had blown the roof clean off. The exterior was chewed down to a patchy gray veneer. Fitz had made a deal with the owner to paint the building if Mitch won the election.

Inside wasn't much more attractive. Plaster walls had been replaced by drywall blistered from the leaky roof. Still, who could tell with the amount of snipe material that layered all vertical surfaces? Volunteers, mostly young women, were scattered about at gunmetal office-surplus desks, and the telephone lines were a massive tangle atop carpet held together with silver duct tape. Fitz had come to call it home. Ground zero. Dutton Central. Every couple of hours he would wander down to rub elbows, give pep talks, and schmooze, schmooze, schmooze. After all, most of these people were working for free.

When Mitch showed up, he would usually enter from the rear. There was a space next to the double Dumpster where he'd park his Volvo. His only office key would fit the back door and he'd slip in undetected, making his way up the stairs to what he called the inner sanctum: a suite of five offices where the real work was done.

On that particular spring Saturday, he had borrowed Connie's Mustang. A breeze had kicked up off the Gulf and he wanted to drive with the top down. So he drove the long way, dropping off the west side of the island down to the Gulf side where he picked up Beach Road, a two-lane highway that etched along the perimeter of the island. As expected, the wind had started up early and left the waterfront air sweet with a salty brine that instantly shot him back to his boyhood, a memory chock-full of shrimp boats and his Uncle J carping at him about wind shifts, weather, the Baptist church, and the evils of redheaded women.

Before he got two steps through the back door, he could smell Rene's perfume. She was coming out of the copy room with an arm-load of the daily press releases. "Ever hear of using the front door?"

"You'd like that, wouldn't you?" said Mitch as he eased past her and into the stairwell. "Shake a few hands, answer a couple of phones."

"Wouldn't hurt. The volunteers work hard. Might show 'em you're part of your own team." Gentle nudges, but nudges all the same.

"How's about this? For lunch I'll buy them all pizza. We can picnic on the roof."

She followed him up the stairs. "It's Saturday. That means some twenty-five volunteers."

"You're kidding me."

"You didn't think you were that popular?"

"News to me," he said, sounding innocent enough, before making the hard right into his office and wondering just how long it would take Fitz to appear. Within a minute, he figured. He could set his watch by it.

Once settled behind his desk, he was surprised to find a pink message slip placed front and center. His first inclination was that it was a message from Connie. Or another from his father. He hadn't called him back. Personal messages always came straight to him. The rest, well, they'd begin downstairs where some volunteer—*any volunteer*—would answer the phone, take down the message, and send it up to Murray, who would filter them to Fitz.

But the message wasn't from Connie. Written in the neatest of handwriting was the name *Shakespeare McCann*.

He picked up the slip and was about to ask Rene about it when Fitz appeared in the doorway with a handful of his own pink paper. Murray was with him. "Glad you're here. Got plenty more where that came from, every last one stacked in order of importance. One call was from Marshall Lambeer from the Hammond Reelection Office. The family has invited you to walk in Saturday's processional down the Strand."

"Of course. It'll be my honor."

"That's good. Rene?" Fitz turned to her and paused. Was it him or were her skirts actually getting shorter? "Let's write up a little release. Let everybody know the candidate's going to walk—"

"I don't wanna make this a campaign march. For Christ's sake, it's a funeral," groused Mitch. "I'll do it out of respect and duty."

"There you go again, sounding like you're in the damn service," said Fitz. "You can walk for yourself, or duty, or for God and fuckin' country. I don't care. Just don't forget the way it sizes up in the eyes of the media. If they're gonna make the most of it, then so should we."

"Fine," he relented. It was too early and he'd started the day too happy. Ten minutes ago he'd had the top down, the wind in his hair, and some damn fine memories. He wasn't about to spoil it by debating over bullshit, considering that Fitz knew what the hell he was doing, and arguing over small matters usually proved pointless.

"Who took this call?" Mitch held up that first pink slip in his hand, turning the neat handwriting around for all to see.

"Shakespeare McCann?" read Murray.

"How'd that slip by?" asked Fitz, reaching for the note. "Damn volunteers. I'm supposed to get *those* messages. I'll give the fellah a call."

"He called *me*," objected Mitch. "He deserves a call back."

"There are channels," said Fitz.

"Sure there are. So this one slipped by you. The least I can do is call him back."

"Candidates don't usually hook up like this. Let's talk about this first," warned Fitz. "Let the managers set some ground rules."

Mitch dialed anyway, smiling all the way. Five times the telephone rang before a male voice answered with a folksy hello. Mitch spoke politely. "Shakespeare McCann, please. This is Mitch Dutton returning his call."

The tip of the week for Hollice Waters came through the *Cathedral Daily Mirror* switchboard, transferred twice before ringing Hollice's house. It was Saturday and he didn't like to step foot in the office unless he was on the clock.

"Heard somethin'," offered the tipster, a woman.

Obviously, you moron. Or you wouldn't have called me, he thought. Instead, he was polite. He wanted the juice. "I'm all ears."

"A meeting. Between Mitch Dutton and that new guy. What's his name. The Republican."

"Shakespeare McCann?" Hollice remembered, the no-name nominee who hadn't a snowball's chance in hell of, at this late date, building any kind of campaign, let alone toppling Dutton in a head-on race. Thanks to an antiquated Texas law, Mitch was about to get a free ride to the House. It bugged the shit out of Hollice.

"That's him. McCann," said the woman. "They're gonna have themselves a little chitchat at a coffee shop out in Benton. You think it's *something?*"

Something. Maybe.

Writing a cross between gossip column and racing form, Hollice owed most of his political coverage to free tips from the anonymous and not-so-anonymous. Friends and foes, it didn't matter. Information flowed. And should new legislation pass that might affect a minority or disaffected group, he was a convenient champion. Racist, race-baiter, muckraker, and political pendragon with a poison pen. He was all of the above and unashamed, just as long as the good folks of Cathedral and thereabouts kept on reading under his byline.

"Interesting," he told the woman on the phone. "You know around when?"

"High noon," she said, a little too dramatically.

"Thanks," was his only concession. And that was the end of the call.

Twelve noon. And all the way out in Benton. What was it? A deal in the works? The tip sounded unusual enough. But newsworthy? A trip that far off the island would mean he was going to miss the

Houston Open on ESPN. Oh well. Information didn't know work-days from weekends.

Dutton vs . . . *McCann.*

Hollice didn't believe in miracles, but he did believe in the power of print. A little ambush action might spark *something.* He grabbed his camera bag and hit the door. If it turned out to be a dry well, he might make it back for the last couple holes of golf coverage.

Mitch knew Benton as a small, poor town that straddled the inter-state. Little more than a truck stop, it was about a forty-minute drive from the campaign office. He used the time on the cell phone, finally braving a return call to his old man. The candidate was relieved to get the machine. "Q. Dutton here. This is my machine, so don't waste my time. Leave a brief message."

Instantly Mitch regretted sending his father the answering machine for Christmas. The gift was so *eighties.* And now he was antagonizing people without even being *present.* "Hey, Pop. It's your only son. Sorry to take so long calling you back. It's been crazy here," was just about all Mitch could think to say. "Best way to get me is at home or on weekends," Mitch fibbed.

After the call, Mitch wondered what his father was up to at that very moment. Had he taken the pleasure boat down to Mexico for some albacore fishing? Or was he hustling a tennis game on one of San Diego County's million or so hard courts? More likely he was shacked up with some surgically enhanced, post menopausal bleached blonde who was suffering her first "Ohmigod, I'm a grandmother!" depression. Q. Dutton, Mitch thought. Granny's answer to Prozac.

As for the telephone conversation with Shakespeare, it had been short and gracious. The folksy voice at the other end of the line had invited Mitch out for a cup of coffee. So polite was Shakespeare that he even offered a small café in out-of-the-way Benton, where, for Mitchell's sake, there would be no media about to tarnish the scenery. Shakespeare had practically conceded defeat in the upcoming general election, referring to himself as a lazy lapdog who'd entered the race against the practiced greyhound and simply gotten lucky.

How could Mitch refuse him?

Fitz had other ideas. The meeting was against his better judgment. "What scares me is the unknown," he admitted. "If we knew some-thing. *Anything.*"

"It's just a hi, hello, and a handshake. I'm certain," said Mitch. "So stop worrying."

The fact was that Mitch *wanted* this ceremonial handshake, something he knew he'd never get from an old political attack dog like Hurricane. Like most American boys born of the fifties, he'd been taught to play fair, an idea seemingly lost on the majority of adults he'd known. Maybe an example could be set. With the little town of Benton the high ground.

So at roughly 11:45 that Saturday morning, fifteen minutes early, Mitch wheeled Connie's Mustang off the interstate and found a place to park at the side of the Mairzy Doats Café. He left his coat in the car, thought twice about it, then finally decided to lose the necktie. No sooner had he stepped from the car when a semi roared past, blowing a load of dust into his face. He winced and brought his hands up to his face a split second too late. Pain scratched at his eyeball as a speck of dust found its way under one of his contact lenses. In a flash he pulled the soft contact out of his eye and stuck it in his mouth to give it a rudimentary cleansing. Instead, it came back ripped and useless.

"Aw, fuck!" he blurted as he piled back into the Mustang with one eye shut. He fished through his glove box for his contact lens case and spare pair of glasses before realizing that he'd driven Connie's car instead of his own. "No."

With his one good eye, he was about to get out of the car, but found a stranger standing in his way. He appeared as a blur in the midday sun. Mitch squeezed his bad eye shut and focused on the smaller man but didn't yet recognize him.

"That's the curse of the contact lens wearer. All it takes is one gust of Texas dirt and you're a blind man." The stranger offered his hand. "Shakespeare McCann. But you can call me Shakes. Everybody does."

"Mitchell Dutton." He blindly stretched his hand out to grab hold of a firm handshake.

"I know," said McCann. "I seen your picture in the newspaper." He swung around to point across the highway. "You know? There's a five-and-dime just across the street here. Maybe we can find you some lens juice."

"It's no good. What I need are some glasses." Mitch stood up and, with his one good eye, tried to get his bearings again.

"What you need is a spare pair."

"It's my wife's car. My spare's in mine."

"Happens to the best of us. Right across the street there. Getcha good and fixed up." Shakespeare was right there at Mitchell's elbow, like the good Boy Scout leading the old gal across the dangerous boulevard.

Mitch was practically blind. Crossing the street, he heard the roar of a truck nearing. For all he knew, it was upon him. Headed for him. Shakespeare would only need to let go, forgetting the Boy Scout oath. Yet the truck blew past right behind him in a roar that chilled him. Why? He didn't know.

The five-and-dime had a prescription counter, upon which there was one of those revolving displays featuring various corrective glasses. Mitch tried on five pairs of the geeky glasses before he found one that slightly resembled his own prescription. And though they were a far cry less flattering than the designer frames that he'd left in the Volvo, for an afternoon in the little town of Benton, they'd most certainly do.

"You look like Buddy Holly," said Shakespeare.

"Or a high school shop teacher."

Seated in a back booth in the Mairzy Doats Café, Mitch finally gathered his first real look at his host. Barely five seven. Wiry, with an acne-scarred face perched atop a sinewy neck, tucked not so neatly into an off-the-rack suit. Wisps for eyebrows. Square chin. The package was topped off by a balding pate with short, tufted, salt-and-pepper hair. Modest wire-rimmed glasses, behind which Mitch found a pair of strangely incandescent eyes. Cobalt blue, but somehow otherworldly. The kind of color rarely found in nature and more likely purchased from his local optometrist, he decided. It was amusing. Contact lenses magnified behind a pair of glasses. A little showmanship, maybe.

The fact was, Mitch found it damn hard to look away.

"Shakes!" blurted out the café's owner.

" 'Scuse me," Shakespeare apologized before leaping to his feet and crossing the room in quick steps to pump the owner's hand and trade a whisper of a private joke. At the punch line Shakespeare's face spread into a practiced megawatt smile—a miraculous salesman's grin that all at once expunged any imperfection that nature had inflicted upon the rest of his face. The scars disappeared and his forehead creased to create a genuine eyebrow, arching over a becoming face. The iridescent smile was followed by a hearty, well-intended laugh that tickled the owner into a free round of iced teas. A waitress brought them over along with lunch.

"So that's what your friends call you?" asked Mitch. "Shakes?"

"You, too," offered the *other* candidate. "If it gets my attention, you must be callin' my name."

"Fine," Mitch answered politely.

McCann was easily into his forties. But muscled under his button-down collar and poly-blend jacket. Before him lay a luncheon of chicken-fried steak with mashed potatoes and a side order of bacon.

"Sure you don't want nothin' more than the coffee?" Shakes offered.

"I'm fine," answered Mitch. "I guess you don't have a problem with cholesterol in your family tree."

"Not that I know of." Shakespeare sawed off another piece of steak. "How about your tree?"

"My mother's side. Heart attacks as far back as I can remember."

"Your old man?"

"Knock wood. He can chase tennis balls with the best of 'em."

"Good livestock on one side. Defective on the other. Where's that put you?"

"I watch what I eat. Caffeine is my one addiction," mused Mitch, surprised to find himself engaged in a conversation of family health and heart attacks with such a stranger. A mystery figure. But with a manner that made talking go down as easy as chocolate milk. A natural politician. No wonder all those old ladies bought the pictures along with the *pitch*. That smile alone was probably worth fifteen percent of the vote.

"Not what you expected, is it?" asked Shakespeare. It was as if he'd read Mitchell's mind.

"I'm not quite sure . . ."

"I mean I know I ain't pretty, like y'all, but looks don't make the man."

"I wasn't thinking that at all."

"Look at us. You an' me talkin' about hearts and attacks and the what-have-ya'll. Sure ain't what I expected. And I'm glad for it, I'll tell you that."

"What did you expect?"

"Bigger 'n life, maybe," said Shakespeare. "I saw your speech at the Hilton."

"You were there?" asked Mitch.

"Naw," laughed the little man. "Taped it on the Toshiba. My VCR."

"So how'd I do?"

"Okay. Whipped up the crowd. They were lovin' you like it was Christmas. And that's what it's about, as far as I can tell. People gotta love ya."

"Believe in you," corrected Mitch.

"Love you," Shakespeare admonished. "Believin' is for God and the Easter Bunny."

"Bigger than life," deflected Mitch. "That's what I always said about ol' Hurricane. Takes a braver man than me to go up against an incumbent in his own primary."

"Aw, hell. Bravery's for the Alamo and there's a thousand scream-in' Mexicans in front of you and no back door." And there it was again. That easy, glowing smile. Well timed behind the old Texas homilette. Mitch was surely charmed. But he still wanted to know why the contact lenses.

"Me?" continued Shakespeare. "I got my print 'n' picture business to fall back on. Just like you got your lawyer business, I reckon."

"That I do."

"You know what else I think?" Shakespeare leaned closer. " 'Cept in the looks department, I think you an' me are pretty much alike. Two peas in a pod, you know what I mean?"

From charmed to unnerving, observed Mitch. A strangeness the other man possessed, a way to which Mitch was completely unaccustomed. Enchanting off the mark, then suddenly familiar to the point of being impolite. And then leaning in so damn close, he was invading Mitch's personal space. Violating the comfort zone.

"See, I look at it this way," Shakes went on to say. "I didn't toss my hat into ol' Hurricane's bullring cuz I figured to take his place in the Washington Big House. There was just some things I reckoned he oughta be thinkin' about down thisaway. I mean, you 'n' I both know the old boy hadn't come down Cathedral way lookin' for nothin' but votes for some twelve years now. Hell, he wasn't even in the damn state for his own election last week. Sure, he done take care of some of the local population on the Island, but like there-abouts where I'm from, down South County and all, we got our problems, too."

"Of course you do. Hurricane had done his duty. Now I think it's time for some fresh ideas. For a new debate."

"Now, there you go. Talkin' like an old-time political hack. When we both know that neither of us has the experience. We owe it to the folks to talk straight at 'em. Give 'em the real stuff, you know? Just like you 'n' me are doing right here. The real stuff." That smile again, then he continued, "Aw hell, listen to me go on. Like I ever thought I'd make it past my own front porch, let alone be my party's nominee for Congress." He held up his iced tea. "Here's to luck and the horse he rode in on."

"Luck," answered Mitch with his own cup.

"Believe in chance, Counselor?"

"Sure I do," Mitch lied, trying not to sound patronizing.

"Then again, my daddy used to tell me something. He'd say, 'Son, the world and all its wonders are afforded the man who sees his chance and takes it.' " Shakespeare punctuated his words by stabbing the steak with his fork.

"I might argue about any wonders associated with public service," Mitch ventured.

"Would you, then?" queried Shakes. Suddenly he was sizing Mitch up again. "You tellin' me you don't *wonder* what it'd be like to be called *Congressman?*"

"I won't say it hasn't crossed my mind, but that's not the point—"

"What *is* the point? Really. I'm curious," shot Shakespeare. "Cuz I thought it was about power and manifest destiny and all that literary gook. I mean, it's just you and me talkin' here. We can at least get some sincerity goin'."

Shakespeare's folksy manner had turned clammy, more crackpot than diligent community man. The smile was gone. Those facial imperfections abounding.

"I've entered politics because I think I can do some real good," Mitch said. "I happen to *believe* in public service. Just like I believe in the draft. And *that's* not a popular political opinion."

"Yeah, sure. You can save that crap for your campaign." Shakespeare grinned, sticking his fork in Mitchell's direction. "And don't you worry. I got myself plenty of my own crap to dish out. Sure you don't want anything else? How about a refill on that coffee cup?"

"Actually, I should go. Gotta go dish out some crap," joked Mitch, dripping sarcasm. Shakespeare laughed at that one. Meanwhile, Mitch reached into his pocket for his money clip.

"Oh, no. This one's on me," said Shakes, shoving the check into his shirt pocket. "Oughta get out and gear up my own campaign, don'tcha think? You've laid some long yardage for me to make up."

"Best to you, then." Mitch stood up and stuck out his hand. He couldn't get out of there fast enough.

"Shake hands and come out fighting," said Shakespeare as he shook Mitch's hand.

"Something else your daddy used to say?" It sounded demeaning. He regretted the comment the instant it left his lips.

"Naw. Just some more bullshit I picked up along the way."

"Well, good luck to you," said Mitch in earnest. Or so he thought.

He turned to exit, but no sooner was he heading for the front door than he saw Hollice Waters rolling up in a cloud of dust, his Buick idling in front of the diner. Mitch stalled.

"Who's that?" asked Shakespeare.

"Cathedral Daily Mirror."

"And I'll betcha think I called him."

"The thought just crossed my mind."

"I gave my solemn word this was supposed to be a private howdy and hello with you 'n' me. Hell, if I'd even know what to say to a newspaper fellah."

"Well, you're about to find out," shot back Mitch.

"Show you I'm a man of my word, I'll getcha out through the kitchen. Back door way, through the alley and right into your wife's little car," offered Shakespeare.

Mitch looked at him, trying to find something to trust. He was a good five inches shorter than Mitch. But his hand was out, ready to guide the way. Hand to Mitchell's elbow just the way he'd guided him across the street to the five-and-dime.

"Let's go," said Shakespeare. "Out the back."

It was all very hard for Mitch to put a finger on. First the invitation. Then the actual lunch itself. It was more than a howdy and hello as Shakespeare had sold it. It was a testing ground. For what, he couldn't figure.

Once into the alley, he could find his own way. "Thanks for everything," he was polite to add.

He found his feet moving quicker, as if something had repelled him from the little man in the button-down collar and poly-blend coat—something Mitch might be able to figure out once he hit the highway and got some wind in his face. He took a hard right turn out the rear door of the diner, instantly trying to put distance between them. His hand up in a thankful wave that said so long, good-bye, and never look back. A thought flashed through his head.

He has everything to gain.

"Oh yeah. Just one more thing," said Shakespeare, his voice still close to Mitch. Right there behind him, shadowing his steps.

Automatically Mitch stopped and turned without thinking, only to find a hammering fist swung overhand and into his forehead, snapping the cheap glasses at the frame. He careened backward into a cinder-block wall, the back of his head cracking against the concrete with a thud. The first thing he thought was that he'd been struck by an object, like a rock kicked up the road by a passing truck. But he was in the alley. There were no trucks. Only the voice. Shakespeare's voice.

Slumped against the cinder-block wall, Mitchell felt a knee brought up into his groin, sending a pain from his abdomen that rolled up through his torso and crashed into his brain. He blacked out. He didn't remember falling to the dirt. Only the boot that swung into his belly time and time again. He couldn't breathe. And when he sucked for air, the dust choked him. In his only defensive move, he rolled over. But the kicking continued as Shakespeare's hard-soled boot dropped into Mitchell's kidney, followed by another shot across his right ear. The tip of the boot bit and stung.

Above him, the alley spun.

The beating was virtually silent. He didn't have wind in his diaphragm long enough to choke out a call for help while Shakespeare McCann relentlessly delivered calculated blows to his victim—blows not of a screaming, shouting, angry motherfucker who's given to violent outbursts, but of someone practiced in serving up that kind of punishment.

Shake hands and come out fighting.

And then the beating stopped. Mitch lay bloodied on the ground. Fetal. Shuddering in primal fear. Then Shakespeare spoke, his face contorting from that charmer's facade into a visage so suddenly malevolent, were there a witness, he might not have recognized the attacker as the sweet fellow he'd just seen exit the café. All that was left of the man was his telltale twang.

"You may got yourself a fancy campaign machine down there on the Island. But lemme tell you, Counselor, this fight ain't over. It's just a beginning. Like young David who slew Goliath, I have faith in *my* Destiny."

How long Mitch lay in the alley was anybody's guess. Shakespeare had vanished, presumably walking the other way and disappearing down the alley. Mitch remembered him whistling "Dixie," the sound receding until another passing truck drowned it out. All he could remember was that after some time—after nobody had called a 911 dispatcher or come to his rescue—his wits finally gathered between the pulse-poundings in his head. He gained his feet, his fingertips finding the mortared grooves in the cinder-block wall until he was vertical and leaning. His diaphragm released and he sucked in a lung-ful of air, swelling his head with oxygen and pain.

Eventually he got hold of those busted dime-store glasses and affixed them to his face. Through the cracked plastic he could finally see his way out of the alley to where he'd parked Connie's Mustang.

He slid his body into the driver's seat, found the ignition, and turned the key. As he reached for the gearshift, fully prepared to barrel the Mustang backward onto the interstate, he caught a brief glimpse of himself in the rearview mirror. Mitch twisted the mirror to frame his face. Without contacts or working glasses, the image was dull, yet still frightening in the damage it revealed. Cut and swelling with a gravel tattoo across the left cheek, the face in the mirror was a mess. Vanity, he thought. He was vain and never knew it until that very moment when another voice called out. It was Hol-lice Waters.

"Mitch!" shouted Hollice, exiting the diner with his hand held high. "Mitch Dutton!"

He found the reverse gear on the Mustang. He touched the pedal, pretending all along not to hear the continued calls as the wheels spun backward against the dirt.

"Mitch, stop! It's me, Hollice!" bellowed the reporter. But his shouting was to no avail as Mitch spun the steering wheel and roared out onto the interstate. Hollice was left with nothing more than a mouthful of dust. He spat at the ground, "Asshole!"

Mitch drove blindly back to Cathedral Island. Without the proper optics, most of the interstate was an alcoholic's haze. Still, he knew the highway. At a pay phone well south of Benton, he stopped to call Fitz. His cellular battery was dead. Timing. The swelling of his lips and jaw were so severe that he could barely pronounce words, yet he was articulate enough to get Fitz to meet him at an outpatient clinic near the campaign office.

"Goddammit, I want him arrested!" mouthed Mitchell from his swollen face, his ire rising with every pained syllable. "I want you to call the county sheriff's office, have them come down here, and I'll swear out the complaint."

"Just relax and let the painkillers do their business," said Fitz, trying the calm and reasonable approach.

In a private back room in the Sanders Street Clinic, an outpatient practice catering to walk-ins and drug addicts, Mitch and Fitz were posted between shelves stuffed with emergency supplies and a crash cart. All that was missing was the brass plaque that should have read: *The Mitchell Dutton Outpatient OR.* For it was his crusading that kept the mini clinic open twenty-four hours a day to the homeless and dope addicts. He had willingly charmed and steered his wealthy corporate clients into throwing open the check books. And it was for just that reason that he chose the clinic for his own medical care. That way the conditions of his visit would remain within his control.

Fitz requested the attending doctor and nurse step outside for a moment while he got Mitchell's full story. "Okay. Let's say you make that complaint," he reasoned. "You got a witness?"

"*I'm* the witness!" Mitch's face stung as the skin was once again splitting at the corners of his mouth. "Ow. Sonofabitch."

"Hear me out, Mitch," Fitz went on to say. And this was where he was good. Real good. He drew the road Mitch wanted to travel both clearly and concisely. "Let's say we go ahead and have the Republican nominee arrested for battery. What's the press gonna say when they get ahold of this? There's gonna be your side and his side. Right? And without a witness, these voters are gonna make up their own minds."

"So let 'em."

"Mitch. You wanna keep the high ground?"

"Don't be an asshole. Of course I do."

"Then keep your mouth shut," answered Fitz. "This is Texas. South Texas. And what I'm saying is that it's gonna look like you took a lickin'. An old-fashioned, down-home ass-kicking where the Democratic candidate got his clock cleaned by the no-name Republican, who, from a single Goddamn incident, garners statewide name recognition the likes of which no amount of money can buy."

"You want to let him off? Just let him walk away?"

"Fuck no. I want to wipe his ass off the slate in November."

"It was assault. That's a felony, Fitz."

"Sure it is. But what's the bigger crime? The SOB makes a name for himself off of your complaint?" Then Fitz couldn't help himself. "I told you not to go."

"You think he planned it that way?"

"Hell if I know."

"Me, too." All the way back from Benton he had asked himself why. Why would a nominee make such a bad move? Some kind of sick and twisted form of manipulation? It was archaic. Medieval. Downright dumb-assed and stupid.

Or maybe not.

"No. He planned it, all right," reasoned Mitch. And the more he thought about it, the more sense it made. The helping hand. The lunch. And finally, a beating designed to get Mitch to run scared to the police. To look like a wimp to the electorate. After all, this *was* Texas.

"I walked right into it," he said.

"Okay. So he's no dummy," added Fitz, tapping his head with his forefinger. "But you 'n' me, we're smarter. And don't you worry. From now on, you won't be getting within ten feet of that cocksucker."

"It kills me to let this guy walk."

"It'll hurt you worse to talk about it. From this point on, it doesn't go past you and me."

"So how do I explain this?" asked Mitch, pointing to his swelling face.

"You were mugged. Hit from behind. Didn't see the attacker," invented Fitz. "In the alley behind the campaign office. Where you park your car."

"In an alley," repeated Mitch. That much was true.

"You called for help. The mugger ran. You found me minutes later."

"Did I get a look at him?" asked Mitch, trying on the lie. It didn't sit well. The last thing his conscience wanted was to swear out a false complaint.

"He was medium height. Black."

"He hit from behind. The hell if I'm going to give the Cathedral PD reason to pick up a couple of their—quote, unquote—'male usuals.' I'll say I didn't see him."

"Fine. And when they ask about his voice, say he hit you so hard, your ears were ringing."

"I hate this."

"You'll live with it."

"Now, Hollice Waters is gonna know I was up in Benton." Mitch was thinking aloud. "He had to know about the meeting. Probably tipped off by McCann himself."

"Fine. You were invited. You had a nice little meeting and you both went your merry way," Fitz finished. "The attack came upon your return to the office. Timing's right. It all fits."

Mitch ran it over again in his mind. "Yeah. It works. Are you sure this is the only way?"

"You're the boss. We can take our chances with the newspapers. But remember. You'd be doing just what *he* wanted."

Mitch nodded. He was stuck. No two ways about it.

"Just think of what that little prick is gonna think when he reads it," said Fitz, trying to lighten the moment. " 'Candidate attacked behind his own office.' Not a fuckin' mention of his silly-assed name."

Mitch was chilled. Only hours ago he'd driven up to Benton so hopeful and smitten with an ideal. Two men. A handshake. And the race would be on. A race, he would admit, that was stacked heavily in his favor. But a race run by honorable men. Now, as Fitz let the nurse and doctor back into the room to stitch Mitchell's cut face, the candidate felt sullied and ashamed.

At a distance, he could only watch and listen as Fitz made the telephone call to the South County Sheriff's Office to make the initial report. A terrible lie of a report that Mitch would have to corroborate and embellish upon. *How many times?* he thought. For how long?

Shakespeare McCann had fouled Mitch. Now Mitch would foul himself further with the falsified police report. The first time Mitch had ever lied to the police.

The horse race was on.

6

The Sunday funeral for the Honorable Congressman George Alexander Hammond was over two weeks in the making. Not since the death of former Cathedral senator Samuel Watson, an Islander from birth to grave, had there been such a processional. The Strand, the Island's main drag, was stacked with Islanders three deep and two miles long to watch the original horse-drawn Trolley Car Number One roll at a meager mile or so per hour, carrying the flag-draped casket to St. Anthony's Cathedral, where a memorial service would follow.

The Gothic cathedral that gave the South County island its name was the antique prize of *all* Islanders, Catholic or not. And where tourist guides called it a "must-see," locals simply called it "the Church," even though the Island had four others, three of them Baptist. Built by a settlement of Spaniards in 1524, St. Anthony's was topped by a gleaming limestone spire that had provided a sure and welcome landmark to distressed seamen for centuries. Pirates, shrimpers, inexperienced day sailors, and even the occasional wayward Cuban refugee had sought her hallowed sight through many a raging Gulf sky.

The funeral procession was led by six uniformed cops on motorcycles, a horse brigade in full regalia, and the two new fire engines old

Hurricane had federally financed through a rider on a piece of Safety Fund legislation only nine months earlier. Behind the trolley followed a black limousine, its windows tinted a dark gray, which carried the immediate family. The rest of the processional was on foot, consisting of pallbearers, more distant relatives, politicians, friends, and respected enemies.

The spectacle was awe-inspiring. A morose rehearsal for Cathedral's famous July Fourth parade, an event in which Hurricane had usually participated, sometimes riding western style on a borrowed horse, or in recent years, on the backseat of a convertible.

Candidate Mitch Dutton was invited to walk in the death march, a solicitation that he was sorry to decline. Complications with his injuries had left him bedridden for nearly a week with a bruised kidney.

On that Sunday, though, he was up and out of the house. Baseball cap on his head, large sunglasses masking his puffy face, he was going to make some use of his downtime. He was going to prison for a date with a killer. Still, the visitors' guard instantly recognized him.

"Hell. That you, Mr. Dutton?" said the guard. "Man, you really did take a lickin', didn't you?"

"What can I say? Every dog has his day," he lied. "And he was a big ol' dog."

"I think I read about that bad boy," said the guard. A fierce reminder of the real reason for Mitch's being a no-show at Hurricane's Sunday funeral. "They ever catch him?"

"Sorry to say, no," he said, looking for a way to dodge any more questions. The local and state media had picked up the manufactured story and run headlong with it. Fitz had ordered up copies of the police report and distributed them to just about anybody who'd bothered to ask. For an entire day a campaign volunteer was principally assigned to faxing copies of the falsified report to all news organizations statewide, insuring the reportage would be uniform:

> Candidate and de facto front-runner Mitchell Dutton was violently attacked near the private entrance to his campaign office. The motives are still unknown and the perpetrator is still at large.

Miraculously, the police report seemed to be all that was required. Respectfully, the media left the candidate alone in his suffering. Fitz's insistence on Mitch granting no interviews passed with barely a whisper of impropriety; the beating would be better served if aired without photos or film. Leave the violent images of their beloved candidate to the public's imagination, Fitz had decided. The actual sight of Mitch might be all too scary for mass consumption and open a new can of worms. A symbol of street crime victimization. Fitz reminded him that he wanted his candidate portrayed as a congressman, not a martyr.

"How you been?" deflected Mitch.

"Can't complain," returned the guard. "Been a while since you've been around. Guess you been kinda busy."

"I have," he said with a smile. "You vote?"

"I vote every time the white man gives me an opportunity," joshed the affable guard, sealing the envelope in which Mitch had just placed his keys, pens, cell phone, pager, wallet, and money clip. The guard *knew* Mitch. He was just priming the pump for a little fun.

The candidate, on the other hand, was still stumping. "So who'd you vote for?"

"Like you're gonna get me to say I voted for you."

"You're a Democrat, aren't you?"

"Twenty-five years," chimed the grinning guard.

"But Hammond was your man," Mitch confirmed, dropping his voice a somber half octave.

"Had my vote every November," said the guard. "Gonna miss him this year, that's for sure."

"Not to worry," said Mitch. "I'm sure TCPOA will tell you how to vote come November."

The TCPOA, short for the Texas Correctional Peace Officers Association. Half union, half lobbying group, which usually got the government they paid for. Powerful in Texas and aligned with similar groups throughout the nation. Mitch was on their side. But so had Hurricane been for his entire congressional tenure. Their support was now up for grabs.

So Mitch was politic. "I'm glad you voted. That's what's most important."

"Don't get me wrong. I'm Democrat my whole life. I vote Democrat for president. I vote Democrat just about every time I can. Just ol' Hurricane, he done good for all us pokey police."

"Too bad you had to work. You could have gone to the funeral."

"Back at you on that one," said the guard. "Why didn't you go?"

"With this face?" joked Mitch. "I think his family's seen enough grief."

The guard laughed, then got down to business. "Name of the prisoner you want to see?"

"Shoop de Jarnot."

"That's what I thought. What's you got to do with him?"

"He's a pro bono case." Mitch smiled. One of his few cases.

"Some charity work, huh?" said the guard, his tone a tad disapproving.

"Charity's where you find it."

"Hell of a way to spend your day off." The guard leaned closer. "Folks know you do this shit?"

"I'm his lawyer. And he has rights." Mitch shrugged. "That and I left my politics back at the office."

"Kinda risky, don'tcha think?"

"You gonna call a press conference?"

"Who, me?"

Enough said by the guard. Mitch gave an appreciative smile. He obviously didn't want anybody sniffing around. Especially when he was dealing with his prize pro bono case, Shoop de Jarnot. A confessed killer who'd called the South Texas State Reformatory his home for the last seven years.

"Have a seat," said the guard. "Your boy's in the shower, so he's gonna be a while."

Mitch checked his watch. It was five minutes past noon. So have a seat, he did. He found a folding chair parked next to a small table and waited. At that point he wasn't in a rush. In a law practice that consisted mostly of corporate and special-interest matters, this was his idea of fun and relaxation; the dabbling in criminal and constitutional law when he had the inclination or time.

A conflict for a politician? Maybe, he mused. But in the back of his mind, candidate Dutton was still hoping to be appointed to the bench one day. Even better, a federal court. From there Mitch could deliver justice and fairness on issues that mattered to him—the environment, healthcare, free trade, and immigration.

"If you don't mind me asking," called out the guard from his Plexiglas-enclosed booth. "I know some lawyers who like to, you know, lend their time. But you know who you're working for? That boy's bad news. Deserves what he gets, too." He ran a mock knife across his own neck. The implication was clear.

"Deserves what he gets?" Mitch found himself asking. "Who says?"

"I say. God says, too. Eye for an eye."

"But is it the state's business to kill?" It was his stock on-ramp to the debate.

"I reckon so. That's if nobody else is willing to do it." The grin returned to the guard. "And I know plenty of boys that's willin'."

"Screws or cons?" asked Mitch.

"Both," offered the guard with a sinister wink.

That's who Shoop was afraid of. The guards as well as the cons. If the state didn't kill him, he thought surely somebody on the inside eventually would. And if Shoop had the choice, he'd rather the state did it. Painlessly.

In the case of *Texas v. Shoop De Jarnot,* the state wanted an execution by lethal injection. Years earlier, the case had crossed Mitchell's law desk as a back-page newspaper clipping from the *Cathedral Daily Mirror,* sent anonymously for his perusal. The story was pretty simple. Shoop, a native of New Orleans, had chased his wife and her lover along the Gulf Coast for some five hundred miles until he'd caught up with them in one of Cathedral's famous shoreline no-tell motels. He'd shot dead both her and the man she'd run off with.

But the issue wasn't murder. Shoop had done the deed and never, ever, denied it. What was at issue were the words that had passed in the motel room long before shots were fired. Earwitness testimony revealed excited shouts and breaking objects. Yet a Texas jury had still seen fit to convict Shoop of plotting the crime. The evidence being the distance he'd traveled. Their verdict? Murder in the first degree. A crime that, in Texas, carried an automatic death penalty.

Shoop, a poor Creole boy with no means whatsoever, filed his first appeal with the help of a court-appointed attorney who, in Mitch's opinion, botched the action by citing erroneous case law. Even worse, the appellate judge had no guts. He should have returned the action back to the legal sender for another try based on malpractice of law. Instead, the judge upheld the first court's decision and left it for the Texas Supreme Court to decide.

The facts of the first, fouled appeal infuriated Mitch, matched only by his loathing of state-sanctioned executions as a means of punishment. His opinion put him in a vocal minority. But in his bones, he believed a civil society required a moral ethic. The state's sponsorship of murder was the worst example a government could set for its citizens—not exactly the popular view in Texas. It had given Mitch's opposition an easy target in the primary. The issue produced an early match of wills between Mitch and Fitz:

"It'll be what buries you, Mitch. They'll hang you by your fucking balls."

"You want me to lie? You want me to say I'm for it?"

"I want you to spin it, pal. Talk about *justice*. Talk about crime and punishment. But for Christ's sake, don't say you're against the death penalty!"

"But that's who I am. That's part of the package."

"Why not say this: While you're against some of the principles behind capital punishment, you'll uphold the mandate by the people—"

"The people are wrong."

"Then they'll brand you some kind of an elitist. And they'll kill you with that."

"Let 'em kill me, then. I won't change how I think to get elected."

"Listen to Mr. High and Moral Character. You like saying you want to win. But if you won't do what it takes, you're a loser. Plain and simple."

"The high ground, Fitz. We had a deal. If you don't want the job, there are others who do."

Shoop appeared in the meeting space. He was a large man. Solid features. But with melancholy eyes. Hardly looking like the killer he'd confessed to be. His face was drawn as if he hadn't slept in days. Still, his smile betrayed the way he looked and felt. He liked Mitch and was always glad to see him. Mitch was hope, and hope was all he had left.

"What happen ta you?" asked Shoop, his native Creole infecting his English.

"Had a run-in with a bad guy. That's all."

"Fellah dat deed it? Mebbe he oughta be in de jail. I'd show 'im de right side a de line ta walk on."

"Someday. Maybe," said Mitch. "You been okay?"

But Shoop didn't answer. He had something else on his mind. "I watched you on de TV las' week. Guess dis means I'ma gonna be needin' a new lawyuh?" He rubbed his hand across the smooth, metallic surface of the table that separated him from Mitch. "But I can deeg a man's ambition, ya knew?"

"Won't matter who presents the case. An appeal is in the writing," Mitch assured him. "And I'm gonna write you a ticket back to New Orleans."

"Yeah. I'ma gonna be home?"

"That's the plan." Mitch gave an encouraging smile, despite what he knew as fact. Death penalty verdicts were almost never overturned even with evidence of bad legal counsel. And a successful writ of habeas corpus was a rare bird indeed.

In Shoop's case, not only would Mitch cite the correct case law, something a first-year law graduate would know enough to do, but he would also offer up a juicy morsel of jurisdictional evidence. Voters in Louisiana had recently passed an anticrime referendum that tied the recent purchase of a gun to the felony committed with the weapon. Shoop had bought his gun retail, waited the legally allotted time before possession was granted, and then done his crime in the week that followed. Mitchell was not only going to argue Louisiana law, but also that all characters involved in the crime were Louisiana natives, Creoles at that. And coupled with the new Louisiana gun law, Texas's right to the case was only a matter of geography. There had been no crime against the state or its constituents or property. Thus there was no jury of peers; instead it was made up of some of the local unemployed and retirees who looked down upon Shoop and his swamp-flavored diction.

"Dem Supreme Court judges. How dey gonna look at de Creole man?"

"They're not gonna look at you. They're going to listen to the lawyers and read."

Read, they would, but within the brief would be a carrot. Mitch had already worked out a plea agreement with the New Orleans DA. Shoop would plea to first-degree murder and live out the rest of his days in a Louisiana prison. Time to think about what he'd done. Time to live.

"You gonna win an' be one a dem political fellers?" Shoop asked, leading to his next point. "Yeah. I had me an uncle dat was in the Loosiana State House. Man, dat mister walked himself a crooked road. Make my doin's look like Sunday school. Whooeee."

"Well, maybe there's a few of us that think we can make a difference."

"Dat be the truth or is dat some of dem campaign fixin's?"

"What do you think? If you were gonna vote, who'd you pick?"

Shoop gave Mitch a hopeful smile. People *needed* hope, Mitch had learned. They *needed* to know that tomorrow was going to be better than today, for themselves and for their children. It was that hope they would entrust to Mitch by casting a vote. Not altogether different from Shoop's *hope* that Mitch would succeed with the writ.

"Just got a few papers for you to sign." Mitch fanned the papers out in front of Shoop. "These will waive your right to appeal the verdict. It's risky, but it signals the court that should they go simply for the change of venue, you're willing to do the life term in Louisiana."

He handed Shoop the felt pen provided by the guard. Shoop signed them, but held them back from Mitch. "Gotta promise me somethin'."

"Sure. Anything," said Mitch, feeling his remark sounded more like that of a politician than an attorney.

"This ting don' fly and dey go ahead, you know? And kill me like dey's plannin'?"

"Not gonna happen. You're going back to Louisiana. You gotta believe that."

"But if I don't. And I die like some say I should. You gotta promise me you'll see my way back home. My momma will be comin' to da funeral. I want you tah say you look me in dee eye and I told ya tah say tah her that I loved my momma. More den God, even."

"It's not gonna happen."

"Den you so sure, you make dee promise."

"I promise," said Mitch. "Now can I have those papers?"

Shoop handed them over, obviously pleased with his negotiating abilities. "You easy, you know."

"I'll be in touch," Mitch said warmly, shaking his client's hand good-bye.

"I be right here," was Shoop's cryptic retort, arms crossed with an ever-so-big grin. He obviously wasn't going anywhere.

All the Cathedral news stations ran segments on the Hammond funeral, with similar images and sound bites, sandwiched in between national news of the labor secretary's dubious tax difficulties and local sports scores. But cable Channel 44 thought they might sell some cheap commercial time by rerunning the whole taped processional during the dinner hour. Mitch watched it with his feet up in the den.

"Damn," said Mitch aloud. "Go back, go back!" commanding the TV camera to reverse direction on the processional. He had seen something. A familiar face. "C'mon. Go back!"

Eventually the TV camera reversed direction, panning the walking processional once again. Mitch was on his feet, his eyes on fire.

Shaking hands with the mourning crowd, chitchatting away with the other marchers, and not sparing a solitary watt of that practiced, salesman's smile, was Shakespeare McCann. In the flesh. He was wearing another button-down shirt, blue tie, and a black jacket, in Mitch Dutton's place, his face stuck on the TV screen for all to admire and wonder, "Who's the charming fellah with the unmistakable smile?"

That chill again—it shot through Mitchell's spine as if his eyes were a direct link to the electrical impulses in his motor memory. His fists clenched with the rage that had been building minute by minute ever since that evil day. Shakespeare McCann had suddenly come to represent a dent in the armor of Mitchell's manhood. And yet, watching the televised parade, he felt, once again, that he was impotently standing by.

Diving for the cordless phone, he dialed Fitz. It rang only once before, almost telepathically, Fitz picked up. "The sonofabitch is on the goddamn TV. He's in the funeral procession. *In my place!*" shouted Mitch over the phone.

"Who's on TV?" Fitz could barely hear Mitch over the lousy cordless reception.

"Don't you get it? That was the fucking plan all along. Get me out of Hurricane's shadow so the symbolic fucking torch would be passed to him!"

"McCann?"

"Yes! Channel Forty-four. They're rerunning the processional."

He waited for Fitz to switch on his TV. In moments he was back on the line.

"Now, let's not give the little prick too much credit. Just calm your damn self," cautioned Fitz. "It's only a funeral. It's only cable. And the most the nightlies will give it is ninety seconds. Anyway, he's obviously getting advice from somewhere. Lemme find out who and see what we're up against."

"You do that." Mitch's fear of the unknown had become powerful, the aching bruises on his face an omen of what might be ahead.

"Once we get a bead on this piece-of-shit candidate, we'll step on him like the little bug he is," returned Fitz over the phone. "Just take yourself a breather and don't bust any stitches."

Mitchell tossed the phone into the couch cushions, whirling back to the TV only to find his vision interrupted by Connie standing in his way. "What was that about?" she asked.

Taking a moment to compose himself, he answered with the grit still in his voice. "Nothing."

"Mitch. You were practically screaming. I could hear you all the way into the basement."

Mitch forced himself to calm. He didn't want to talk about *it* with her. Not with Connie. When it had come time to confess, he'd told her *the lie* along with everybody else. He didn't want her to know how he'd gotten the shit kicked out of him. And he certainly didn't want Gina to know.

"Politics, hon," he assured her. "Just silly old politics."

"Your face is red."

"It is? I'm sorry."

"What are you sorry about? You didn't do anything to me."

"I'm sorry I yelled."

"Are you all right?" She cupped his face. Kissed his stitches. She'd been nursing him all week. Treasuring the time alone with him.

"I'm fine. It was just Fitz. I got mad."

"Wanna talk about it?"

"No."

"You want dinner?"

"Fine." Subject closed, he prayed.

"Okay. Dinner." She headed back toward the kitchen.

Then Mitch called after her. "I'm sorry."

Connie stopped and shrugged again. "What for?"

"For everything."

Fitz was right on top of it. The next morning he had the door to his office shut with only Rene alongside to lend a hand. It was time to find out just who this Shakespeare McCann really was *before* he was allowed to define himself to the media and the public.

Stu Jackson ran an opposition research team called Source Finders, Inc. Private Investigators for political hire. Fitz had Stu on the phone at his in-home office over in nearby Jennings.

"Shakespeare McCann," mused Stu Jackson. "Heard his name around, but nothin' else along with it. So the Republicans are gonna run him?"

"Didn't have a choice," answered Fitz. "Our initial research tells us he cut up just enough of the South County pie that they *had* to run him."

"I'll check around." Stu stopped asking questions and was in lockstep with Fitz. "Got a girlie up in Houston that lets me run TRWs on just about anybody I please. We'll get that ol' recta-scope working on this Shakespeare fellah. Find out what all matters."

"Talk to ya." Fitz hung up the phone and turned to Rene. "Who do we know on the other side who can give us some real dope?"

"There's a couple of professional turncoats who owe me favors. I'll make some calls and see. But it's gotta be an outside fax line," she said, already on her feet and headed for the door.

"We don't need the whole shebang. Just who he's got in his back pocket, if anybody. I wanna know if this guy's for real or just a one-trick pony."

She returned to her office—temporary digs in a nomadic trade. Hastily personalized. The tattered Kandinsky poster that followed her everywhere. Cappuccino machine. Boombox. She began making calls. She knew plenty of players who knew plenty more players. All of them in politics. Somewhere along the way those relationships crossed party lines to make new connections where information could be funneled. Loyalties be damned. Everybody in the game liked to talk. All anybody needed to know was which buttons to push. Rene had them all listed on her PowerBook.

"Freddy," she cooed into the phone. "How ya doin'?"

"Fine, fine. What's the trick to beatin' that Texas heat?" answered back Freddy.

"Hair spray," she fired back. "How's the Cape?"

"I can think of tougher places to sit out an election year." Freddy was a fellow media consultant for a Detroit candidate that had gotten creamed in the primary. So far he hadn't hooked up with another crew. "Hey. I saw your old man in the airport."

"Nantucket-bound, I'm sure. He wasn't wearing those ugly red pants, was he?" she asked, referring to the strange custom of summer natives wearing a muted pinkish color known only as "Nantucket Red."

"I remember he looked good."

"Quadruple bypasses can do that for you."

"Still kicking ass, huh?"

"And then some," she said, referring to her indestructible father, Marv Craven, an old-league corporate lobbyist with more connections than Delta Airlines.

"Mom?"

"Same as always."

"Sorry. And your sisters?"

"Still married. But between bottles and babies, they're still greasing those hallowed Jackson halls with the best politics money can buy," she said, semiproud of her pro forma political family. Rene was the breakout child, picking the uneven, gypsy life of campaign work over a settled, fixed-income existence working over the same old State House hacks.

She switched subjects. "Any prospects for November?"

"Not yet. Got anything for me down thataway?"

"Willing to work for free?"

"That tight, huh?"

"We're hoping to get the party to kick in something. But that won't happen until July, so . . ."

"So what can I do for you?"

"I need information."

"Who's the victim?"

"It's our opposition. His name is Shakespeare McCann."

"You gotta be kidding me. A candidate named Shakespeare McCann?"

"Colorful folks down here."

"What do you need?"

Rene found herself smiling. That's all she needed to hear.

Fitz would say, in political races, as in so many other endeavors, information is power. An organization's ability to quickly amass potent information is critical to its operational success or failure. The enemy would need to be assessed. No matter how large or small the threat. And on a cool, gray afternoon, under the live oaks and white flowering dogwoods of Mitch Dutton's backyard, Mitch, Fitz, Rene, and Murray sat poolside in comfortable lawn furniture and appraised the competition. Rosa, the Dutton household maid, served flavored iced tea, coffee, and scones baked from Connie's grandmother's historic, butter-based recipe.

"No, thank you," said Rene when she heard the list of ingredients. But Fitz and Murray were both game.

"Where's the missus?" asked Fitz.

"It's subscription time at the station," he answered, referring to one of Connie's charitable pastimes, the local public radio station, KLUD.

"These are phenomenal," said Murray of the scones.

"Clog your arteries," said Rene.

"I'm young. I'm dumb. This is my time to be reckless," fired back Murray.

"Eat now, pay later." She smiled. "See you at your local coronary care unit."

"Leave him be," said Mitch, wanting to get on with the work. "So who is he?" The question referred to Shakespeare McCann.

"A nobody," answered Fitz. He flipped through Stu Jackson's opp-research report. "Owns a chain of print shops. Then there's that photography stuff that we know about. What else? Gives to the church, but doesn't attend. Rents his house. Neighbors don't see him much and, for the most part, don't seem to care. We're still clueless on much of anything else other than what's been filed with the local and federal election commissions."

"What about a criminal record?" asked Mitch.

It was Murray's turn. "Not under Shakespeare McCann. We tapped sources at the local PD. I even got a college pal at the DOJ to do a run through the FBI computers. Not even a traffic ticket."

Rene cooled her mouth with an ice cube, wondering how long she could keep the item against her trademark tongue before it numbed her mute. She was sitting next to Mitch, at the edge of the lounge. Long legs crossed. So far, Fitz was the only one who was sneaking looks at the spectacular gams.

"I think he's even more of a nobody than we anticipated," she volunteered. "I think he got lucky with those fifteen points he took off Hammond. And I also think that jumping you in the alley was the most creative thing he's got in his little bag of tricks."

Jumping me in the alley?

Mitch swiveled a nasty look toward Fitz. He told. Nobody else could've.

Fitz was ready. "They're part of the team, pal. Had to know what you were up against."

"It's okay, Mitch," added Murray with an understanding nod. "Secret's safe with me."

Rene noted Mitch looked like he'd been sneak-attacked. She put a comforting hand on his knee. "And nobody talks about it again after today. Am I right?"

"God's truth," volunteered Fitz, mixing his oath with a Boy Scout salute. "Murr?"

"The candidate was assaulted by an unknown assailant."

"Just stop it," barked Mitch, burying his shame and changing gears again. "Sum and total, we don't know shit about McCann." It was the lack of information on McCann that scared him.

"It's early yet," said Fitz. "Campaigns tend to strip the veneer off a fellah. Give it a little time. Until then, we'll steer clear."

"Treat him as if he doesn't exist," voiced Rene.

"Hell. He's such a nobody, I bet the Republicans don't give him a stinkin' dime," added Murray.

Mitch laughed to himself. Murray. Twenty-some years old and he already knows the Texas Republican party strategy better than the Republicans themselves.

Lip service, he told himself. They didn't know a damn thing and that was that. "We stay the course. And I continue to define the debate."

"What debate? Other than the one stunt, he's a blip on the radar," said Fitz.

"The public debate. The issues. What I got in this for," corrected Mitch. "I didn't decide to run just so I could sling mud with old Hurricane or trade fists with the likes of McCann."

The high ground.

"All I'm saying is that I'm not worried about McCann," countered Fitz. "You're in. All we gotta do is, like you say, stay the course. Come November, you're a congressman."

"Don't bet the farm," finished Mitch. "He's Texas-smart. And that obviously counts for somethin'."

Texas-smart. The kind of fellah who seemed to know which way the coin would fall on a toss and bet against the Cowboys whenever he felt lucky. The description fit when the image of Shakespeare McCann came to mind. It fit like a glove.

7

"Shit!" Hollice Waters slammed the phone back into the cradle. Since early May he'd been trying to get in touch with Shakespeare McCann, but the numbers he'd been given had never panned out. Phones would either turn up disconnected or would ring endlessly without an answer. And now as the Memorial Day holiday approached the intrepid reporter was starting to believe the rumors: Shakespeare McCann was nothing more than a local crackerjack who caught a minor fifteen-point wave in the primary. Luck, and luck alone, had dropped him into the big race. The new candidate had probably seen the insurmountable campaign before him and had either dropped out or been paid off by his own party not to embarrass them. When Hollice had moved on to another tack with his campaign coverage, Shakespeare found him.

"It's time we talked, don'tcha think?" Shakespeare announced. As for his absence, he merely answered, "Was putting together my campaign staff. Didn't figure I was in the horse race till weeks ago. You know how it goes."

Hollice knew as much, yet said nothing. Instead he dutifully took down the directions to Shakespeare's office in nearby Cathedral City. It promised to be the candidate's first official interview. With luck, Hollice could stretch it into two columns.

Shakespeare McCann's center of campaign operations was a single-room walk-up with an empty secretarial space. Faux brick veneer and wood-grain paneling. Shakespeare greeted Hollice at the door, apologizing for stinky wet carpet from the air conditioner leakage, then retreated behind a barren, mesalike desktop with a high-powered PC to his right with multiple modem cables snaking into brand-new wall jacks.

"That's a helluva computer setup," remarked Hollice. "Looks like you're connected."

"Building a Web page for my campaign," said Shakespeare. "Callin' it 'Shakes On-Line.' "

"Campaigning through the Internet. Sounds a little broad-based for a small congressional district, don't you think?"

"Yup. But you never know if there's a fellah in Decatur with ten bucks and a stamp to spend on better government." Shakespeare grinned. "Can I getcha somethin'? Iced tea? Dr. Pepper?"

"I'm fine, thanks." When Shakespeare dove underneath his desk to open an ice-filled cooler, Hollice caught a look at a large cork bulletin board on the wall behind the candidate, colored with three-by-five cards, each bearing an indistinguishable scrawl. "What's that?" asked Hollice, nodding to the corkboard and cards.

Shakespeare popped open a Dr. Pepper. "Oh, that? That's my campaign."

"How's it turn out?"

"You gotta stay for the end of the movie to find out how it turns out," said the candidate with a wink and that smile again. "But I'll give you a hint. The dark-horse candidate wins."

"Really?" said Hollice, already amused. He'd seated himself across from the desk in a folding chair Shakespeare had fished from the broom closet. Hollice took that to mean the candidate wasn't accustomed to visitors. He made a note and asked, "And your campaign staff? Day off?"

"Front-office gal, she's out to lunch. As for the rest of the staff, you're lookin' at him."

"On the phone you said you're putting your staff together."

"Ain't done yet. But November's a long way off."

"Okay. So let's talk about your campaign."

"What's to know? I'm the Republican nominee," responded Shakespeare, rocking back and forth in his leather office chair, eyes straight ahead at Hollice. "Didn't expect to be here. Guess neither did you."

They shared a laugh with that one. Hollice suddenly felt sorry for the man, certain that McCann didn't have a clue as to what he was in for. "And the dark horse wins. Your words?" he returned.

"You can quote me on that," said the candidate. "Got a right to be optimistic, now, don't I?"

"You're free, white, and American," tempted Hollice, seeing if McCann would bite.

Instead, Shakespeare sat back and got himself a good look at the reporter. His eyes narrowed and hardly wavered. "You wanna bait me, don'tcha?"

"Don't know what you mean."

"Oh, cuz I'm the right-winger. Y'all just wanna know how far right, I reckon."

"Fifteen percent off of Hurricane Hammond. I don't see much of that coming out of the middle ground."

"Fair enough. But when it comes to the colors of the rainbow, I'm an equal-opportunity candidate. South County, yessir. Can't deny my own Texas dirt. As for the rest, I'm free, I'm American, but the white part was God's doin'."

"Got a platform? Got a stand on anything?"

"Sure do. But I'm afraid the sign reads, 'Under Construction.' "

"This is your interview, Mr. McCann. Folks are gonna wanna know what you stand for."

"For a start, let's just say I'm the law-and-order candidate."

"Okay. But so is Dutton. Your opposition. At least he says so. In fact, he's got a strong record of support for law enforcement, and they for him."

"So he says. But he's anti–death penalty. You 'n' I both know it. To me, that ain't law and order. That ain't Texas."

" 'That ain't Texas,' " said Hollice, amused. "I think I remember Hurricane saying that."

"I steal from the best. And Hurricane was the best."

"If he was the best, why'd you run against him?"

"Oh, I had some things I wanted to bring to the party, so to speak. Thought I'd try my hand at the great American debate."

"But now that he's gone, is that your campaign strategy—to reinvent yourself as the second coming of Hurricane Hammond?"

"I'm not that lucky and I'm not that smart. Just like Popeye says, 'I am what I am,' " retorted Shakespeare, happy with his answer and looking more like a cartoon character than a candidate.

"Can I quote you on that?" said Hollice, leaning on every syllable of sarcasm.

"As long as you let your readers know that I speak with grand humility," returned the candidate.

"Okay, all right. So let's cut the crap." Hollice sat forward, switching off the tape recorder. "Ain't no love between me and your opponent. He's the odds-on favorite and will probably kick your ass come November. Now, if I'm to be correct, your campaign isn't even out of the gate and he's already in the backstretch. You're short of money. And you're short of support, not including the South County Old Home Society, who I hear are real happy with their family portraits."

Shakespeare stopped rocking. The smile faded and he stared dead ahead at Hollice. "You want straight talk. I can talk straight. What's on your mind?"

"You need a friend," said Hollice without so much as a blink. "I could be it."

"A friend in the press?" Now Shakespeare's tone was sarcastic. "Why do I need a friend in the press? So you can build me up to tear me down? I don't think so. Not when I got the power of the Almighty Republican party behind me."

"Don't gimme that. I've heard they're gonna pass you by. Save their money to put on a candidate that counts."

"Well, that's where you're wrong," said Shakespeare, rocking once again in that dwarfing leather chair. "They're behind me one hundred percent. They don't wanna lose the seat to a lefty like Dutton."

Hollice stalled a moment before reaching out and restarting the tape recorder. "I find that hard to believe. I talked to Bill Ziegler just last week." Bill Ziegler was the state Republican party chairman. A man with old ties to Cathedral and Hollice Waters.

"What'd he tell you?" asked Shakespeare.

"You tell me."

"What would you say to a canceled check for seventy-five thousand dollars?" teased Shakespeare, paying off the smile on his face with a photocopy of a canceled check from his top drawer. The check was cut from a Dallas bank, dated two days prior and made out to the Shakespeare McCann for Congress Committee. The familiar Texas Republican party logo of an elephant standing on a state seal appeared in the left-hand corner as sure as day.

"Is that for real?" asked Hollice, not thinking how stupid it would be to assume that McCann would show him a faked check.

"Real as rain on a tin roof," sparked Shakespeare, picking up the phone and handing the receiver to Hollice. "Call the bank if you like."

The story didn't wash with Hollice. Less than a week ago he'd had conversations with Bill Ziegler, who hadn't said a damn thing about Shakespeare McCann other than the fact that he'd surprised the hell out of just about everybody up Dallas way with his fifteen-point pull from the Hurricane Hammond pool. On the contrary, Zig had implied that financial support of *any* party candidate against Mitch Dutton would be throwing good money after bad.

"Go ahead. Call Zig, if you don't want to call the bank."

"Why would I?" said Hollice. "It's clear you're their candidate and they're behind you."

"Clear as crystal," Shakespeare answered.

The little clichés were grating on Hollice. That *and* the check. Was it enough to print, though? All he needed was to call Bill Ziegler to confirm the support. But party politics weren't always made for public reading. And seventy-five thousand could be seed money or the only payday Shakespeare would ever see from up Dallas way. If denied, Hollice would have to print such a denial.

Why take the chance? he thought on his drive back to the Island. Seventy-five grand worth of support was seventy-five grand. The interview had garnered him little else that was tangible. Like a slot machine that returns two quarters for every one wagered, Shakespeare had returned two questions for every one he answered, revealing little in the process.

Seventy-five thousand dollars.

"That's real support," he'd told Shakespeare. "I'm impressed."

"Impressed enough to print it?"

"Not up to me. Up to my boss. The editor."

"Charlie Flores. Yessir. Give him a howdy and hello from me," quipped McCann.

Charlie Flores was a staunch Republican. And hell if Hollice was going to give a howdy or hello from anybody. As for the check, that wasn't really an issue. Real or not, it *appeared* to be real support. That would be worth printing. The Grand Ol' Party, behind the new man from South County, Shakespeare McCann.

Hollice looked forward to waving that in front of Mitch Dutton, who by luck was getting a free ride to the Hill because some fat, drunken incumbent couldn't stay on his Goddamn horse.

*   *   *

For the Dutton camp, June passed through in quiet gusts of activity. The state party had released funds to all its favorite nominees, sending Mitch's staff on a spending spree. More office phones. More colorful pins and bumper stickers. More TV buys. Mitch and his message were regular, thirty-second spots at six and eleven. Business as usual, thought Fitz. It was full steam ahead, with the Shakespeare McCann campaign barely visible in the wake, fueling the rumor that the South County candidate was nothing more than a one-joke Johnny-we-hardly-knew-ya.

But July. That was a month hot enough for its own headlines. The ever-present Gulf breezes faded, leaving afternoons so sticky with perspiration, the local power utility rolled out a last-minute radio campaign that pleaded for reduced energy consumption. The mercury soon tipped the Cathedral Island one-hundred-year record.

Polling-wise, the month was far cooler. Fitz had kept a keen eye on the numbers, employing the bean counters at Electioneering USA to run weekly tracking on his candidate. As expected, the unlikely passing of George "Hurricane" Hammond had boosted Mitchell's viability and acceptability to a whopping seventy-four percent. Name recognition was even higher at eighty-two percent. Still, amongst likely voters the most comforting figure was in the category of trust. There stood a huge gap between Mitchell's name and that of the still unknown Shakespeare McCann. Mitchell's score was in the seventies, where Shakespeare's was just over fifteen points, not so coincidentally the same figure he'd garnered against the incumbent in the primary.

"These are the kind of numbers that make my week," e-mailed Fitz to Martin O'Roarke, a colleague working a state senate race up in Portland, Oregon. "They prove my theory that the opposition isn't anything more than an amateurish, terrorist threat, leaving my candidate without the muddy, rhetorical entanglements campaigns are fast becoming famous for. That, and it leaves me, his genius campaign manager, to focus on the road ahead. In other words, I'm feeling like a winner."

The e-mail response was envious. "Fitz. Wake up. It's July. How far away is November?"

Mitch, on the other hand, nearly fully recovered from what he would only refer to as "the incident," was back on the stump. He didn't want to see the tracking numbers, preferring to run his campaign as he'd always intended—on the issues and new ideas for change in government.

The high ground.

He wrote his feelings in a Sunday guest column in the *Daily Mirror* that touched on everything *but* crime and, more important, Mitch's none-too-popular view on capital punishment. Fitz had red-penned it.

"I'll make you a deal," said the campaign manager. "You leave out the death penalty stuff and I'll buy you and your wife the best dinner on the Island."

"That'd be at Portofino," ventured Mitch, "but it's officially off-island," referring to the pricey Italian restaurant on the mainland side of the Span.

"Done."

"What do you think that'll cost ya?"

"Two bills."

"Swell. Take that two hundred dollars and write out a check to the Cathedral Children's Hospital. Right now. Then I'll cut out the stuff on capital punishment."

Fitz grudgingly wrote the check with one arm twisted behind his back. "Now you're learning."

"The trick with the check. I'm going to remember to use that," mused Rene. "You had leverage and you used it."

"I have my persuasive moments," said Mitch. "And then again, I don't." He was thinking back to the botched speech he'd just given to a South County chapter of the American Association of Retired People. It ended with an old woman, big enough for two whole chairs in the grade school auditorium, shaking her fist at him and bellowing, "You're not gonna take away *my* Social Security!"

"I'm not talking about *your* Social Security," he had too rationally countered. "I'm talking about your grandchildren. The system is going bankrupt and it needs rethinking."

"Hard enough feeding three dogs and a husband with Alzheimer's with what I got!"

Mitch swallowed uncomfortably. Seemingly his big mistake was when he decided to ply the meeting with fact. "Did you know that between the ages of sixty-five and seventy, you'll have spent just about everything you've paid into Social Security?"

The shouting from the old lady rose way over the collective deafness of the forty-six attendees. Afterward Fitz threw an arm around Mitch. "Way to go. You just alienated the single most consistent voting block in America."

"I told the truth," said Mitch, knowing he'd gone about the question and answers all wrong.

"Next time save the truth for those who want to hear it."

Fitz had a meeting in Cathedral City after the event, so it was just Mitch and Rene on the drive home. But an accident involving an overturned semi closed the Span. There was no way to get back on the Island until traffic cleared. Rene suggested dinner. Mitch's convenient answer?

Portofino.

A valet parked the Volvo. As they entered the tiny cliffside restaurant, Rene turned the usual heads. Men, mostly. All of whom were either sitting or standing, waiting for a table. "I forgot," said Mitch. "They don't take reservations."

Taking his hand in hers, she weaved the way over to the maître d'. Instead of asking how long the wait was, she whispered. Instantly the maître d' looked past her, his face beaming with sudden recognition. Menus in hand, he led the two of them to a corner table with a spectacular windowed view of the channel, and beyond, the Island. The Span above. The starry sky. The carnival-colored lights of Cathedral mirrored in the glassy green water. It was a table reserved for millionaires and heavy tippers.

In all his years of anniversaries, birthday dinners, and special occasions, thought Mitch, he'd never rated such a table. Or even knew he could ask for it.

And he was there with another woman.

He found himself doing a defensive scan of the room to see if anyone was watching. If anyone had noticed. If there was anyone he *knew*. Or anyone who looked as if they recognized him.

"So tell me. How does it feel?" asked Rene.

"How does what feel?" He swung his attention back to her. She was close enough to kiss.

"Celebrity," she prompted.

"You told the maître d', didn't you?"

"That you were Mitch Dutton? The candidate? Sure. Now, are you going to answer my question?"

"Celebrity?"

"Uh-huh."

"I try not to think too much about it."

"Good boy. A little denial goes a long way." She winked. "Just make sure you watch yourself. Or one day you'll wake up and the grass won't be green enough, the sky not blue enough, or the girl in your bed not young enough."

"Ah, the evils of power," he said cynically.

"Power corrupts."

"Absolutely," finished Mitch. "Lord Acton, if I recall. He musta been for term limits."

"I know what I'm talking about, Mitch. It happens to every candidate."

"You know this from experience?"

"I was the girl in the bed."

Mitch practically choked on his breadstick. That and the images that came to him plugged his ears and stalled the conversation. Rene was stretched out on a unmade bed. Naked and wanting more. Across the room, a fat-assed, hairless candidate, drunk on Chivas. It didn't fit. But that picture of her, naked, needing . . . someone.

She broke back in. "Power's an amazing aphrodisiac."

"You're talking to the original Boy Scout," defended Mitch. "True and blue."

"Boy Scouts grow up." She leaned in, but let her eyes flick around the room until she'd picked out a man. Classically handsome. Nice suit. "Look at him. The guy in the pinstripes. You think he has what you have?"

"I wouldn't know."

"Looks good. At a glance, a girl might be interested. But then she takes him home and finds out he's more into his La-Z-Boy lounger than a good roll in the hay. I'll bet he only gets off to pictures of Cindy Crawford."

"Be my guest," tested Mitch. "Ask him. See if he isn't tempted to give you the back of his hand."

"Oh, he wouldn't hit a woman. He's *scared* of women." Once again she gazed about the room, finding another victim. "The guy in the blue blazer, green tie. Now, there's a wife beater if I ever saw one. I'll bet he thinks missionary has something to do with the Catholic church."

"You are cruel," he joked. "You don't know these people. For all you know, he may *be* a priest."

"Wouldn't mean I'm wrong." She gave him a mischievous smile. "Now it's your turn."

"My turn to what?"

"The woman. The blonde with Bubba over there. The one in the hat."

"What about her?"

"You tell me."

The look Rene gave him spelled out her little game. A sort of sexual "What's My Line?" Mitch held eye contact with her for a few seconds. Challenged. If he could've thought of a way to politely deflect, maybe he wouldn't have turned to give the blonde with the hat act another look.

"You're too nice."

Mitch just shrugged.

"Go ahead."

"Okay," he began ever so slowly. "She picked him because he's got some dough. But. She's afraid that sixty words per minute won't get her the Cadillac she's always dreamed of."

"And?"

"And . . . she loves him. You can tell by the way he smiles back at her. Comfortable."

"But . . ."

"When he gets up to go to work, her best friend's her vibrator."

Rene howled and clapped her hands. "You got it."

"I made it up."

"It's just a game, Mitch."

"Okay. Your turn," he said, seeking out her next target. "The guy with the bad hairpiece. Sweater vest. Under the painting. See him?"

"Easy. Tries hard. Comes too fast. Entertains the kids by making balloon animals out of condoms."

They laughed some more. It was a cruel game. But it made Mitch feel connected to someone in a way he hadn't in months. It had nothing to do with anything, he told himself. It was just a bit of twisted fun, plain and simple.

"My turn," said Rene. "Back in the dark corner. She's got her hair pulled back. The one with the scarf, see her?"

"Got it," he said, zeroing in on the unsuspecting wife. "Miss Proper Yuppie. She's good off the gun, but gets bored quickly. Afraid blow jobs might spoil her makeup. And twice in one night—"

"Oh, out of the question!" agreed Rene, giggling over her appetizer.

They were laughing so hard, when the maître d' appeared, he thought the joke might be on him. "Excuse me, signor. Mrs. Dutton is on the telephone."

Cold water. That's what it felt like. As if a wave of the stuff had broken through the plate glass and washed away all their fun. Mitch was blanketed in sudden guilt. He excused himself, rose from the table, and followed the maître d' to the house phone.

How Connie knew Mitch was at Portofino turned out to be a

kind of detective work reserved only for married couples. She'd seen on the news that the Span was closed and, certain he wouldn't wait until he got home to eat, called the three restaurants she knew of near where the Span joined the mainland. Portofino was last on the list. The call itself worked out to be relatively uneventful. One of their two golden retrievers had gotten into a tangle with a neighbor's cat. Connie was at the veterinarian's and wanted to know if Mitch could pick up a half gallon of nonfat milk on the way home. No problem, he told her.

Throughout the remainder of the dinner, both Mitch and Rene kept the conversation on track, working out the small daily details of the campaign, mixed with a little talk about family. Mitch confessed to her that he'd been trading calls with his father for some two months now. It was par for the course, he told her. As a rule, his old man didn't like lawyers. They were second only on the shit-pile to politicians.

The Span cleared and the two-minute drive across was practically silent. Parked in front of the campaign headquarters, they said their good-nights. Then as Rene was crawling out of the car, she turned back to him. "I'm sorry," she apologized.

"Sorry for what?" he asked.

"Earlier. At dinner," she confessed. "I'm a tease when I drink."

That hair, he thought. That amazing hair, it strung over her face, her eyes peeking through it. Brave and embarrassed all at once. Mitch brushed it out of her face and kissed her. Full on, just like he'd been tempted to for so many damn months. Rene, she didn't retreat, her lips softly held to his as long as he dared.

And when he finally broke contact, "I'm sorry," he found himself apologizing.

"What for?"

"For wanting to." For wanting to *so badly,* he corrected in his mind.

She shrugged with resignation. "I'm the girl."

"I better go."

"See you tomorrow," was all that was left to say. Rene smiled, retracted herself from the car, and shut the door. Mitch watched her as she disappeared inside the old whorehouse building.

In that old manse on Flower Hill, Mitch usually woke to the sound of newspapers flopping one by one onto neighboring drive-ways. For years the *Cathedral Daily Mirror* had been delivered by Harvey Gooden, a sixties burnout, in his original '64 Volkswagen bus. The drive up to 532 Broughton formed a canyon where even the smallest sound would carry. Even from the south-facing master window, Mitch would hear the newspaper call and ease ever so gently from the bed, careful to not wake Connie. Once downstairs, he would read the morning paper with a single cup of coffee before his five-mile run with their two golden retrievers, Merle and Pearl.

But that Wednesday morning, Mitch didn't run. In fact, he'd barely slept, thinking all the night about Rene, the kiss, and whether his slumbering wife had even the faintest clue of what he'd done. Downstairs, in the kitchen, the poor dogs sat idle, watching all the while as he read and reread Hollice Waters's single-column piece on Cathedral's newest underdog, Shakespeare McCann. *Seventy-five thousand dollars in campaign funding?*

How could they? asked Mitch. Did the party leaders know what they were doing? This man was crazy. Worse. Psychotic. Violent. How dare they validate *his kind of behavior!* For over a month now, he had done his best to forget about the beating, finding what comfort and distraction he could in just about every way possible. In the campaign. In hard work. In those welcome, praising handshakes from just about everybody he'd run across. But in that moment at the breakfast table, the morning sun twisting upward through the backyard dogwoods and oaks, he was alone with the recollection of an assault so vivid that he didn't realize the coffee cup was at his lips and he was gagging. He dropped the cup and it fell, splintering across the ancient tile floor.

Connie arrived downstairs in time to find him kneeling and sweeping the splintered china into a dustpan. "Well, I hope it wasn't one of Mother's."

He looked up to find her smiling. "I think that leaves us at seven." They'd broken four cups since their wedding day.

"I guess when they all break, we're done for," she quipped as she crossed to the fridge and removed a carton of orange juice and a loaf of whole wheat bread.

"Your mother's twisting in her grave."

"Let her twist. I'm already looking for a new set. Thinking about redoing the whole kitchen, actually. Would you mind?"

"I like it fine as is." Mitch dumped the remains of the broken cup in the garbage pail in the pantry.

"It's my mother's kitchen. It's her house, when you think about it." That's when she moved in on him from behind and put her arms around his waist. Her hands were cold from the refrigerator. "Don't you think it's about time we made it *our* house?"

"Anything you want," he said.

"Did you run?" To her touch, he felt dry, absent the usual stickiness that followed his morning runs.

"Not yet. And now I'm late. Gotta shower, then a campaign to win." Mitch kissed her ever so briefly, then turned to head back upstairs. Connie, though, held on to him.

"How's it going?"

"What?"

"The campaign," she ventured. "Are you really going to win?"

"Between you and me? Yes." Another kiss and he was off.

Yes.

The word stung.

Yes.

He was going to win. He was going to be a congressman. And yes, they would have to move, leave the Island . . . leave her *home*.

There would be no point in changing the kitchen or anything else.

Born on Flower Hill to a family as old as the Island itself, Connie had never exactly felt a need to grow up in the traditional sense. The Island had always taken care of her, as had the magnificent Victorian home that had been built by her great-grandfather and left in her name by her deceased parents. Still, there had been no money in the will. Her parents' extravagant lifestyle and apparent inability to deny themselves any luxury had provided their only daughter with a fairy-tale childhood. Private schools. European vacations. It had also devoured every penny they had, and then some. Connie had inherited her parents' debts and the house.

When she was introduced to Mitch, she was a paralegal pulling hours equal to the partners in the law office of Gade, Seaton, and Peacock, just to make the payments on the second and third mortgages she was carrying. Mitch, on the other hand, was the new associate making the jump from another firm, and she was assigned to his desk. The romance that followed was like a prairie fire, she'd told all her girlfriends. Mitch and Connie instantly burned up the customary dating rituals and shot straight into cohabitation. After all, they *were* working alongside each other. Why not live together? They saved on rent and gas and just about every other expense. Plus she had great digs, he would proudly tell his law buddies. Just her and that big ol' house. The neighbors talked and talked. Let 'em, he said. They were in love and that was all that mattered. That would surely be enough.

Connie remembered how Mitch had encouraged her to go to law school and cross that bridge into the *real* legal game. Instead she crossed a threshold in his arms and became Mrs. Dutton inside year one, forgoing her family name in exchange for the unspoken promise that he would never take the Island from her, or her from the Island. The same went for the house on Flower Hill where they would live forever, raise their children, and one day hold court to gaggles of grandchildren.

Such was the fantasy. Such was a promise that was about to be dashed against the seawall that had become their marriage, where surging currents moved in opposite directions along a rocky ocean outcropping. Everyone knew Mitch was the front-runner. And front-runners usually win. And winners leave home, just like old Hurricane had, never to return for anything more than a free meal and a promise to play an honest game.

Alone now save for Rosa, who would come and clean on Monday, Wednesday, and Friday, Connie was left to fill her days with charity work: the local public radio station. The annual March of Dimes telethon. Leukemia Society functions. Heart of the Gulf Foundation. And whenever she could, tending the large camellia garden and greenhouse her father had built at the rear of the property. Other times she would silently cry about the dream she and Mitch had failed to fulfill—to bless the big house with children.

Ten A.M. Gina arrived in her new Mercedes convertible with the top down and her hair in a mad tussle. She leaned on the horn and shouted, "Connie! We're gonna be late!" It was five more minutes before Connie appeared at the side door, dressed and made up for a day in Houston for the quarterly sorority luncheon.

"What's wrong with you, girl? You been crying?"

"He says he's gonna win."

"So what if he does? Nobody ever said you had to go with him," shot back Gina with a confident grin.

"What about the house? Who would live there?"

"The house isn't going anywhere. And neither are you if you don't want to," assured Gina.

They were only words meant to make her feel comfy and cared for, and Connie knew it. Deep in her heart, though, she felt the struggle begin. A war was about to be waged between her home and her heart. *The House on Flower Hill v. Mitch and the Congressional Seat.* She was afraid for herself and the part of her that would undoubtedly lose.

Crossing the Span into Cathedral City, Gina put the hammer down in the Mercedes and racked a new CD into the deck. The music thumped. And Connie tried to roll a joint without losing too many buds to the wind. "Shit!"

"Don't forget to flush the seeds," joked Gina. "Maybe we'll get pulled over for speeding. Get busted. It'd be in the papers."

"That would be mean."

"And what's he being to you? Mr. Wonderful?"

"He's being Mitch."

"Rhymes with sonofabitch."

"He is not," defended Connie. "He's just never home. I hardly ever see him."

She bit her lip and went with her gut. "If I were pregnant, I betcha he wouldn't be running for office. He'd be where he belongs."

"And you think that's the reason?"

"He's just bored, that's all."

"Bored with you. And you know what that means."

"Not Mitch. He's too principled."

"He's controlling."

"He's my *husband*, G."

"He's a *man*. Men have *penises*. And when they're *bored* they *play* with them," said Gina. "I swear it's true. I read it in *Cosmo*."

"You should try reading a book."

"What happens when he wins, Connie? Seriously. He'll want to move. He promised you he wouldn't make you leave the Island."

"We'll cross that bridge when it comes."

End of subject. But all the way to Houston, inside Gina's perverse skull, were the beginnings of a plan. A plan that would surely release Connie from the internment that was her marriage.

North of Houston is Dallas. And thirty years earlier, Dallas had but one downtown. Little more than four corners, it was flanked on one side by a modern, eight-story jail, and a schoolbook depository on the other. With a curvy little drive that swiveled in between grassy knolls and park benches, retreating westward and underneath a railroad trestle, Dealy Plaza gained an identity all its own one November day in 1963. Soon after, the city fathers had seen fit to abolish any master plan to further develop the west end of Dallas, and focused eastward in creating their business mecca. Eventually the old downtown was dwarfed by sparkling structures built from glass and steel. By 1975 Dallas had its own skyline as distinct as any modern Ameri-

can city, leaving Dealy Plaza as little more than a painful reminder—
a landmark, frozen in time and political infamy.

Like so many organizations before them, the Texas Republican
Central Committee had long since abandoned their Dealy Plaza offices in exchange for the entire eleventh floor of the Union Bank
building in the lustrous new downtown.

William "Zig" Ziegler was late getting into the office that Friday
morning the *Daily Mirror* had touted the party's generous contribution
to the McCann campaign. Forty-nine and the father of five, he was
a picture of new health with a thick head of hair and a body recently
leaned on doctor's orders by a home StairMaster and HealthRider.
At the ding of the elevator, he stormed through the lobby with barely
a nod to the receptionist before vanishing into the maze that was the
Central Committee's base of operations.

"I want a copy of the *Cathedral Daily Mirror* on my desk. Now!"
said Zig in place of his usual cheerful "Good morning." The door to
his office slammed, leaving the air behind him still. The day was not
off to a good start.

His office was well appointed, but tackily adorned with a wall
plastered with cheaply framed pictures of Zig with Republican celebri-
ties, including Barry Goldwater, Bob Dole, Ronald Reagan, and Colin
Powell. Perched on a credenza behind his desk were family pictures.
Mostly of his eighteen-year-old daughter, a tawny blonde with Miss
Texas, U.S.A., sort of features. A real local beauty. The black-and-
white eight-by-ten head shot showed the girl had modeling prospects.

Zig was calling Hollice Waters for the fourth time that morning.
He'd started just after seven, dialing from his Fort Worth home, trying
again at eight and eighty-thirty with no returns. If Hollice didn't answer this time, Zig's next call was going to be Charlie Flores, Hollice's editor. Someone needed to be the unfortunate recipient of his
vitriol. Instead, before he finished dialing, a message scrolled in green
letters across the screen of his Amtel.

—Shakespeare McCann is—

He cut off the message by hitting the code key that returned to
his secretary a message that read:

—Call back—

Hollice's line at the *Daily Mirror* was ringing at the other end of his line when a new message scrolled by:

—Shakespeare McCann is here to see you!—

The message momentarily shook him. He'd avoided McCann's calls for months. The Republican nominee whom the Central Committee's chair had refused to even acknowledge was now standing outside Zig's closed door. He wasn't the Committee's choice. Or even the People's. The man beyond the door, in the eyes of the Central Committee, was lucky. Nothing more. In a time when campaign cash was always better spent on *candidates who could win,* and when the Committee was expecting tight races all over the state come November, Shakespeare McCann was less than an afterthought. He was a total write-off.

"Sonofabitch," said Zig to himself. He'd have preferred to talk to Hollice first. Get the reporter's story straight before facing off against the candidate who'd fraudulently *asserted* to have been given seventy-five grand of the Central Committee's cash.

Then ding. Another message scrolled across the screen:

—Mr. McCann has brought you a copy of the Daily Mirror—

Reluctantly he crossed to the door that only moments earlier he'd slammed shut, opening it slowly and drawing a smile across his face. "Mr. McCann. I'm glad we finally have the pleasure of meeting. I'm sorry it's taken us so long."

Shakespeare was out of his seat and pumping Zig's hand, that patented salesman's smile on his face and contact-blue eyes showing zero sign of the utter contempt he felt for the Republican chair. Not only had Zig not returned his numerous calls, but he'd passed Shakespeare by as he'd breezed into the office. Hadn't even noticed him chatting it up with the office staff, telling jokes and generally keeping anybody within earshot entertained. Yet he accepted Zig's hand as if it were the friendliest of encounters.

"Pleased to make your acquaintance, Mr. Ziegler." Then he followed the chairman back into his office. Once again, the door was closed.

"You brought me a copy of the *Mirror,*" said Zig, seating himself across from the candidate. "Only minutes ago I'd asked my secretary for a copy."

"I know. I was there," said Shakespeare, finding a comfortable seat. He let the insult roll off, crossed his legs, and seemed as relaxed as a house cat.

Zig had sat across from hundreds of candidates in his years at the Committee. That was his job. All of the candidates with their hands out for money. Hearing their practiced pitches. It was a power position for Zig, holding the purse strings to so many political futures. But something about Shakespeare had him off kilter. Suddenly he didn't feel so powerful.

"I haven't spoken to Hollice Waters yet. But you can bet I will." Zig watched the strange man, wondering why the candidate wasn't squirming.

"All he's gonna tell you is that I showed him a canceled check from your Committee to my campaign," said Shakespeare.

"Not from my Committee. Because I didn't sign it. We didn't give you seventy-five thousand dollars."

"Take a look for yourself." From his inside coat pocket, Shakespeare handed over the canceled check.

Zig examined the check, his brow furrowed in a sudden, worried stare. It looked real enough. And the signature was dead-on perfect. "This isn't real. It's a forgery."

"And a damn good one if you ask me," said Shakespeare, as if he were expecting a compliment.

"You're proud of it?"

"Got your attention, didn't it?" The candidate smiled, obviously pleased with himself.

"Was that your intent? To get the Committee's attention?"

"Here I am."

"So you are," acquiesced the chairman.

"So let's get to know each other. I'm your candidate from South County. You give me five minutes, I'll betcha I can make that phony check as good as gold."

Ballsy, thought Zig, briefly charmed. There were plenty of wannabe candidates who'd tried to get through his door. Few of those uninvited had made it past the lobby. Shakespeare was clearly an exception. "Have you thought of how it might look when we deny ever giving you a check?"

"I have," said Shakespeare. "But it goes both ways. How's it going to look to the faithful in South County when they find out their own party won't support the rightful nominee?"

"The Committee already weighed that risk against our own limited resources." Zig shrugged.

"Five minutes. That's all I ask."

Zig turned the clock around on his desk to face McCann. "Five minutes."

"Betcha I won't even need that."

"Clock's running."

"I'm a people person, Zig. I *can* call you Zig can't I?" asked Shakespeare. But he wasn't about to wait for an answer. "I know what's in folks' hearts. I got a feeling for what they're lookin' for in a representative. Their hopes. Dreams. The world ahead for their children. How else can you explain how I pulled fifteen points off ol' Hurricane?"

"There's always a fringe vote willing to go the other way."

"I did it with zero party resources and my own humble dollars. I talked to people. They told me what they wanted and I listened. I'm a good listener, see? And most every one of those good folk I talked to down there rewarded me with their faith and votes. Ninety-two percent by my count."

"Who did your polling?"

"I did."

"Scientific, was it?" Zig couldn't wait to hear this. "How large was your sample?"

"One hundred percent." From his briefcase Shakespeare produced a computer-printed diary. He fanned the pages in front of Zig. "I made a record of every registered Republican voter whose hand I shook or shared a cup of joe with. I also included their family names, church affiliations, and the likelihood that they would go to the polls and pull a lever."

Zig stared at the sheaf of paper. He had never heard or seen such a thing as the Bible-thick log. Elections were modern. Polling. Tracking. Advertising. The way Shakespeare made it sound was that practically every person he spoke with had gone into a voting booth and cast a ballot for him. "You must have a winning personality," was all he could think to say.

"That, I do. Imagine what I can do in a general election. Me up against this fellah Dutton? He's nothin' but a Ken doll. Me? I'm the real thing. A genuine people's candidate. I can deliver."

"Different animal, a general election," shot back Zig. "Taking fifteen points off an incumbent in a primary is one thing. You had a low turnout for an obvious winner. The general requires military-like tactics and the dough to see it through. Let alone name ID.''

"I'm resourceful. I've got ideas.''

"I'm sure you do. How's this? Get out there, put some of your ideas to work. We'll track you when we can. Start putting up some numbers, maybe we'll make good on the check.''

"A carrot on a stick.''

"Let's call it incentive," said Zig, now feeling confident. It was an obvious brush-off. "We're busy up here. Lots of campaigns. And I'm afraid money's tight, Mr. McCann. What can I say? We have to spend our cash on candidates that can win. Show me you can win, then we'll talk.''

For a moment those sharp blue eyes just stared back at him. "You didn't even ask my views. What I stand for. Hell, as far as you know, I could be for open borders and a Mexican in every kitchen.''

"Are you?''

That smile again, the ice in his eyes gone. "Just pullin' your leg.''

Impatiently Zig pushed on for some kind of closure. "I'm sure your politics fit the platform.''

"How about I tell you about my business?''

"Five minutes, Mr. McCann. Maybe we can meet again?''

"Oh, the rest of it won't take long.'' Shakespeare sat back again. "I'm in the printing business.''

"Makes sense.'' Zig nodded toward the bogus check. "Forgive me for being short, but for now, the decision stands. The Committee has met on your candidacy, and financing is not appropriate. I'm sorry.''

"Rivers flow. Preachers know. And decisions can be reversed,'' spun Shakespeare. Confident. Like he knew something Zig didn't. "To bet against me would be as dumb as eating soup with a fork. I'm full of surprises—''

"Damn right you're full of surprises!'' Zig waved the check in front of Shakespeare's face. "You can go to jail for this. And you want our support?''

"It's good work, that check.''

"You're proud of it?''

"Like I said, printing is my business. Started out with one shop. Built it up to six. And the technology, now. Whooey. It's amazing. With high-resolution computer imaging. You can manipulate just about anything. Checks. Signatures. Pictures.''

"Check forgery's a felony.''

"So's blackmail and extortion. But that doesn't stop smart folks from makin' hay outta hooey." Shakespeare opened up his briefcase, lid forward so Zig couldn't see inside.

"You can leave right now."

"You gonna call the police?"

"If I have to."

"That'd be a good story. Republican Committee chair has Republican candidate arrested. There's some PR for ya. Betcha the honchos back in D.C.'ll love that in an election year."

"You can just go," insisted Zig. "How's that? No cops. We'll forget about the check. Just go."

"Pretty little girl you got there." Shakespeare gestured to the framed pictures behind Zig. "Her name's Erica, am I right?"

"How'd you know my daughter's name?"

"Texas Tech?"

"I asked you how you knew—"

From his briefcase Shakespeare withdrew a folder. He laid it before Zig. "I know your daughter from her pictures. Looks like she's done some modeling."

Zig opened the folder. His heart stopped. He gasped at a singular black-and-white photo of his daughter, nude, reclined with her legs spread while some other, faceless female performed some acrobatic, oral copulation. Utterly pornographic and . . .

"Now, before you get all worked up—"

"That can't be my little girl."

"Well, it is and it isn't. It's a fake, if that's the word you're lookin' for."

"Yes. It's a fake! It has to be!"

"A good fake, too. Just like the check."

Zig ripped the picture in half and tossed it at Shakespeare, standing and shrieking, "You sonofabitch! How dare you make smut out of my little girl! I oughta—"

"Siddown, Zig. You have a heart attack, you can't write me a check for seventy-five thousand dollars," eased Shakespeare. "If you don't, I swear I'll plaster this little picture all over Texas Tech. I'll put it on the Internet. I'll stuff it in your neighbors' mailboxes."

"You won't blackmail me!"

"You selfish SOB. All you're thinkin' about is you. Instead you should think about Erica. Her years in college. What her friends think of her. A lesbian. Oh my." Carefully Shakespeare retrieved the faked photo from the carpet and reassembled it in front of the chairman.

Nearly apoplectic, Zig stood over his desk and heaved. His chest rising as he sucked in more air. His heart clanging against the confines of his rib cage. Veins swelled.

"Your face is as red as a fire truck," warned Shakespeare. "I'm serious, Zig. Please. Sit. I didn't mean to scare you *that* bad."

Simon says. Zig actually sat down. After which he sort of listened. Shakespeare spoke quietly, but with a sudden firmness. He was in charge. "You know what your problem is? You look at me and think it's not possible to exceed the limits of possibility," said Shakespeare, standing and waxing political. "Me? I look in the mirror and see *your* future."

"Erica," Zig found himself whispering.

Shakespeare went on. "Now, let's look at this like the two smart fellahs we obviously are. What I know about politics, you can stick up a gnat's ass. But like I said. I know people. I know what they *care* about. Generally speaking, it's what other people think about 'em that matters. Stigma, I reckon they call it. Well, some stigma, real or imagined, can stick like a three-day-old Band-Aid. My guess is, when the smoke clears, you and your pious folks on your little Committee'll come around and make good on your commitment to me and my candidacy."

Zig didn't know whether to hit McCann or stand and suffer the indignity of worse threats to come. Then came the big finish.

"Now, I would guess that in a candidate, you're always looking for the reasonable man. And I'm the first one to say that I'm not. But look at me this way. Where the reasonable man adapts himself to the world, the unreasonable man persists on trying to adapt the world to himself. Therefore all progress depends on the unreasonable man. Am I right, or am I right?"

"George Bernard Shaw," Zig found himself recalling despite the ringing in his ears.

"In my humble opinion, it's the definition of a successful politician," capped Shakespeare, pleased to have hit the right nerve.

"You might make a congressman yet." From underneath that shelf where Zig's daughter's head shot reigned so pristine and prominent, the Republican party chair withdrew a large check binder. "Seventy-five thousand?"

"Why don't we make it an even hundred?"

8

The Texas State Court of Appeals' hearing for Shoop De Jarnot's writ of habeus corpus was less than two months away. And Mitch, anticipating an ever-taxing political schedule, and never one to wait until the last minute, spent most of his late nights in the early weeks of July on the written portion of the appeal. He decided, however, that the oral arguments to the high court would be performed by someone else. He didn't need that kind of exposure, and neither did Shoop. The writ needn't be compromised by a Texas Supreme Court justice who, for whatever reason, didn't care for Mitch Dutton, the candidate.

Chosen to deliver the words was *Public Defender Extraordinaire* Alex Bernardi. The two had linked up on many pro bono sojourns over the last five years, having met through mutual friends in the Texas Legal League, the Longhorn State's centrist-leaning answer to the ACLU.

"You can step off, now. I'll put my name on it," said Alex.

"You just want all the credit," Mitch said, smiling.

"And you do? I'm not a politician, but I know this could hurt you."

"Thanks, but Shoop was my client long before I decided to run for office. If my name's not on the writ, it'd be as if I'd jumped ship."

"In name only."

"It's like signing a contract. And I *believe* in contracts."

It was moments like this when Alex was reminded why he'd grown such respect for Mitch. Pro bono work, as much as it was part of an attorney's supposed credo, had long been lost in the maze of soaring fees and TV advertising. Most lawyers were in it for the buck. Mitch was clearly in it for something else, though Alex never bothered to ask what that might be.

"It's gonna need editing," Alex commented. "Don't get me wrong. It's looking real good. There just seems to be more verse than chapter, if you get my meaning."

"Like I've been out on the stump too long," figured Mitch. "I know, I know. What can I say? I'm just another windbag running for Congress."

The meeting was in the law offices of Gade, Seaton, Peacock, and Dutton, only two blocks from the Strand's trendy west end, with a fourth-floor view. The suite occupied the entire floor, with elevators that emptied into a sumptuous, mahogany-paneled lobby with dual receptionists, a far cry from the funky, around-the-corner-from-the-free-clinic digs where the campaign was waged. Mitch took refuge here with his diplomas and dog-eared criminal law books. An ancient oak church door turned horizontal for a desk. The wall behind it held family pictures, including a faded color still of a father and son standing before the Dutton fleet of shrimp boats.

"How's your old man?" asked Alex during a reading break.

"Okay, I guess. Can't get the old fart on the phone," Mitch fibbed. Fact was, neither was working very hard at the connection.

"And your partners? They cool with the campaign?"

"At first they were cautious." He made a couple of quotation marks in the air. "But now that I'm the *front-runner,* they're thinking *Congressman Mitch Dutton* would look good on the letterhead."

"What's the other guy's name again?"

"Shakespeare," answered Mitch, who kept his head on page sixteen of the appeal brief. "Shakespeare McCann."

"That's it. There's a South County name if I ever heard one. The Republicans are really gonna put money on this dog?"

"That's what I hear. Ask me if I'm worried."

"*Are* you worried?"

"If I were, I wouldn't be here doing this," said Mitch, thinking he'd rope Alex back into the appeals process. The less he talked about

Shakespeare, the better. Naive? Yes. Mitch knew it, too. He'd better get used to the name. He was in a race with the scumbag.

"You met him yet?"

"I have," he answered sotto voce, eyes still boring into the page.

"So what's he like?" pressed Alex.

Mitch stopped what he was doing, stood, and crossed to the door, opening it briefly enough to ask, "Could one of you women bring us some more coffee?" Then he shut the door and turned back to Alex ensconsed in a leather couch pushed up against a floor to ceiling window. "Had only a brief chat with the guy. He was gracious, I guess. A little strange."

"You know where he's setting up shop?"

"Ask me if I care."

"Couple of blocks from here. Saw a sign down there this morning. Right *on* the Strand. Big banner with that stupid name of his," noted Alex. "Republicans gotta be throwing bucks at him like crazy. Believe me, rent down there ain't cheap."

Mitch turned and looked out the window. There, two blocks to the east, was an eager-looking crowd gathering right on the street. Cars stalled. Traffic was backed up.

"Two blocks? Which way?"

"East, I think," answered Alex, joining him at the window to point out the direction. He, too, saw the commotion below. "Right about there. What do you think that's about?"

Mitch shrugged. "Beats me."

"Wanna go give it a look?"

"Let's not," he said, returning to his desk. "How about we get back to it?"

It was even hotter than the local weather gurus had forecasted. Four floors down outside Mitchell's air-conditioned suite and just minutes after noon the temperature had already cracked the hundred-degree mark, with the humidity at ninety-one percent.

Two blocks to the east, before an empty storefront with a banner reading SHAKES strung from end to end was the *other candidate,* digging out scoopfuls of ice cream from a keg-sized tub. The lunchtime crowd, along with the tourists, were flocking onto the boulevard for a taste of both flavors: vanilla and Shakespeare McCann. Around each free cone was wrapped a red, white, and blue napkin with the slogan printed in bold:

SHAKES CAN!

The Strand was getting so congested that the Cathedral PD had to move in with three cruisers and six officers in white gloves to control traffic. Shakespeare gracefully complied with their requests, booming over the crowd with "That's me! I'm the law-and-order candidate." The ice cream lovers laughed and asked for more. Soon after, the policemen were a little less obstructive, bought off with Shakespeare's good humor and ice cream cones to ease the sweat under the brims of their navy blue baseball caps.

TV cameras mobilized. Crews scrambled with tape and cable, trying to get close enough to catch a few sound bites before the ice cream melted. And that's just what they got. Bites. Morsels from the new candidate as he answered a question about his campaign's theme. Shakespeare was quick. "Early to bed, early to rise, work like hell, and advertise!"

Then came the obvious question about Shakespeare McCann being a neophyte candidate. The newcomer shot from his charismatic hip. "The trouble with experience as a teacher is that the test comes first and the lesson comes later."

The crowd grew larger and lapped him up just as they did the ever-softening ice cream.

McCann on the economy: "If all the economists in the world were laid end to end, they still wouldn't reach a conclusion."

Even the damn hot weather made great hay for the cameras: "Sure, if I could fix it, I would. But the fellah who's smart enough to control the weather? I figure he'll have done messed up the last safe topic of polite conversation."

Finally, from somewhere in the swelling crowd, someone began chanting, "SPEECH, SPEECH, SPEECH!!!"

The chant caught hold long enough for the candidate to hold his arms out wide. "Nope. No more talkin' today. I'll be dishin' out plenty of the meatier stuff in good time. Today's just a little somethin' for your sweet tooth," teased Shakespeare. "Now, who wants more?"

It was enough to draw spontaneous applause. Meanwhile, the man who'd called for a speech, starting the chant, escaped the crush and moved around behind the ice cream truck to wait the scene out.

The man was Marshall Lambeer, George "Hurricane" Hammond's former campaign consultant. An expensive pro. He was charging Shakespeare five thousand a week for his services.

"Somebody get out and *chum* the crowd," ordered Marshall to a gaggle of *paid* volunteers. Chumming. The practice of bucketing out loads of campaign buttons and bumper stickers to cheering masses. "Let's go, let's go!"

Along for a ride on the Shakespeare McCann gravy train were more from Hammond's campaign committee. Bob Owens in charge of press relations. Shirley Rosensweig handled polling and research. They were followed by more pros who followed the Republican party's promissory note as it was FedExed from Dallas to Shakespeare's Cathedral City office. Barney Cropper was media consultant. And along with him he brought Candy Mishner, who, on the heels of a recent fiasco with the Christian Channel, would be in charge of fund-raising.

From across the street, watching the scene through his usual cynical perspective, was the one and only Hollice Waters. In his shirt and tie and trademark baseball cap, he leaned against a lamppost and watched with unrestrained awe.

He recognized most of the faces in the background as former and recently unemployed staffers from Hurricane's campaign. "All the best talent the Republican party could buy," he would write in his follow-up column to his initial McCann interview.

9

If ice cream was the tonic to tame the overheated locals, alcohol was the buffer against the monthlong crush of tourists who sought the Island's famed beaches and bars. With eighteen miles of beaches, Cathedral had it all. Deep sea fishing. Surfing. Seaside cabanas. And miles of newly poured cement for the building wave of in-line skaters. A Zamboni couldn't have cut slicker sidewalks. In swimsuits and Winnebagos armed with Coppertone and bug repellant, the summer vacationers poured in from the north to dip themselves in the water, baptizing another summer season with daily doses of hot dogs and saltwater taffy.

And in a state whose oil revenues had all but dried up—and which supported an ever-increasing influx of illegal immigrants to the welfare rolls—the July deposits to the South County coffers were crucial. So the welcome sign was out with a gentle plea: *Bring money to spend.*

Spend, they did, packing hotels and motels all up and down the interstate and Gulf highways. Folks from all walks of life were there to walk barefoot on the beaches or stroll along the Strand. Finally, as the sun would set, casting its long shadows across the Gulf, crowds would gather nightly at the seashore to drink, dance, or simply stare out at the twinkling lights of the pleasure boats that dotted the bay.

As tradition would have it, the most spectacular of those boats belonged to a Texas media zillionaire named Vidor Kingman, owner of five television and nine radio stations broadcasting statewide. And he was expanding. For sixteen summers he'd been anchoring his boats off Cathedral Island for the month of July, doing business from the foredeck and fishing off the stern. No boat was bigger than Kingman's. He liked it that way.

As coincidence would have it, July had been the favorite summer month for old Hurricane to make his nonelection-year appearances. Most of them on Kingman's boat. The old man was fond of saying, "If Kingman's big boats were hats, he'd wear 'em."

But Hammond was dead. Now Kingman was looking to throw his weight toward a winner.

Enter Rene Craven.

The door was wide open and Rene wasn't shy about walking through it, even if it appeared that she'd be dancing topside on a freshly dug grave. Such was politics. And the never-married Kingman was known to have a keen eye for women. At an Austin charity ball for a local university, she arranged to be seated at the table next to Kingman's with the back of her gilded chair pushed against his. It took barely ten minutes before he'd made the first move, and the rest was up to her.

Before she left, a casual dinner was to be arranged on Kingman's anchored cruiser for a July weekend. Rene would gladly be his date. The candidate, of course, would be accompanied by his wife.

"It's just a dress," Connie said aloud to herself. But well within earshot of Mitch.

"Whatever you wear, honey, I'm sure it'll knock 'em dead," he called from the bathroom.

But she'd fretted for days over the right dress, misreading her husband's anxiety over Vidor Kingman's dinner invitation and concluding that it was an important evening. She was trying hard to be as close to the perfect wife as possible. If she only knew he didn't want or need the perfect wife.

He wanted her not to go.

Since *the kiss,* Mitch and Rene hadn't spoken about anything personal. It was left unsaid, but hardly forgotten, buried in a shallow grave inside the candidate's nervous sexual psyche. The thought of Connie and Rene seated across from a dinner table gave Mitch the kind of pause that would burn a hole in most men's stomachs.

He chose to simply focus on the task at hand. Bagging the elephant.

"I'm having second thoughts," said Connie.

"What's that?" He couldn't hear her over his electric shaver.

"I'm having second thoughts," she said louder.

About the evening, he thought. *Thank God.* If she decided not to go, he could dodge that most certain emotional bullet.

"About the dress," she said, framing herself in the bathroom doorway.

The morning of the fateful dinner, she had still been without a suitable evening dress. She and Gina had shuttled to visit a Dallas couturier who thought he had the perfect combination of gown and gangplank—a shimmering strapless number that would disappear in the dinner candlelight, yet still stay afloat upon her small bosom as she stepped from the shore craft to the steps that would lead sharply to the main deck. "Smashing," said the couturier, his faux British accent sounding like a sales pitch

"That King-man is gonna eat *you* for dinner in that dress, darlin'," said Gina, her tiny butt cozied into a slipcovered chair in the couturier's private salon.

"It's not *him* I want to feed," said Connie, turning one way and then the other in the mirror. "I've got competition."

"Who?"

"You haven't seen her. But it's Mitchell's publicist." She mouthed the word in the mirror. *Wow.* "You don't think I need more up here?" she asked, referring to her breasts. Lately she'd been wondering if she should've gotten breast implants when Gina had, only months before the FDA banned the use of silicone.

"It's made for you, honey," Gina added. "Little tits 'n' all."

"Elegante," drawled the couturier, switching to a faux Parisian accent.

"How much?" Connie said, nervously watching herself in the mirror.

How much indeed.

That's exactly what Mitch asked when he saw her stalled in the bathroom doorway.

"Just tell me you like it," she worried.

"I'm sorry, honey. You look phenomenal." He stepped up and kissed her. "The dress doesn't look half-bad either."

She knuckle-punched him on the arm, and he responded with the requisite *"Ouch."* He was trying to keep it all fun and games between them. A little love and a lot of sleight of hand might keep the evening afloat and the hole from burning through his stomach lining.

"Not the red tie. That's the candidate's tie," advised the missus. She went into the closet and returned with a festive Nicole Miller tie. She laid it out against his shirt. "That's the one. It says the candidate wants to have fun."

Mitch turned to the mirror to get a look at the tie against himself. "This guy Kingman. He and Hammond were way up each other's asses. I think I should go more conservative."

"This *guy* is the immortal *bachelor*. At least that's what Gina says. If he'd been married just once, then I'd say he was conservative."

Ah, the world according to Connie. Sometimes her philosophy was dead-on in its simplicity, he thought. A brief reminder of why he really loved her. She was real. Leave it to Connie to cut through the bullshit and double talk. The sky is blue, the grass is green, and the flowers in the backyard are the color of the rainbow. That was Connie's world and she was sticking to it, God bless her.

"And I'm your husband," he added to the list, the words shocking him as they came from his mouth.

"That you are, so you do as I say. Wear the tie," she said, tying the knot for him as he faced the mirror, finishing it off with a kiss to his neck. "You need a haircut."

"Naw. I'm just trying to court the sixties vote," he joked. And that was the end of the brief banter. Soon after, they were downstairs locking the dogs inside the house and on their way in Mitchell's sedan.

The short drive to the shore-boat landing was longer than expected. The tourist traffic had jammed the Island both coming and going. Mitchell, never one to enjoy stalled traffic, nervously spun the AM radio dial looking for some interesting talk.

"Why don't you find some music," pleaded Connie. "It's a beautiful night. It might ease those ants you got in your pants."

Ignoring her, he stalled on a weather report that told of the impending doom expected in the eastern part of the Gulf near Cuba. A whimper of a hurricane named Howard had swung west and was bearing down on the already beleaguered island. It was a cue for Mitch to roll down the window and inhale the damp air.

A good sailor can smell a hurricane from a thousand miles, Uncle J used to say.

Hurricane Howard, by Mitchell's calculation, was maybe thirteen hundred miles away. Still, as he drew the warm air through his nostrils, he wondered if he could actually smell the storm. If he could sense a shifting wind.

At the shore-craft landing, a cigarette speedboat with DARLING stenciled on the stern waited for the Duttons. The yacht called *Deandra,* named after Kingman's mother, was anchored barely a quarter mile offshore. The white lights outlining its profile aptly foretold that it was indeed the biggest vessel, short of a commercial ship, in the harbor. Blue-black sky overhead. The mainland beyond, a flattened shadow trimmed in the yellow lamps of Harbor Road. Connie pulled tight to Mitch as if to warm herself, even though the evening temperature was well into the eighties. Then, as if the thought had popped into her head for the very first time, she said, "Now that I think of it, I've never actually met Rene."

"Rene?" was all he could think to respond.

"Rene Craven? Is that her name? Your press person," she explained. "I mean, I *know* Fitz. Murray, I've met a bunch. But Rene, I've seen her. I just realized that we hadn't really met."

"I thought the two of you had spoken the night of the primary."

"We missed each other."

"I'm sorry," he said. "I hope that doesn't make you uncomfortable tonight."

"It doesn't matter. Just as long as she's not as drop-dead gorgeous as she looked from afar, I won't have a jealous bone." It was clearly needling and nothing more. She poked his ribs to remind him so. Still, it was like a knife in his kidney and she was twisting it for effect. The guilt in him raged, flushing his face. Thank God for the darkness.

If she knew he'd kissed her, she'd break into a million pieces, thought Mitch. What a prick he was.

And in that brief moment, during those last hundred yards from the speedboat to the yacht, he found himself shamed and vowing to purge his mind of *the kiss.* Simple as that. He could quit wanting her just the way he had quit smoking some eighteen years ago. One day he had just decided, and had stopped smoking by the power of his own sheer will. He would reach down deep and do it again, removing the bullet from the chamber, and never play Russian roulette again.

Then again, in another remote corner of his conscience, he thought this sudden compulsion utterly ridiculous. The evening ahead would probably go swimmingly. Rene was a pro. She and Connie would dish and life would go on as it had, unfettered *and* without need of a rearview mirror. Still, his palms were damp. And for a man who wasn't inclined to nervous behavior, he considered it a cryptic premonition of danger ahead, and once again repeated to himself the vow. His marriage was too important.

Connie was too important.

A pudgy second mate was at the ship's gangway to tie up the cigarette boat and assist the passengers onto *Deandra.* "Do I look okay?" asked Connie, mostly to get him to look at her one more time.

"You look heavenly," he assured her. With that, they started up the ramp.

Topside they encountered a tall, imposing figure on the first deck. Lanky, L.B.J. features. F.D.R. round glasses. "You must be the candidate," boomed Vidor Kingman, his voice resounding in a Texas twang.

"Mitchell Dutton." He outstretched his hand cheerfully to meet his host's. "And this is my wife, Connie."

"So pleased to meet y'all," said Vidor, shaking Mitchell's hand and giving an imaginary tip of the hat to Connie. "And you know my *fiancée,* Rene Craven?"

Connie bit. "Your fiancée? Mitch, you didn't tell me!"

"That's because he's joking," whispered Mitchell.

"And most certainly, I wish I wasn't," said Vidor. "Hell, I'm thinking of running for office just so I can give her a job in the office next to mine."

Suffice it to say, this was Rene's introduction to Connie. She appeared at Vidor's side in her usual Armani *über* suit, but stripped of a blouse and brassiere for a spectacular evening effect. But it was Rene's eyes that caught Mitch off guard. Gone was her normal behavior of detached ease. Her posture, vocal inflection, everything, spoke of impropriety. She should, thought Mitch, stick out her hand to Connie and make an introduction. Instead, it was Connie with an ever-so-polite "Hello there. I'm Connie Dutton. I don't think we've met."

"No, we haven't. I'm Rene," returned the media consultant, her long red nails accepting Connie's sudden and confident handshake. Then, stepping closer to Mitch and Connie, she said in a hushed phrasing, "You'll forgive my manners. This is a terribly awkward moment."

Mitch found his larynx constricting.

What the fuck is she doing?

For the five months he'd known Rene, there'd been nary a wrong tenor in her silky voice. Not a forgotten social grace or a trick she'd missed. And in the days since *the kiss,* he had marveled at her effortless swagger of indifference, knowing the peril of a misstep in their mutual attraction—something she was all too careful to avoid. But now it was all he could do not to reach across and clasp her throat, just so she'd know what he felt like at that very delicate moment.

"We have ourselves a fifth wheel," breathed Rene.

"Why, yessir we do," snapped Vidor. "Y'all have met, I think, the *other* candidate, Shakespeare McCann?"

With a genial "Howdy," Shakespeare McCann appeared, crossing from the opposite railing, a bottle of Dr. Pepper in hand and a smug grin on his face. "Forgive me, I'm sorry. I was just wrapped up in all them pretty-colored lights on the water. Like Christmas in July. Hi there, how are ya? Shakes McCann." He crossed and took Connie's hand. "Pleased to meetcha, ma'am." Then he turned to Mitch. "Your wife's a first-class beauty, Counselor."

Connie might've blushed, but the blood that rose in Mitch colored him red, his face bloomed in an instant flush of anger. He looked to Rene. "I thought we were *four.*"

"Don't look at me. I'm no party crasher," Shakespeare was quick to respond, laying his hand out for Mitch to grasp in a sort of challenge. "Mr. Dutton. I must say I'm so sorry about your accident. Crime is a perilous problem."

"Accident?" asked Vidor.

"The mugging," answered Shakespeare. "Terrible thing. You know, it was all over the TV."

"Hell, I *own* TV. Don't mean I watch that crap," howled Vidor with Shakespeare right alongside him.

Rene was speechless. Kingman had clearly sandbagged her with all the sweet talk and supposed interest in giving an audience to Mitch and his political leanings. Now her momentary loss of joie de vivre had suddenly placed the weight of the situation squarely on Mitchell's shoulders. As the blood in his face cooled, he drew his sights down upon Shakespeare. His dormant school-yard hackles obscured behind those fine features, his hand outstretched toward the enemy in a cordial gesture. Suddenly Shakespeare looked his size. Smaller than Mitch and, in his eyes, a mutant. With that in mind and possibly a slight adrenaline push, he took hold of Shakespeare's hand and squeezed it like a vise.

"Owweeee!" feigned Shakespeare at the handshake. A disingenuous squeak. "I guess you've recovered from your accident, all right."

"After I'm down in the first round, I like to come out swinging," added Mitch. "Something *my* old man taught me."

"Sounds like you 'n' me had the same daddy," howled Shakespeare, drawing three of the fivesome into his ring of laughter. Mitch smiled falsely.

"Hows about a drink, Candidate Dutton?" offered Vidor. "And something for you, Mrs. Dutton?"

"Connie," she insisted. "And I'll have a champagne cocktail if you're so inclined."

"I am so, madame." Vidor snapped his fingers twice without taking his eyes off her. Then to Mitch, "And you, sir?"

"Dewar's rocks," he ordered, forgoing his patented Perrier on the rocks. He found Connie's hand once again in his. It squeezed him back and felt soft, comfortable. Easy. Mitch was back in control as they both tracked Vidor across the foredeck of the 150-plus-foot vessel. By the time they reached the outer bar, the drinks had already been prepped, served up by a white-suited black gentleman with graying temples. Mitch made a mental note. Vidor Kingman was old-world Texas, not unlike the old families from Cathedral Island, Connie's family included.

"Would it be too much to ask for a tour?" asked Connie.

"Hell no." Vidor stuck out his ever-charming arm. Mitch thought to follow, but then Rene was conveniently there at his ear.

"I'm sorry. I didn't have a clue," she whispered.

His instinct was to keep his back to her and chase on after his wife and Kingman. Proximity to her might hint of impropriety. But Shakespeare had returned to his perch at the far railing to gaze out upon the water and sparkling lights of the Island.

"We can always just say our good-nights and go," she went on to say. "We didn't need Kingman from the start. Who says we need him now?"

"And leave him to the *Good Humor Man* over there?" he quipped in hushed tones. "No, thank you. I think I'll bury the creep right here. Tonight. If Kingman's as smart as he's supposed to be, he'll see through McCann's charade before the main course is served."

"Well, if it's not the renewed Mitch Dutton. *Touché*," she said, impressed. "And by the way, Shakespeare's right. Your wife *is* beautiful."

"Yes . . . she is, isn't she?" He'd meant it to hurt Rene, and for the record, it did. She'd fucked up on the evening and maybe compromised his position with Kingman. Maybe this little dart would put some distance between them so he could get on with being Mitchell Dutton, candidate for Congress and ever-faithful husband.

Dinner was served on the top deck of the yacht, with even more black servants in white shirts and ties attending. A carved teak table with inlays of ivory and ebony had been assembled under a canopy, leaving all guests, no matter where they sat, a spectacular, unrestricted view of the harbor and all the accompanying boats. The table, arranged for five, left Vidor at the head, flanked by Mitch and Rene. Connie was to Mitchell's left. And Shakespeare to Rene's right. The scene was magically lit with a string of white Christmas lights looped lazily about the canopy. Citronella candles burned around the perimeter.

Vidor insisted on pouring the wine himself. "A toast to the winner," he boomed. His eyes swept left and right to catch the reactions from Mitch and Shakespeare.

"I'll drink to that," said Mitch with little hesitation.

"Hear hear," added Shakespeare. "And record turnout at the polls." He nudged Rene, his touch making her skin crawl. Then she glanced across at Mitch, who made sure to clink glasses with Connie first.

The conversation remained light and airy through the first course of foie gras and into the second course of baked scallops in cream sauce. Vidor was polite enough to entertain Connie, being sure to keep her at the center of attention before the conversation eventually left her in the political dust. Such was the bane of political wives. Valued only until the real discussion began.

Meanwhile, Mitch kept a close eye on Shakespeare, curious about his seemingly untamed interest in Connie's affairs.

"Now, lemme get this straight," Shakespeare would ask as he followed Vidor's lead into Connie's academic history. "You say at Southern Methodist U, by most educated accounts, Texas's answer to the Ivy Leagues, you spent most of your time goin' to fraternity and sorority parties insteada stickin' your head in a book?"

"Well, I still got A's," answered Connie, a bit flustered.

"Of course you did," he continued. "Ain't a good ol' boy west of Arkansas that don't know that Texas women got both the beauty *and* the brains."

Connie blushed from the oh-so-obvious bullshit flattery, tugging at Mitchell's hand all the time just underneath the tablecloth.

"Hows about you, Counselor?" asked Shakespeare. "Where'd you do your contriculations?"

"Junior college in Cathedral City," said Mitch. "UT after that. Then I did my law at Stanford."

"Out there in California? Well, that answers it," Shakespeare declared.

Mitch knew better than to bite on such an obvious baited hook. But unfortunately, Connie didn't. "Answers what?" she asked.

"Where your husband got all them crazy ideas of his," answered Shakespeare. "Pardon me, Mrs. Dutton. But have you been reading his campaign literature? Because I have."

With that, the conversation turned.

"Well, I haven't. But I don't think I need to," Connie said. "After all, I live with him."

Rene laughed unguardedly, cueing Vidor. It was tantamount to her shoving a sharp elbow between the old man's ribs.

"Forgive me for talking over the meal, Mr. Kingman. But this stuff is just bubblin' up for me," Shakespeare went on. "I guess I'm just a horse stuck in the gate."

"And I'm the gatekeeper. I thought we could wait until dessert," said Vidor. "Leave the ladies to themselves."

"Forgive me, Mr. Kingman," said Mitch, his juices primed for a debate, "but we gave women the vote back in 1920 with the Nineteenth Amendment. I think it's about time they participated." With those two Dewar's in him, he was ready to drive a stake through McCann's heart. "Go on, *Shakes*. Speak your mind."

"Thank you, Counselor." Shakespeare nodded. "Now, like I was sayin', I've been readin' all this stuff from your mostly unopposed primary campaign. Direct mailers and the like, the kind you send out to the local populations lookin' for a vote. And frankly, it just don't swing with me."

"Exactly what?" prompted Mitch. "Let's be specific."

"For example. How you figure to go marrying the business folk with all them environmental crazies we got runnin' around? I mean it this way. The business fellah's got it tough already. He's got all kinds of government restrictions to put up with, and his competition's goin' south of the border cuzza NAFTA, or overseas and up a Chinaman's kazoo. Now, you wanna go puttin' these hurtin' folk with the same ones that've been puttin' them under?"

Vidor sat back. The curtain was raised and the actors were onstage.

"Okay. You want an example? How's this?" asked Mitch, turning away from Shakespeare, ready to deliver the rest of the answer to

Kingman, the only audience that mattered. "You all know Pete Peterman, don't you?"

"Sure I do," answered Kingman. "Played in a four-man scramble with him last week."

"Out at The Links, I'll bet," said Mitch.

"Hell of a golf course," Kingman added.

"I'm sure it is. But I'm afraid I don't play," said Mitch. "Anyway, about three years ago, Pete came to me with a problem. He'd purchased the old landfill down off of Lucas Landing, with plans to build a championship golf course and country club."

"That's probably because he'd screwed over so many of the old boys on bad investment advice at Cathedral Country Club."

"I'd heard that," said Mitch, unfazed. "The logjam on the progress of the golf course was a small environmental group I'd worked with called The Earth in the Balance Campaign. They were blocking the construction with some rather tart legal maneuvers. It seems since the city had stopped using the property as landfill, some rare local waterfowl had begun to flourish there in sinkholes caused by the natural settling of the site."

"I'll tell you right now, Mitch. I believe in the environment, but I'm not big on environmentalism," said Kingman. "Or a buncha ducks, for that matter."

"Fair enough," said Mitch. "And for the record, I'm not on the side of any group that takes the extreme. But I knew these parties to be reasonable. So I offered a solution."

"Which was?" cued Rene.

"One. I suggested they hire a golf-course architect with the experience to incorporate the existing wetland into the design. Secondly, to help Pete with some of the severe overages that such a huge change would incur, I hooked him up with an offshore financial group looking to invest in Gulf Coast resort properties. The hotel was added to the plan, and if I remember, it should open by the first of the new year."

Kingman was impressed. "Created some local employment in the process, I take it."

"Four hundred new jobs," said Mitch proudly. "Proof it can happen. It just takes someone willing to do the hard work."

Both Connie and Rene applauded. It was biased support, but it drew smiles from both Mitch and Vidor Kingman.

Mitch settled into his chair more comfortably. "You see, my theory is that politics is nothing but other people's agendas. Everybody's walking around, carrying their own soapbox. Quick to get up and tell everybody else how they should live their lives. What I propose is to ask them to share the platform. Suddenly human nature takes over. Things get worked out."

It was at that moment Shakespeare applauded, all by himself, his hands clapping together inches above his cooling entree. He kept it up until he was certain he owned the floor.

"You know, it's funny about applause. Folks do it wherever they go. Hell, they even do it at weddings. Right after the bride and groom kiss. The whole congregation gets all excited and puts their hands together. And over what? A kiss? The couple ain't been married ten seconds and folks are ready to say, 'Congratulations. Y'all done a good job.'" Shakespeare zeroed in on Mitch, then panned his gaze left and over to Connie. "How long you been married?"

"Ten years," answered Connie.

"Kids?"

"Not yet." She was squeezing Mitchell's hand again.

"Six outta ten marriages in Texas don't last past twelve years, Mrs. Dutton," continued Shakespeare. "And the few that do last, who's around to applaud that?"

"What's your point?" prompted Vidor.

"*His* point is," Mitch interrupted, "that a marriage of any kind, be it between people or competing political interests, shouldn't be expected to last."

"You got that right!" finished Shakespeare. "Intentions make for a pretty package. *Time* is the only true judge of a man."

"You'll forgive my opponent, Mr. Kingman," said Mitch. "He doesn't offer a very hopeful picture of the future. Yours. Mine. Anybody's, save for his own, I might venture."

"I second that motion," piped in Rene.

Shakespeare just smiled proudly for a moment. "Look. All I'm sayin' is that good ideas are like dog food. Until the dog eats it, you ain't sure."

Enough time for Rene to sharpen her Mississippi tongue. "Cute, Mr. McCann. But when you're talking, I don't know what you're selling. All I know is that I've already got a used car."

"Girl's got some bite, don't she?" Shakespeare winked at Mitch. "Looks like you got the woman's vote, Counselor."

"Hell. And I thought we were going to get to talk about that TV cable bill back in Washington," said Vidor. His little dinner debate was dangerously close to turning nasty, so he tried to save it. "Whaddayou think, Ms. Craven? Shall we dance before dessert?"

"Love to," Rene answered, taking his hand and rising from the table.

Vidor gestured to his lead servant. "André? Hows about a waltz on the aft deck?"

"Yessir," said the servant, snapping his fingers for his small staff to attend to the chairs of the other dinner guests. Mitch, Connie, and Shakespeare rose from the table and followed Vidor's lead down a brass-railed stairwell to the aft deck, adorned with Japanese paper lanterns illuminating a parquet dance floor. A Strauss waltz was already drifting off hidden speakers like the ocean breeze through those cherry-blossom lanterns.

Much to the cook's dismay, the chocolate-crème brûlée that Vidor planned for dessert would never be served that particular evening. The host wisely chose not to antagonize either candidate by seating one across from the other for the remainder of the evening, choosing his dance partner instead of his candidate. The old Texas son of a gun swung Rene around the dance floor with his large, generous steps, making the waltz about as intimidating as a Texas two-step.

Mitch and Connie took up the invitation to join in the party, leaving Shakespeare to a lone barstool and a snifter of cognac. From that comfortable seat, the sharp-eyed man kept a watchful eye upon the spinning twosomes, keener still on the subtleties of his opponent: the practiced dance steps from Stanford days, when Mitch had dated San Francisco ballerina Holly Madigan, the easy smile he showed Connie when their eyes met—and the way his eyes would wander when he pulled her close, catching Rene's passing glance at almost every turn. Shakespeare studied those awkward glances, looking for the giveaway.

Then he found it.

The tell, as it was called in those days. Con men and thieves, waiting for that point when the mark gives away his cards. The inside track to a man's soul was never through his eyes, but in what they were lookin' at. And Mitch was looking at Rene.

Mitch felt a tap-tapping on his shoulder. He turned to find Shakespeare behind him, asking in a gentle voice, "May I have one dance with the most beautiful lady?"

The hair on Mitchell's neck stood on end. Bristling, like a dog's. Always from behind, he thought. It was like the mongoose that patterned all its attacks from the rear, always lying in wait for the prey's attention to wander. First it was the beating in the alley. Then Hammond's funeral parade. Tonight and the impromptu dinner debate. In his mind he could see himself mowing over the twisted man on the spot, lifting Shakes by the throat and hurling him over the railing, only to toss him a life jacket when it appeared the SOB might actually be drowning.

But that charismatic, folksy manner was hard to deny. Shakespeare continued, "I feel like a fifth wheel. Hell, I *am* the fifth wheel. Then again, I figure it's a social event. Correct me, Counselor, if I'm out of line."

"No. Of course, you're not," answered Connie, giving Mitch's hand a reassuring squeeze as she left for her new partner.

"I'm not a dancer," said Shakespeare. "So would the pretty gal be so kind as to show me the way?"

And off they turned, Shakespeare and Connie, spinning away from Mitch and his jilted posture.

"Here, son. Take on your Media Mistress," coined Vidor, ignorant of the implication of his words. "I'm afraid she's fired her arrow and punctured a lung." It was obvious that Kingman had hit on Rene and, by the wounded look on his face, been shot down on the spot. "All yours, partner," he offered.

Mitch let his eyes meet Rene's. And for the first time that evening, he looked at her in the way he was accustomed. Pleasingly. Clearly she knew better than to offer herself in a near-public dance. So instead, Mitch offered a rocky salvo. "I think Ms. Craven likes tequila. And I'll have another Dewar's."

"That I can do," said Vidor, who gestured to the bartender. From there, the evening withered. The waltz ended at precisely the moment the compact disc ran out of music—and Mitch found an excuse to leave early. The return to the Island by shore craft was quiet. Yet the evening had turned remarkably chilly and Connie cuddled close to her husband with her hands inside his jacket. Rene stayed clear on the other side of the shore craft, keeping her eyes to the Island lights and her thoughts to herself. That left Shakespeare. Without room for four on the cigarette boat, he stayed on the yacht with Vidor and his multitude of servants.

"I don't want to guess what the two of them are talking about," were Rene's only words from the bow. She was in business mode.

Mitch's response was plain. "I don't care." And the subject was closed until Mitch and Connie crawled into bed.

"His wife and kids are dead. Did you know that?" Connie volunteered.

"I didn't," said Mitch, stripping naked and reaching for a pair of pajama shorts.

"Drunk driver killed them. The children weren't even five yet."

"He told you that? In one dance?"

"Why not?"

"And you believed him?"

"Why would he lie?" she asked. A question he couldn't quite answer offhand.

He crawled into bed. "Why would he tell you?"

Connie rolled up close to Mitch, her arms stroking his back. "Maybe it was the touch of my hand," she giggled. "It's a kinda truth serum."

"You want the truth?"

"Uh-huh."

"Don't trust him. He's a bad guy."

"Don't get me wrong, Mitch. He gave me the creeps with all that divorce stuff at dinner," she reasoned. "I just thought he deserved our sympathy."

"Because of his dead wife and kids, right?" His cynicism was thick.

"Everybody's got a past. Why not him?"

He turned to her. "Sweetheart. In two months' time the Texas State Supreme Court will review my appeal for a change of venue for a convicted killer. This guy had a past. He had a motive. But he still chased his wife and lover across a state line and blew their brains out in some sleazy beach motel. My doing the writ doesn't make him any less a bad guy. And if he asked you to dance, I might wanna kill him, too."

"You wanted to kill that charming man? Shakespeare McCann?" she laughed.

"The thought crossed my mind."

With that she kissed him, still giggling, but appreciating the sick sentiment.

"He's harmless. And you'll beat him in the election," offered Connie, words of encouragement that were rare from her lips. At such a moment, the boy in Mitch clung to her as if she were salvation itself.

Still, the man in him wondered aloud, "That's what worries me . . . *I'm going to beat him and he* knows *it!*"

PART

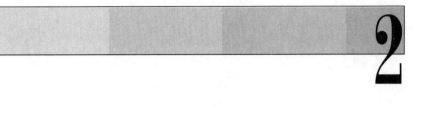

2

"**I**'ve got somebody I want you to meet." Pete Peterman had his arm around Mitch, weaving him through the several hundred party guests who'd braved the dough-baking temperatures and ankle-biting grass chiggers to ogle the financier's spanking new estate. "Somebody who can make a big difference for y'all."

"If it's Vidor Kingman, I've already had the pleasure," said Mitch, half joking.

On the less-developed outskirts of Cathedral City, the ten-acre site boasted a museum-sized house, a petting zoo, pool house, game house, stables, and a canal, complete with a Venetian-style gondola, which serpentined around a landscape of lush, freshly rolled turf. Twenty-five horses worth of electric pumps may have kept the canal water from going stagnant, but that didn't keep the huge mosquitoes from party crashing. No doubt it was all designed and built by the same golf-course architect who'd done such spectacular work for Pete on The Links at Lucas Landing. *Kickbacks?* wondered Mitch. Peterman had most likely constructed and paid for most of it with contractor rebates from the resort.

"The Koreans seen this place?" Mitch asked.

"Seen it. Loved it. But see, that's how it's done over there. Business is relationships, everybody looking out for each other."

"Sounds more like the mob. Anyway, as your attorney, I'd rather not know the details."

"So about Vidor Kingman. Not a bad guy, if you want my opinion," said Pete. "But he cheats at golf."

"But does he cheat and win?" asked Mitch.

"Took me for an easy coupla thou," said Pete, the not-so-sore loser, leading the way into a green, glass-encased dome of a structure across the canal. "We're in the solarium."

The solarium was cooled with tropical plants and an automatic misting system to moisten the air. At center was a marble fountain atop a stone deck, littered with ornate iron-worked garden furniture. Fitz was waiting there with Sandy Mullin.

"Sandy Mullin. Mitch Dutton," introduced Fitz, arms wide as if bringing together two heads of state.

"Nice meeting you," said Sandy as he shook the candidate's hand. "Heard great things about you."

"Heard a few things about you," answered Mitch with a wary smile. Oh, he'd heard all about Sandy Mullin. He'd just never met the industry maven. Younger than Mitch had imagined, he was edging up on sixty, rail-thin, with skin like a newborn's and bleach white hair.

"It's all true," joked Sandy. "Unless you heard it from one of my wives."

"Everybody. Let's sit and have something cold to drink," said Pete. From an ice tub filled with canned brew, Pete served Bud Light and Dr. Pepper. Then after some meaningless chitchat about divorce lawyers, Sandy made his pitch.

"I'm the CEO and the principal stockholder of New Century Industries—" began Sandy.

"I'm familiar with the company," said Mitch, wondering if Sandy was more famous for moving a tool and die foundry to Mexico and leaving five hundred–plus South County residents on the local unemployed rolls, or living the life of Elizabeth Taylor and marrying seven times in his sixty years.

"We're multinational," continued Sandy. "But we're still Texas. Now, I'm here to tell you I've got nine thousand employees total. And eighty-one of those are senior managers. Each of whom, along with their wives and a little lobbying on my part, want to give you and your campaign the individual maximum contribution of one thousand dollars each."

"That's a hundred and sixty thousand dollars," added Fitz, revealing an envelope in his pocket.

All were smiling but Mitch. "In exchange for what?" he asked.

Sandy looked at Fitz, then Pete. "Why, for some good Goddamn government. What do you think?"

"I'm sorry if I seem cynical," said Mitch. "I'm more curious than anything else, considering that I'm on record for opposing the pullout of Standard Tool from South County and sending all those jobs to Mexico."

"And I respect your opinion on the matter," responded Sandy. "But on a corporate level, I felt it was the right move. I got stockholders to think of. Many of whom are fellow Texans, I might add. That doesn't mean we can't disagree and get on with it."

"Get on with what?"

"Good government," said Pete.

"You're the man for the job," said Sandy. "I like what you have to say. So do all my managers. We want to help."

"And help is appreciated." Fitz gave Mitch a hard look.

"And if I'm elected?"

"You will be elected," said Sandy.

"After which . . ." The candidate was waiting for the other shoe to drop.

"You'll give us good government," said Pete again.

Good government, my ass.

It was code. As an attorney, Mitch was attuned to the double talk, insinuations, colored innuendo, and code-speak. He'd used it plenty himself. It was part of the trade.

"Cut the crap!" moaned Mitch. "There's some quid pro quo somewhere in this good-government garbage. Why doesn't somebody just spit it out so I can politely say no?"

Fitz shrugged and backed off, as if he didn't know a damn thing.

Pete, on the other hand, was exchanging subtle gestures with Sandy. Should they tell? Shouldn't they tell? Finally Sandy angled forward in his chair. His voice in a lower timber. "I have friends in Washington who tell me you've already been pegged for an assignment on the Commerce Committee."

It was news to Mitch. Flattering, even. He was already being spoken of on the Hill. Sandy went on, "New Century has recently acquired a Texas-based company and retooled it at considerable expense to manufacture brake pads specifically for SUVs."

"Sport utility vehicles," chimed Pete.

"Parts for these vehicles are becoming a huge market. Lots of jobs," said Sandy. "But these SUVs? They're basically cars built on truck chassis. And where we're making brake pads specifically for this kind of vehicle—"

"You've got a foreign competitor," prompted Mitch.

Sandy almost beamed. "You know it. German operation based in the Philippines. They make brake pads for trucks. Their labor peaks at a dollar per hour."

"Gee, Sandy. You ought to understand those kind of wages," shot Mitch. "Why not move your operation next door to your plant in Mexico and flat out compete?"

"I'll bet you already know the answer."

"Because you don't *want* to compete," offered Mitch. "You want the tariffs raised on truck parts."

"Only because it's not fair. They're getting in under the present trade rules where some truck parts aren't taxed the same as auto parts. But these SUVs aren't trucks. They're *family* cars."

"And once in office, you'd expect me to send a vote your way."

"I'd expect you to vote for *Texas* jobs and *Texas* employment," answered Sandy.

"But not South County jobs."

"Congress is a federal office. I expect you'll be voting on stuff that affects the Eskimos in Alaska."

"And if my opponent were the front-runner?"

"He's not. You are," said Sandy.

Mitch stood. He was about to say no thank you and good-bye when Sandy added more fish for the frying pan. "You know, Mr. Dutton. Those same eighty-one senior managers of mine might also have a mind to contribute to a political action group of my making, say, let's call it the South County Citizens for Good Government Committee. That'd be a hundred and sixty-thousand more dollars that my committee could put toward anything it damn well pleases. Could buy some TV time in your name—"

"Whoa! Stop right there," interrupted Fitz. "What you and your PAC do in the name of good government or the Good Witch of the West is up to you. But the Federal Election Commission rules are clear. The candidate cannot and will not be a part of such dealings."

"So be it." Sandy smiled. He'd gotten his message across.

"Pete?" said Mitch. "It's been fun. Thanks for having me." The candidate turned to Sandy Mullin with a reluctant handshake. "On the record, Mr. Mullin. No and thank you. I'll get to the Hill on my own."

Once outside, the heat hit Mitch like a hot blanket. And if it weren't for all the hands he was compelled to shake on the way to his car, Fitz would surely never have caught up with him.

"I got something to show you," said the campaign manager, ushering Mitch around the corner of a catering truck. Fitz pulled out that envelope.

"No. I don't want to even see it."

"You're gonna see it," demanded Fitz, opening the manila flap and unfolding the envelope. "Tell me what's in here."

Mitch was forced to look. Somehow he expected to see something dirty. Like used twenty-dollar bills wadded into rubber-banded stacks. Instead Mitch found a rainbow of different-colored personal checks. From different banks. Some personalized. Some plain. Each made out to the *Mitch Dutton for Congress Committee* for one thousand dollars.

"You know what this is?" asked Fitz. "A hundred and sixty-two checks from a hundred and sixty-two different *individuals*. Taxpayers, Mitch. Each of them wanting to support *your* election to office. You can't just put 'return to sender' on them."

"It's a payoff, Fitz."

"It's a legal political contribution. And those go only one way. Into the campaign kitty."

"If elected, I won't vote to raise tariffs just so *he* can make a bigger profit."

"Then don't. And when you get to Washington, you vote your heart. And if Sandy Mullin doesn't like it, come your reelection, he'll back the other guy. That's how it works. It's a great country."

Over the past ten years, Fitz Kolatch had liked to joke that he wished he'd had a drink for every time he wondered if he was an alcoholic. The line would draw guaranteed guffaws from whoever might be listening, usually a local PAC or some deep-pocketed special interest group from whom he was about to ask for money. Yet deep down, Fitz truly missed the days of the pocket politician, the *money boys,* smoking up those famed back rooms. A deal was a deal then. And campaigns were plain fun to run.

But the Byzantine laws concerning campaign funding had since been structured by lawmakers themselves. And where money had never been a worry in most respectful campaigning, show runners like Fitz now were forced to spend less time making deals and more time hustling the big dollars required to win a seat for their candidate.

The old days were gone.

The deal Fitz was working now was for the front-runner to agree to speak to the entire membership of the Latino Businessmen's Alliance in a fund-raising forum. What remained was negotiating the ticket price of the meal that would be served.

"Two fifty," said Fitz. "Campaigns aren't cheap, gentlemen. You wanna know what thirty seconds on Channel Three during the dinner hour costs us?"

"Our membership is not a wealthy membership," stated Carlos Rodriguez, the leader of the local alliance. "Mitch knows that. We're mostly small businesses. But we are a good-sized membership. We can buy lots of dinners."

But Fitz was playing hardball. "Two fifty per member. That's what it costs to put a man in Congress."

"Maybe against Hammond. But you're practically running unopposed," chimed the fat man to Carlos's right. Bad move.

"Did I hear you right?" said Fitz. "Because we're ahead in the polls, that's reason for you to go cheap on a candidate?"

"If Mitch were here," pleaded Carlos, doing his best to be forgiving of his old friend for letting Fitz throw the fast balls, "he'd say two fifty's not a fair price."

"Well, Mitch isn't here, friends. He sent me to cordially ask you to put up two fifty a head. Mitch knows what he needs to win. And that's the price of a ticket."

The table was silent, the members looking blankly at each other. Carlos broke the silence. "Can you give us five minutes?"

"Sure thing." Fitz stood and gestured that he was headed toward the bar, giving Carlos a friendly pat on the shoulder as he walked off. He had 'em and he knew it. The members would complain to Carlos about the ticket price, but they'd eventually sway to their leader's opinion. Giving money to a front-runner was too good of an investment. Two fifty was cheap.

At the bar Fitz ordered another vodka and gave a look-see as to what was on the TV. It was just after five o'clock. "Care if I switch channels?" he asked.

"Go ahead," said the bartender, sliding the remote in front of him.

He channel-surfed until he found some local news. A live press conference was under way. The cameras were focused on Shakespeare McCann.

"That'll be four bucks."

But Fitz didn't even hear him. He was too busy turning up the volume.

In front of the First Cathedral Bank, Shakespeare McCann stood before an eager gathering, holding up a Xerox copy of a canceled check. "Made out to the Dutton for Congress Campaign Committee!" he announced, as if he were the cat who'd just eaten the canary.

Marshall Lambeer had successfully coached Shakespeare on everything but the timing of the press conference. Five o'clock on Friday would leave the opposition no time to respond before the weekend when news and information ratings tumbled. But McCann insisted on Thursday.

Copies of the Xeroxed check were passed among the press while Shakespeare continued, "One thousand dollars. The maximum contribution. And signed by Jamal La Croix himself."

The media buzzed. Jamal La Croix was a black nationalist and a former member of the Nation of Islam. Considered a crackpot by most politicians, and *extreme* in the eyes of African-American leaders, locally and beyond, La Croix was most famous for a march he'd led through Cathedral Island only three years earlier. A protest that soured, turning into a riot, trashing a good part of the Strand, and practically killing the tourist trade for the following two summers.

Jamal La Croix was political poison.

And there it was, held up high by the grinning man running against Mitch Dutton, a copy of a canceled check to the Dutton campaign for one thousand dollars. "I think this is a good example of what I've been talking about. This is the kind of support my opponent seeks. These are the kind of sick people he believes he will represent in Congress. Dangerous men. Extremists. Communists. Black racists."

"How'd you get the check?" called out one reporter.

"Right behind me is the First Cathedral Bank. Inside work loyal McCann-of-the-People supporters. But most important, citizens of Cathedral who watched in horror as our beautiful island burned three summers ago. All because one man, Jamal La Croix, marched through here with a band of hooligans and thugs from the Houston welfare projects."

Hooligans and thugs. *Buzz words.*

But the worst buzz word came in the form of Jamal La Croix, a Texas black-activist so extreme and corrupt the Nation of Islam had tossed him out of their organization. Three years ago, he had found a cause in a proposed Cathedral liquor ban, which was a thinly veiled reason to sweep the tourist beaches of black teenagers. Sources said La Croix had wanted to make a splash. Something with headlines.

Gathering bodies and muscle from the Houston projects, he bussed them down to the Island in a convoy, joining protesters on the beach and picking a fight with the cops. Tear gas canisters flew. Then as the mob fled the smoke and megaphones, they ransacked the Strand, overturning cars and setting a torch to shops and businesses. The Governor called for the National Guard. Overall, there were over fifty arrests, including La Croix. Most were convicted of civil disobedience and released on probation.

But Jamal La Croix never spent a day in jail.

"This man is a danger to our community," spouted Shakespeare McCann. "And by association, so is Mitch Dutton."

"Have you talked to Mitch Dutton about this?" asked another reporter.

"That's your job," answered Shakespeare. He grinned broadly.

The siege that followed the press conference quickly overtook the Dutton campaign office. The doors were locked. The phones went briefly unanswered until Fitz and Rene could figure a way to spin the situation back the other way. TV trucks and radio cars camped outside and waited for the return volley.

"In the name of God, how the hell did that check get cashed?" fumed Mitch. He was walking circles, around his desk, then behind the two chairs where Fitz and Murray sat.

"It must've slipped through," answered Fitz.

"I don't find that very satisfactory."

"Checks have been piling up. We average forty to fifty a week. Then there was the stack we got from Sandy Mullin . . ."

"Candy is *really* sorry," said Murray, referring to the campaign treasurer, Candy Anne Frost. It was her job to do computer checks against every campaign contribution, just in case.

"Sorry doesn't cut it," said Mitch.

"Wanna fire her?" offered Fitz.

"Of course not." Mitch had known Candy for years. She'd done his taxes since law school.

Fitz took the offensive. "Question, then. Do you know Jamal La Croix?"

"No."

"Ever met him?"

"No."

"Any of his family?"

"Not that I know of."

"Then that's what we say." Fitz turned to Murray. "See where Rene is on the statement."

Murray left the room while Fitz worked his theory. "It's another trick."

"McCann?"

"Has to be. Why else would this guy give you a thousand bucks? Probably wasn't his money."

"But Marshall Lambeer—"

"I know. It's not his style. But he doesn't sign the checks, does he?" said Fitz. "Think back to the alley. It's the same old shit. Hit and run."

Hit and run indeed. A sharp contrast to the Dutton campaign, wherein, over the last weeks, the *Mitch Machine,* as volunteers were calling it, seemed to roll along with a consistent ease, leading the way with endorsements from the Texas Teachers' Association, the South Texas Police Chief's Council, and the South Coast Commerce Alliance. TV and radio spots were politely dispersed along with direct mail drops and personal appearances. Meanwhile, the McCann of the People campaign would awkwardly vanish for a week, then pop up wherever and whenever the TV advantage might lead, always with a grin for the camera to defuse the lightning-rod rhetoric.

—At a news event covering the arrest of three school bus loads of illegal immigrants, McCann was there. "China has the Great Wall. And that old wall is *great* because it keeps out the unwanted and the unwashed."

—When TV cameras arrived at a textile plant closing, McCann was there to shake hands and give his two cents. "Where are these jobs going? South of the border, where pay is cheap and profits are big. What about these folks? What has NAFTA done for them but screw up next Christmas?"

—Then there was more populist rhetoric at a rally protesting the closing of a Cathedral homeless shelter. "In my daddy's day they were called bums and tramps. They'd show up at the door and offer work in exchange for food. But now we call 'em *homeless*. I tell you, that's a word engineered to make y'all feel sorry for 'em. I say let's change the language. Call 'em what they are—tramps and bums again—then let's see if the taxpayers wanna keep payin' for it."

Hit and run.

It always looked cheap. It most certainly sounded crackpot. Yet people would surely remember the name behind the sound bites. Shakespeare McCann.

"What should we expect?"

"Another spike in McCann's name tracking. And your first big bump in negative numbers," answered Fitz. "But that'd be up from zero. I'm only worried about the timing."

"What about the timing?"

"It's Thursday. If they had the check, a smart man would've dumped this on us Friday. We wouldn't be able to counterpunch effectively till Monday. Marshall's too smart for that, so something is up."

"But Marshall doesn't sign the checks," reminded Mitch. "Has anyone heard from La Croix? I'd love to hear what he has to say."

"Best I could find out was that he's over in Africa, seeking peace and revelation."

Rene breezed in, handing off her statement to Mitch. He read it to himself. "It sounds careful."

"That's you." She smiled. "Counterpoint to *reckless,* which in a nutshell defines our opponent."

At nine o'clock on Friday morning, Mitch conterpunched, reading from a prepared statement. "The assertions by my opponent are reckless and careless. The support for my nomination has been broad, and with so many campaign contributions my underpaid campaign staff has had to sort through, it's no wonder a single check was overlooked."

Mitch was reading the statement in front of the offices of the Cathedral City NAACP. Backed by a genial, racially mixed group of local supporters, Mitch trudged on. "I have never met or spoken to Jamal La Croix. And by no means do I agree with a single word of his angry politics. Martin Luther King said we will walk up the top of the hill, black and white, hand in hand. I truly believe in those words. Jamal La Croix does not.

"If anything, I'm here to say thank you to the First Cathedral Bank employee who brought this simple error to my campaign's attention. And to put an end to this matter, we are returning the contribution of one thousand dollars."

The front-runner didn't take any questions and gave no impromptu answers. Instead he said thank you and was on his way to a calendar full of one-on-one interviews on the matter.

"The high ground," rumbled Fitz as he watched the press conference. "How long can it last?"

2

The Texas facility where Shoop de Jarnot awaited word on his appeal was named after a former Texas corrections chief named Carlton C. Abbot. During Abbot's twenty-year tenure, he'd built four prisons, leaving them as his legacy, and him with the moniker the "King of Corrections." But the inmates at Carlton C. Abbot State Penitentiary had another word for the concrete stockade.

El Rincón.

One of the few seaside prisons in the country, it boasted ocean views and its own lighthouse on the jutting outcropping of land it stood upon. Prosecutors affectionately said of El Rincón, "It's where the joint meets the point."

Shoop couldn't afford a room with a view. Those were mostly reserved for trustees, cons who'd made deals, or those who'd had so much "good time" logged that it was either release the old boy or upgrade him to a scenic suite. But Shoop's space was a single bunk, ten by five feet, built from cinder block with indoor plumbing. And since he was a prisoner with a pending death penalty appeal, he wasn't allowed to mingle with the facility's general population. Instead he spent all his hours in solitary confinement, except for the occasional infirmary visits for chronic sinusitis. There he would actually find conversations with various patients and nurses, a tonic he sorely missed when the infections would clear.

Television was Shoop's greatest comfort. It was monitored and rationed; the day for most of America's incarcerated revolved around three square meals, brief respites of fresh air, and two sessions of TV—early prime, i.e., before dinner, and prime time, between seven and ten at night.

It was on the ten-o'clock news when Shoop first caught wind of Mitchell's most recent *tête-à-tête* with the news media. On Thursday he'd watched excerpts from McCann's news conference. And that Friday, Mitch's rebuttal. He was thrilled catching his lawyer on the news.

"Das my lawyuh," Shoop would proudly point out to a guard named Tyler Tubbs.

"Hate to burst your bubble," sparked the guard, "but you ain't gonna win him any votes from here."

"He da good man. Mitch Dutton."

"Sure he is." Tyler nodded. "You finished with your tray?" Shoop slid his barely eaten dinner tray through the slot. "Hate to tell ya, Shoop. But starvin' your Creole ass ain't the best way to get yourself to the infirmary."

Shoop hated Texas and its love of barbecue sauce and everything chicken-fried. To him, they couldn't cook without a flotilla of grease and some salty sauce to smother the flavor.

"My lawyuh say dat dah food in dah Loosiana prison is much better."

"Still thinkin' you're gonna make it out, huh?" Tyler tried a forkload of the stew. *Not bad,* said his expression.

"I got mah hope."

"And what if you don't?"

"Den ah die." It was that simple. Shoop was momentarily resigned to the either/or of the proposition. Prison had done that to him.

"You trust this politician guy?" Tyler seemed more than just curious. A new swing guard, part-timing it between the correctional job and night school, he was a Louisiana native sidetracked to Texas by way of a failed pro-football career. Shoop shared nothing with Tyler other than a former common geography called Louisiana. "You really don't wonder he'll leave you hangin'?"

"He won'. He mah lawyuh. He made me a promise."

"Yeah? So what kind of promise?"

"Dat if dey kill me in Texas, dat he gonna see me back tah Loosiana and my momma."

"Even if he's elected? He's gonna leave Washington, D.C., and go to some killer's funeral?"

"Promise is ah promise."

"You crazy."

"Not me."

"Yeah, you. For one thing. You gonna trust some white man to deliver your dead black ass to your Creole momma. And two, this white man's a politician." Tyler gulped back what was left of the tripe stew. "Maybe they just wanna kill you cuzza you're so dumb."

Connie Dutton no longer read newspapers. To her they were little more than a daily bundle of bad news on cheap, recycled paper. Not the best way to wake up, she thought. It was no wonder that she didn't recognize the face of the man shaking hands with her husband in the picture that came over the fax machine on Saturday morning. She delivered it to Mitch at his usual postjogging perch. Kitchen table. Hunched over a bowl of cereal, a cup of coffee in hand, with the newspaper spread out in front of him as if he were a lost tourist scouring the local road atlas.

"Came over the fax for you." She knew better than to wait for him to look up. She just slipped it under his nose.

"Thanks, sweetie." He took the fax, briefly set it aside as he finished an article by a *Daily Mirror* guest columnist on the state of municipal bond funding throughout the Southwest. Only when he was done did he give the item a once-over. That's when his blood went cold.

Mitch Dutton and Jamal La Croix, warmly smiling, hands firmly clasped in union.

"It's a fake!" bellowed Mitch from his study. Fitz was at the other end of the phone. "Yes. That's me. But I swear, that's not Jamal La Croix. I have *never* shaken his hand!"

"Then who the hell is it?"

"Hell if I remember. There's not enough detail in the picture."

"I knew it," said Fitz. "I should've seen it coming."

"Seen *this* coming?"

"The Thursday press conference. I couldn't figure out why McCann did it Thursday instead of waiting until Friday."

"Because they wanted me to come out and say without equivocation that I'd never met Jamal La Croix." Mitch was quick to catch on.

"You got it."

The Call Waiting beeped. "Hang on, will ya?" He switched lines. "Hello?"

"Mitch Dutton?"

"Speaking."

"Kevin O'Sullivan from Channel Five."

"I'm sorry. I can't talk right now."

"I just want a statement."

"It's a fake. That's all I can say right now." He switched lines back to Fitz. "Channel Five. The bastard must have had a field day faxing it to all the media this morning."

"How'd they get your home number?"

"It's a small town." Then his line beeped again. "Shit."

"Don't answer," advised Fitz.

"I have to. Connie just left to get her car serviced and I'm waiting to see if I have to pick her up." The line beeped again. Mitch depressed the switch. "Hello?"

"Mitch. It's Hollice Waters. I'm on vacation in Colorado, but somebody just faxed me—"

"It's a fucking fake, Hollice. I've never met the guy."

"Can I quote you?"

"On everything but the Goddamn expletive."

"If it's a fake, then who did it?"

"That's your guess."

"So if it's not La Croix in the picture, who're you shaking hands with?"

"I don't know, Hollice. Now, I gotta go." Mitch switched back to Fitz again. "Hollice Waters calling from his vacation, for Christ's sake." The phone beeped *again.*

"Goddammit, don't answer it."

But Mitch was already gone. "Hello?"

"Mitch Dutton."

"Listen. I can't talk right now."

"Mitch. It's Wilson Pendercost."

Wilson Pendercost?

The name struck Mitch funny. He'd heard of it. Had some good feelings from it. But he couldn't place him. "I'm sorry, but I don't remember . . . Help me out."

"I understand. It's been a while since we've met. And it was only the one time," said Wilson Pendercost. "I was the CCSD teacher of the year five years ago. That's when you were on the school board. You presented me with the award."

Mitch's mind slingshot backward. Then the face came to him. A smiling, friendly fellow with the kind of visage only great teachers achieve. Full of trust and love and patience. Wilson Pendercost had been honored with the Cathedral City School District Teacher of the Year award. Mitch was the master of ceremonies that night, handing out the award to the city's best. Wilson Pendercost. Suddenly Mitch found himself looking at the faxed fake.

"That's me in the picture," said Wilson. "Right after you gave me the award. Me shaking your hand."

"You're right. That's where I remember this."

"It's a fake."

"Damn right it's a fake," said Mitch, putting a cork in his fury. "How'd you get it?"

"My sister. Some type of fax chain letter."

"I expect all of South County must have seen it by now."

"Well, I have a copy of the original if you need it. You know. To debunk the faker."

"Where do you live?" asked Mitch.

"I'm still on the mainland."

"Hang on, will you? I have someone on the other line who's going to call you. His name is Fitz Kolatch."

"Okay. I'll hold."

Mitch switched lines again. "Wilson Pendercost."

"Who?"

"The man in picture. He's on the other line. He has the original."

"Okay. I wanna talk to him. But I want you on the phone to Rene. You're gonna have to make another statement."

"The sooner the fucking better."

"I'm not so sure about that," reasoned Fitz. "I don't want any hasty counterpunching. If McCann was behind this, we've been sandbagged good."

"It's fraud, dammit."

"So was filing a false police report. But that's the game you chose to play when you decided to run for office."

"Not this game, Fitz."

"Grow up, Mitch. You're in it. I'm calling this guy Willy Pendergrass—"

"Wilson Pendercost," corrected Mitch.

"Whatever," said Fitz. "I'm calling him and then Marshall Lambeer. It's time we made diplomatic contact with the other side."

Somehow Texas never felt like home to Marshall Lambeer. The sixty-four-year-old political warhorse hailed from Maine, and ever since moving to Cathedral thirty-one years earlier, he had tried to summer down east every other year. The odd summer, of course, was given to *The Show,* as he'd come to know it. Having managed twelve successive Hammond campaigns for reelection, he'd found barely a week or two to sneak away when it came to election years. Even with old Hurricane's seemingly bulletproof incumbency, the job wasn't exactly slack, requiring more than its share of shaking all the old hands and dressing up Hurricane's status quo politics in the occasional new suit.

Cathedral, though. Marshall never figured to stay. The bugs were too big and the tourists too tacky. From day one he'd planned to return to his native Maine, expecting the Hammond gig to someday end. But after thirty-one years, from when he was Hurricane's thirty-three-year-old administrative assistant until the very day Hammond died on his Virginia farm, Marshall had stayed. For the kids, he'd often told himself. Three girls, all grown and through college, the youngest having graduated just last June. Marshall and his wife, Eleanor, were experiencing the twilight years. All the readable road signs told Marshall to quit, retire, move on!

Go back to Maine.

Yet in the scorching that came with July, Marshall found himself working for a candidate he hardly knew, let alone spoke to. At double his previous salary. Yes. Extra pocket change for the permanent retirement account. Nonetheless, Marshall felt somewhat less than sanguine about the chore. The surrounding faces were all the same. Good Republicans, all. Dedicated. Family folk. Except for one strange-looking guy who stood on top of Marshall's campaign heap with an unfamiliar face that gave away little more than a trademark smile.

But who in the name of God was he?

The question plagued Marshall each and every night when he curled up against his wife and closed his eyes. To get to sleep, the old campaign mule would have to remind himself that Shakespeare had the state party endorsement or else they wouldn't have funded that initial one hundred thousand. After all, Zig Ziegler, the state party chair, had given Shakespeare McCann the official thumbs-up. No explanation required. Marshall would later admit that he didn't think enough to press Zig for details on the candidate. Maybe it was because of the money they'd given the campaign. Or maybe it was the eighty thousand that Shakespeare had promised Marshall, twenty thousand of which had already been deposited into Marshall's account.

Maybe, maybe, maybe . . .

"Fitz Kolatch on six."

When Fitz's call came through the McCann campaign office switchboard, Marshall had first thought to return the call later on, after he'd ascertained just where the faxed photo had materialized from. Instead, he had Fitz hold, got up from a crowded desk covered in scheduling markers, and walked the short, paneled corridor to Shakespeare's office. He excused himself as he squeezed past a couple of volunteers blocking the hallway. Shakespeare had gathered himself a loyal and zealous flock. Buzzing minions devoted to the man who would be *their* congressman.

Shakespeare had furnished his Strand office in the bare necessities and little else. A desk, a couch, a computer. No family photos or familiar memorabilia to give any clue to a past. And as usual, Marshall found Shakespeare seated on his desk, back to the door, staring upward at that bulletin board covered in that rainbow of three-by-five cards, each with a scribbled text that nobody but Shakespeare could understand.

"Shakespeare," started Marshall.

"Marshall," acknowledged Shakespeare without turning his head.

He stood at the threshold, trying to find the right words. "I've got Fitz Kolatch on hold."

"Did you talk to him?"

"Not yet. I'm sure it's going to be about this fax thing."

"So what's to say? You don't know *where* the picture came from. But you're awful glad some good citizen thought well enough to distribute it."

"He's a smart man. He's gonna want to know if we had the picture *before* we made an issue of the check."

"That so?"

"Yessir."

"And what'll you say?"

"That we didn't have the picture."

"That's good, Marshall."

"Did we?"

"Did we what?" asked Shakespeare.

"Did we have the picture?"

Shakespeare finally turned with just enough shoulder so he could get a clear shot of Marshall. "Of course not."

"Because if we did, I'll just pack it in. There's sandbagging and then there's—"

"Marshall," interrupted Shakespeare, swinging his stare to his cards. "We didn't have the picture. And if we did, does it make Dutton's lie any better?"

"I don't know."

"You've been in this business too long. Anything else?"

"No, sir."

"Hear what he has to say, then tell 'em what I said directly."

Marshall stood at the threshold another beat before turning to exit.

"Oh, Marshall?" called the boss. "You think Dutton loves his wife?"

"I . . . I wouldn't know," he answered, returning to the threshold.

"Find out. And shut the door."

The door latched closed. Afterward Marshall hustled right back to his office and the blinking phone line where he'd left Fitz on hold. "Fitz, ol' friend. How ya doin'?"

The faked photo was front page on Sunday *and* Monday in both Cathedral's newspapers. It also led the evening newscasts. Candidate Dutton, shaking hands with local enemy *numero uno*. Proof positive of the lie. And even though news editors and directors had been informed Saturday of the fraud, the picture was too hot. The story, too juicy. The denial would have to wait until Monday, when the maligned candidate, Mitch Dutton, stood before a crush of cameras and swinging boom mikes. He held up both pictures for all to see, the original and the fake, and from both Rene's and Fitz's perspectives, sounded too damn controlled and lawyerly in his indignation. The hurt and anger from Saturday's fax attack had been buried too deep for the candidate to ever retrieve it.

The retracted story was on Tuesday's *Mirror's* page six, below the fold.

"I'm sorry to call you at home, Mitch."

"Who is this?"

"William Ziegler," said the Republican Central Committee chair from his own home telephone.

They'd met only once before, Mitch and Zig, at a charity auction in Dallas where they'd bid against each other over a football signed by Cowboy great Roger Staubach. Both lost out. Afterward they'd shared a friendly word or two, and that was that.

"It's not too late to talk, is it?" asked Zig.

Ten-thirty and Mitch was finishing up his daily reading. "It's okay. What can I do for you?"

"What I have to say is off the record," said Zig. "Are you talking on a hard line?"

"Yes," answered Mitch.

"Good," said Zig. His voice was low and even, speaking from a deep reserve inside his soul. "If you repeat what I say to you, I'll deny every word."

"I'm primarily a corporate lawyer," said Mitch. "I have more secrets to keep than I'd like to admit."

"I'll take that to mean we understand each other."

"It won't go past me."

"Politics aside, man to man," stated Zig. "Your opponent, Shakespeare McCann . . ."

"Yes?"

"Just watch your back. That's all."

"You know something I don't know?"

"I think he's dangerous."

"And you gave him seventy-five thousand dollars," Mitch found himself saying.

"Something I'll always regret. But I'll learn to live with that."

"I hope so."

There was an awkward silence. Through the phone, Mitch could hear the swirling of ice in a tumbler.

"That's about all," said Zig.

"I appreciate your call."

"Think nothing of it." He hung up.

A good two hours passed before Mitch packed it in for the night. Between the phone call and David Letterman's first guest, he had replayed the cryptic conversation with Zig over and over in his mind. The message. The motivation. No matter which way Mitch processed it, he got the same answer from every angle.

The high ground is crumbling.

In August the rain crashed into Cathedral Island with five straight days of thundershowers to wipe the streets clean and leave the Island with a sweet ocean smell that many hoped would erase the sweltering hell that had been July. As the cooler temperatures prevailed, Charlie Flores hoped so would cooler heads. As editor-in-chief at the *Daily Mirror*, he'd watched as July practically cooked his precious Island to a crisp. Tourism was down. Crime was up. And the local cops were threatening to strike over the issue of summer uniforms.

It would've been a banner month for most newspaper editors, with plenty of news from which to pick and choose. But for fifty-four-year-old Charlie, who liked to tell his interns that he'd already had his heart attack, he preferred a targeted approach to news gathering. Instead of the news coming to him, he'd rather send his crew out to get the news. "Beat the bushes," he'd say. "Come back only when you have something. Until then, stay out of my hair."

"So is he in the race or not?" Charlie asked Hollice, nudging the reporter's feet off his desk and replacing them with a stack of Cuban cigars. Cohibas, Romeo y Juliets, and Partagas.

"Havanas?" asked Hollice.

"A gift from my brother-in-law," confirmed Charlie. The cigars were his last vice in a life dictated by the laws of Pritikin and Covert Bailey. "So is it a horse race or not?"

"Depends on how you look at it."

"Just gimme the spin. Granny's gonna be askin'."

Granny, otherwise known as Granthum Baxter, publisher of the *Daily Mirror*. Eighty-eight years old, like clockwork he'd fly for quarterly visits from his house in the Grand Caymans to get the grislies on his newspaper business.

"McCann's up twenty-five points from nothin'. But then you can also say he's thirty points down when you put his numbers against Dutton's."

"So we can go with the dark-horse story. Candidate with momentum and all that."

"Or with the dead-horse story. Candidate throws rocks, hits a few targets, but nobody really knows what he stands for. He's stuck in the gate. All he's really done is up Dutton's negatives and, in doing so, built up his own dubious reputation."

"I like the dark-horse story better."

"Obviously."

"When we had Dutton versus Hammond, that was going to be our tack."

"And I was ready."

Damn right he was ready. The story would've been a doozy, too. Hollice had already finished the Mitch Dutton profile. He'd had it filed since high school. Everything since had just been basic follow-up work.

MR. CLEAN VS. MR. MEAN.

That was the banner headline that Hollice had hoped the *Daily Mirror* would have run as a postprimary piece under the Hollice Waters byline. It would have included photos of Mitch and Hurricane Hammond pasted on either side of the story, facing off in obvious opposition. The tenor of the story was to have been Hollice's perspective on Mitchell's Neverland Politics versus Hurricane's Washington Wrestling Match. It would have been certain to raise eyebrows in both camps and set the standard for each man's reputation.

Of course, Hollice had planned to follow with those rumored allegations of Mitchell's personal improprieties, i.e., the candidate's matriculations into social groups on the political fringe, including some leftist academics whose writings bordered on what Hollice thought he'd label *neocommunism*—this in a state where the Red Threat was still associated with the likes of Lee Harvey Oswald and the assassination of President Kennedy. Then there would have been the rumors of Mitchell's affair with one or even numerous campaign staffers, allegations that were hard to substantiate, yet impossible to deny without a considerable tarnishing effect.

And Mitch would be Mr. Clean no more.

Not that Hollice would have been one-sided about any of this. He'd planned similar trashing of the incumbent candidate, whose list of actual and factual indiscretions was a mile long and wide enough for ten newspapers. Hollice had planned to keep up with this planned pumpkin-smashing all the way to Halloween and thereafter.

Enter Shakespeare McCann. A man, so much as Hollice could discover, without a past. A man who (if anyone was to believe his press kit) sprang from the ground to act as duelist's second for George Hammond like an orphan weed amongst the scrub. A man Hammond never knew. A man nobody seemingly ever knew before 1982. At least, nobody living.

"You think McCann can win?" asked Charlie.

"I've seen stranger things," said Hollice, snitching a Diet Coke from Charlie's personal refrigerator. A perk of the position, Charlie's little icebox was famous inside the *Cathedral Daily Mirror*. Located underneath the second-floor window, it also made a fine stool for Hollice to seat himself while he popped open the soda and guzzled. "One thing for sure, Dutton's a wimp. McCann's not. And November's still a ways off."

"How about another profile on the both of them?"

"There's my problem. McCann's all about what he says. Not who he is."

"Then find out."

"Easier said than done."

"Why not go at it through the Dallas connection? Republicans gotta know something. I mean, Zig Ziegler and the rest of those Dallas boys wouldn't go throwin' so much good money after bad."

"Listen to me, Charlie," said Hollice. "So far, I can't find a living soul who knew McCann before eighty-one. And those that are alive and talking refer to McCann as if he's the holder of the Holy Grail. Now, name me anybody you've ever met who fits that description."

"He's obviously hiding something."

"No shit."

"Look harder. That way, when we find out something, you can run this fellah's laundry up the flagpole and see if anybody salutes. Until then, let's lay some more hot coals for the front-runner."

"So what? When he goes to cool his feet we can see if he walks on water?" joked Hollice.

"Just keep a stash of life preservers nearby. When it comes time for Granny to give an endorsement, I don't want to see any floating bodies," said Charlie, amused with his own metaphor. After which he broke open one of those cigar boxes, snipped a double corona, and lit up without offering so much as a taste to Hollice.

Stu Jackson would've joked that he'd never actually seen a metaphor, but he'd seen plenty of floating bodies in his forty-eight years. Working for the DEA, he'd seen more *real* bodies wash up on the Gulf beaches than there were cousins in the Klan. Colombians. Bolivians. Mexicans. It was his job to ID the Juan Does of the Texas drug war. That was the beginning of his pedigree as a private investigator, later starting the opposition research business as a sideline. So successful were Stu and his team at digging up the DNA on Republican candidates, he'd gone full-time by the mid-eighties, turning the PI gig into an afterthought, and opposition research into a valuable tool for the Texas Democratic party.

"So let's get on with it," said Mitch. He'd decided it was time somebody found out the who, what, and where about Shakespeare McCann.

Laconic in just about every aspect of his manner, Stu opened a file folder. His long black fingers sifting through notes and printouts while everyone else waited around the conference table in the Dutton campaign office. Mitch, Fitz, Rene, and Murray. But instead of coming up with a dossier on the opposition, Stu found what he was looking for and laid it out in the middle of the table. It was a check.

"What's that?" asked Fitz.

"Your money back."

"What for?"

"Doin' a crappy job for you."

"It's been two months," said Fitz. "You could've said you weren't up for the job."

"Oh, I was up for it. And I did what I could in the time I was given," answered Stu, his voice as lazy as his languid looks. "But I've dug up body parts with longer histories than Shakespeare McCann."

Mitch picked up the check for fifteen thousand dollars. A lot of money, he thought. In his law practice, he'd worked with plenty of private investigators. They did the real dirty work that was later turned into a legal judgment. But hiring a PI to look into the political opposition's past? Fitz reminded Mitch that paying Stu Jackson was a legitimate campaign expense, commonplace in modern campaigns. A necessity.

"I can give y'all another month, if you like. On the house," continued Stu. "Maybe I'll find some buried leader and reel in somethin' you can hang a hat on."

"Jesus H. Christ. What's he hiding?" asked Fitz.

"It's gotta be bad, whatever it is," added Murray.

"Oh, it's bad, all right. Nobody erases half their life for no reason at all," said Stu. "And it'll catch him someday. Bite him in the ass. Always does."

"Sure. Look what it did for Clinton," said Rene with her trademark cynicism.

The candidate had been quiet throughout. Looking at the check. At Stu.

"Sorry." The investigator shrugged.

"Just give us what you got," said Mitch, sliding the check back over to him. "We'll see if there's any more later."

"Good enough." Stu smiled, appreciating Mitch's trust and patience. He filed the check back into his folder and turned back to page one. "Okay. Shakespeare McCann. Both parents deceased. Foster parents deceased. Aunts and uncles unknown. Schools listed in McCann's bio were either burnt down or came under a wrecking ball. Found a strip mall where one of 'em once stood.

"Military history," Stu went on. "Field mechanic, marines, Philippines. That's in the bio, too. Now, we got the Marine Corps to acknowledge Shakespeare's fulfillment of duty during that period in history, but they've been slow in finding a file on Motor Pool Sergeant McCann, and have yet to make available a copy to Hollice Waters, who's applied for the documents through the Freedom of Information Act."

"He applied? You didn't?" asked Fitz.

"Got a little girlie in his office doing duty for me. She'll fax me when it comes in," said Stu. "From there it gets vague again. His bio glosses over the two decades after his military service. Soonest we come back into contact with him is when he'd apprenticed as a print shop monkey somewhere in 1980."

While Stu talked, Mitch browsed the printed version of the report. Most of it, he knew. Toward the end of that print shop job, Shakespeare claimed to have found the religion of Jesus Christ while stamping out the weekly liturgy for the First Presbyterian Church of Cathedral City.

The *Power of God* is to what Shakespeare attributed his rise from ink *meister* to entrepreneur. Through the church and the business connections that followed, he'd opened his own print shop and copy center. Soon there was a small chain of Shakespeare's Quick Copy shops, totaling four in all. Two in Cathedral City. One in nearby Meyers and another up in Houston. It didn't take much legwork for Stu Jackson to recognize that where there was a Presbyterian church, one of Shakespeare McCann's Quick Copy shops would be nearby. From interviews with various parishioners, Stu garnered that Shakespeare McCann would manage his Sundays around his print shops, giving himself over to each church only once per month, and leaving the rare fifth Sunday for fishing.

Good business, Mitch thought. Smart.

"The rest is still up for grabs," said Stu. "I've run him through databases from here to Hanoi. It comes up zip."

"Shakespeare McCann comes up zip," confirmed Mitch.

"There you go. But if there was an alias? Well, then he could be anybody from anywhere."

"Social Security?" asked Rene.

"He was born Shakespeare McCann. In South County." Stu shrugged back at her.

"TRW?" asked Fitz.

"That's where we started. He's got a good credit history after eighty-two, but no credit history before that."

"FBI?" pushed Rene.

"Get me some fingerprints, I can call in a favor. No guarantee of results. In the meantime, we ran his picture through as many computer identi-kits as I could get my hands on. Nothin' there yet."

Reading further from the report, Mitch noted that Shakespeare's flock was rock solid on the candidate. Stu's "girlie" had lifted transcripts from audiotaped interviews Hollice had made with early supporters. "God's example" were words often used. "He's been a savior," said a crippled man whose wheelchair had been maliciously crunched by an errant teenager in a four-by-four pickup. Instead of calling the police, a bystander named Shakespeare McCann had volunteered his print shop to manufacture some thousand posters that were hung on lampposts and telephone poles. It had taken only days for somebody to recognize the boy's truck from the description on the posted sheet. A day later the boy had turned himself in to the police, offering restitution to the crippled man for repairs to the wheelchair.

"Courageous," said another parishioner, a single woman with two children whose husband had up and vanished without a trace, leaving them penniless with a mortgage to pay. With the help of fellow church members, Shakespeare had organized a dragnet to run down the deadbeat father who'd absconded all the way to Montana. Described by the couple as a "miracle," the man eventually returned and, with his wife, sought the counseling of a minister in the salvation of their marriage.

There were pages more. A man who'd lost his job due to false charges of theft. An elderly woman whose Social Security checks were being stolen and cashed by an evil nephew. A young hooligan with a drug habit who found work and training inside one of the candidate's print shops. All ages and colors and genders.

Mitch spoke up. "The big question is, why doesn't anybody seem to care that this man's a total mystery? Where's the press? I mean, my life's on open book. Part of the public record. Him? He's a ghost."

"Voters don't care so much anymore as to who you are or where you've been," said Rene, hosing Mitch off with the political ice water. "Voters only care what you're gonna do for *them*."

"Or if you've had a criminal record," chimed Murray.

"And that depends on the crime," finished Fitz.

Mitch stood and tossed the report into the center of the table. "So let's make an issue of it. Who's Shakespeare McCann?"

"An issue of what?" asked Fitz.

"The fact that he's got the Grand Canyon running smack through his life story."

"In other words, make something from nothing?" answered Fitz rhetorically. "You see the dilemma? We can make a mountain out of a molehill. But when there's nothing there . . ."

Rene added, "If his numbers were better. If he was closer, maybe. It's an ad campaign. Who's Shakespeare McCann? Until then, he's nothing more than a double-digit demon in your rearview mirror and that's it. You're way ahead in the polls. You don't want to look like you're running scared."

Unsatisfactory, thought Mitch. *We can do better!*

"If I'd said it, he'd have argued with me," joked Fitz to the rest of them.

"And I may yet argue with it," said Mitch.

"Well, while you're planning your great debate, lemme say that Rene's right. Your numbers speak for themselves and they don't lie. You got better'n twenty points on the little shit. So don't look back. Full speed ahead. Leave the paranoia for the professionals."

"Thank you," said Stu, accepting the second chance.

"Fine," relented Mitch. "Full speed ahead. Let's get out there and light some fires." He slapped the table, bringing smiles to the crew. "I wanna move on the Prisons for Schools concept. I'm thinking we can get endorsements from state corrections commissioners *and* school superintendents. That and I think it's time to frame an election finance reform platform. I have some ideas that're gonna curl Sandy Mullin's hair."

Mitch could light all the fires he wanted, thought Fitz. But numbers—they were the intravenous prick strapped to his forearm and stuck deep in a pulsing vein. There were the weekly tracking, the midweek tracking, the nightly tracking, and the morning report.

By any informed account, Mitch had great Goddamn numbers, despite his own view of himself as nothing more than a boy with a sling and a pocket full of rocks. During the primary he'd been scoring just under forty percent in the category of likely voters for the general election, a practical guarantee to have given Hurricane a serious run for his money. And even after the old man's untimely death, the digits were those Fitz could only dream of. Name recognition alone was at eighty-two percent for candidate Dutton. If the election had been held a week after Hammond's death, the numbers revealed that Mitch would have closed with seventy-nine percent of the likely voters, taking into account that most of the Republicans would have stayed home in sheer protest.

4

Wanda Kennedy liked to tell interested folks that she had some distant relations in the Northeast, up Massachusetts way. But without a family tree, she couldn't quite prove her theory that the famed Kennedy clan had left a piece of the family to root and prosper in South Texas. So important to her was the Kennedy kinship that when she married Jimmy Joe Huggins back in 1963, she'd declined to take his surname, thus causing an uproar between respective in-laws that lasted nearly a lifetime. Still, Wanda loved Jimmy Joe, and when he died in 1991, she secretly spread his ashes along the Cathedral Island postal route that he'd walked nearly twenty-five years.

A Dutton volunteer, and tireless worker, Wanda was the kind of woman to lend her hand to just about anything labeled *Democrat*. From voter registration drives to dressing in clown makeup on hundred-plus-degree days and gathering petition signatures door to door all up and down the Gulf Coast. And when called a political zealot, she'd always cite that all-important Kennedy coda:

"Ask not what your country can do for you, but what you can do . . ."

On the first Sunday in August, the 10:00 A.M. mass at Cathedral City's St. Cecelia's ended in a gorgeous, choir-enhanced rendition of "Nearer My God to Thee." As Wanda exited the church, dipping her hand into a marbled cistern of holy water and crossing herself, the good

Father Philip Samuels put a kind hand on her shoulder. "Dearest Wanda. How are you today?" Then he leaned closer and whispered importantly, "Could I see you for just a moment? In my office?"

The good father's office was small and stuffed with books, a fax machine, an old IBM Selectric typewriter, and the coatrack where he hung his robe. "Wanda, you're going to have to explain this to me."

Wanda was giggling. She knew exactly why she'd been called on the carpet. "What can I say, Father? Sometimes I just can't help myself."

On Father Samuel's desk was a collection plate. And in it, amongst all the quarters and cash, were five "Dutton for Congress" buttons. "I also made a donation. There's a twenty in there with my dearly departed husband's name on it."

"Wanda," said the priest, hands clasped patiently under his chin. "We can't have you campaigning during the church service. Believe it or not, we've got Republicans in some of those pews."

"Republicans always claim God is on their side. Can I help it if I believe God is on Mitch Dutton's side?"

"Please . . ."

"By the way. I don't see more than five badges in there, and I musta put at least a dozen in. That should say something to you."

"Wanda. You can't do it again. Now, I had planned to talk to you about last Sunday's—"

"That wasn't in church. That was *after* mass."

"You were giving away bumper stickers on church property. The event was to collect donations for the children's hospital and—"

"Mitch Dutton is for the hospital. And if you help elect him, I'll bet he could get matching federal grant money so we can build a new wing."

"The Mitch Dutton Wing, I'm sure." Father Samuels smiled.

"Not while he's in office. That wouldn't be politically proper."

"Listen to me, Wanda. Church is for God. We're there to worship Him, not Mitch Dutton. Am I understood?"

Wanda shifted in her seat. She was no more than five feet, frizzy bleached hair, and stubborn as an old stain. But would she obey? "Just tell me who you're voting for."

The priest squirmed. "Probably Dutton. I don't even know the guy he's running against."

"Shakespeare McCann. And I can personally guarantee you, Father, that Shakespeare McCann runs with the devil. I got personal knowledge."

"Glad to hear it. Now, I've Sunday school classes." Then as Father Samuels was showing Wanda to the door, she pinned onto his black tunic a "Mitch Dutton for Congress" button. After which she left with a winning smile. She'd gathered one more vote for the Democrat, Mitch Dutton—a man so good-looking, he may as well have been a Kennedy.

Shakespeare McCann runs with the devil.

About that, Wanda was absolutely certain. It was a solid-state fact she'd dutifully passed onto the volunteer coordinator, Murray Levy. And what she'd said was enough to send ears burning all the way to Dallas.

Wanda's twenty-three-year-old daughter, Trudy, worked the reception desk in the Cathedral City Planned Parenthood office. The clinic, victim of countless antiabortion rallies, was otherwise known to be quiet and confidential. Trudy's job was to check in the young women who'd made appointments for pregnancy terminations, assign them the various legal forms to fill out, and establish a method for payment. Planned Parenthood was not just a cash business.

On July 26 the clinic had what they called a "door-swinger": a young girl, under eighteen, without an appointment. Typically a door-swinger would sit in the parking lot, either building up the gumption to get on with the deed or engaged in a fight with her boyfriend. Eventually she would burst through the doors and ask for an abortion on the spot. It was Trudy who had the unfortunate job of informing these poor girls that Planned Parenthood required an appointment. That and they might be better off thinking for twenty-four hours about the procedure. As the pregnant teen would invariably begin to sob and beg, the doors would still be swinging.

Jennifer O'Detts was a door-swinger.

The sixteen-year-old walked through the door, bruised and sans makeup—not even attempting to hide the familiar red and blue marks of a beating. The teenager had demanded an abortion and uncrumpled her only three hundred dollars for the procedure. When she was informed that an appointment would be necessary, Trudy Kennedy kindly asked her to come back the following Tuesday.

"I want it out!" shrieked Jennifer, her pretty mouth swollen from a harsh blow. "Look what he did to me! All I wanted was the money for the abortion! Three hundred fucking dollars!"

"You can have the procedure," continued Trudy. "Tuesday is only four days away."

"This is all I have," Jennifer said of the money. "Please. He's an evil fuck and I don't want his baby!"

"If he hurt you, you can file assault charges. I can give you a number—"

"File charges against Shakespeare McCann? *Puh-leease,* sister. Do you know who he knows?"

As a rule, Trudy didn't give much of a damn about politics the way her mother did. Trudy thought the whole game was a sham played by crooks and rich businessmen. She was a registered Democrat because her mother had seen fit that an absentee ballot had been filled out in her name in time for the last primary. She'd barely heard about Shakespeare McCann. The name rung a very small bell.

"Let me make you an appointment," urged Trudy.

"Don't think I can't do this myself! I know some girls who did it themselves. Or went to Mexico to have it done."

"That would be extremely dangerous. We're only talking four days."

"If you knew him, you'd understand. You'd understand *everything!*" sobbed Jennifer, before rushing away from the reception counter and plowing back through those swinging doors.

In a passing remark while waiting in line for a dollar-ninety-nine movie, Trudy told her mother. And when Wanda pressed for details, the most Trudy could do was give her the patient's name, easily remembered as Jennifer O'Detts, who, like most door-swingers, never appeared for her Tuesday appointment. Odds were that she'd driven up to Houston where there were more clinics and, for a few dollars more, abortion on demand was a thriving business.

When Wanda approached Murray, his first inclination was to sit on the information for a few days. He'd scribbled the name—Jennifer O'Detts—upon a desktop notepad and sent Wanda back to the volunteer pool with a pat on the back and the promise to keep the name to herself. Murray would handle it. What made him wait two days before telling Fitz was his allegiance to Mitch. A clean campaign was the candidate's first and foremost marching order. From the start, that's what Mitch had commanded. And Murray, still wearing his idealistic youth like a badge of political courage, had become a true believer, even though he'd heard loose talk of striking back at McCann over the Jamal La Croix hoax. Fight fire with fire.

If Jennifer O'Detts was real—if she'd come forward—it would be all over for Shakespeare.

Jennifer O'Detts was hot.

So hot that Mitch might have no alternative but to turn her out against McCann. And once done, corrupt the campaign and corrupt himself in the process. Even worse, he might blame Murray, destroying the young staffer's chances at a postelectoral position in D.C.

The dilemma was resolved when the man who'd hired him, Fitz, asked Murray, "So what have you done for the campaign this week?"

"Jennifer O'Detts," said Murray, finally shaking loose the monkey.

"Jennifer who?"

"Jennifer O'Detts. And she's hot."

"Hot how? Hot like you wanna jump her?"

"No. Not like that," corrected Murray. "She's sixteen. And she was raped."

It took Stu Jackson less than an hour to find the girl. O'Detts, it turned out, was a local name, easily found in the Greater Cathedral registry. The family was spread throughout South County, and most hadn't moved in a hundred years. Jennifer was described as sixteen, and at first, didn't appear on DMV records, voter lists, or tax rolls. Most likely, he thought, she'd still be in school. From another case, he had the number and password for the Cathedral School District. Ten minutes later it was a certified bingo. Jennifer O'Detts. Oakdale High School, Cathedral City. Residence: 458 Lake View Terrace.

The plan wasn't easy. But since the rewards might be so great, Fitz decided to risk it. Mitch was not to know about the initial query. Nor was Rene. She might slip the name to him. Or even disagree with Fitz. She was too close to the candidate ... how close, Fitz didn't want to know.

Stu's fax relayed that Jennifer O'Detts was living with her parents and two younger brothers in a middle-class section in neighboring Acre Lakes, a planned community in the Cathedral City outskirts. Even better, a search using her Social Security number came up with an IRS W-2, listing her as an employee of Carol's Sunny Nails Salon.

"I'm looking to speak with Miss O'Detts," said a very polite Murray Levy, trying his best to conceal the nervous shaking in his chest. Fitz had picked Murray to make the introduction. After all, she was *his* idea. The salon owner was smiling right off the mark. Carol's heavy makeup cracked at the creases as she looked Murray up and down the way a mother would survey the potential father of her grandchildren. His navy sport jacket and button-down collar were decided signs of an educated man. The kind she would want to meet her little Jenny. Not the usual boys with the buckled boots, nose rings, and tattoos she'd seen so many times before.

"She's in the back. I'll go get her," offered Carol. "She's expecting you?"

"Uh . . . not exactly. My name's Murray."

Jennifer didn't know Murray from Michael Bolton. She first peered at him through the plastic shower curtain that divided the salon from the back room where the girls would smoke and hang their smocks.

"Never seen him before," she said. "What's he want?"

"Why don't you ask him?" said Carol.

"But I don't *know* him."

"I didn't know my Pauly before he walked into The Blue Tattoo."

"I thought you said that was a strip place."

"So what if he was a customer? Get a look at the boy, hon. He's cute. He's wearing a *jacket.*"

Jennifer deposited her smock and applied a fresh coat of lipstick in the mirror tacked over the sink before making her entrance. The bruises on her face were all but gone. Only a chapped split on her lower lip was still visible. The lipstick covered that just fine.

Murray and Jennifer walked around the corner to a Taco Bell and sat outside at the concrete-formed picnic tables. An afternoon sea breeze was kicking up. Her long strawberry blonde hair was the kind that took well to the wind. It kicked up attractively and he was instantly struck. Sixteen and a real humdinger. Any man would be attracted. He wondered if she had a brother.

"You're not here to ask me out, are you?" Jenny cut to the heart of it. She was good at sizing up both boys *and* men. And Murray showed a different kind of nerves.

"I want to talk to you about Shakespeare McCann."

"Fuck you." She was on her feet and headed back to the salon.

He tried to save it. "We know he hurt you . . . I mean, *I know* he hurt you!"

That stopped her. "Are you like a reporter? Cuz if you are, I don't wanna talk to nobody."

"I want to help you."

She was still standing as if at any moment she'd bolt and be gone for good. "Like how can you help me? I already got the abortion if that's what you want to know. It cost me seven hundred and that was everything I'd saved. That was my ticket to New York."

She'd given him the opening. He saw it and took his chance. "Ever been to New York?"

"No. I'm barely seventeen," she lied.

"I have. Went to college there. Columbia University."

"Really? I want to go to NYU. But I know I don't have the grades." She sat down again. "My parents, *they* definitely can't afford it. Least that's what they say. I know they got money. They just don't want me to get outta Texas, that's what I think."

His nerves briefly intact, Murray talked up New York City for about as long as she would listen. The subways. The culture. The colleges and museums. He didn't forget the arts, either. Jennifer was a budding actress and New York was her calling, or so her high school drama teacher had told Stu Jackson. She had dreams. And Murray understood dreams. His was a career on the Hill. With Mitch Dutton to tie his wagon to, he was almost there. The conversation finally returned to home.

"So you wanna get Shakespeare, huh? You work for that other guy, don't you?"

"He's a good man, Mitch. You'd like him. He's fair with people our age. I mean, sure I'm a little older than you. But look at me," said Murray. "Guy like me wouldn't have a chance at working on a major campaign. But Mitch said yes."

"I seen him. He's cute and all that. But my dad, his boss is like a Republican. They had a barbecue at the plant for Shakespeare. A party, you know? To raise donations, I guess."

"I know."

"That's where I met him. I mean, it was either go to the party or watch my little brothers. And I hate my little brothers. They're shits."

"So what happened at the party?" He tried to sound as benign as possible. The nerves were back. He was still afraid she might up and run.

"Nothing much. There was some beer. My dad lets me have beer sometimes. I mean, I'm almost *eighteen*, right?

"Right," said Murray.

"So that's where I met him. And he was really funny, you know? Nice smile. It's not that he's really ugly, either, he's just older and knows a lot. Talks good. Like you. About New York. Acting and stuff. He said he knew folks who could help me once I got there. He said once he became a senator—"

"You mean congressman?"

"Yeah, sure. *Congressman.* He said he'd be able to help a lot. But like he got more busy as the party got kinda late and we didn't talk no more. At least, not till we were leaving and he asked me to stay and like help as a volunteer."

"And your dad, he let you?"

"Sure. He thinks politics is good for me. Give me some values, he says." The contempt on the girl's face was obvious.

"So you stayed behind," cued Murray.

"Yeah, I stayed. I had some more beer. He offered to give me a ride home, so I said okay. And then he fucked me." The blunt language made him blush. And she liked the rise it got out of him.

"Who?"

"Fucked me? That guy Shakespeare."

"Did he rape you?"

"I was drunk. I don't know. I mean, I didn't like it, if that's what you're asking. But I didn't exactly say no. He was gonna help me in New York."

"Did you tell your father?"

"No way!" That look again. She hated him. "You think he'd believe me? My dad's like angry about everything, you know? Mexicans. The president. He thinks Shakespeare McCann . . . it's like he's all my dad talks about. But hey. Like he'd believe *me,* anyway. He sees the guys I go out with. And he *knows* I'm not a virgin no more."

"But you got pregnant."

"Yup. First time, too. I wanted to get an abortion, but that was gonna cost three hundred at the clinic, and that was almost half my savings. So I went to Shakespeare for the money. I mean, what's three hundred to him when he's gonna be a senator?"

"Congressman."

"Whatever. But that's when he kicked the shit outta me. Hit me hard. Kicked me hard. I hate him!"

"And you didn't tell anybody else?"

"Not a soul. And my dad? He didn't even ask. He just called me a slut and told me I was going to hell."

Now came the hard part. She'd told Murray. But would she swear to it?

"Would you tell anybody else?" he asked.

"Like I'm telling you?"

"Would you go on the record? Sign an affidavit?"

"What's that?"

"A statement that says what happened to you."

"No way."

"Not even if I could help you get to New York?"

Magic words . . .

Jennifer was suddenly thinking. "I don't know. Could Shakespeare do anything about it?"

"You mean, could he hurt you?"

"Yeah. Could he hurt me?"

"I don't think so. Give me a day or two. I'll see what I can put together."

"With Mitch Dutton, you mean?"

"With the campaign. You see, it's like this. Mitch is the good guy. Shakespeare is the bad guy. It's really that simple. And as I see it, the world will be a lot better off as soon as Shakespeare exits the picture. You could help. Maybe we could help you in return." Murray got up to leave. "I can find you at the salon?"

"Monday, Wednesday, Friday. Just don't call me at home."

"Don't worry. I won't."

And as Murray was leaving, she couldn't help but ask one more thing. "Hey. Is this what they call dirty politics?"

5

T he candidate sat stock-still behind his desk, listening while Fitz
and Rene ran down the details. According to a young girl named
Jennifer, she was raped and later beaten by Shakespeare McCann
when she'd asked for abortion money. Murray said she would agree
to swear out a sexual assault complaint in exchange for two thousand
dollars cash and a bus ticket to New York City.

Street money. Campaign cash. Won't be traced.

"Name your suitor," said Fitz. "Sandy Mullin. Pete Peterman.
I'll betcha we could get Vidor Kingman to make the payment."

Rape. Assault. They weren't talking about Candidate McCann.
Instead they were talking about the violent man Mitch knew from
the alley behind the Mairzy Doats Café. His insides ground as Fitz
went on, secretly regretting he'd never sworn out his own complaint
against the bastard.

"I know this is against every fiber of what you are, Mitch. But
it's bigger than you. It's about her."

"You know, Mitch. The cash doesn't mean she's lying, either," offered
Rene. "She's sixteen. She's scared of her father. This is her ticket out."

"We're doing her a favor," said Fitz.

"Or she's extorting money from us in exchange for the complaint," said Mitch. "We're complicit in a crime."

"Now you're sounding like a lawyer," said Fitz.

"I am a lawyer."

"It's McCann who broke the law. *He* had sex with an underage girl. *He* beat the crap out of her," said Fitz.

"And if we let this go?" said Mitch.

"More than likely? He gets away with it," said Fitz. "No guarantees the young lady will make a complaint, swear out an affidavit, or even stick around to see the general election. She's on her way to New York, for Christ's sake!"

"With our help, she is," reminded Mitch. He was simply arguing, though. He knew Fitz was right. The longer they waited, the more likely the crime wouldn't be reported. Jennifer O'Detts would bury it like a dead pet and move on with her young life.

"So it's the money that's got you worried?" asked Rene.

"I'm trying to be circumspect."

"Networks pay for stories every day," she said. "They say they don't, but they do."

"Why shouldn't we?" added Fitz.

"Because I didn't want my campaign to go negative."

Fitz was on his feet now. The opening was clear. "Listen to me closely. Primary Tuesday, Hurricane falls off a horse. Suddenly you're the front-runner. You pick up his slack. Your positives hang at a solid seventy-plus percent and your negatives are around twenty. Where are your positives now?"

"Pretty much the same."

"Yes. And that's good," continued Fitz, insisting that Mitch hear the ugly truth. "But your negatives are up to forty. And that's Shakespeare McCann. He's not out there building himself up as much as he's trying to tear you down. Calling you everything from a communist to a nigger lover."

"I don't like that word," said Mitch.

"Live with it. Now, McCann's positives are thirty, but his negatives are only twenty. That's because nobody knows about him."

"You want me to get in the mud and throw it. I can't. We're better than that!" intoned Mitch, sounding less forceful than earlier. The candidate was not convinced. He could feel the earth eroding from underneath his feet.

"Let's get one thing straight, Mitch. *We're* not better than anything. *You* are," snapped Fitz, his finger pointed.

"You're not in the race."

Fitz moved in, leaning over the desk. "Hear me good, mister. The only high ground in this great country is on Capitol Hill. That leaves the rest of us to fight it out down here in the dirt and mud of the floodplain.

"Now, your opponent. He's got the momentum. He started at less than ten and now he's at almost thirty. And he's bringing your negatives up with him. The time to draw blood is now. Let him know you aren't scared of his bite."

"He's right, Mitch," said Rene, too diplomatic to add much more. This was between Mitch and Fitz. The candidate sat with his feet up on the windowsill, staring out at a smoked sunset. Deciding. The pragmatist inside him trying to make it all fit.

"We got the girl at the clinic," said Murray. "She saw the bruises. She heard her dump on Shakespeare."

"Hearsay."

"This ain't court and you ain't counsel," argued Fitz. "This is politics and we don't have to do a Goddamn thing. There's so many leaks inside Cathedral PD, how the story leaked and to whom, nobody can point the finger at us."

"People will ask why she didn't tell her parents," Mitch tested.

"Shakespeare beat the crap outta you and you didn't even tell your wife," was Fitz's cutting response.

The room went silent. Fitz had spoken sacred words that had been tucked neatly in a drawer since June. Words that made Mitch feel like a coward. The rage swelled inside him again.

"I'm sorry," added Fitz, knowing the apology was a notch too late.

"The truth hurts," said Mitch.

Fitz looked up at the ceiling in a mock prayer, spun around, and ended up back in his seat with a resounding thud. "I'm still sorry, okay? Listen. It's up to you. It's your campaign. We work for you. You're the boss—"

"Shut up," barked Mitch, his eyes slamming shut.

Fitz tried his last shot. "It's a Goddamn silver bullet, Mitch. It kills McCann dead."

The Silver Bullet Theory. Mitch had heard of it. It's the shot that, once fired, explodes the heart of the opposition's campaign. Certain death. Game over.

"And how many silver bullets have you fired in your career?" asked Mitch. It was a gut test for Fitz.

"I've had a few. Mostly twenty-two-caliber. Not much penetration. But this one. It's a forty-four, and we're gonna fire it point-blank right into the fucker's skull."

"Sounds messy. But I'm the one who has to pull the trigger."

Fitz relented, his arms up in the air in surrender. "It's your call. I just need to know what it's gonna be."

The candidate's lips pressed together, then finally released with a heave of air. "Do it."

"Do what?" asked Fitz.

"Whatever you have to do."

"You serious?"

"Just get out and do it. I don't want to hear any more about it," ordered the candidate.

Exchanging looks, Fitz got up, gestured for Murray to exit in front of him, then waited for Rene. She nodded for him to leave first. "Mitch?"

"Yeah?"

"McCann deserves what he gets."

"And so do I."

She had to think about it. All she could come up with was, "Yes. I guess you do."

"Shut the door, please."

She left the room, easing the door closed behind her. That left him alone with his thoughts and the sunset. With his eyes closed, he reeled back to the Mairzy Doats Café and the concussion of blows suffered at the hands of Shakespeare McCann. One shot after the next. The kicking and the dust in his throat. Busted glasses. And then that squeaky voice:

"I have faith in my Destiny!"

When Mitch's eyes popped open, the sun was gone, leaving a tortured sky, black against the ever-darkening blue.

Revenge, he thought. *Revenge.*

The word floated into his consciousness just as Fitz's words faded back into his ears. "This is politics," he had said. "Love it or leave it. They hit you, you hit back."

Revenge.

"Look at the shit he pulled with Jamal La Croix and that phony picture."

"Deserves what he gets," Rene had said with that Mississippi lilt and soothing rhythm. "He's a bad guy. He's a violent guy. He oughta be in jail."

Revenge.

The word had muscled its way front and center in the candidate's psyche. It was a powerful desire. A visceral want as if for food or sex. Without intellect or remorse. He would screw the ethics and screw Shakespeare and his home-fried homilies and South County wit. The blood that he was tasting in his mouth was no longer his own, but the opposition's. The other guy's. The bad guy's. Mitch was emotionally resolving that it was time for Shakespeare to go down. And go down hard.

"Fuck him," he cursed.

The deal with Jennifer was done the next day. She'd told Murray that she didn't like the idea of filing the assault complaint against Shakespeare. In fact, she'd said it scared her to death. But Fitz was convinced that without a formal charge, even with a signed affidavit, the accusation might not stick. Through Stu Jackson, Fitz learned he could time the complaint in such a way that, if filed at any midnight hour, the girl could be safely on a bus and out of Texas well before a judge would issue a warrant.

On Wednesday afternoon a hand-delivered package with Jennifer's name on it arrived at Carol's Sunny Nails Salon in Cathedral City. It was a coffee-table book filled with big, glossy photos of New York City. On page sixty-four the sixteen-year-old found an envelope containing two thousand dollars in cash and a ticket.

She was on a bus by the next morning.

As was his tendency, Charlie Flores was going ballistic. A leak inside the *Mirror*'s rival publication, the *Cathedral Evening Breeze,* had called him just before the lunch hour and informed him that Superior Court Judge Coretta Tyson had signed a warrant for the arrest of Shakespeare McCann. The charge was sexual assault on a sixteen-year-old minor named Jennifer O'Detts. Charlie wanted to make sure that Hollice Waters was in it up to his ears.

"I pay you to dig this shit out," barked Charlie. "Now the *Breeze* has got it!" The subtext was that the *Breeze,* an evening edition published off-island, would break the news by four. After that, TV would saturate the story throughout the evening's newscasts. By the time the story would appear in the *Daily Mirror* the following morning, the arrest of the Republican congressional candidate would be old news. After that, the election and the fait accompli result. The horse race would be over.

"I got my people working on it," answered Hollice, sore and obviously beaten by the news. Dutton was going to Congress. "All I know is that the source was inside the PD."

"You don't have sources inside the PD?"

"What can I say? I write a good story, the source gets shit-canned."

"If there's an angle nobody's got, I want in. I'll pay for it. I want the *real* story in tomorrow's edition." That was style *à la Charlie Flores.* Irritate. Inspire. Then bark the marching order. "I don't care how you do it. Just get it done."

Hollice took the orders with him back to his office. That and not much else. Once there, he eased his angst with one of Charlie's precious Cuban cigars, one of the three he'd stolen while the boss was out to lunch. With feet up on his desk, he drew in some of the Havana smoke and took to his habit of tossing sharpened pencils into the acoustic tile ceiling. Those two-by-two-foot soundproof tiles were better than a dartboard, making for an excellent distraction when he found himself clueless and without a solid lead on a story. Like a circus knife thrower, he'd stick the pencils in the ceiling, one by one.

Shakespeare McCann, Arrested for Sexual Assault.

So what? thought Hollice. Shakespeare screwed and beat up some sixteen-year-old slut-puppy. Probably some groupie who wouldn't go all the way with him. Hollice understood those kinds of feelings. Teenagers, too young to be legal, but sexually active and willing as hell. They looked of age, drank like whores, carried fake IDs that'd fool any cop, and fucked like the Energizer Bunny.

So what? The reporter needed a headline.

Shakespeare McCann, Populist, Plagiarist, and Pugilist.

Did Shakespeare have a violent history? As far as Hollice knew, he had *no* history. Hollice had already dug deep and found out next to nothing about McCann, other than what the candidate had published himself. There was *without a doubt* a story there. But dig up the whole enchilada by the next morning? Next pencil. *Thwack!* The number 2 stuck into the ceiling tile.

Mitch Dutton, Congressional Shoo-in.

Hollice's old school chum Mitch Dutton, a.k.a. the front-running Democratic nominee, and now a certain-fucking-winner—in a congressional contest against the soon-to-be-arrested-for-rape dead horse, Shakespeare McCann. How would the Democrat react? Did he already know? Surely. Mitch Dutton had many fans inside the Cathedral PD. Mitch must have known before the *Breeze* did. All other media would be looking to Mitch for some kind of statement. A well-spoken sort of statement. Rehearsed. Not too gleeful. The Dutton camp would be feverishly hammering it out as Hollice impaled another pencil into the acoustic tiles above his head.

Hollice Waters Explains to Charlie Flores Why There Is No Other Story than the Obvious.

The phone rang just as Hollice impaled another pencil into the tiles above his head. "This's Hollice" was how he always answered his telephone.

"Hollice. It's Marshall Lambeer."

Hollice Waters's position changed instantly. His feet were off the desk as he instinctively reached for a notepad. "Marshall. Good to hear from you. Been a while—"

"There's an all-media press conference tonight at eight. McCann HQ."

"Why so late, Marshall? By that time your boy's gonna be trashed from here all the way down to Corpus Christi. The TV's gonna eat you up. Now, if you were to give me an exclusive before—"

"We're way ahead of you, Hollice. We *want* the bad press. After all, we've got the girl. And we're willing to give you her first interview."

"The girl? The O'Detts girl? I heard she was already out of state."

"Untrue. She's right here in town. She feels bad about what she's done and wants to get things straight, if you get my meaning."

"I'll quote her, all right. But it's just me. Only me. Hollice Waters, *Daily Mirror* exclusive."

"For your morning edition. Sure. Then it's open season."

"Where and when?"

"Four-thirty out in Acre Lakes. She lives with her parents at 458 Lake View Terrace. Don't be late." Marshall hung up the phone.

Hollice didn't hang up. He simply switched lines and left a terse message on Charlie's voice mail. "Charlie. It's Hollice. Hold tomorrow's front page and save me about twelve inches *above* the fold." Hollice thought that should do it. A helluva tease that guaranteed Charlie a second heart attack if he didn't hear from Hollice by 7:00 P.M. By then the news wave over Shakespeare's arrest warrant would most likely have already crashed on Cathedral's political beachhead, only to recede with a powerful undertow written by Hollice himself. Who that undertow might pull underneath was still uncertain. But none of that mattered. In the ebb-and-flow game played between the media and politicos, there were always casualties and cannon fodder.

The willful soldier along with unwilling victim. Such was life. Such was politics. Such was the philosophy of Hollice Waters.

Acre Lakes was one of those middle-class communities born from seventies' tax deals and the early eighties' real estate boom. Half-acre lots spread across ten square miles of South Texas flatland. Seventy-five prefab homes surrounded a man-made lake with a still undetermined drainage trouble creating a stagnant hazard that was so bad, the EPA had forced the developers to drain it permanently. Soon after, the guilty parties filed for bankruptcy protection and fled for the indemnity-rich shores of Florida.

After a short but disastrous venture in Oklahoma City, Miles O'Detts had moved his family back to South County for a dream construction job that was to last through the end of the century. But after ten years of backbreaking struggle, all he could show for the move was a pending workmen's comp claim, the terrific deal he'd gotten on his three-bedroom stucco house in Acre Lakes, and a job as a loading foreman at a newly relocated cardboard plant. Like his father before him, Miles was Republican red, white, and blue. He thought Reagan was close to God, Bush got a bad deal, Barry Goldwater had lost his mind when he advocated for gays in the military, and the *Cathedral Daily Mirror* was a leftist rag on par with the *New York Times*. Yes. Miles was an *Evening Breeze* man, and before Hollice had a chance to interview his daughter, there would be some ground rules set.

"The pinkos took advantage of my little girl. They bought her liquor, filled her head with crap, and paid her to sign some damn paper that was nothin' but lies. That's what you're gonna print," demanded Miles right off the gun. They were all seated in the O'Dettses' lakeview kitchen. Hollice was struck by the huge hole that lay outside their garden window. Mrs. O'Detts was serving instant lemonade.

"If that's the truth, that's what I'll print," said Hollice. "Can't do you better than that."

Marshall Lambeer thanked Mrs. O'Detts for the lemonade and sat next to Hollice. "Miles. I called Hollice Waters because I knew he was fair. I knew he wasn't political either way and he'd write it as it should be."

"Those Dutton people are telling just about anybody who'd listen that Shakespeare knocked my little girl up, then kicked her ass. I just wanna know if that's what your paper's gonna say, too."

"Not if it didn't happen," repeated Hollice. "Is she here? I've got a deadline." It was almost five o'clock. If Hollice was going to file the story, he'd have to see the girl, get her statement, and check some facts. All by seven.

"Go get Jenny, will ya?" asked Miles of his wife, though he sounded more like a drill sergeant ordering a recruit.

In less than a minute young Jennifer appeared. On her face was hardly a hint of makeup—not even a smudge of lipstick to leave an imprint on an iced glass of lemonade. *She was sixteen, but looked more like fifteen*, thought Hollice. A real daddy's girl. Not at all like the *Lolita* he'd pictured.

By six Hollice still had some facts to check. Driving back from the interview, he ran it around in his head over and over again. Murray Levy of the Dutton campaign had approached Jennifer O'Detts. The girl had just received an abortion, not at Planned Parenthood, but at the North Cathedral Reproductive Rights Clinic, where the procedure was paid for by her boyfriend, a seventeen-year-old named Willy Nichols. Easy enough to check. From the car Hollice called his assistant, Shelly, and had her start the fact check.

Next there was the plot.

"This guy Murray?" Jennifer had said. "He said he'd found me out through some like prochoice people? They were for Mitch Dutton."

"What was he like?" asked Hollice.

"Nice. Kinda cute. But I think he's gay," said Jennifer. "Not that I have a problem with that."

Jennifer had been feuding with her father, garnered Hollice. Probably about the abortion, and maybe, just maybe, supporting the Democratic candidate might be the way to get back at her right-wing father.

"After I told him about the fight with my old man, that's when he offered me the money. Two thousand dollars. That's a lot, you know?"

"It most certainly is," said Hollice. "Whose idea was the bus ticket?"

"His idea."

"Dutton's."

"I never talked to him. Just that guy. Murray."

Two thousand dollars and a bus ticket far from her old man in exchange for a sworn statement and a signed assault complaint against Shakespeare McCann. That part, Hollice knew would be her word against Levy's. The cash he'd seen was unmarked, and the bus ticket had no name on it.

Still, Jennifer's story seemed convincingly told, with just enough contempt and regret to make it all real. Her tale ended after she'd further claimed to have gotten on the bus and made it only as far as Houston.

"That's when I got scared to be so far from home."

"And you called your dad?"

"I called my mom. I was too scared to talk to him."

"What happened then?"

"They drove up to Houston and picked me up."

"Your dad and your mom?"

"Uh-huh."

"Was your dad as mad as you thought he'd be?"

Jennifer didn't answer that question. She looked away, nervous, then shifted in her seat as a silent reminder of the licking she'd gotten when they'd arrived home.

Later, Miles O'Detts had added that his daughter had wept in the presence of Shakespeare himself, getting on her knees and asking his forgiveness.

"Questions," said Hollice into his tape recorder. "Why would a front-runner with a surefire lead risk the race on such a stunt?" He flipped off the tape recorder and answered the question himself. Mitch probably hadn't known about it. He was an elitist. And a lawyer, yes. But this down-and-dirty shit wasn't his style. Mitch fancied himself a high-road moralist.

"Question. If Dutton knew the girl was lying, what has him so scared of Shakespeare McCann? Is there dirty laundry in his own closet he fears will hurt him down the backstretch?"

Mitch could be having an affair. Hollice himself had floated the rumor all the way back in May, and nothing solid had come back to him. Still, so what if he was? This was the nineties. It hadn't hurt Clinton.

"Question. If Dutton didn't know the girl was lying, who did? Is Dutton in control of his campaign? Or is he a willing puppet of a national party that would prefer throwing money at needier candidates who were still on the political bubble?"

Too cynical, decided Hollice. He shut off the tape recorder and switched his mind over to talk radio to see if anything was swelling on the Shakespeare McCann arrest. Rolling down the window, he twisted the dial to AM 970 and caught the last bits of "The Mark Shilts Show." Calls were coming in from all over. The believers and the disbelievers. And even some who'd never heard of Shakespeare McCann. Who said there was any such thing as bad press? he wondered. This was going to make Shakespeare McCann a household word.

He drove on and left the tougher questions behind. And also the ones he'd completely overlooked. Such as the brand-new Cadillac in the O'Dettses' driveway, complete with factory window sticker. Or the sideways glances Jennifer would give her father when he was correcting her story. Looks that Hollice mistook as contempt instead of guilt. Nope. It didn't matter as long as the horse race was on. It didn't matter as long as Hollice would be getting those twelve column inches above the fold he'd most surely pocket in less than an hour. Tomorrow he would once again be Mr. Exclusive, leaving everyone else in his turbulent wake.

Then he flipped on his tape recorder again. "Reminder. Next week ask Charlie for a raise."

6

T he South Texas Democratic League dinner wasn't quite the distraction Mitch needed. With all the hoopla surrounding the Jennifer
O'Detts story, the five-hundred-per-plate fund-raiser put on by the
local party faithfuls was awash with the day's buzz of arrest warrants
and Shakespeare McCann. He had prepared a speech for that evening
that touched mainly on the national economy and political reform.
It was a serious effort that he'd hoped would carry him through the
event without so much of the usual ear-bending and glad-handing.
There were young minds in the room to inspire and even some old
hands who could use some lift from Mitch's fresh ideas. He was
the front-runner and the podium would be his bully pulpit. Or so
he'd thought.

Instead, the news of Shakespeare's folly only cemented in everyone's mind that once and for all, the congressional seat that had been
the property of Hurricane Hammond and the Republican party for
so long would now be flying Democratic colors. The evening had
quickly turned from a fund-raiser to the coronation of Congressman
Mitchell Dutton. The well-wishers descended upon him. Among
them, the party lounge lizards. Die-hards of local politics with a
shared fantasy of riding Mitchell's coattails to Washington, D.C.

Yes, he wanted to win. And yes, he surely wanted Shakespeare to fry in hell. But at what expense? The election was ten weeks away. It was presumptive and downright unfair of them to treat him as if he'd already won the popular vote.

"Good evening," he began, once he'd finally made it up to the dais. But that's all it took. The room erupted with shouts and applause.

"Thank you," he offered with a smile and hands raised high. He resigned himself to letting them applaud. Then he would begin the lecture. Instead someone began singing "God Bless America." And so followed the rest of the room. Yet it seemed more like a crowded stadium singing "Happy Birthday" to a famous ballplayer. They weren't thinking about the song they were singing. They were just wrapped up in the happy emotions of the moment.

Mitch Dutton. Congressman. The real thing.

He looked left from the dais and caught sight of Fitz swaying and singing along. An ordinary party speech had turned into a big surprise party for Mitch. And when they were finished with "God Bless America," they followed with a chorus of "For He's a Jolly Good Fellow."

Still, as hard as he tried and as loud as they sang, he found it all so disingenuous. What had made him rise up from an afternoon funk rife with guilt and anger over the entire Jennifer O'Detts deal was his speech. Every word was from the heart. And every punctuation mark revised to emphasize the importance of the issues he would be discussing. And now he could see all they wanted were jokes, platitudes, and thank-yous.

The speech can wait.

Fitz had quickly scribbled the note and passed it up to Mitch. But he already knew what it said. He could feel the undertow. So, like a gentleman annoyed by the lateness of his dinner companion, he waited for the crowd to settle. Then, with aplomb, he returned to the microphone and said, "I accept your mandate."

Pandemonium. And once again, it began. The singing and rejoicing and applauding so hard, some would later wonder why their hands were so sore and their throats hoarse and scratchy. Meanwhile, while waiting for his next cue, Mitch neatly folded his speech and replaced it inside his coat pocket.

10:54 P.M. Mitch made the last turns onto Flower Hill and the tree-lined drive up to the old Victorian house. The windows were rolled down and he could smell the late oleander's bloom. It was an odd phenomenon that gave Flower Hill its name. There was never an off-season and there always seemed to be some kind of new budding and scent in the air. Azaleas. Magnolias. Especially the white oleanders. They bloomed late on the high island knolls. Another mystery.

He could see the television flicker coming from the high right rear of the house. This meant Connie was awake. She couldn't sleep with the television on and often used it to stay awake until Mitch came home. He turned off the engine, but sat in the car for a moment longer as he tried to ease his mind. The evening he had left behind was a whirl of emotion. All love and hate and mixed feelings. The unused speech was still in his pocket. Suddenly his thoughts switched to Jennifer O'Detts. *How far had that bus taken her? All the way to New York?* he wondered. *Or did she stop for the night in Chicago, or maybe Baltimore?*

Climbing up the stairs toward the master bedroom, he could hear the familiar voice of Channel 9's eleven-o'clock anchor, Bobby Gonzales. He couldn't quite make out the words. But then again, maybe he was still trying to tune it all out. Connie was propped up in her usual position amongst the goose-down pillows, her knees pulled to her chest and reading glasses pushed against the bridge of her nose. She didn't say "hello" or even a "how-are-you?" She was simply pointing at the TV and saying, "Did you see this?"

He turned the corner into the bedroom until he caught a good angle of the TV. All he could see was a reporter outside the police station doing a live wrap-up.

"What'd I miss?"

"Wait. I taped it for you." She was quick with the remote control. He suddenly recalled how it was a wonder to him that she knew how to program the VCR. He barely knew which end of the tape to load.

"There," she said, after she'd rewound the tape. "I can't believe you haven't seen this."

"Seen what?" he asked, nearly irritated. He sat on the edge of the bed with his jacket draped next to him.

The videotape rolled. Shakespeare McCann was making his formal appearance at Cathedral PD, complete with handcuffs. A small crowd had gathered, no doubt marshaled to the station by Shakespeare's campaign staff for a visual show of support. Then, before being brought inside, Shakespeare was quick with a quote. "The evidence will show that this is a cynical attempt to smear my name by my opponent, Mitch Dutton. I will be exonerated. Now, stick that in your hat and cook it.''

A woman's voice called out from behind the camera, "If what you say is true about Dutton, can you say how close he is to the mark?"

"Depends on the marksman. If he's a fellah who shoots first, and whatever he hits he calls the target? Then that's my opponent. That's Mitchell Dutton!'' Shakespeare finished with a flourish, winking at the camera and raising his shackled fists into the air like a martyred leader of the revolution. "This injustice will not stand!"

"Did you know about this?"

"All day." Mitch was back on his feet and on his way to the bathroom. He wanted to throw up.

"They said he raped some sixteen-year-old girl."

"I told you before, Connie. He's a bad guy and gets what he deserves.''

"But I just can't imagine . . . A guy like him . . .''

He was back at the bathroom door. "You have one dinner with the guy and you think you know him?"

"I was only saying he just doesn't seem violent."

"Don't judge a book," was all he could say, and he was back in the bathroom.

"What about the part where he said you were responsible?" But Mitch didn't hear her. At least he pretended not to. The shower was suddenly running and he'd escaped into a sanctuary of hot water and steam.

Thursday, Mitch's morning run with the dogs was a full two hours earlier than the usual 7:00 A.M. At five he was awake after a night plagued with poor sleep and a nightmare about his father. It was the same scene as when he had gotten home. The stairs. The voice of Bobby Gonzales on the TV. Connie propped between the pillows, pointing at the TV set. On-screen was Shakespeare McCann, hand-cuffed with his hands held high in martyred victory. But the words were different. They were from the speech Mitch had failed to deliver the previous evening. The crowd was rapt and listening to McCann. Laughing at Mitch's jokes. Stirred at his thoughts for government reform and a spiritual awakening to public service. Even the cops dragging McCann along thought it was a good speech. When the news story switched to the arrest warrant and alleged beating, the photo that appeared on-screen wasn't of Jennifer O'Detts. It was of

Mitch's father, Quentin Dutton, bruised and battered by the fists of Shakespeare McCann.

After he woke, he rose from bed, washed his face, and tried to return to sleep with the specter of the dream still haunting him. At the first signs of daylight, he got back out of bed, quietly dressed for his run, and encouraged the sleepy dogs to follow him downstairs.

The morning was balmy and cool. The air was wet and a good fifteen degrees below the temperature of his sweat, making for a brisk run. Mouth closed. Air through the nostrils equalled no swallowed insects. Mitch had mastered the art of jogging in South Texas. The dogs kept pace at either side of him, turning corners as was their habit. God forbid Mitch would change routes. The poor animals wouldn't know what to think of it.

Mitch and the dogs had started so early on the run that the morning paper hadn't yet arrived. Though it might not have mattered. It was another of Mitch's morning habits to pick up the paper only *after* his run. That way his mind would be fresh and unaffected during the workout. But had he not started so early, maybe he would've seen the headline staring up at him as he ambled down the front walk with the dogs. For when he got home, it was staring up at him like a cursed voodoo doll tossed upon his stoop.

DUTTON CAMPAIGN CAUGHT IN PAYOFF SCHEME!

And then the kicker underneath . . .

Alleged Victim Recants Arrest Complaint Against McCann

At first Mitch thought he'd misread the headline. Or that it was all some awful mistake. He picked up the paper and tore into the story following Hollice Waters's byline.

Jennifer O'Detts, interviewed at her family's home near Cathedral City . . .

But she was supposed to be in New York. Murray had put her on the bus only yesterday morning. Shakespeare had raped and beaten the shit out of her and she'd filed the complaint, for Christ's sake!

. . . alleged that the Dutton volunteer coordinator, Murray Levy, arranged for the payment of two thousand dollars cash and transportation

to New York City in exchange for filing battery and rape charges against Shakespeare McCann . . .

The dogs were barking. Mitch stopped his reading to look down the drive. The morning calm was busted wide open by the sound of an accelerating truck up the cul-de-sac. A news van was checking addresses, obviously looking at number after number until it would arrive at Mitch's address, where in moments it would find the guilty candidate standing sweaty, shirtless, and chagrined on his front stoop, the *Cathedral Daily Mirror* in hand.

"Merle, Pearl. In the house! Let's go," he ordered as he found the front door handle and pushed inside. The retrievers scurried past him, certain breakfast was next on the agenda. Instead, their master locked the front door and cut a quick path into the study. He speed-dialed Fitz, who answered before the phone returned a ring signal.

"Who is it?" asked Fitz. He was up. He was alert. And instantly suspicious.

"Your silver bullet backfired, Fitz."

"Mitch?"

"Wanna tell me what's going on?"

"I don't know anything yet. I'm on the other line."

"It's not even six in the Goddamn morning. You wanna tell me who you're on the phone with?"

"I got Hollice Waters at his house."

"Fitz. The guy beat her up and practically raped her. It was a cold deal. Are you telling me they got to her?"

"I don't know anything yet. But I got a hunch we were set up from the start. I'll call when I know more." Fitz hung up and left his candidate hanging. When Mitch finally hung up, he dropped back into the armchair in stunned silence. This was all so new to him. All these horrid feelings. Confusion. Frustration. Guilt. He'd never been there before. Everything for him had an answer. Action, reaction, action. It was physics. The way of his universe. But at that very moment, he was without a single, solitary move.

"Do you know there's a TV truck out in front of our house?"

He swung his chair around to find Connie in a bathrobe, standing at the threshold. He lied. "No. I didn't know." It was a dumb lie. But all he could muster at the moment.

"It's six in the morning. Who were you on the phone to?"

"Fitz. There's a problem."

"What kind of problem?"

"We don't know yet." The dogs were suddenly at his feet, licking the sweat from his legs. They were hungry. "Sorry, guys. Somebody forgot to feed you." He was up on his feet, sliding past Connie and heading for the kitchen.

Two cups of food for Merle plus a hard-boiled egg for his coat. That was his morning meal. On the other hand, Pearl had a weight problem despite her morning exercise, so she was relegated to a special diet of low-cal kibble and vitamin supplement. Mitch felt sorry for her every time he served up breakfast. Little Pearl would plow through her meal, then hover near Merle's bowl in hopes that his good nature would spill a morsel, or that distraction would get the better of him and he'd leave his bowl altogether unprotected.

Mitch was adding cans of water to a pitcher of frozen grapefruit juice concentrate when Connie appeared once again. This time she had the morning paper in hand. What possessed her to even look at it was beyond him.

"Is this true?" she asked.

He didn't look up from what he was doing. "Is what true?"

"Don't play dumb. You know what I'm talking about. That's why you were on the phone to Fitz! That's why there's TV people in our driveway!"

"The fact is, I don't know if it's true."

She started reading, " '. . . Dutton volunteer coordinator, Murray Levy, arranged for the payment of two thousand dollars cash and transportation to New York City in exchange for filing battery and rape charges . . .' "

"That's what it says."

"Is it true, Mitchell?"

"That she was paid? Yes. In exchange for filing the complaint? It seems that part's up for grabs."

"Murray paid her off?"

"McCann beat the shit out of her and raped her. She was afraid of her father and wanted out of Texas. A friend of the campaign helped. . ."

"A friend?"

"What? For seven months you want to know zip about the campaign," he snapped, "and now you want details."

"So this means you won't tell me. I'm too late to your party?"

" 'A friend of the campaign' is another term they use for an NDX."

"What's an NDX?"

"Independent expenditures. Money that doesn't come directly out of the treasure chest. The same way a university alumni association breaks the NCAA rules in its support of a sports program."

"So this was illegal?"

"Not exactly. There're a lot of gray areas in the campaign finance game." He looked winded, as if the air had been sucked from his lungs. He leaned against the kitchen counter and finished, "As for this girl, she told Murray she'd been raped and beaten by McCann."

"And he told you."

"And Fitz and Rene. But that was before she apparently changed her story."

"But the payoff. This NDX. You approved it."

"It wasn't a payoff!"

"It says here that you paid her to tell lies about Shakespeare McCann. That nice funny man—"

"Whoa! There's nothing nice about Shakespeare McCann."

"You forget, Mitch. I met him. I had dinner with him. I think I could tell if he was a rapist."

"Take my word for it. He beat that little girl," warned Mitch. "Now, what happened between the time she told us the story and this morning's paper is anybody's guess."

Connie crossed to the breakfast table and put down the paper. "You know something? I don't think he's violent at all. I think you're afraid of him. I think you like being the front-runner and want to keep it that way."

He burned. It was bad enough that she didn't believe him. She herself had seen him bloodied and bruised from one of Shakespeare's surprise attacks. Even though he'd lied to her about what had happened, couldn't she hear the truth in his voice now?

"You think that's all I care about?" he asked. "Being the front-runner?"

"Winning, Mitch. That's what you care about."

"Where'd this come from?"

"Just because I haven't said it before, that doesn't mean it's not true."

"Me and winning?"

"I told you I didn't want to go to Washington. That I didn't want to leave. But you did it anyway."

And she was right.

"Listen, Connie. I don't need this kind of crap from you right now," he cautioned. "If you can't be supportive, don't talk to me."

"In other words, if I don't like what I see, I can just stuff it? Is that it?"

"It's complicated." Mitch crossed to the table to stir his grapefruit juice.

"Fine then. But gimme the last word, okay?"

"You got it, babe." His tone was meant to cut her off, but it had no success. She just took a brave step forward.

"I may not like the campaign," she started, "and I may not want to go with you to Washington *if* you're elected. But at least I believed in you. That you stood for something."

"And now you don't? Is that it? After one newspaper article?" He picked up the paper and stuck it in her face. "You don't even *read* the paper!"

"You want to win, Mitch. That's all you care about. No matter who you have to screw."

"As in Shakespeare McCann? Is that what you're saying?" he pushed. "Well, fine. You vote for him. Wear his fuckin' bumper sticker on your ass, for all I care." With that, he threw the newspaper. It fluttered in sections around the kitchen.

"I hate you!" Connie burst into tears and hurried out the door. As he stood there, flushed from anger and betrayal, he could hear her footsteps pounding as she returned to the bedroom upstairs and slammed the door so hard it shook the house.

7

Gina had been sleeping only three hours when the phone rang. "It's me." Code for Connie. There were tears in her girlfriend's voice. "Did I wake you?"

"Of course you did," she said, fumbling with the cordless phone and reaching through the darkness for a cigarette. All the leaded curtains were drawn in a day-for-night effect. "I guess I had another night with stupid."

More girl-code from the college days. *Another night with stupid.* It was all about excessive drinking and bringing home the fabled faceless stranger. A time when unprotected sex meant a girl could get pregnant, VD, or both. And that was it.

"I'm afraid Mitch has turned into a bastard," said Connie.

"What kind of bastard? Not the kind I described?"

"Did you read the paper?"

"Puh-lease. I just woke up. Is it about politics?"

"He cares more about it than me."

"Well, girl. That's what I've been trying to tell you."

"He paid this young girl to lie about the other candidate," proclaimed Connie, as if the more she said it, the more she would believe it.

"Shakespeare McCann? Didn't you—"

"Have dinner with him? Yes. And it was nice. I thought he was kinda sweet."

"Wake up, Connie. That's politics. There are no nice guys."

"I know that. But Mitch said he was going to be different."

"Is he there?"

"He just left. There were TV trucks in my driveway, G!"

"Are they gone?"

"I think so."

"Then I'm on my way over."

"Gina!"

"I'm here."

"I'm afraid I don't know him anymore."

The conversation soon ended. When Gina hung up her cordless phone, the Radio Shack utility scanner signaled the call was over. The placid investigator, seated on the driver's side of a car parked in the back alley of the cliffside estate, stopped the tape player, marked the audio-stamp onto his time log, then waited for Gina to appear in her convertible Mercedes. The investigator's orders were to follow her, monitor and record all her cell and cordless telephone calls, and report back twice a day. At noon and midnight. It was 7:42 A.M.

Once again the Dutton campaign team was assembled for damage control. By nine that morning, they'd met at Mitchell's law office in an effort to avoid the phalanx of media camped outside the campaign HQ. Both Rene and Murray were instructed by Fitz to take the service elevator to the fourth floor and enter through an unmarked door that led through a small kitchenette at the back of the attorneys' suite. When all were present, Mitch appeared, crossed silently to his desk, and sat in the two-thousand-dollar leather chair that was a gift, some time back, from an appreciative client.

"By all rights, the lot of you should be fired," he began.

"Mitch. I'd just like to—"

"Shut up, Murray. You're on a short rope with me. This started with you and maybe that's where it ends."

Rene sat coolly on the green leather sofa. Legs crossed. Immobile. The chips would fall where the chips would fall. She deserved what she got. No better, no worse. And she wouldn't complain. Meanwhile, Fitz stood up to speak. "You're right. By all accounts, we should be fired. We set it up. We gave bad advice and, overall, fucked up. Most of all, me. I'll take the rap if that's what you want."

"I don't know what I want. Not yet. I've let you carry the Goddamn ball so much lately, I wouldn't know which way the wind was blowing with a wet hard-on stuck in the breeze."

"Well, that's graphic," teased Rene. Mitch wasn't usually so coarse.

As for the reference, it was what Mitch's old Uncle J would say to confused first mates. If he hadn't been so mad, he would've apologized for the off-color remark. Rene's silent grin said it all, though. It turned her on.

"I advised poorly," Fitz continued. "I can only promise not to make such a mistake in the future. That's the best I can manage at this point."

"At this point, I've got only one question," asked Mitch. "Did he rape the girl or not?"

"My guess is no," said Fitz. "I got Stu Jackson all over this and I expect answers by the afternoon. It looks like a complete setup. He tied on the bait, let out some line, and we took it hook, line, and sinker."

"It's Jamal La Croix all over again."

"Only we struck first. Same game. Different opening move."

"Silver bullet," groaned Mitch. "Forty-four. Point blank."

"Guilty as charged. Am I fired?"

"Not yet. First I want a damage assessment."

That was Rene's cue. She recrossed her legs, looked to her notes. "My best guess is a twenty-point swing at best. We lose ten. Shakespeare gains ten with your negative hiking into the mid-thirties. That will leave us with just under a nineteen-point margin. His forty-one to our fifty-nine."

"You're still the front-runner," added Fitz.

"But we just let him into the race. That's what you're saying?" finished Mitch.

"Pretty much. Yeah," said Rene. "He'll play the martyr all the way to November."

"And what about the girl? What side of the fence does she land on?"

Fitz laughed. "Try the California side. When I talked to Hollice Waters this morning, he told me he did his whole interview with the girl in the girl's parents' kitchen. But when he called this morning to get a reaction from the family, figuring to run a follow-up in tomorrow's *Mirror*, her mother said her daughter's run off and called her from the airport. Seems she caught the red-eye out of town."

"New York?" asked Mitch.

"Hollywood."

"Can you believe it?" offered Murray nervously.

Mitch didn't answer.

"The sum and total is that by day's end she'll be yesterday's news. I figure McCann's story won't stand the scrutiny of a serious investigation," capped Fitz. "It was their dough that paid for the first-class ticket, no doubt."

Rene added, "McCann took his shot and scored big. But not big enough by my account. I'll remind you, Mitch, that South Texas has seen its share of dirty campaigns. And when the dust settles, it's still going to be substance over style. I really believe that."

"We learned our lesson. No more funny stuff," said Fitz. "We stick to the issues."

"That your way of asking if you still have a job?" said Mitch.

"I guess so."

"I'll tell you when I get back from D.C."

Fitz slapped his hands together. "The Congressional Candidates' Workshop. Good deal! I was hoping you'd give that a go. There's about fifty good Democrats there who want to throw some money at you."

"It's a good time to go," said Mitch, his voice dropping an octave as his fight with Connie crept back into his consciousness. But that was none of their damn business. "Rene. Before I go, I'm going to want to make a statement."

"Where and when?"

"In time for this evening's *Breeze*."

"I'll get on it."

"And pack a bag."

Rene was struck. Did she hear right? "What was that, Mitch?"

"Pack a bag. You're coming with me," he said, turning back to face the three of them. The implication of his demand was unmistakable and brave, considering none of them, including Rene, had heard him make such a remark before.

"Fitz. Murray. You'll excuse us for a moment."

"C'mon, Murray. We got ourselves a day's worth of damage control to contend with." Fitz ushered Murray from the office and shut the door as he left.

Now that Mitch and Rene were alone, she waited a moment before speaking up. "You want to tell me what that was about?"

"I want you to come. Simple as that."

"Simple as that."

"It's business. You know the territory. I'm gonna need you." He sounded cold. Zero warmth. He'd caught her totally off guard.

"Okay," she said. If there was subtext to his invitation, she'd have to wait. "How many days?"

"Three, including travel."

Two nights, she thought. She looked for something in his eyes to tell her which way the wind was blowing.

"I think we should prepare that statement," he said.

"Okay, then. But the media's going to want more than that. They're going to want to ask questions."

"Good. I want to answer the questions. Bring 'em on."

"I'll make the calls."

"Everyone but Hollice Waters. You leave him to me."

"Here's what I know. Jennifer O'Detts was assaulted. *She* was the one who pointed the finger at Shakespeare McCann, and it was through the encouragement of members of my campaign staff that *she came forward* and filed the rape and battery complaints."

Damage control.

Mitch maintained an even strain during the course of that very long day. Over the telephone, then later on camera, he repeated himself, all variations on the same theme, and most emphatically he pushed the point with Hollice Waters.

"Were we set up? I don't know. Is the girl telling the truth? Well, it's true that we arranged the money for a bus ticket to New York. But that was at her request. It was McCann who upped the ante and bought her a first-class seat to Los Angeles. You can figure that one out by yourself."

"Be straight with me, Mitch. Was this whole thing your idea or not?" asked Hollice from his office at the *Daily Mirror*. Feet up on his desk, phone at his ear, pencils in the ceiling, and puffing on that second stolen Havana cigar.

"What can I say? This is my first race and I'm supposed to be in charge of a small army of staff and volunteers. That *and* keep my head above water and the issues in front of me."

"What you're saying is that shit happens."

"Off the record?" asked Mitch. "Yeah. But it's not that I can't deal with the shit. It's only when you and every other son of a journalist whips it up into a *shit storm* that it makes me wonder if it's all worth it."

"Is it?" asked Hollice.

"Is it worth it?"

"Yeah."

Mitch thought about his answer. His voice remained cautiously distant. "Ask me in November."

"I will."

"Gotta go, Hollice. Nice talkin' to ya."

Mitch returned to Flower Hill shortly before six with barely fifteen minutes to pack and start for the airport. All day he hadn't spoken to Connie. He wasn't in the mood for confrontation, but he most certainly could've done with a bit of consoling. But she wasn't home. Had been gone all day. He guessed she was probably with Gina at some shorefront tourist bar drinking double margaritas and trashing him. Well, let 'em, he thought.

Upstairs, he tossed three suits in a garment bag, overnight clothes, two pairs of gym shorts, running shoes, and the requisite accessories. At the last minute he exchanged one suit for a tuxedo, recalling something about a black-tie event. Then moments later, cursed the decision when he couldn't find the dry cleaning that contained his tuxedo shirt. With little time to spare, he finally opted to forgo the shirt. If needed, he could always have Rene pick one up for him when in D.C. That's what she was there for. To assist.

The house felt cold, lonely, and empty. He couldn't get out of there fast enough, saying his angered good-bye on the telephone answering machine. He pressed the Memo button, it beeped, and he began speaking. "Hi, Connie. It's me. Had to catch a plane tonight and go back to Washington for a Candidates' Workshop. I should be home by the weekend. Maybe we can talk about things then . . ." Mitch paused too long and the machine automatically shut off. He pressed Memo one more time. "Me again. I'll call when I get in and leave the number where I'll be staying."

Once in the car and on the way to the airport, he recalled that he'd forgotten to say the requisite "I love you." That was how they usually ended messages on the machine or on the phone.

This time Mitch hadn't even thought to say it.

Connie hadn't gone out drinking. After Gina had left, she'd spent the entire afternoon phone-soliciting for the Cathedral Children's Workshop, a nonprofit theater group for disadvantaged kids. For five hours and without a break, she dialed and pleaded, cajoled, asked kindly, gave friendly reminders, and even occasionally sounded like

Mitch as she rose upon the soapbox and decried Congress for cutting funding for the National Endowment for the Arts.

The campaign had been harder on her than expected. Where she'd come to regard Mitch as her hearth and home, now she was sharing him with Fitz, the campaign staff, and the better part of South County, it would seem.

Then there was the damned subject of children, which Mitch now jokingly referred to as the Royal Breeding Program, a failed science experiment.

"Hi. This is Connie Dutton and I'm calling from the Cathedral Children's Workshop. Am I talking to Mrs. Jo Anne Thomas?"

"Didn't somebody call me about this six months ago?"

"I'm sure they did, ma'am. But with the cutbacks in crucial NEA funding at the Workshop, we're forced to call our subscribers twice a year now. The lease is up on the theater space, so we're trying to raise enough funds for a down payment."

Connie knew the drill by heart, so she barely listened to her own words. All she could think about was the Royal Breeding Program, her guilt over a childless marriage, and Mitch's reluctance to adopt. She knew Fitz feared adoption and was glad that his candidate was cold on the idea. He'd counseled Mitch that any sudden move into the baby game would appear a cynical attempt to curry favor with the Family Values Crowd.

And Mitch had listened to him!

The theory was that children could wait. And should the couple change their minds, as a part of the House of Representatives, Mitch and Connie would be first in line for their pick of birth mothers seeking adopting parents. She cursed Fitz for making that decision for her.

She dialed another Workshop subscriber. "Hi, this is Connie Dutton and I'm calling from the Cathedral Children's Workshop. Am I speaking with Mrs. Allison Reyes?"

"Yes?"

"Due to cutbacks in NEA funding—"

"Aren't you married to Mitch Dutton?"

Connie wanted to say no. She wanted to get on with the call. "Yes, ma'am."

"He's a sonofabitch, your husband! After what he did to a good man like Shakespeare McCann."

"I'm sorry you feel that way. But I'm calling today about the NEA and the Children's Workshop."

"Do you believe in God, Mrs. Dutton?"

"I do, yes."

"Then pray for your husband. He needs to be saved."

Connie hung up on the woman.

Save Mitch.

Hardly, she told herself. Her hopes for a baby and the marriage it would *save* had pretty much been left on the back burner to go bad. Their house was now stinking of her arrogant husband and the musty odor of isolation. Mitch was the front-runner. By most accounts, he was going to win. Next he'd be demanding that she pack up her precious home and move east.

"The hell with him," she said, further soured by the cheap note he'd left Memoed on the answering machine. The time stamp on the machine spoke electronically, marking the moment of Mitch's message at shortly after six. It was now seven-fifteen. They'd missed each other by barely an hour.

Merle whined that he needed to go out, and Connie released the latch on the rear door. Merle pushed it open and he and Pearl gladly escaped her gloom. Her next stop was the liquor cabinet.

The *Cathedral Evening Breeze* reported that the sun would set that August evening at exactly 7:52. It was true, although the *Breeze* remained unread on the Duttons' front porch, complete with a front-page story carrying an apologetic photo of Shakespeare McCann with his uncuffed hands engaged in an exonerated thumbs-up to the camera. By eight, Connie was drunk on tequila.

Eight-fifteen, the doorbell rang. Connie rose from the darkness of her sitting room and made her way to the foyer. Vanity forced her to regain some sort of balance before she swung the door open, without so much as checking the peephole.

"Look who I found," giggled Gina, pulling Shakespeare up onto the porch, flush in the face of her girlfriend. In his own self-mocking gesture, McCann held up the *Evening Breeze* Connie had left on her front doorstep, and gave the same silly grin he'd given the camera.

And Connie laughed.

"That's the papers. Always catchin' your best side," he smirked.

It was funny and hilariously ironic. The hated husband gone. The abandoned wife, rescued from her gloom by her best pal and the charming opposition himself.

"Don't look like she's gonna invite us in," mused Shakespeare. "Maybe she's too looped to know it's us on her stoop. Maybe she thinks we're Jehovah's Witnesses."

Gina laughed. "Well, don't stand there looking dumb and drunk, girl. Invite us *inside.*"

"That's if the pretty lady'll have us," offered Shakespeare, who withdrew from his coat pocket a Baggie of cannabis. "California-grown. Guaranteed to getcha happy."

Without further thought, she swung open the door with an inviting "Come on in. *Mi casa es su casa.*"

"She's drunk already," said Gina, entering first and kissing Connie on the cheek.

Shakespeare followed. "Started the party without us? Makes us party crashers, I reckon."

"No," said Connie. Shutting the door and automatically latching it. "It just makes *you* late."

8

Apart from the delay in Houston, the American Flight to D.C. was uneventful. The entire trip, Mitch and Rene were seated side by side in the first-class cabin, enmeshed in work. Fitz had finagled the round-trip seats courtesy of some national party sponsors. The other half of the deal was a Potomac-view suite for the candidate at the Watergate Hotel. Flowers. Fruit basket. Complimentary champagne. Rene's smaller room was booked three floors down and near the service elevator.

"Very nice," said Mitch of his suite. "Fitz is obviously trying to get back in my good graces."

"Is it working?" she said from her room phone.

"Jury's still out. Now, what about dinner?"

"It's late. Why don't I talk to the concierge and get a recommendation."

"Why don't I talk to room service and we can eat in?" Mitch hadn't said, "in my room." Only because he hadn't yet decided. She waited for the invitation. "We could eat here."

"Or my room," offered Rene.

"My room's bigger."

"Shall I bring the laptop?"

"Let's leave the work for tomorrow."

"Okay," she said. "Should I order now, or when I get to the room?"

"What do you want? I'll order from here."

"Any old pasta will do."

He thumbed through the room service menu. "Caesar salad?"

"That'll be nice. And a glass of Merlot?"

"I'll order a bottle."

"I'll be up in a minute."

"A real minute or a female minute?"

"A woman's minute."

Mitch smiled, depressed the switch on the phone, thought of dialing Connie, but hung up instead. She'd cut him up good that morning. Spoken her mind, letting the lion loose and telling him that she didn't believe in him anymore.

To love, to honor . . .

His stomach churned. Picking up the phone again, he dialed home. Three rings and he got the machine. She's still out, he thought. Out bitching with Gina Sweet. "Well, fuck her!" he said. He hung up without leaving so much as the number of the hotel where he was staying.

Next he dialed his father and got *another* machine. "This is Q. Dutton and you got my machine. So don't waste my time. Leave a brief message."

"Hey, Pop. It's Mitch. Sorry to miss you *again*. If you want to try me back, I'm in Washington, D.C., at the Watergate of all places." Had he actually hooked up with his father, Mitch wondered what he would've said.

"Hey, Pop. I'm in the seat of government. No, no. Connie's back at home, hanging out with a sorority sister. They're probably taking turns going down on a bottle of tequila. Me? Oh, I've got this woman on the way up to my room. A real dish. Dinner's ordered. Bottle of wine. What's that? Am I gonna screw her? Well, Pop. I actually haven't decided yet. What do you think I should do? Oh, really. So your philosophy is 'Do as I say, not as I do'? Is that it? Is that what you told Mom before she died?

Quentin Dutton had never made it a secret, nor had he apologized for his pathological love of the ladies. Not while he was married. And not after his poor wife died. If she'd lived, Mitch would sometimes try and imagine her. Alive. What she'd look like. What she'd have thought of Connie. Or her later years without grandchildren. It seemed to suit Quentin just fine. Progeny were nothing more than a biological by-product of an active libido.

He called room service, ordered up the meal, then cut the air conditioning and opened all the windows, expecting, maybe, some kind of breeze off the Potomac. There was none. The air was thick, still, and smelling of the city. Dinner arrived thirty minutes later, wheeled in on a service cart by a bright, smiling Jamaican gentleman. Mitch tipped the waiter, shut the door, and checked his watch. It was ten o'clock straight up. Nine o'clock in Cathedral.

"You should lock your door."

He swiveled from the window. Rene was already in the suite, the door closed behind her. She threw the dead bolt. "You are in the big, bad city, you know."

"Otherwise known as the seat of democracy."

"I need an invitation."

"But you're already inside."

"I can always go back to my room."

"Please, come in." He crossed from the window and held out his hand. He drew her further into the room. "What do you think?"

"I think Fitz is kissing your rump."

"And he should."

"I'm likely to agree."

Rene was wearing a long prairie dress, casual and very cool. Sleeveless and backless. Mitch followed her as she eased over to the dinner cart, leaning at the waist to lift the covers off the entrees and give them her nose.

"Hmmm," she said. "Smells okay for room service."

Moving in behind her, he placed his hand on the bare small of her back, then slowly, with just two knuckles, traced her spine, all the way up to her neck. Her hair was still wet from a shower. Her makeup, slight and fresh, as she turned an eye toward her candidate.

"That felt nice," she said, holding the pose. She locked herself at the elbows and gripped the cart.

With his left hand he found himself lifting her dress. Not by any direction or intent, but by instinct. The subconscious doors were open, and desire was bubbling up to a surface temperature of ninety-eight point six. The right hand moved from the easy curve of her neck, back under her arm and inside the loose dress. Once there, he found a small breast that was moist from her sweat, the nipple sharpened by the wandering fingers.

"That's nice, too," she said.

"Stop me," Mitch found himself saying.

"Oh, I don't think so."

It was his game and she was the willing contestant. She arched her back and swayed subtly up against him. He carried her dress higher until she was exposed. A glistening ass. No panties. It shocked him. And he took a step back.

"Oh. You stopped," sighed Rene, failing to hide her disappointment.

"You wouldn't. So I guess I will."

"Before you do something you'll regret?"

"You were expecting me to make some kind of move, weren't you?"

"Expecting? No. But optimistic? Yes," she said. "A girl can pray for only so much."

"And if I didn't?" he asked.

"If you didn't what? Wanna fuck me?"

"If I didn't *want* to."

"Then I'd continue to play the fantasy in my head," she answered, moving barely a muscle. "Then I'd just finish myself off later."

Mitch backed off even further. The magic plane was shattered. Reality had returned. "So you fantasize about me?"

"Sure. What about you? Any fantasies, Mitch?"

"About what?"

"Do you fantasize about me?"

"From time to time. Yeah."

"How's this, then," she offered. "*You* watch *me* having a fantasy about *you*." She was still bent over the cart. Stock-still. Arched back. Facing away from him. And now she slipped her own hand up between her legs. She caressed herself.

"No," he said.

"Do it, then."

"Wait."

"Don't wait! Just do it!"

"Is that what you want?"

"Forget about what I want. Jesus. I want what you want. Don't you know that?" She shuddered with frustration. Stuck. She'd taken it too far. If his answer was no, she didn't want to see him again. She'd lower her dress, turn and walk out the door. It would be over. The ill-fated affair. The campaign. All of it. She begged, "Please, just tell me."

"What I want," he finished.

"Yes!"

"I want you to turn around and look at me."

A long moment passed before she reluctantly released herself from the dinner cart, straightened up, brushed the hair from her face, then turned. Her eyes were red and full of rejection.

"Now. I want you to walk over here and kiss me," he said.

A nod from Rene. She kept her eyes on the floor as she walked the five short steps over to Mitch. When she got there, she looked up. "Kiss you how?"

"Like you love me," he said. "Like you *believe* in me."

It wasn't a hard part to play. She pushed off from her toes, inching up to his lips. She gave her mouth to him, and with it, all of the heart and heat she could muster.

"How was that?" she asked, her lips parted, ready to give more.

The kiss stirred the candidate, filling him with a brief reserve. It was enough for the moment *and* the night. He looked at her, regretting every word he was about to utter, and every dirty idea that he was about to unleash.

"That'll do," he said. "That'll do for now."

By nine the impromptu party up on Flower Hill was in full tilt. The stately Victorian already had the wafting smell of marijuana applied to the antique upholstery, and the sound of the seventies thumping in a bad disco eight-track flashback. Actually, with a little urging from Gina, they'd forgone the compact discs and had dug in for the long-lost needle-in-the-groove taste of vinyl.

Shakespeare, on the other hand, had proven his worth as a master roller in the art of joint making. By the time the first record got pumping, he'd licked and twisted a neat row of little white bullets that only required a smoker and a match. And though he didn't fancy himself a dancer, he joined in long enough to get the girls on their feet before settling into a comfy spot on the couch to watch the girlie show he'd so fiendishly started. Gina and Connie were quite the pair. Engaging themselves in some recklessly bad dances. Shakespeare would call 'em out.

"Do the Bump!" And the girls would try.

"Okay, now. The Hustle. Y'all remember the Hustle!" The girls remembered the Hustle the best they could.

"Now the Grind."

"Aw, hell. That one's for strippers," said Gina.

"I think it goes like this." And Connie was grinding away with her best simulation of what a dance called "the Grind" implied. She'd never seen a stripper, though somewhere in the deep recesses of her worst mind she remembered an episode of "Charlie's Angels" in which Farrah Fawcett and Jaclyn Smith went undercover in a strip club to bag some pockmarked bad guy.

So there she was. Connie Dutton. In her own living room fearlessly doing her "Charlie's Angels" Grind for Shakespeare McCann. Eyes closed with the music thumping:

That's the way, uh-huh, uh-huh. I like it, uh-huh, uh-huh . . .

"Whoooee. You're givin' me a hard-on, Mrs. D."

"Excuse me?" Connie stopped and opened her eyes, locking looks with Shakespeare. Stretched out on the couch with his arms splayed left and right, he tried to defuse her with that charming-assed grin of his. Steeled by the cannabis, she stayed locked in the gaze, then coyly tilted her view down a notch to see if she could actually detect a rise in his pants.

"Oh, don't look. That's what he *wants*."

"You're a sweet tease, Gina," he shouted over the music.

"I'm hungry," said Connie.

He was on his feet. "Don't stop dancing. I'll getcha some food."

"There's frozen pizza in the freezer," she called. Then Gina was grabbing her belt loop and they were back to dancing, trading a fiery joint between the hammering beats.

"Think he's cute?" asked Gina.

"I thought so. But now I think he's a little sleazy."

"Just a little?" The two burst out laughing. "And the plastic surgery. Gawd."

"I didn't notice anything other than the contacts."

"Well, look close. I think I see scars here and here." Gina gestured around her eyes. "And the nose and chin? Puh-lease. Gimme some good sunlight and I'll tell you the surgeon."

Shakespeare yelled out from the kitchen, "No tellin' any jokes 'less I'm there to hear 'em!"

It only made them laugh all the harder, drawing up around them that wall that leaves all men out. Girlfriends to the end.

"Gawd, if Mitch were here," snorted Gina.

"He would *die*."

"I mean, what's his problem? Shakes is just a guy. That's all. So they disagree. That's what politics is about."

"Know what I think?" Connie leaned closer to her. "I think Mitch is scared of him."

Gina squealed with laughter. "Big Mitch afraid of that little guy?"

"Not so little," laughed Connie.

"You saw it, too?"

"I got pizza in the microwave. But look what I found in Mrs. Dutton's kitchen . . ." Shakespeare returned, braving the blasting wave forms of disco. He carried a silver tray, upon which were three Waterford flutes and a bottle of Dom Perignon.

"Oh my God. That was a gift . . ." Connie's hand went to her mouth, leaving the joke for Shakespeare to finish.

" 'From the Democratic Party of the Great State of Texas,' " continued Shakespeare, reading from the card that was still affixed to the bottle. "May I?"

"Be my guest," she said, her voice suddenly sharpened to a hard point.

Bang! The cork ricocheted off the nearest beam and rolled underneath the couch while Shakespeare was quick to pour. Gina raised her glass. Then Connie. And Shakespeare made the toast. "To Mitch. Hope he has a good ol' time with all those jackasses in D.C."

"Fuck him," said Connie under her breath, before guzzling the champagne. And as inaudible as her words were, Shakespeare was looking at her as if he knew exactly what she'd said. As if he'd actually heard. Had she said it? She was drunk, then stoned, then sweat-soaked from the dancing. Control was gone. Was she suddenly speaking out of turn?

That's right. Fuck him.

That was the look Shakespeare gave her. It was powerful. Something she hadn't quite seen from him. It unnerved her deeply.

"Gotta pee," said Gina, as if her announcement was newsworthy. She tripped out of the living room.

Alone with Shakespeare, Connie lost her lust for dancing and flopped into the big, wing-backed chair. "My feet can't take this." Her eyes shut, only to open again as she found gentle hands caressing her arches. Shakespeare was on his knees, her feet held against his chest, thumbs digging down toward her heels.

"Now, don't say you don't like this? Cuz it'll hurt my poor-boy feelings."

She answered by withdrawing again, behind closed eyelids, floating a sigh that sounded like a bare hum against the silence. The music had stopped. And the footrub felt too good to resist.

"Been awhile, has it?"

"Since what?" asked Connie.

"Since Mitchy rubbed your pretty feet."

Connie instantly tugged both feet up to her chest. "I didn't like that."

"You said it, not me."

"I said what?"

"Who turned off the music?" asked Gina, returning from the bathroom, oblivious. Without a second thought she stumbled over to the turntable and flipped the record over.

"Fuck him," answered Shakespeare as soon as the music returned to volume. From his pocket he pulled another joint, lit the number, and held it out for Connie.

"So who's dancing?" begged Gina.

"I am." Connie accepted the offered joint, sucked back the mind-numbing smoke, and returned with Gina to the dance floor.

"It's not adultery if you're on location," said Rene, lying naked across the king-sized hotel bed, her face over a plate of cold pasta.

"What's that?" asked Mitch, who wasn't hungry. He'd pulled himself up to the headboard, pillows behind his head and on his lap.

"It's not adultery if you're on location."

"What's that supposed to mean?"

"I'm told it's something they say in Hollywood. I heard it from some camera guy I met in Florida who was doing a commercial for a candidate."

"So we're on location. Is that it?"

"If it makes you feel better."

"Can we change the subject, please?" The deed was already done. There was no taking it back. For two hours they'd fucked each other sore. It was break time. The lights were on, the food was cold, and the temperature hadn't changed a lick.

"Tell me about your father." Rene switched direction.

"You know about my father. You wrote the campaign bio."

"Hey, I know bullshit when I write it."

"Oh, I wouldn't call it bullshit," he said. "I'd call it none of the public's business."

"Ooh. Watch your mouth, now. You're a public figure," she said sarcastically. "And the public has a right to know."

"About me, maybe. But not my old man."

"Do I hear a few skeletons rattling?"

"Nothing that could hurt me. He taught me that the facts of life were up for interpretation."

"He bent the rules, then," she tried to confirm.

"Wherever he could. A classic hypocrite of a parent."

"You must have one story to tell your little Rene," she teased, never leaving the pasta, but sliding her foot up the inside of his thigh and wiggling her toes.

"One story."

"And forever I'll hold my peace."

Mitch slid away from the headboard, taking the pillow from behind his head and placing it on her butt. Resting his head back on the pillow, he stared at the ceiling.

"Okay. I was eight. It was a Little League game. The one game my old man decided to show up for. I was playing catcher. Hollice Waters was at bat—"

"Busted. You're making this up."

"Honest to God, truth."

"Hollice Waters? Mr. Poison Pen?"

"The one and only."

"But you weren't teammates."

"Not that year. Anyway," he continued, "Hollice knocked one down to third base, but on his way to first, he threw the bat. He didn't know I was running right alongside him."

"You were going to back up the throw to first."

"Very good."

"I'm not as much of a girl as I look."

"Where was I?"

"The bat."

"Right. Anyway, it caught me right in the mouth."

"Ouch."

"All it did was chip a tooth. A little blood. No big deal. Batter's automatically called out."

"Hollice was out."

"Yes. But that wasn't good enough for my old man. He wanted Hollice out of the game. He walked right out onto the field and started screaming at the umpire. I remember it was some poor high school kid whose dad worked on one of my dad's shrimp boats."

"So what happened?"

"My dad said that either the umpire throws Hollice out of the game or he was taking me home right then and there. Now, Hollice and I are standing there. Both of us want to play. And my old man is out in the middle of the field, screaming at some seventeen-year-old who's scared his father's job's on the line."

"He threw Hollice out of the game."

"Damn straight he did."

"Then what happened?"

"I wanted to walk off the field in protest. But my father said that if I walked off the field, I'd never play baseball again." Mitch shrugged at the thought. "So I stayed and played. Hollice went home and *he* never played baseball again."

"No way."

"That's how it happened."

"A parent could argue that it was just your worried father protecting you."

"It was an accident. And it was all about him," said Mitch. "It was always about getting his way. In business. With my mother. With me. He'd win at any cost. Arguments. Finances."

"Yeah. But did he ever lose?"

"Yup. To a bunch of lawyers who'd invested in a bogus shrimp distributorship. So when they couldn't collect on the judgment, he married some hooker he'd met in Las Vegas, put all his assets in a trust with her name on it, then filed for bankruptcy protection. The marriage, of course, didn't last. He retired to San Diego. End of story."

"He must've loved it when you told him you were going to be a lawyer."

"When I graduated from Stanford, he sent me dead flowers and a note saying that I was now one of them."

"It's a wonder you ever talk to him."

"We don't talk, really. We trade phone messages. He'll occasionally ask for legal advice."

"Do you give it?"

"Sure. But I send him a bill."

Rene laughed so hard, the bed shook. "You send your father a bill?"

"What's worse is that he never pays."

Harder, she laughed, her casual cool breaking wide open. This was Rene Craven. Naked to the teeth. Earthy and sexually inclined. When the laughter died, she curled herself around him in such a way that he could smell her sex. His arousal was swift. Rene had him in hand, sitting astride his hips, guiding him deep inside her until they were joined. Candidate and cohort. She straightened up and looked down at him. "So *this* is the high ground?"

"Is that supposed to be funny?"

"Just checking out the view, mister."

"And how is it?"

"Getting better all the time."

They screwed for the last time that night, with Rene falling off into an exhausted and snoring sleep. Mitch lay awake for some time, then finally resolved to call Connie . . .

. . . and confess?

Hardly. He stuffed his guilty conscience. He was being courteous. Connie didn't know where he was, and should she have needed to talk to him, God knows she'd have been loath to call Fitz and ask *him* which hotel he had landed in.

He crept from the bedroom, slid the door shut, and dialed from the phone next to the sofa. Connie'd probably be asleep. Would she wake or let the machine pick up? He was conflicted. The machine would be easier to deal with. He'd apologize for leaving without talking to her, then leave the hotel and scheduling information. Then again, there was a tugging deeper inside him that wanted to hear her voice.

But the phone rang and rang and rang. There was no machine to pick up and no answer from his wife. Ten rings. Eleven rings. In that brief time he wondered, had she turned the machine off out of spite. Or was it not be picking up due to something so simple as a power outage?

Fifteen rings.

Clearly she wasn't going to answer no matter what the problem. Still he hung on, deciding to give it twenty rings and try her again in the morning.

Eighteen, nineteen, twenty rings.

Mitch hung up, noting the knuckles on his hand clutching the receiver had turned white in a kind of death grip. Rene caught his eye. She was standing in the bedroom doorway, naked as a new day.

"Everything okay?"

"Everything's fine."

"Then please come back to bed."

he skies over Cathedral were clear and without a cloud to interfere with the brilliant three-quarter moon. As for the telephone machine, it wasn't malfunctioning, nor had Connie turned it off.

The party had lasted until around midnight when Connie's body had finally succumbed to all the abuse. With the Bee Gees still pounding over the stereo, she'd suddenly had enough and bid her guests a speedy good-night. Somewhere in her memory she recalled reminding Gina to lock the door behind her and leave the key in the mailbox. Then she'd started up the stairs for bed.

It hadn't crossed her mind to ask Shakespeare to keep the evening's festivities from her husband. Or even Gina, for that matter. Caution had been left in the ashtray. As she shut out the downstairs music with the door to the master suite, all she was hoping for was a dreamless sleep and not too big of a mess to clean up the next morning. Her head was already hurting from the thought of the oncoming hangover. So shortly before tumbling into bed, she followed Gina's remedy of two full glasses of water, one B complex vitamin, and two aspirin to thin the blood. She dropped her work clothes in exchange for one of Mitch's T-shirts and crawled into bed, making sure to leave the bathroom light on as was her habit when her husband was gone. She checked the clock before closing her eyes. It was a blurred 12:16 A.M.

Downstairs, the party was far from over. Gina had made up her mind that it would serve Mitch right to fuck his worthy opponent on the floor of the very room where he read his Sunday paper: a screened sun porch off the living room. With the records stacked on the turntable and the music turned down to a moderate decibel, she and Shakespeare spilled the lounge cushions to the Astroturf floor and began a sweaty tangle of wet tongues and groping hands.

Gina fancied herself a sexual stalwart, despite the scuttlebutt that she was a notoriously lousy encounter. All awkward legs and arms, she had a habit of making sex a wrestling match. Shakespeare was quick to handle her, reaching underneath her tennis dress and tearing her panties clean away with a single tug. She reached for his belt buckle. But he stopped her cold.

"What?" she pressed.

"You're too easy."

She took her heel and poked it hard at his chest. "Is that what you want? A fight?" She poked him again.

"I want to be teased." His blue eyes gleamed, his eyebrows raised.

"I know." Gina smiled. "You want more money. But you forget. I've already contributed the maximum legally allowable to a po-li-ti-cal can-di-date."

"Money, I don't need," sneered Shakespeare. He unzipped his pants and pressed against her, teasing her without mercy. "What I *need* is information."

"Like the nasty about Mitch Dutton?" She grinned at the idea, groping for his erection with her fingertips. "So you got any rubbers?"

From his shirt pocket he removed a very small white envelope. "I got better than rubbers."

"Yeah?"

"I got the best sex you'll ever have." From the packet he let slip two blue capsules into the palm of his right hand.

"What is it?" she asked, already having forgotten about the condom.

"Gotta fuck me to find out." Shakespeare put one capsule in his own mouth and left the other for her to beg for. Gina's mouth opened wide and he let the bomb drop.

There wasn't much to remember after that. If it was the best sex she'd ever had, she would never recollect. After she'd swallowed the blue capsule, it was two more minutes of tumble and tease before her lights went out.

Shakespeare had never swallowed his capsule. He'd left it between his cheek and gum like a wad of tobacco, quickly spitting the capsule out while he briefly went down on her.

Leaving Gina unconscious on the sun porch, he methodically gathered up his pants and shoes, tying them up with his jacket and leaving them on the kitchen counter. Next, with a bottle of Windex and paper towels, he moved efficiently and with remarkable memory around the downstairs and wiped away any traces of his presence. Fingerprints. Saliva samples. All evening he'd been careful of his hands, keeping them to his sides, drinking only from the same glass.

Leave no evidence of your crime, friend.

Once he felt confident that he'd wiped the house clean of any evidence, he stepped briefly out the kitchen back door with two New York steaks he'd earlier removed from the freezer instead of pizza. He'd time-defrosted them in the microwave, and now it was time to feed them to the dogs, Merle and Pearl. Shakespeare hadn't figured them for any kind of serious guard dogs, but chose not to take any chances. The dogs lunged for the raw steaks, allowing him time enough to reach up with a push broom and pull down the one telephone wire that connected the Dutton household to any kind of emergency services. Afterward he circled farther left to the unlocked electrical box located near the outer doors of the study. Once there, he easily found the master switch and cut the power to the house.

Rubber surgical gloves.

The last item on Shakespeare's list. Once totally undressed inside the Dutton kitchen, he removed them from the buttoned rear pocket of his trousers, worked them onto his hands, and then started up the stairs. The floorboards creaked. Most likely, though, if Connie heard him, she'd think he was Gina.

She loves me. She loves me not. She loves me. She loves me not.

In the dark, his instinct prevailed. It was a Victorian house, large and open with all upstairs rooms off the hallway at the top of the stairs. There was just enough moonlight for him to venture that the double doors to the right and down the hallway from the stairwell would be the master suite. No longer the candidate—or the exonerated con—he was now the predator.

Connie's eyes opened and blinked. The battery-powered backup on the digital clock read 1:36 A.M. Everything else was blurry, unfocused, and darker than she remembered. She rolled over. It took her another fuzzy moment to realize the bathroom light was out.

But she'd left it on . . .

Then again, she'd been drunk and stoned and . . .

A hand across her mouth. She wanted to scream! But nothing came. It was, after all, only a dream!

"Ain't no dream, little missus," said the intruder. "This is really happenin'!"

A burst of adrenaline focused her eyes upon Shakespeare straddled atop her. His rubber-gloved hands over her mouth and forehead.

"Are you awake?" He slapped her face. "Cuz you gotta remember this. I'm askin' if you're Goddamn awake!" Another slap! She tried to answer. But there was his hand across her mouth and the weight of him on her chest. "I said wake the fuck up!" Shakespeare slapped her again. "Now, answer me! You blink twice if you hear what I'm sayin'!"

Connie blinked twice. An almost autonomic response. Her eyelids slamming down over her wide eyes to get the message back to him in the clearest, most succinct way.

"That's right," said the intruder. "See me as I am. I know I ain't so handsome, but I'm twice the man. I promise."

She realized that the covers were off the bed. Had he done it or had she kicked them off while she was sleeping? The T-shirt she wore was pulled up well above her waist, and the intruder was already forcing her legs apart. Instinctively she bucked against him, using her legs to try to kick him off of her. Then crack! Shakespeare quickly hammered an overhand blow across Connie's left ear. It shook her like a loud gunshot. In her entire life, she'd never been struck. It so disturbed her synapses, she was instantly distracted and lying limp from the shock and the pain.

"I'm gonna be raped?"

The deadly obvious spilled from her mouth in a sad commentary that sounded strangely out-of-body. Even to Connie.

Shakespeare stuck his teeth to hers and hissed a response. "Missus. Ain't no such thing as rape between a man and woman. But if that's what you want . . ."

With a powerful twist of her leg, he snapped her to her belly and crawled over her back. Those large teeth suddenly at her left ear. "Rape? Now, that *always* comes from behind. With your eyes closed and a ten count in your head just hopin' the nigger fuck that's givin' it don't hold back and make it too slow and painful."

"Please, no," she pleaded, her eyes squeezed shut and bleeding tears.

"You want rape? This is rape!"

"No," squeaked Connie.

Shakespeare rolled her back over, shoving her legs apart and thrusting himself deep without getting so much as a quiver of defense. Remarkably, she lay motionless as he ground away inside her, a twisted smile affixed on his surgically repaired face. And no matter what the intruder called it—rape or not—it was an unspeakable violation. Degrading and without consent. All Connie hoped was that it would soon end. She looked to the right. The phone was there and certainly within reach. She thought of dialing 911, wondering if the operator could hear a rape in progress. But how many sick couples dialed and screwed out of their own twisted exhibitionism while the emergency operators listened vacantly with a voyeur's ear?

"You know, it costs more to send a man to prison than it does to get a law degree at Stanford," he said.

She hadn't noticed that it had ended. Didn't feel the little man ejaculate or remove himself. He was back astride her.

"Betcha didn't know that," he offered.

Her voice was barely audible. "Know what?"

"That I was the best fuck you'd ever have," barked Shakespeare. "And that's just what you're gonna tell him."

"Are you gonna kill me?" wheezed Connie.

"No. But you tell the police before you tell your husband, I swear I'll kill him." He brought those teeth close again. So close she could smell his foulness. "Unless you *want* me to kill him. Is that what the missus wants?"

"No!" she cried. He'd just raped her, and only now did she find herself begging. But not for herself. For Mitch. "Don't hurt him, please."

"Looks to me like he's done some hurtin' to you."

"I'll do what you say. I'll tell him first."

"Tell him what?"

"That you were the best."

"The best what?"

"The best fuck I ever had."

"Smart girl. Now, lookee over here." From atop Mitchell's nightstand, he picked up one of those blue capsules with his rubber-gloved fingers. He held it over her mouth just as he had for Gina. "Now, you swallow this and say good night to your handsome sugar man."

"What is it?" she asked without thinking, same as Gina.

"You women are all alike." And with that, Shakespeare forced her mouth open and dropped the capsule, holding her jaw shut until he was certain she'd swallowed the pill. "Now I'll just lie down here with you until you go nighty-night."

And lie with her, he did. Right alongside as if he were Mitch holding her tight. All Connie could do was stare at the ceiling and pray. Pray for survival. Pray that Mitch was safe, wherever he was. And pray the blue capsule she'd swallowed wasn't a lie. It could have been poison. Some kind of death pill. Darkness would soon come. She wouldn't know the truth until she woke.

Stranger still. As the certain sleep was taking hold, for one nightmarish moment she imagined it *was* Mitch lying next to her. He was holding her close, whispering nursery rhymes to her with his own silly words added just to make her giggle. Private time. In that momentary flash of time, it might've been Mitch next to her in the August moonlight. Much like that rarest of nights, only a week earlier, when husband and wife lay, postcoital, back to front. When silently, before falling asleep, she'd whispered another prayer and asked Christ for a miracle. Asked him for what she'd been told was practically impossible. A child of her own.

Mitch woke up alone sometime after seven. Rene was nowhere within earshot. She probably went back to her room to change, he thought. He swung his legs over the bed and ran a hand through his hair. It smelled of Rene. Then before he could summon a guilty thought, he noted the flashing message light on the telephone. He picked up, followed the instructions for message retrieval, and silently hoped to hear his wife's voice at the other end. Maybe she'd called Fitz after all. She wanted to apologize.

The voice mail recording spoke. "Room 1254, you have one message. To play, press the star key. To return to menu, press pound."

Mitch pressed the star button. The message was cued and played back in the unique voice that was Shakespeare McCann's. "Hickory dickory dock. Your wife has joined my flock. She'll vote for Shakespeare. And come this time next year. I'll be punching the congressional clock."

The twisted motherfucker! How did he know where to ... And what was that about my wife?!

He fumbled and forgot the menu instructions on the voice mail. He wanted to play it again. The voice was saying, "You have no more messages."

Three. He pressed three, certain it was for playback. Instead the recorded voice answered, "You have erased your message. Thank you."

He slammed the phone down in frustration. Picked up and dialed Rene. *What the fuck is her room number—919?* He dialed, woke up some poor, hungover hotel guest, apologized, and then called the front desk. "Yes. I need to dial the room of Rene Craven . . . Okay. Thank you."

The line paused and he thought he'd been cut off. He was about to hang up when the phone started ringing. Rene answered on the second chime. "Hello?"

"Get up here right now!"

Mitch depressed the switch. He dialed nine, then one, followed by his area code and home phone number. There was another long pause as the hotel computer registered the room charge. Then he could hear the phone ringing on the other end.

Pick up, Connie. Please pick up the phone.

Just like the night before, the line rang endlessly. No machine. No answer. Nothing. He stopped counting rings, because the next thing he recalled was the knocking at the door. He hung up, threw on his trousers, and headed for the door. Rene was there in the same dress she'd worn the night before.

"We're going back to Cathedral."

"Excuse me?"

"Something's wrong."

She followed him back into the suite, careful to close the door behind her. "What?"

"Cancel everything. Then get us the next flight home."

"We can't cancel *everything*."

Mitch vanished back into the bedroom. Something in Rene told her not to follow or panic. Just do as instructed. She dutifully went back to her room and her PowerBook to arrange the return trip to Cathedral and deal with *the problem*.

Whatever it was.

Murray Levy lived on Sheffield Avenue, Cathedral's former red-light district turned bohemian enclave. The street and surroundings offered mostly coffeehouses and beat bars, inhabited by a gay population and perpetual hipsters who thought it was cool to "hang homo." Recently the Sheffield Renters and Property Association had voted to close the avenue to weekend traffic and install wrought iron on every corner to give it a New Orleans look. Suffice it to say, rent prices on Sheffield were going north.

When the phone rang in Murray's apartment before 7:00 A.M., he crawled over and lifted the handset from the cradle. And though his voice cracked from an evening of breathing secondhand smoke, he answered like a true political diehard who was all too used to Fitz waking him at all hours for various and sundry tasks. "Murray here."

"It's Mitch," said the voice at the other end. "I want you to go over to my house and check on my wife. Don't ask why. Don't talk to anybody else. Just go. Now."

"Mitch. It's six-thirty—"

"You haven't earned back my patience, Murray. Now, repeat what I told you."

"Go to your house. Check on your wife."

"If she's okay, tell her you were delivering overnight numbers. So take an envelope."

"And if she's not? I mean, I guess that's why you're calling for—"

"If there's no answer, call the police and break down the fuckin' door! You got me?"

"Got it." Murray was sitting up by now. Ron was awake and stroking his back, but he shrugged it off as he hung up. "Gotta go." He was out of bed and throwing on last night's clothes.

"Don't tell me," groaned Ron. "Another of Fitzwater's milk runs?"

"It's not Fitzwater. It's just Fitz. Plain fucking Fitz. Anyway, this is something for Mitch."

"I thought he was in Washington."

"He is. Don't ask me any more questions."

"Oh, I get it. Campaign secrets. You give your skinny little body to me, but your heart belongs to Mitch Dutton."

"You don't understand. I thought I was out. Now he needs me to go to his house and do him this favor."

"The only thing *out* about you is your shirttail." Ron helped Murray tuck his shirt into his pants, then gave him a slap on the butt as if he were being sent in for the big play. "I'm sleeping in. So don't come back before noon."

"Fine. Lock up, will ya?" He was out the door.

"Without a kiss?" called Ron after him.

"Feed my cat!" Murray shouted back. Ron could hear his footsteps recede down the stairwell. After that, he had everything down pat. Ten seconds to get to the car. Five seconds later Ron would hear the Honda's engine turn over. A count of two followed by six seconds of whining reverse as Murray backed out of his parking space. Finally, first gear and the Honda would wind its way out onto Sheffield Avenue.

Then it would be safe.

Ron reached across the bed and picked up the phone and dialed a number, long tattooed in his head. It rang five times before an answer. "It's me. Dutton just called and asked for some big favor. Murray had to go to Dutton's house for something. He didn't say what for."

The voice didn't respond immediately. And then simply said, "Thanks. Check's in the mail."

By the time Mitch and Rene reached Dulles Airport, it was nine forty-five in the morning. The flight was at ten-twenty sharp. With no bags to check, they retired to the American Airlines Admirals' Club where they'd have fifteen minutes with the national party's Brad Pustin and Kevin Cronyn.

Rene'd warned him in the cab. "Don't kill me over this, okay?"

"I'm not exactly in the right frame of mind," Mitch complained. He felt as if he'd been jumped from behind.

"Fifteen minutes. Smile and listen. These two think they're God's gift to first-time candidates."

"And if I say no?"

If you say no, I swear, I'll tell your wife about last night.

"Just don't," she pleaded. Then she braved the big question. "Is this about last night?"

"No," he said, lying only in part.

"Because if it is, we can just forget it ever happened."

"Just like that."

"I've been here before. I can just walk away. Can you?"

"You're amazing," he remarked. And it wasn't a compliment. "You think this is about you, don't you?"

"Okay. So it's not." The neurotic in her had escaped. She screwed the lid back on. "It's about your wife, isn't it?"

"Let's stop right here, okay? We're out of my comfort zone."

"Okay, then." Rene took a deep breath. "And the meeting?"

Mitch didn't have a ready answer. So he let her stew.

Brad Pustin and Kevin Cronyn were waiting for them inside the Admirals' Club lounge. And though she hadn't lied when she'd told

Mitch they'd gone so far out of their way because they were so excited to meet him, she hadn't said what else she'd promised to make the meeting happen.

Promises, promises . . .

One of the many currencies of national politics. What followed was the casual arm-twisting, followed by a million machinations of salutations, assertions, and character assassinations if a promise to an insider or party leader was not met. Mitch knew little of this, temporarily seeking shelter in the ignorance of the idealist. He promised nothing he couldn't deliver. But Rene. She'd promised she could *deliver* Mitch Dutton to D.C.

"Charm them," she'd pleaded.

And charm, he did. He talked them out of nearly five hundred thousand dollars in National Committee investment in exchange for a double-barreled caveat. Brad Pustin was first, leaning in over the small cocktail table covered with coffee cups and stale pastries.

"Word is, Mitch, that you don't like to play dirty," said Pustin. "Afraid to get a little mud on your suit. Is that right?"

"We had a bad week," said Mitch. "But so did Bob Leuchesi."

"Ooh. He got us with that one," said Kevin Cronyn, his ruddy complexion hiding his Irish from no one.

Mitch had been following the news. Bob Leuchesi, the chairman of the Democratic National Committee, had just been indicted in New Jersey on extortion charges. The rumor was that he would resign before the weekend.

"Don't look so happy, Brad," goosed Mitch. "Or should we be calling you Mr. Chairman?"

"If nominated, I will not run," joked the finance director. "And if elected, well, I'll think about it."

Everybody laughed. And Mitch continued, "Let me answer your question with a question. I wonder if a campaign *negative* isn't unlike when a marriage turns bad. Can you ever get back to where you started? Can trust be salvaged? Can love ever prevail?"

Rene started hacking with a bite of muffin caught in her throat. Where in God's name was he going with this?

"You okay?" asked Kevin, offering her his glass of water.

"Fine. I'm fine. Sorry," she said, glaring at Mitch the whole time.

He ignored her. "What I'm asking is if the relationship between a candidate and the voter isn't like a marriage. There's a public trust about which I'm concerned," he said. "I've been public about taking the high road."

"Nothing wrong with the high road," said Brad. "And I'm likely to agree. But as far as we can tell, nobody knows squat about this guy McCann. Who he is, what he's capable of, et cetera. But the kinda crap he's pulled on you so far is making you look bad."

Kevin took over with a more laid-back approach. "The money we're giving you serves two masters. Master number one wants to make you a member of the House. Master number two wants to crush the opposition. Do you know what the word *campaign* means?"

"I believe it's defined as *war.*"

"Exactly," said Kevin.

"All's fair in love and war," blitzed Brad, his toothy, frat boy grin cracking at the corners.

"So I've heard." Mitch smiled. "And close only counts in horseshoes *and* hand grenades."

"That's a good one. Can I steal that?" asked Kevin. "I got a candidate in Maryland who could use it."

"Be my guest." He didn't tell him the quote belonged to the deceased Hurricane Hammond. "Gentlemen. I have every intention of kicking my opponent's ass all the way back to South County. Your money's on the right horse."

"It better be." Brad returned in the guise of the bad cop. "We've got plans for you here. It's *all* in motion, if you get my meaning. And with only ten weeks left in the race, voters could give a good Goddamn about what Mitch Dutton has to say. At this point, all they care about is who hits the hardest." He snubbed out his cigarette for punctuation. "Do us all a favor and bury him, Mitch."

A pretty Admirals' Club attendant appeared. "There's a telephone call for you, Mr. Dutton." Mitch was out of his chair in a shot, leaving the rest of the gang in Brad Pustin's lingering cigarette smoke.

Rene assured the two men, "He's in. He'll do what it takes. I can promise that."

"Woulda been good to hear it from him," said Brad.

"We did." Kevin smiled. He patted Rene on her thigh. "We most certainly did."

Murray was calling from a campaign cell phone while parked out in front of Mitchell's house.

"Is she okay?"

"I didn't see her. I talked to Gina."

"Gina Sweet."

"Yeah. The girl from primary night."

"So what'd she say?"

"Well, I must've rung the bell and knocked on the door for ten minutes before anybody answered. Then Gina answers. She looked real hungover and really pissed. But that's just my opinion."

"What about my wife?"

"She said Connie was upstairs sleeping. I told her the phones were out and you were trying to call. That's when she said it."

"Said what?"

"I mean, I'm only paraphrasing. But she said she wouldn't blame Connie if she'd cut the phone wires—knowing that you'd be calling."

"Thanks, Murray. Looks like I worried for no reason."

"Anything else?"

"Keep this to yourself. Thanks again." Mitch hung up the phone, briefly reevaluating his panic. Connie was home, sleeping off one of her benders with the evil Gina Sweet.

I shoulda known.

Gina hit the road right after her short and testy talk with Murray. She'd woken at the pounding on the door, searched madly for her panties, only to find them torn and useless, answered the door, then lied about seeing Connie upstairs and sleeping. It was a reasonable assumption. Where the hell else would she be at that unholy time of day?

Meanwhile, the continued brownnosing from Fitz materialized in the form of a helicopter ride, returning Mitch and Rene to the Island by early afternoon. When Mitch rolled up his Flower Hill drive, the Southwestern Bell Telephone truck was already parked out front.

Having rehearsed the apology a hundred times on the return flight, he gathered himself in the car. He planned to be contrite. He planned to reach deep. And most of all, he planned to resolve the matter *that day* so he might get on with his work.

So much for planning.

He found Connie in the kitchen, cleaning up the mess from the night before. Bottles in the garbage. Twice she'd vacuumed the living room rug for leftover weed and seeds. Anything else found amongst the cushions and pillows would go down the garbage disposal. She'd made a new resolution. A candidate's home should be clean. Who knew who might be snooping in the garbage?

"You're back so soon. You miss me or something?" she joked, kissing him briefly on the lips before moving quickly past him to the pantry. She wanted to appear as if she were in cleaning mode. Dusting. Dumping. Any excuse to turn her back to him. Because if he caught her eyes, he'd surely see the damage from the night before. He'd see Shakespeare.

"I did. I missed you," he said, looking for his moment. But she beat him to it.

"I'm sorry about yesterday. I've done a lot of thinking. I decided I wasn't fair to you. You're working hard to try and accomplish something. And I shouldn't question how you do it." Mitch moved to the pantry, only to have her duck under his arm and cross to the fridge. Connie was *not* going let him catch even a glimpse of the agony that she was shoving deeper and deeper with every willful breath.

He followed, trying to get in a word. "I'm the one who should be sorry."

"Please, Mitchell. This is *my* apology." She continued, "I want you to win. I want you to do what you have to do. I want you to kick that little bastard's butt all the way back to wherever he came from."

"Whoa. Wait a minute. Whatever happened to 'that charming man'?"

"I was mad at you. I wanted to hurt you. And it worked." She folded herself into his arms, so close he wouldn't be able to see the hurt.

But could he feel it?

"You were mad at me because I lied to you. Am I right?" Mitch was still looking for a way in so *he* could apologize.

"No. I was mad at you because you were going to win." She could feel the wreckage boiling up from inside her. She needed to hang on. Keep the tremor out of her voice.

Calm, Connie. Calm!

"I'm sorry, too. I'm sorry I left without—"

"Please, Mitch! There's no need. I'm ashamed of myself and I've been no help to you. You're in a tough fight. I know that now."

He knew that Connie always made things far too easy for him, putting his needs before hers. He'd convinced himself it was her way of loving him. "Okay. I'll stop with the apology on one condition."

"Okay."

"Why the sudden change in attitude?"

"Like I said, your leaving gave me time to think." Then she came as close to the truth as she could without totally breaking down. "He's a bad man, isn't he?"

"That he is."

The voice inside her screamed, *Yes, he is an evil, horrible man! He raped me just so I would tell you! Well, fuck him! I won't give the little bastard the satisfaction!*

But Connie covered before breaking down. "I'm late, sweetie. Got my annual with Dr. Simmonds. And it's always better to shower before he gets me in the stirrups, if you know what I mean." It was another lie. She had already showered, scrubbing herself raw from head to toe. But the shower was the only place quiet enough for her to get away from Mitch and cry. After that, she would go see Dr. Simmonds and tell him the truth. She could trust the old gynecologist with just about any dirty secret. He was better than any shrink, priest, or lawyer.

As she tried to escape upstairs, he stopped her with one more question. "What happened to the phone?"

"Windy last night. I think a branch fell and pulled out the line. Should be fixed just about now." She gave him another kiss before exiting. "I know you tried to call. But it was better that we missed. I do my best thinking when this house is quiet."

"I love you, Connie," he found himself calling after her. "You know that, don't you?"

"Of course I do," she singsonged back, out of the kitchen and up the stairs. Once in the privacy of the master bath, she turned on the shower. What followed were shakes and a violent series of abdominal convulsions. After which she curled up on the cool tile next to the toilet and let her pain loosen a pitiful wail into a bundled towel held tightly to her face. Her muffled cries never made it past the bathroom door. For some twenty minutes she didn't move, blowing off what emotion she could and sucking back the residual. Makeup and Visine would mask the rest.

And Mitch will never know.

Downstairs, the dogs were scratching at the back door. Mitch loosened his tie and let them in. As he opened the door they jumped all over him, doused him with wet, hairy kisses.

"All done," said the young telephone repairman. "Just need to check out the handset inside here."

Mitch let the fellow pass by. "You think maybe I oughta get those trees trimmed?"

"Hell no. The trees are fine. Looks like somebody just reached up and gave it a good yank. But I already said that to Mrs. Dutton."

Momentarily dumbstruck, he tried to recall Connie's explanation about the tree branch. Did he hear right? "Cut? Excuse me, you said somebody pulled this down?"

"What I said." The repairman picked up the kitchen line, got a dial tone, and nodded. "Nice neighborhood up here. Don't see much of that kinda stuff unless somebody was trying to disable the alarm. Should get yourself some steel conduit and run that phone line underground. Could do it for you this weekend if you like."

"Yeah. Sure. You got a card?"

"I'll just call you. Telephone company, ya know? We got yer number," said the repairman with a wink. "I must say, Mr. Dutton. I still ain't figured out who to vote for yet."

Mitch shook the repairman's outstretched hand and plastered on his candidate's smile. "Shaking me down for a vote in exchange for fixing my phone line?"

"Well, I ain't fixed that other guy's phone line. I figure it this way. You want the job. I want the job. That's politics, ain't it? A little give and take?"

"Something like that. I'll call . . . Wait. You'll call. Just let my wife know you're coming round."

Cut phone line? And Connie's lie. What really happened last night?

The repairman gone, Mitch looked to the dogs, circling and sniffing the new smells on his trouser legs. They would surely have been in the house last night. They knew the truth and remembered how it all *smelled.* If only they could tell him about the funny weed brought in by the night visitor. The kind man who smelled of sweat and cologne, who fed them raw meat and petted them kindly with his odd-feeling rubber gloves.

The dogs remembered Murray at the door and the foul, angry breath of Gina Sweet. Later, relegated to the backyard, they remembered dancing around the flames as Connie soaked the bedroom sheets in kerosene and lit a match to them. The burning had filled the air with smoke and ash. What smells they were. Right for dogs. But awful for Connie, whose salty tears were so tasty to the animals. Both Merle and Pearl got their last licks in just before the phone man arrived.

If only they could talk.

10

F or a month that began with eleven straight days of rain, August looked as if it was going to end up a scorcher like July. As a promotion, FM radio station Hot Hits 98 was cooking eggs on a specially poured concrete sidewalk, serving them up any way you liked 'em. Scrambled, over easy, and with grits. Across the street, the free ice cream served daily at the Shakespeare McCann headquarters was an ever-popular Cathedral treat. As its own sort of promotion, it was cheap. In addition to those "McCann of the People" napkins, they'd added red-white-and-blue-wrapped waffle cones. The flavor was always vanilla, imported at a bargain from Costa Rica.

Shakespeare was spending less than a nickel a scoop to buy those smiles out on the sunbaked sidewalk. A nickel a scoop that might someday return $5, $10, or $50 donations to his campaign.

But the smiles were few and far between inside McCann headquarters. On top of the daily tirades Shakespeare was accustomed to performing in front of the staff, the shit had been flowing downhill for the past week. From Shakespeare to Marshall Lambeer, then with a Reagan-like trickle effect, the building began to reek. It began with the news that the Democratic National Committee was committing a half million dollars to the Dutton camp, with half the cash targeting the Republican candidate with a "Who's

Shakespeare?'' media campaign scheduled to hit by the last week of August.

Then there was the bad news of the day. A camera crew from Channel 13 had appeared outside the ice cream stand, asking the happy recipients just how they felt about eating ice cream from Central America wrapped in red, white, and blue waffle cones. The Shakespeare campaign had been busted for going cheap on the ice cream and not buying American. The news piece would hit by five. More camera crews from other stations were expected.

In one of his hourly closed-door sessions with Shakespeare, Marshall wanted to pull the ice cream. Have the candidate publicly put the blame on some faceless campaign staffer and, within twenty-four hours, replace the cold stuff with some low-budget American brand. Shakespeare was more interested in the leak. ''We wanna know who leaked it! And we want his head on my desk by six!''

''It coulda been anyone. It might not have even been in-house. The FEC requires us to report all expenditures. All it would take is an opp-research team and a little legwork—''

''Dutton? You saying the opposition did this?''

''I'm saying it doesn't matter. We fix it and move on. That's politics.'' Marshall knew he was dealing with a neophyte, who at one moment seemed to know close to nothing about politics, then at other times, saw the campaign as if it were through a crystal ball. A Machiavellian kind of genius, at his heart neither Republican nor Democrat. He was his own brand of politics. The dangerous kind. A man who had more than once put fear in Marshall's heart should he ever consider leaving the fold.

The biggest problem was, Marshall still didn't know what motivated the guy. But at five thousand a week, he tried not to care.

''You know what this says?'' Shakespeare pointed at the bulletin board, filled with those three-by-five cards. He'd shuffle them daily, then lay them out as if he were reading tarot. ''This says we should be ten points off the pace by now. Closing the gap. But we're how many points behind now?''

''You're sixteen,'' said Marshall.

''*We're* sixteen,'' corrected Shakespeare, who wanted everything concerning his campaign couched in collective terms. He wanted fingerprints on everything.

''I'm sorry.''

''It's okay. But now we got us a new negative. Because some dumb ass leaked this ice cream bullshit to the TV.''

The contempt Marshall felt for this man was overwhelming. He thought, *You're the dumb ass. You wanted to go cheap on the ice cream. You get what you deserve.*

Instead, he was more diplomatic. "You want a sacrifice. Fine. I'll find you someone to sacrifice."

"I want the SOB that betrayed us," barked Shakespeare.

"Done." Marshall even made a note so his boss would see that he'd taken the command seriously, scrawling it all onto a legal pad. He then cleared his throat. "Speaking of negatives, this is just the beginning. Dutton's preparing to hit us with those 'Who's Shakespeare McCann?' spots in a week. I would expect them to follow with a request for a debate. Now, it's my recommendation that we hit him spot for spot with negatives in the order of his left-leaning policies. Especially his anti-death-penalty stance."

"I'll debate. But on *our* terms," groused Shakespeare. "Now, what about these commercials?"

"There's the issue of money. We can't afford it. With only 'official support' from the Republican State and National Committees—"

"Don't you worry about money. It'll come during the All-American Ice Cream Road Show. We're gonna take it to the people."

But Marshall didn't figure Shakespeare's planned bus and ice cream truck show to raise more than twenty-five thousand dollars. Tops. And they were up against *two hundred fifty thousand* in negative spot-spending. If there was more money coming in, Marshall would need to know about it. The Federal Elections Commission's reporting requirements were complicated and needed daily attention.

"I've had an interesting financing offer," said Marshall.

"Let's hear it."

"The CBC."

"What's that?"

"Conservative Business Consortium. They want to make your campaign—"

"It's *our* campaign, Marshall," corrected Shakespeare.

"They want to loan *us* one hundred thousand dollars."

"Do I have to pay it back?"

"Not entirely. First, *you* must request the loan. After *they* meet the requirements as a lender, we can collect the dough. Spend it as we please. Pay it back . . . *whenever.*"

"And the catch is?"

"Whatever your imagination can conjure."

Shakespeare didn't need time to think about it. "Good. Let's do it."

"I'll tell them."

"Now, Shoop de Jarnot," said Shakespeare in one of his patented non sequiturs.

"Excuse me?" asked Marshall. He didn't think he'd heard right.

"That's the name of the Creole nigger that Dutton's secretly written some death penalty appeal for." Shakespeare pointed to the card on the bulletin board that represented Shoop de Jarnot. Marshall couldn't make out the scribbling.

"What about him?"

"You work on those anti-death-penalty commercials. But leave this one fellah outta the mixture. We got us some other plans for him."

"Leave him alone," noted Marshall. "Done." He was out of his chair and headed for the door.

"As for who I am?" added Shakespeare, responding to the forthcoming Dutton spot campaign. "I am what I say I am. Understood?"

"So you are," said Marshall in a way that should've followed with a bow. He made a fast exit, leaving the little man and his damned colored cards on the other side of the door.

Oh, but the cards had such meaning for Shakespeare. Something useful he'd learned from the old days and the place where time stood still unless a man made a stand and knocked time off its Goddamn feet. Management was the key. Mastering the inner universe. Mastering came only with a plan. For that, a visual aid was required. Each architect's step of the plan built from singular sheets of starched toilet paper, each pasted on the wall using tired chewing gum. That was the first plan ever.

The plan born before a man could afford a bulletin board, colored cards, and brushed-metal push pins. Each little sheet of tissue, pasted upon a slab of vertical concrete, had a purpose that organized the mind and kept a man from certain madness. Kept him on that straight-and-narrow path that would lead to a future without pain or punishment.

All he had to do was stick to the plan.

But plans go wrong. And part of Shakespeare's blueprint was that Connie would confess to her husband about the rape. Such a violation would surely rip a massive, spewing hole inside the front-runner's facade. An open sore at which Shakespeare could prod and poke at will. Yet, ten days after the dreadful act, he had heard nothing. Not a peep from one of his many spies.

Could she have liked it? Hardly. But could she have hated her cheating husband so much that she wouldn't have told him? Not likely. If she hated him, she would've told him out of pure spite!

Answer: She loves him too much to hurt him.

Shakespeare tasted blood! He'd miscalculated. The more he thought about missing the mark, the more his insides wept. It left a sour taste in his gullet that made him spit red into his linen handkerchief every time he coughed.

The voice cast a reminder. *Change the plan. Move the cards. Play your game and win the war. That's it. Put the bastard's neck into the noose and kick out the chair!*

The certain meltdown that was in store for Connie never seemed to materialize. At least, not in August. The fragile wife was far stronger than her husband, or anybody, might ever have imagined.

The key was Gina.

It'd been two entire weeks since they had talked. Gina had called and called, but Connie couldn't look in the face of anything that might remind her of that awful night. Gina showed concern by showing up at the house. Connie answered the door, dressed in nothing more than a T-shirt and bathrobe. At first sight, she wanted to kick the door shut in Gina's face. But the Elevil had kicked in and she was feeling hospitable.

"So, what? You're not talking to me anymore?" asked Gina.

"I've been sick. I'm sorry." Connie started up the staircase, but fatigue made her turn and sit on the steps. Then came the tears.

"That prick," said Gina under her breath. "What's wrong, sweetie? Gina can make it better."

She kneeled in front of Connie, trying to get her to look up. But no luck. Just the sight of Gina brought it all back. To look at her would let loose a tumult. And if it came, Connie was sure there'd be no return. The best she could do was to shake her head no.

"Is it Mitch?"

Of course not! It's that rapist you brought into my house!

"C'mon, girlfriend," pressed Gina. "You can tell me."

Connie bit her lip and nodded, hoping that Gina would simply drop it. But that's just what started it.

Gina was back on her feet. "That fucker!"

"Please, G," begged Connie. She'd misled her with the nod, but now was time to reel her back in. "It's not that bad."

"Is he making you cry?"

More leakage. Connie tried to cover her mistake. "Leave it alone, please. He's my husband."

"He's killing you. Don't you see that?"

Shakespeare McCann killed me. I'm the walking dead. Can't you see, you dumb bitch?

"Go away, Gina. Please."

"You need me."

"Get out!"

Gina gave her a long look, got the message, picked up her bag, and charged out to her car. The tires spit gravel as she peeled out of the driveway.

Alone again. The way Connie wanted it.

Gina fumed. She was angry at Connie, but most of all, at Mitch Dutton. He was the reason for all of this shit. From the easy comfort of her air-conditioned Mercedes, she dialed information and got the McCann of the People campaign office. She memorized the seven digits in her head, redialed without having to take her eyes off the road, and after a brief tangle with a campaign volunteer, was put through to Shakespeare.

"I know that Gina's sweet, but does she have something more than sugar for her daddy?" spun that folksy voice.

"You gotta date me to find out," she teased back.

For the inmates at El Rincón, the second heat wave was just one more form of punishment. Surviving the staleness of each morning was routine for the prisoners, and the ocean breezes were the closest thing they had to air conditioning. As the sun rose high and the temperatures escalated past ninety, somewhere north of two o'clock, in would come the breezes, and the sea air would lift spirits over those old stone walls. But in those latter days of August, as flags hung limp against their poles, the boys at the Point were ready to riot. The stink was high. The joint reeked of contraband smoke and glue smuggled from the wood and metal shops. Anything to beat the heat. A con would rather fry his brain on paint thinner than sweat over the crimes of his past.

Shoop spent much of the time trying to keep his mind clear. Despite the scorched air that reminded him of cooking over hot griddles in back-bayou kitchens, Shoop was two days from the *decision*. He wanted to stay focused. He wanted to hear it *straight* when the news came.

With Mitch stumping, Alex Bernardi kept in close touch, shuttling information to Shoop and leaving voice-mail messages in the Dutton campaign office.

Shoop was warned that there would be no news until there was an actual decision. But appeals judges have staffs. And staffs talk. The word getting back to Alex Bernardi was very positive. The legal aides had been impressed by the writ, the use of the new Louisiana gun law, and perhaps the signature of the presenting attorney and congressional front-runner, Mitch Dutton. He was news. He was running for office. And taking such an unpopular stand in Texas during an election, well, that showed balls and a conviction to the writ. It just might impress the justices along with saving Shoop's life.

Ever hopeful, Shoop prayed and, for the first time in five years, felt a lightness that was a far cry from the rage of the night he killed his wife and lover. That rage had left the deadly weight of conscience upon him. After the crime, he had wanted to kill himself. Put the gun in his mouth and have it done with. But the rage had been supplanted by a sudden apprehension. He cursed the fear. It was what made every passing day that brought him closer to his legally sanctioned end a living nightmare.

When he wasn't afraid of the end, he was dreaming about it. The frigid stainless steel tabletop upon which he'd be Velcro-strapped. The intravenous drip line, needled into a vein, throbbing helplessly from a heart that did not want to die. Then would come the lethal injection and, afterward, the hell described by his mother. A hot iron to his forehead that would brand upon him the mark of Cain, followed by the eternal torment of his burning flesh.

Just two more days.

The inmates prayed that day would hurry into night and cool their restless souls. Shoop requested to shower early and asked the duty guards if he might return naked and wet to his cell. That way the moisture on his skin would act like a coolant. Hold him off until night came. The guards granted the wish, and Shoop thanked them for their mercy and grace.

Night fell, and along with it, the temperature. Ten degrees. Enough to take the stink off the place. The meal that night was more putrefied grease, and Shoop refused to eat it. He'd rather starve. Fifteen minutes short of lights out, Tyler arrived and wasn't at all surprised to find the tray of food uneaten.

"Got somethin' for ya, Shoop."

He thought he was dreaming. The smell had hit him so hard, he thought it had to have been a subconscious concoction of peppers and cayenne.

"C'mon, ya dumb Creole. Meal's on."

Bolting upright on his bunk, Shoop sensed the dream wasn't real. Eyes open, he saw Tyler, big Louisiana grin on his face, sliding a steaming tray through the slot. His nose prickled.

"Can' be!"

"Sure is," confirmed Tyler. "Takeout all the way from Loosiana."

Shoop knelt at the tray, hands to his chest in amazement. There was a cup of buttery tomato bisque with baby crawdads, jambalaya, mashed potatoes with Hot Fanny sauce, and a fish and rice gumbo. He broke a sweat just looking at the tray.

"How you get dis?"

"Came in dry ice and a Styrofoam box marked Shoop de Jarnot. Return address said it was from Molly's."

"In dah quarter?"

"Only Molly's I ever heard of," said Tyler. "I had the boys in the kitchen nuke it. Oh, and there was a note." Tyler pulled a slip of paper out of his breast pocket, the one just above his name tag, and unfolded it. "Want me to read it?"

"Please." Shoop lifted the tray to his bunk, holding his head over the steamy spices and sucking back the smells of home.

"It's from Mitch Dutton," lied Tyler. "Says, 'Looking good. Got my fingers crossed. You do the same. And in two days you'll be on a bus back home.' " He folded the note and stuck it back in his pocket. "Ya know, I don't think it's his writin', though. Look like a woman's. Maybe Molly, ya think?"

"Ah think ah god dah bes' lawyuh in dah whole worl'!"

"Well, eat up before it gets cold."

"You wan' some?" Shoop offered his first spoonful of gumbo to the messenger.

"Sorry, man. Too spicy. My stomach can't handle it. Why do you think I moved west? Cuz the food was milder."

"No Mexican food?"

"Now, that's somethin' else. I like them chips and margaritas." Tyler picked up the uneaten prison meal. "Enjoy, brother. I'll come back in a while to get the leftovers."

"Won' be none!" Shoop smiled.

He made the meal last well beyond lights out. By then, he was eating by smell alone. But that was the Creole style. His nose told him which dish he would sample next. The jambalaya. Yes!

It was practically pitch-dark when he got to the dessert. Bread pudding. And when it was all gone, he licked the tray until all there was left to taste was stainless steel.

Naked and still, Shoop lay stretched out across his bunk, the water from his shower replaced by beads of spice-induced sweat. He was hot on the inside. Cool on the outside. His mind, though, was clear enough. Thinking that tomorrow would make it only one day until the decision. And though the day might be the longest of his life, it would be only a day. One day. A rising and setting of the sun. Then he would be going home. The sudden burst of optimism led his mind drifting. Then came the dreamy Seconal sleep.

First there were the guards who opened his cell door, leading Shoop naked through the prison. Alex Bernardi was there to give a warm smile and shake the prisoner's hand, as were the warden and the judge who presided over the first trial. Shoop was handed a telephone. He could hear Mitch at the other end. It was his voice, all right. But the words were strange. Another language? Angry. Some kind of warning. Shoop found himself congratulating him on a successful election, certain that had something to do with this sudden pardon.

Shoop's sleep was deeper, still.

He was to be set free without consequence. Naked and dripping wet from one last shower, he was led to a double set of tall, riveted doors. A bolt was thrown and the doors swung outward onto a bayou of placid water and tall, lingering trees. A breeze touched his face. He was home. It smelled of boiled shrimp and spices. All he had to do was follow his nose. Just as he'd done with that special meal. He sniffed at the air, which had suddenly turned hot and burned his nostrils. Through his mouth he inhaled, scorching his lungs. He gasped. Held his breath. Then turned back toward the prison. Only he was no longer in the bayou. He was on the shiny table. Guards Velcroed his arms and legs. A nurse jammed a dirty needle into Shoop's vein. Blood issued in a brief geyser, then came the IV drip connected to the lethal injection machine. The archaic-appearing device sputtered and smoked and smelled of Creole spices.

There was a gallery to watch. From behind splintered glass sat Mitch, Shakespeare McCann, his mother, his dead wife, her murdered lover, and Tyler, who was wearing street clothes instead of his usual guard's uniform.

The warden said, "Ready?"

Shoop couldn't speak. Velcro was strapped across his mouth.

As the dream faded, Shoop could hear the applause.

Shoop de Jarnot never woke up. He was found dead on the floor of his cell, curled in a fetal ball around the empty dinner tray. His eyes wide open. His mouth open as if in a wretched gasp.

11

Some date, complained Shakespeare to himself. The bitch was too damn easy. He'd picked her up in a car borrowed from a willing McCann of the People volunteer. And there she was, waiting for him at the predetermined place and time: 10:45 P.M. Standing on a Strand street corner like some twenty-five-dollar prostitute, Gina tongue-kissed the candidate hello just to get a rise out of him, then suggested one of the local no-tell motels down on the coastal route. In what was nothing more than a twisted coincidence, the sleazy flophouse was less than a mile down the strip from the same dive where Shoop de Jarnot had finally caught up with his wife and her lover.

As Gina paid for the room, Shakespeare stayed in the car, keeping his baseball hat brim low on his forehead and an eye out for anyone who might recognize a Republican candidate on the prowl. Teasing and trashy, she finally stepped from the motel office, jangled the room key, and gestured at her date to follow. He tracked from the car, parking at the farthest outpost from the office. The door was wide open when he got to the room: 211. Gina was already on the bed with her shirt unbuttoned and her surgically enhanced breasts looking as if they were about to burst from a black satin bra.

"Like 'em?" she said. "Right off the showroom floor. And I'm not talkin' none of that Dallas Cowboys Cheerleader stuff. These are Beverly Hills, bought and paid for."

"How'd someone with your kind of money end up so cheap?" he asked. Not that he cared a whit. He was just making polite conversation, if talking *tits* was polite.

"Practice," she giggled. "Takes a lotta cash to make me look this cheap."

"I don't get it. You and Connie Dutton."

"Class and Trash. That's what they called us in school."

"College girls?"

"Sorority sisters," she corrected. *"I Felta Thigh."* Then she fell over on the bed laughing at herself.

"You got something for me?"

Tina dried her eyes. "Maybe."

"Don't fuck with me, sister." And when Shakespeare went to his belt, it wasn't to take off his pants. He slid the thin strip of brown leather away and wrapped it around his knuckles. He was in no mood to be teased.

Gina called his bluff. This wasn't the first cowboy with a handful of leather she'd faced. "What're you gonna do? Spank me?"

"Haven't decided yet. It depends on what you got."

"Let's get one thing clear, Mr. Candidate. We're both on the same side. We both wanna see Mitch Dutton crash and burn."

"Talk is cheap and my time is getting shorter," he said, easing closer to the bed. "So give it up."

Suddenly she noticed there wasn't a single crease in his face. It was a blank slate, ready to be chalked with pleasure or hate. Utterly without expression. Just waiting for her answer. She teased once more. "What do I get?"

"A big kiss from your new congressman."

"Is that *alllll?*"

"You want some political pork? Is that it?"

"Wasn't so bad the last time."

What last time? thought Shakespeare. *She was out cold on that little blue bombshell.* "I'm waiting."

Gina's lips drew back into a wide grin. Oh, she had something, all right. Something she was sure and willing to tell the world. On TV even. An eyewitness account, sure to screw Mitch in the biggest, baddest way. Even if it *was* a lie.

"The gentleman from Texas recognizes the lady with the new,

improved titties." He smiled. His grin was infectious. The promise of things to come.

"Okay," she said, sitting up and crossing her legs. Those Beverly Hills miracles of plastic surgery heaving one more time before she let loose with the goods. "Mitch and I had an affair." But the smile on Shakespeare disappeared back into that creaseless face. She shifted uncomfortably, drew back her arms and arched her back so that her breasts jutted even further, as if they were proof enough. "And Connie doesn't even know."

"You lyin'?" he asked.

She shook her head. But her eyes briefly darted away with her answer. A telltale sign of a liar. "If I'm lyin', I'm dyin'."

It was an awful mistake, Gina's lying. Shakespeare let loose with that leathered fist right across her forehead. The impact sent her tumbling clear off the bed, finding herself ass-first on the floor. She was stunned, dazed, and stupid to show her anger. "You cocksucker—"

He already was upon her, grasping a fistful of her hair. He yanked her back to her feet and dumped her onto the bedspread. She crawled, but still he wouldn't let go.

"Please . . ." she pleaded, trying to sell the lie with her own pain. "Mitch and I *really* had an affair."

"Sure you did. And the wife didn't know?"

"I swear she doesn't."

"You bet your ass she doesn't. That's 'cause it never happened."

"I'll swear to it. I'll go on TV."

"Yeah, sure you will. Yessiree-bob! You and your new titties." Shakespeare let go of her hair and pushed her backward as if to get a better look at her. "You know what Mitch Dutton is?"

She was scared to answer. She just tried to catch her breath.

"Okay, I'll tell ya since you didn't ask," he continued. "He's a Goddamn elitist. Know what that is, college girl? Means he thinks his shit smells like birthday cake. And most of all, he don't like to get his hands dirty. Now, you think a fellah with that kind of bead on himself gonna dip in some trailer trash with a fat bank account?"

"Okay. So *he* wouldn't," said Tina, trying to turn the insult around. "But you would."

"You got no idea, sister," he seethed. "Pick up the phone!"

"It's not ringing."

"Pick up the fuckin' phone and dial him! Call fuckin' Dutton right now!" Shakespeare picked up the phone and threw it at her.

She jumped in fear, but eventually dialed. The simple task finished, he snatched the handset from her.

The phone rang and woke Mitch. He found himself sitting up in bed with the light on and glasses askew on his face. There was homework on his lap. Debate homework. He was preparing for the as-yet-unscheduled public forum with McCann. As election day drew closer, there would be less time to prepare. Meanwhile, Connie mumbled from her sleep, "Are you gonna get that?"

He caught the phone on the fourth ring, cleared his throat, and answered. "Hello."

"How's the wife?" asked the voice.

"She's fine," he found himself saying automatically. That was before he realized he was talking to Shakespeare McCann.

"Got a question for ya, Counselor," continued Shakespeare from that dirty motel room, Gina curled up at the headboard with a pillow scrunched in her arms. "Correct me if I'm wrong, but you're against the death penalty. That right?"

Mitch gathered his wits, pausing briefly before his answer. "I thought we'd wait for a more public forum before we debate. Are you calling to confirm?"

"Off the record, Counselor. Are you or aren't you?"

"Off the record, I think you're a twisted SOB."

"How about on the record? I'll tell you where I stand," said the undaunted Shakespeare, giving a wink to Gina. "Myself? I believe in the death penalty. Eye for an eye's what the Good Book says. For example, that Creole they got locked up in El Rincón. The one you wanna send back to *Loooo*-siana?"

Mitch turned away from Connie, fearing he'd disturb her. Lowering his voice. "What about him?"

"Let's just say I wanted to even up the debate."

"There is no debate yet. Is that what this is about? You wanna negotiate terms?"

"No. I just wanted to tell you about the favor I've done you. This Bayou bitch? We both know he's the Achilles' heel of your campaign. And we both know in a public debate I could crucify you for writing that little ol' appeal that would release a killer from his noble appointment with death."

"Fine. Do it then. A place and time. You and me and everybody watching." But Mitch was missing the entire point.

"Maybe I should make it crystal-clear. This is a public-service call. Shoop de Jarnot is no longer a campaign issue. Justice was served."

Shakespeare coolly hung up and turned his gaze back to a very frightened Gina. "Now, with that done, what do you think I should do with you?"

Her skin twitched and spasmed. The fun and vengeance in her had long since gone the way of the dinosaurs, substituted by a terror she thought only existed in *other* people's lives. "I can help you," she squeaked, her voice quivering and barely audible. "Please, *let* me help you," she finished, realizing only then that she was begging for her life.

"When the timing's right, I'm sure you will."

After Shakespeare hung up, Mitch had held the phone for a moment before quietly laying it back into the cradle.

Justice has been served? By whom?

Mitch looked at the clock. It was 11:18 P.M. Too late to call the prison. Or even Alex, for that matter. Alex had a newborn baby and his hours were bad enough. He didn't need to be disturbed by Mitch on some ruse. Shakespeare was a liar and manipulator. Mitch was not going to spend another sleepless night suffering the little bastard. Resolved to getting a decent night's sleep, he put aside his worries and turned off the light, rolling over to lay a cozy arm across Connie. Only she wasn't in bed.

The bathroom light was on and the door was closed. He could hear the water running. All he could assume was that the call had woken her and she'd gotten up to wash her face. She often did that on hot and humid nights. But he hadn't a clue. His mind was still with the cryptic call.

"You okay?" he called out.

"Just cramps," she returned.

"You need anything?"

"I'm fine. Go back to sleep."

According to state prison officials, the cause of Shoop's death was either a case of premeditated poisoning or an allergic reaction to something exotic served in that special meal, sent him by an anonymous Mitch Dutton supporter. It took the state prison coroner over forty-eight hours to show up at the prison morgue for the postmortem, extracting the standard selection of stomach contents, blood, liver, and kidney samples from Shoop's body. But the poisoned tissue never arrived at the county SID. Somewhere along the scientific assembly line the materials were either lost or intercepted.

Covering for the error, the county coroner's office officially listed Shoop's death as an allergic reaction to an unknown, exotic biological toxin.

Molly's in New Orleans's French Quarter was informed.

The investigation was picked up by the New Orleans City Health Department.

And that was the end of the inquiry.

Nobody thought or cared to check with Tyler Tubbs, or made notice that he'd called in sick, quit school, and left the state altogether.

12

"He knew. I don't know how, but he knew. And not just that. I think McCann had him killed just to mess with me," said Mitch, pacing across Fitz's office.

Fitz crossed the room to close the hollow door. "You wanna tell what precipitates this kind of paranoia?" he asked calmly.

"You think I'm paranoid?"

"No. I think we're down to eight and a half weeks and you're looking for explanations into the unexplainable."

"He called me. He knew."

"So he's got somebody inside the prison. Ally, campaign supporter, volunteer. So what? That's allowed," said Fitz, who chose to sit on the rented, upholstered couch instead of behind his desk.

Mitch was shaking his head. "No. It was a threat."

"Coulda been. McCann's an opportunist. We know that much. But it certainly doesn't mean he did the actual deed."

"Play along with me," said Mitch. "What if he did? Think about it. What would it mean?"

"I'm not gonna go there, Mitch." Fitz had his hands up. And until that moment, he'd been holding back on how he *really* felt about Shoop. The poisoning. Mitch's involvement with the con. But now it was ripe. "I'll tell you where I will go. McCann's smart. Can we acknowledge that?"

"Make your point."

"Your weakest position in every track and poll is your death penalty position. Agreed?"

Mitch didn't need to answer.

"Okay," continued Fitz. "That appeal you were writing was political dynamite. You know my reservations with it. But it's something you felt compelled to do, so I never pressured you to lay off it."

"You were always clear." Mitch was looking impatient.

"I'll get to the heart of it. The appeal was looking good. Shoop was going to get shipped to a Louisiana facility. And guess who'd be responsible. You. Candidate Mitch Dutton got the killer off."

"In jail for the rest of his life. I don't call that getting a killer off."

"You don't think Marshall Lambeer's got a thirty-second TV spot ready to go? One that makes it look like you, Mitch Dutton, *personally* screwed with the death penalty? The law of the fucking land? This is Texas!"

"I don't need you to remind me—"

"Listen to me. If Shoop is dead, that means the *issue* is dead. No more political dynamite. The bomb's been dismantled."

Mitch was shaking his head. "It doesn't make sense."

"Life doesn't make sense. Food poisoning doesn't make sense. Or cancer. Or criminal behavior." Fitz was back on his feet. "But you still don't get it. Your buddy Shoop and his lucky supper was the best campaign donation you could have imagined!"

"You're a heartless SOB—"

"That's why I get the big bucks," joked Fitz.

"Shoop de Jarnot meant something to me."

"Well, that's between you and him." Fitz calmed himself. "Just as long as he doesn't mean anything to the enemy. That's all I give a shit about."

"Then why the phone call?"

"Emotional terrorism. That's all the cachet he had left. McCann knew Shoop was his only shot at catching you. He was waiting to spring it on you, counting on your genius appeal. But now that he's dead, he's lost. He's got nothing to hang you with." Fitz was in fine form, putting all the pieces together. "The phone call was nothing more than sour grapes. Now can we put this behind us and get on with the dog and pony show?"

Mitch found a seat behind Fitz's desk. Fitz, on the other hand, wanted to take a bow. It was a hell of a performance in the art of political perspective, thought the show runner. But the compliment never came from the candidate.

"I'm gonna need the weekend," said Mitch. "All of Friday, too."

"What for? You need some time off? You know, all of us are working real hard trying to get you the whole month of November off. You're gonna need it to pack for the big move to D.C."

"Just three days. Then I'm yours until election day."

"Permission granted," authorized Fitz. "We'll move some stuff around. Just as long as I get a hard week's work from you beforehand."

"That's a deal."

"Mind saying what for? Gonna take the wife for a little three-day *whatever?*"

"I'm gonna keep a promise," said Mitch, his voice grave and resolute.

The Dog and Pony Show.
Watch Mitch be phony show.
But it's my only show.
The Dog and Pony Show.

The singsong verse ran through Mitch's head. From the very beginning, Fitz likened the long days of a campaign to an old dog and pony act. For a while Mitch was amused by the pomp and circumstance of it all. Then one day he made the verse up in his head while pumping hands and grinning his way through another faceless gathering of local political fringe dwellers. From that day on, the verse never left him. He would shake a hand, giving some lucky well-wisher his best "Hi there. Mitch Dutton. Pleased to meetcha." But that silly song would be what always played in his head. Like some bizarre cue for him to put up a smile and *be the candidate.*

The Dog and Pony Show.

Mitch was forced to make a deal with Fitz about his planned attendance of Shoop de Jarnot's funeral. Being that it was in New Orleans and out of the campaign's province, let alone the state of Texas, Fitz gave his okay as long as the trip was quiet. Nobody else would know. Mitch would slip out of town with the missus and merely show up at the memorial to pay his respects and leave. No public appearances. No speeches. In and out.

Mitch promised.

Next was convincing Connie to accompany him. It would hardly be a vacation. A couple of days. A funeral, after all. But it would be time away from the campaign grind. Just the two of them. Alone, for at least a little while.

Watch Mitch be phony show.

Due to the bureaucracy of shipping prison corpses interstate, the funeral was three days away. And a deal was a deal. So *Candidate Mitch* knuckled down to work in the few days that were left. That meant more endless handshaking at shopping malls and supermarkets. Meetings and greetings. And sleeves rolled to his elbows as he beat the pavement, door to boundless door, through South County subdivisions.

But it's my only show.

"Hi. How are ya?" He would start with that line, followed by, "Mitch Dutton. I'm running for Congress."

The drill would go as follows. A campaign thrasher would work one or two houses ahead. Knocking on doors, ringing bells. Finding the registered voter in the house. By walkie-talkie, the name of the pigeon was radioed to Rene. The groundwork thus laid for the candidate to appear from the sidewalk with trademark loosened tie and rolled-up shirtsleeves. Then Mitch would offer his hand and that rehearsed smile. The one that Rene had taught him. Not a grin, not aloof, nor contrite. Just enough teeth to look genuine, the *campaign smile*, always served up with a firm handshake—two hands if the voter was a woman. "Hello, Mrs. Addison. Mitch Dutton. Pleased to meetcha."

The Dog and Pony Show.

And those three days were merciless. Humid. Precinct after precinct.

In the rear of the campaign van, Rene kept a fresh box full of starched, white shirts. After only an hour of door-knocking and handshaking, she'd have Mitch strip in the air-conditioned van. Once there, he'd towel off, shower himself with baby powder, pull on a fresh shirt, and go at it again.

"Mr. Gaines. Can I call you Walter? Swell. I'm a new Democrat," he would charm. "I want you to call me in Washington—I want you to have my number—I'm running to make sure Washington runs for *you!*"

So many hands to shake. So many people to meet. It was candidate as faith healer. God's disciple and charitable hand. A role Mitch found easier with every newly starched shirt Rene would peel from shrink-wrap.

* * *

It had been forever since Connie had packed *anything* for Mitch. The politics of packing, she'd complain to herself. Suitcases would be strictly his and hers, prepared respectively at different times. And where she was usually prepped and ready a full twenty-four hours before departures, Mitch would always wait until the last minute, raiding closets and drawers until the wee hours of the morning. Sometimes the racket would be so annoying that she would take to sleeping in the guest room.

Yet two days before the weekend, he surprised her with an uncommon request. He called from the campaign HQ and asked her to pack for him, giving her a short list that included one black suit and bathing trunks. He would entrust her with the rest.

"Where are you going?" she asked.

"New Orleans. I thought we'd drive the Gulf route. Mustang. Top down."

"Who's we?"

"You and me, babe. How about it?"

It was meant as a surprise. And Mitch had wanted to see her face, but his plans had only formed within the past hour. There was the promise and there was New Orleans. The getting there was what he hadn't figured out until the moment before he called. It warmed him to think that he and Connie would have three days to themselves, maybe finding something they'd lost along the way. Each other.

She held her breath. She needed to ask one more question. "Is this about the campaign? Or is it about us?"

"It's about us, Connie."

"I'm sorry, Mitch. I don't mean to be paranoid. I just need to know."

"Do I have to say it twice? It's about us. That and some personal business which I'll explain later."

"No politics?"

"Nope."

"We're not meeting anybody in New Orleans?"

"Nobody from the campaign," he assured. "Now, do I have a date?"

She had to think about it. Caution was her new credo. An emotional look before leaping. Then she said sweetly, "Of course you do."

"Good," he said, his voice smiling back at her.

"I'll start packing."

"And I'll try to be home for dinner. No promises, though."

Connie hung up and turned instantly to Mitchell's request. Her mind quickened. A trip along Route 87. A random motel stop. An oceanside dinner. God was talking to her. The scene would be perfect. Already she had her own surprise to spring. She would go shopping. Buy Mitch some new clothes. And quite possibly, when the timing was right, somewhere along the way she would tell him about the baby.

13

On the rare and recent days when Hollice Waters ventured downstairs to what they called *the dungeon,* he was reminded of how much he missed the smell of newsprint. No longer, though. Gone were the massive presses and tumblers from which newspapers were spun and creased for delivery. Nowadays, news stories were composed in a cyber-world called RAM, downloaded as megabytes, digitized, then lasered onto recycled bond with color pixelized photos and software-generated graphics, and finally run on a massive copy machine.

"Any slicker, we'd be a daily magazine," shouted Maynard, the shop manager, over the din of the newspaper stacker. Maynard might be the only familiar face left over from the good old days.

"If we were a magazine, the pay'd be better," answered Hollice, lighting up the last of those Havana cigars he'd stolen from Charlie Flores.

"So why you down here in the dungeon?"

Hollice waved the cigar. "They finally did it. The communists four-walled the offices with no smoking signs. I mean, even Charlie Flores went along with it."

"That one of his stogies?"

"He'll never miss it."

Maynard moved closer to Hollice. "Well, I won't tell on you, then."

Hollice's pager sounded. He automatically scrolled the number. He didn't recognize it. He had a memory for numbers, especially the ones that showed up on his pager.

"Got a phone?" he asked.

"There's a pay phone next to the time clock."

"What? There's no inside line down here?"

"Oh, there's plenty of lines. But each one's someplace where you'd have to stub out."

"Watchin' out for me, Maynard. I won't forget it." Hollice waved his good-bye with the smoking cigar and headed off toward the time clock.

The pay phone hung on the wall between the rest rooms. He set his cigar atop the phone, fished in his pocket for a quarter, and came up with two dimes. A five cents savings, he thought as he dropped the change in the slot and dialed the strange number. The phone rang once before a voice picked up and said, "Hollice Waters?"

"This is Hollice Waters. Who'm I talkin' to?"

"Shakespeare McCann. I think it's time we talked. You know Fill's Famous Barbecue?"

"Which one? Cathedral City?"

"I'm having lunch there at twelve-thirty. You come along. I'll buy."

"I'll be there."

As barbecue went, Fill's Famous was just about okay. The original establishment was a delicatessen owned and operated by a New York émigré named Howard "Fill" Fillstein. Soon after opening, Fill discovered that deli wasn't going over big in San Antonio, so he switched the menu to barbecue, and business picked up. So much so that he later opened a second franchise in Cathedral City called Fill's Famous II. With its central air conditioning, plastic plants that looked almost real, serene poster art, and tabletops laminated from actual Mexican bullfight posters, it served three times the floor space as the San Antonio original. But too bad for Fill, it only served one quarter the customers. Friday was Fill II's last day of business.

"Whatever you do, don't order the house special," said Shakespeare, sliding into the booth.

Hollice found Shakespeare's hand inside his own, giving it a solid shake. "What *is* the house special?" he asked.

"Barbecue," joked Shakespeare. "Poor SOB who started the joint shoulda stuck with deli and moved his dumb ass back to New York City."

"Well, sir, you picked a swingin' place to talk."

"Closin' their doors tomorrow. Thought this would be quiet. So we could talk, you know? Anyway, if you ask real nice, they serve up a helluva pastrami on rye. Hot mustard. The works."

The hostess showed them to their seats, taking her time to educate both gentlemen on the day's specials.

When she left, Shakespeare went about setting the ground rules. "I liked what you did with the Jennifer O'Detts story. You're a guy that can play ball."

"Depends on the game."

"Your game. Headline. Byline just below that. Then you write what the people want to hear, right there in black and white."

"I'm not for sale. I write what I think." Hollice loved the role of *El Journalista.*

"Sure you do. Like I said, I like how you handled that whole thing with Jennifer—"

"That was a setup, wasn't it?" interrupted Hollice. "Dutton was running low on negatives, so you had to invent some. The girl was bait and he took it hook, line, and sinker. You used me to reel him in."

"I thought you wrote only what you think."

"You didn't answer my question."

"I will. In good time. I'm fixin' to give you the exclusive interview."

"When?"

"When I'm closer. Me 'n' Dutton. Neck and neck."

Hollice had to laugh. "I don't know. You've made up a lot of ground. But there's still a helluva a gap."

"Depends on whose numbers you're lookin' at."

"And yours are different than Dutton's?"

"Numbers don't mean diddly. It's about what's in the air. When I'm close, you'll be able to smell it."

Hollice pulled on the slack. "Okay. I guess the gap is the unknown factor. Nobody knows the real Shakespeare McCann. They only know what you say. Comes a point when every politician has to open up."

Shakespeare knew he was right. Marshall had cooked the numbers enough times to make the answer clear. Shakespeare McCann needed to seem more accessible to the voters and less like a populist bomb thrower.

"I'm working on access," he agreed. "But don't forget for a minute that I'll always be the dark-horse candidate. The underdog. And I need all the strategy I can figure on."

"Theoretically. Sure. I see your point. But I'm just a reporter. Campaign strategies are for guys like Marshall and Fitz Kolatch to figure out."

"That's right. Your job's to call 'em the way you see 'em," Shakespeare confirmed.

McCann hailed the waitress to take the lunch order. As expected, he requested a pastrami sandwich. Hollice ordered a hamburger, barbecue fries, and another large iced tea.

"Tell me about yourself," asked Shakespeare.

"You first," countered Hollice.

"In good time."

"Oh, I forgot. The promise of things to come."

"Really," said Shakespeare. "I'm interested. Why's someone smart as you writin' for some little Island paper?"

"I like the sea air."

"Got that in L.A."

"Been there, done that," said Hollice.

But Shakespeare knew that. In fact, he knew everything. The story hadn't been hard for his investigators to run down. After four years of college, Hollice chased a would-be actress by the name of Carol Anne Finch out Southern California way. They rented a Hermosa Beach apartment and married soon after. By day he worked as a copywriter for a large advertising firm, while by night his wife stripped at a club in Gardena. After she spent both their paychecks on cocaine, Carol Anne sidetracked into heavier drugs and porno films.

"Married?" asked Shakespeare.

"Twice. The first one was way back when I was young and dumb."

"And wifey number two?"

"Remarried. Moved up to Oklahoma City with her kids."

"Yours?" asked Shakespeare. He knew this answer, too.

"Hers from marriage number one."

"You know how to pick 'em."

"Least I gave it a ride. More than I can say for you."

Shakespeare leaned closer and whispered, "I was savin' it up for Jenny O'Detts."

Hollice burst out laughing.

Shakespeare leaned back into the vinyl and smiled broadly. When Hollice returned to earth, he found a package in front of him. "What's this?"

"My appreciation."

"I can't take a gift from a candidate."

"Call it an honorarium. Just open it and then say no." Shakespeare pushed it across to Hollice.

Too curious to argue, he ripped the gift wrapping off a brand-new Sony Hi-8 video camera. Obviously Shakespeare wasn't aware of Hollice's visceral dislike for technology. "I don't get it." He shrugged.

"What's to get? I know you don't like Dutton any more than I do."

"I never said that."

"I'm giving you the opportunity to bury him," said Shakespeare. "In exchange, though, I will give you the interview you deserve. The whole enchilada. A truthful answer to anything and everything. No time limit. And you can tape it if you want."

Hollice pushed the video camera back across the table. "What does this have to do with me not liking Mitch Dutton?"

"Is it true or not?"

"What do you know?"

"Forget what I know. Look me in the eye and say it's not true."

"Fuck you."

"No. *Fuck* Mitch Dutton," said Shakespeare. "His daddy fired your daddy. So your daddy couldn't get no more jobs. He died of a stroke. Your momma started drinking. Blah blah blah blah."

"Who told you this?" Hollice leaned forward, angry now. "Look. I don't know who you've been talking to. But I'm over it. That's kid stuff. Old news. If I don't like Mitch Dutton, it's on my terms."

"Fine. Your terms."

"And I *hate* video cameras."

"So will Mitch."

"Why?"

"Starting today, Dutton's going on a three-day vacation with his wife. Destination? you ask. New Orleans."

"What? A vacation?"

"He's going to a funeral."

"Who died?"

"A killer named Shoop de Jarnot."

14

Mitch decided to wait to tell Connie about the funeral until they were well down the highway along the intercoastal waterway. The most he'd given *anybody* was his destination. He informed the staff that he'd check in from the road.

As for that first weekend following Labor Day, voters would be obsessed with other things. Labor Day was Cathedral's last tourism gasp of the year. It was a business-friendly choice to leave politics out of the holiday.

Barely two miles down Texas State Route 87, Mitch felt the campaign shackles loosen. They'd forsaken the safety of the Volvo for the devil-may-care attitude of Connie's Mustang. The top was down and the wind was busting through her hair.

She hid her painful secrets behind a pair of dark Persols. Since the rape, they'd become her disguise; she wore them whenever she could get away with it. Always avoiding eye contact, especially with Mitch. If he'd seen her eyes and looked hard enough—just once— he'd surely know. And Connie wouldn't have that. She'd suck back the hurt like a lungful of foul air. Hold it with her head upright, only to release it when she was alone and out of earshot. Mitch will never, ever know, she promised. And that would be that.

From his perspective, behind those designer shades, she didn't look a day past twenty-one. She sat silently, content with her hand waiting for his. He shifted the steering duties to his left and touched her with his right, grazing her cheek with a gentle knuckle, enough to elicit a warm smile. He clutched her hand and kissed it.

"Thanks," he said.

"For what?"

"For dropping everything."

"Don't thank me yet. I may not have packed your underwear."

"That's cold."

"Dem's duh risk y'all takes, hun," joked Connie in her best deep South twang. "Now, tell me why you had me pack the funeral suit."

It hadn't gotten past her, nor had he expected it to. What else had she sussed out? Did she know about Rene? In the joy of the moment, he was suddenly filled with regret. God, he should tell her. Confess now. Get it out and done with. Ruin the moment. Heal the soul.

But these were selfish thoughts. He couldn't hurt her like that.

"Remember the call I got a week back?" he said, forcing his brain back in the conversation.

"The death-row guy."

"Shoop de Jarnot. He died in prison."

Murdered. McCann did it. Mitch knew.

"He was from New Orleans? You know, I didn't know you were close."

"We weren't. But I made him a promise. That if he never made it out of Texas alive, I'd go to the funeral and tell his mother he loved her."

"I knew there was another agenda."

"I told you I had some personal business."

"Yes, you did." Her head tilted backward, eyes closed behind the shades. "So what else haven't you told me?"

"What do you mean?"

"Oh, I don't know. Just making conversation. Long drive to New Orleans."

Mitch fired her a quizzing look. What the hell was she thinking behind those dark glasses? What did she know?

"You want secrets?" he asked, feigning innocence.

"Something dark."

"Something I've never told you?" He was blind to her ruse. Too wrapped up in his own conscience, he couldn't see Connie was keeping the conversation onto *him* and away from *her.* "Lemme think," he said.

"Don't hurt yourself," she grinned.

By her tone, he saw she was game for play. And not for any hardened, painful truth. So he steered clear of the subject of Rene. "When I was fifteen I used to steal cash from my dad's wallet."

"Alert the media!" laughed Connie. "The candidate has a criminal history."

"He caught me," admitted Mitch.

"What'd he do?"

"Whacked me around a bit. Then I worked off the debt on one of his boats."

"Coulda been worse."

"At ten cents an hour?"

She laughed at the image of the fifteen-year-old working for slave's wages on one of Q. Dutton's shrimpers.

"Your turn," he said.

"Oh, I don't think so. This is my game."

"Two can't play?"

She changed subjects. "Three days. All mine?"

"Not unless you tell me a secret."

"I will. I promise." She patted his leg. It was as good as gold. "When's the funeral?"

"*Mañana*. It's just an hour out of three whole days. And you don't have to come, either. The rest of the trip belongs to you. Scout's honor." Mitch made the sign with his right hand, three fingers in the air, thumb crossing his palm and pinning his pinkie. Not that it meant a damn thing. The Boy Scout in him had long run off with the likes of Jennifer O'Detts.

"Oooh, promises," cooed Connie. "Scoutmaster Fitz must have *luuuved* the idea."

"So he wasn't thrilled. But a promise is a promise."

"Not to be confused with a campaign promise."

Two points. "Don't remind me."

"Okay. I won't. No more campaign talk till Sunday night."

"Monday morning. I promised a long weekend, and a long weekend it shall be." He kissed her hand again and she smiled mischievously. Mitch didn't miss it. "What?"

"May as well get off to a rousing start." And off came the sunglasses and the seat belt. "Eyes on the road, cowboy. It's your lucky day."

Surprise was Connie's rarest art.

She leaned over in the seat and began unbuttoning his trousers.

First the top button, then the zipper, then reaching her hand inside to pull him out, exposing him to the elements before devouring him into the softness of her mouth.

"You got me," said an astonished Mitch, attempting to keep his eyes to the road.

Yes. She most definitely got him.

Sweet anonymity.

As Mitch slipped from their French Quarter hotel and went for a run early that Saturday morning, he couldn't help notice that . . . *nobody noticed.* When out in public, he'd just about gotten used to all the sideways looks, whispers just out of earshot, pointed fingers, autograph seekers, and glad-handers after a piece of the candidate. Recognizable as a can of Pepsi, he was product. Packaged, sold, and distributed in the small universe that was South County. But once outside, the celebrity vanished. And he found it strangely liberating.

At a small, corner café he stopped for coffee and a perusal of the local newspaper. Parked at an outdoor table built from the wrought iron that made the French Quarter so distinct, he could sweat and swill his coffee without so much as an offhanded stare. Four blocks away, Connie was still in bed sleeping. Just like it had been on weekends some years back. He'd go run. And she'd sleep late into the morning, waking up to fresh croissants he'd bring home from the bakery. Good idea, thought Mitch. He paid for his coffee and muffin and ordered a couple of croissants to go. Chocolate and almond. Connie would be pleased.

What he didn't know was that the hotel phone would be waking Connie before he'd even thought to stop for breakfast. "Hello?" she answered.

A man's voice responded over a crackling connection. Deep and hollow. "May I speak to Mr. Dutton?"

"Not here," she answered, eyes barely open. "Can I ask who's calling?"

"This is Shoop's daddy, Les De Jarnot. I wanted to see if Mr. Dutton had the correct address for the afternoon service."

"Oh, I'm sure he does," she said, resigning herself to crawling from bed to fish through his briefcase for his Day Runner. "Just hang on a moment."

She placed the phone down, and drawing the sheet around her instead of closing the curtains, dove into Mitch's briefcase. Instantly she realized this was something she never did—look through Mitchell's personal belongings or papers. She never had to. Now she was glancing at every note and paper, reading but not retaining. Just rummaging for that New Orleans address and praying she wouldn't discover something that might lead her down some dark path.

The address was neatly paper-clipped to the back of his calendar. Connie crawled back across the bed. "I think this is it. Twenty-two North Rampart? How far is that from the French Quarter?"

"In New Orleans, nothing is very far. We will see you there?"

"Well, I hadn't planned. Shoop was Mitchell's case. It says two o'clock—I might come along."

"Okay, then. Thank you." The man hung up.

When Mitch returned to the hotel, the shower was steamed and Connie was gone. He'd just missed her, finding a note on the bed that was simple and sweet:

> *You got a date for the funeral.*
> *Gone to find appropriate attire.*
> *Let's meet for lunch at noon.*

Obviously she couldn't have known he was bringing back breakfast. Fresh croissants, still warm from the bakery. All he could do was to eat them himself, reclining on the hotel room bed with the bag of buttery pastries and channel-surfing for any kind of sports programming. All that was on was a spate of Saturday morning children's programming mixed with cooking infomercials and assaultive political affairs reporting.

He was reminded that at that very moment, there were campaigns with candidates galore, running the political gauntlet in every nook and cranny of America. Congressional incumbents and challengers, talking from both sides of their mouths, promising, and cajoling the gullible electorate for precious votes. They even had the same damn trash-talking TV commercials. And the messages all bore the same self-serving uniformity. Only the faces were different.

In the course of two hours, Mitch had gone from anonymous to insignificant. Another cog in the political machine, another rat in the race.

At the northern edge of what locals called the Rampart District, the corners of North Rampart and St. Ann were once four Creole-influenced city blocks. They called it Storyville. Now, the native patois was shared with gang bangers selling Baby T and Big Harry. And the smell of spice had faded along with the government paint on the housing projects. Still, this was hallowed ground for what was left of the city Creole. Trespassers beware.

The church was medium-sized and hollow. High arches. Hardly Notre Dame, but the spirit was intact. Mitch and Connie found seating at the rear right of the cluster, two white beacons in a room of Creole black. He counted seventy-nine mourners in all, including the priest who conducted the ceremony in French. He thanked God that the service was short.

"Mrs. de Jarnot, this is my wife, Connie," introduced Mitch.

Shoop's dear mother was best described as round. Every part of her curved and bulbous, including her short hair, curled into circular ringlets. "You mus' be so proud," said Mrs. de Jarnot.

"Excuse me?" asked Connie.

"Shoop tol' me yo husband was runnin' tah be a congressman." The old woman's eyes were warm and reflective.

"Oh, I am proud," answered Connie, pulling closer to Mitch. "We're all proud of him."

"Shoop say Mistuh Dutton deed his bes' fo him. Ah hope he does good by you, ma'am."

Connie couldn't help but notice the gathering of tall young men surrounding her. Each with his mother's eyes.

"Are these all your sons?"

"Ah am lucky, say? God geev me many boys. I have five boys left ta luv me good."

"May I ask where Mr. de Jarnot is?"

The old woman's face shifted from warm to curiously cold. Had Connie misspoken? She looked up to one of her boys.

"I'm sorry. But was I mistaken?" She turned to Mitch. "He called our hotel room early this morning to see if we had the address all right."

Another son spoke up in an educated voice, without a trace of patois. "My father died of a heart attack on the day Shoop was sentenced in Texas."

She brought a hand to her mouth, chilled instantly to the bone. Horribly embarrassed at the faux pas. But who had called her? She couldn't have been *that* wrong.

Mitch's hackles were up. "Did you get the address, or give it?"

"I got it from your briefcase and read it back."

A disturbance broke out at the back of the church. They were ushering a white man who hadn't bothered to appear in mourning attire. Then Mitch heard the voice. Hollice.

"Hey. It's okay, all right. Don't push. I'm a friend of a friend." Mitch glimpsed the video camera in Hollice's hand just as he was shoved through the double doors.

"Do you know him?" asked Connie.

"It's Hollice Waters," he said, pulling away from her and heading for the front exit. She grabbed him by the arm.

"No. Let's go out the side door. You don't need this right now," she urged.

"I gotta talk to him."

"But he's here *because* of you. That can't be good."

"You're right. It's not good."

"So let's go."

"He had a *video camera!*"

Mitch blew through the church doors, finding Hollice on the steps and fumbling with the camera.

"Hollice!"

Instinctively Hollice brought the camera up to his eye, ready or not, only to have Mitch slap it to the concrete. The camera bounced and burst into pieces. Mitch followed it down the steps, crushing the ejected tape underfoot like a cockroach.

"Oh, that's just swell. You gonna buy me a new one?"

"You oughta be ashamed!" spat Mitch. "Where's the Goddamn story?"

"Candidate grieves over death-row killer," defended Hollice.

"This hasn't a thing to do with politics!"

"We'll see about that."

"And what's in it for you? A little vacation. Charlie know he's paying for this?"

"Haven't turned in my expenses yet."

"You know? You used to be a smart guy. You had a future."

"So'd my old man."

Mitch was aghast. "Is that what this is about? Because if it is, you're about three thousand miles in the wrong direction."

"The view from here's just dandy."

"You're in the gutter, Hollice."

"That's the business, *Mitch.* You're a public figure now. We own you."

"And who owns you? McCann? I don't see you chasing him down any dark alleys."

"That's because I don't have to. But that's next week's story. Shakespeare McCann on the record. I'll send you an advance copy."

"He's an evil guy," warned Mitch, taking a step closer. "And he's more dangerous than you think."

"I'm shaking."

"I'm gonna win this thing. And I'm gonna do it on what's important," said Mitch, cautioning Hollice in as emphatic a voice as he could muster without resorting to a shout. "And when I do, you might want me as something less than an enemy. Don't make me shut you out."

"It's only politics, Mitch. Get used to it. You win? One day *you'll* need *me*. It goes both ways."

"Wallowing in the mud is not the best way of getting clean," said Mitch, sounding a bit too lofty.

Hollice took a step forward, braving himself for the next shot. "If I wanted to throw mud, I'd have staked out that high-end piece of ass you got working media for you."

Mitch burned. "You got something you can prove? Don't be shy."

"She's a real hot potato. And from what I hear, you're not her first candidate—" Hollice stalled. He would've gone further, but he stopped short when Connie appeared on the steps behind Mitch.

Organ music sounded from the church. The casket was on its way, and the mourning mob along with it. Hollice thought it wise to take his leave, turning from Mitch and hustling back toward his rental car with the busted camcorder.

Shoop's five living brothers, plus one uncle, appeared at the top of the steps, the casket raised shoulder-high. Slowly they maneuvered down to the waiting hearse. Connie clutched Mitch's hand and pulled him clear.

"Was it bad?" she whispered.

"I smashed the tape."

"So that means it's okay."

He didn't have an answer.

The picture that ran on the front page of Tuesday's *Mirror* was in grainy black and white, lifted and enhanced from a low-lit piece of videotape. It depicted a somber Mitch Dutton and his wife observing the open casket of a confessed murderer. And though it wasn't the main headline, the photo made it above the *Daily Mirror*'s Sunday crease with a caption that read:

As if to confirm his anti-death-penalty stance, candidate for Congress Mitch Dutton attends Saturday funeral of a death-row inmate.

The technophobic Hollice Waters had *another* tape. All his fumbling and bumbling with the Sony Handycam had accidentally paid off. The first tape turned out to be a boring travelogue of the intrepid reporter's trip to New Orleans. By the time he'd slipped into the back of St. Ann's, he'd filled ninety percent of the first tape with pictures of the French Quarter and some soft-core porn he'd bootlegged off the motel's cable system. Hollice taped only ten minutes of the funeral service. When Mitch caught him outside on the steps, he had already pocketed tape number one and had just injected a fresh cassette.

Mitch had destroyed a blank tape.

For the candidate and his wife, the return trip from New Orleans was long and somber. Most of the drive, Connie played with the stereo, distracting herself and Mitch by surfing radio stations along the Gulf. They played "Name That Tune" games. But the bubble effect under which the trip was concocted had burst with the front-page fax Mitch had received Sunday morning from Fitz.

The weekend was over. The surprise was a sharp instrument named Hollice Waters.

Connie decided that news of the baby would have to wait. When she told him, it would have to be special, she thought. And not to save a botched vacation.

As the newspapers piled up that week, she purposefully kept away from TV news or talk radio, where it seemed every five minutes there was something *negative* about Mitch.

The baby couldn't read, but it could hear.

Hollice's story had set off an avalanche of unwelcome press on the death penalty issue. Like the cycles of the seasons, issues would flower and die based upon the ebbs and flows of the airwaves. For some reason, the media caught hold and seemed determined to rub the subject raw until there was no skin left on the Creole carcass of Shoop de Jarnot.

There were the initial news stories.

Candidate Attends Killer's Funeral.

Those were followed by the hackneyed tabloid takes on the matter.

The Candidate and the Killer: What Price Friendship?

Then there were radio talk shows and angry callers, asking questions of the on-air ratings-mongers.

Who does this Dutton think he is? Is he Texan or is he the devil?

And if all that wasn't enough for the baby's ears, there was the paid advertising by the opposition camp. Shakespeare McCann flooded the airwaves with attack ads about *Dutton and the Death Penalty,* leaving no question in the minds of the electorate where the candidates stood on the issue. Shakespeare was for. Dutton was against.

Which candidate for Congress is a friend of murder? Why, Mitch Dutton is. It's a fact that he thinks first-degree killers should live to see another day. And if they don't, he'll even cry at their funerals.

Shakespeare McCann believes in the death penalty the same way he believes in Texas. Vote McCann for Congress and put killers were they belong. Six feet under.

PART

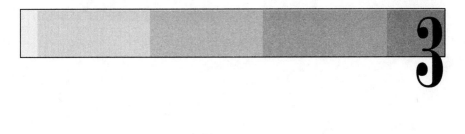

3

1

"That's it," said Rene, the video color bars on the monitor signaling the end of her presentation.

Mitch and Fitz had just endured the entire *oeuvre* of Shakespeare McCann's paid TV advertising. They'd already seen all the commercials in one form or another, catching them here or there. They just hadn't seen them in chronological order, beginning with spots introducing the public to Shakespeare the Candidate. Progressively, the ads had turned the spotlight away from McCann and onto Mitch Dutton, each one tossing another negative on the electoral fire.

"Roughly, we're looking at twenty-five percent Shakespeare-on-the-issues, seventy-five percent trashing Mitch," summed up Rene. "Now, compare that to our own reel, which, to date, runs eighty-five percent Mitch-on-the-issues and only fifteen percent anti-McCann. So congratulations." She poured on a healthy dose of sarcasm. "So far I'd call it a fairly well-scrubbed campaign."

"We didn't check behind his ears," joked Fitz, scratching a swelling mosquito bite on his thick neck.

"Like my daddy always said," joked Mitch, "If you can't say something nice about a fellah . . ."

"Why do I think your daddy never said such any such thing?" Rene said.

Mitch sunk back into the big office chair and threw his feet up on the desk. It was a rare jeans and sneakers day. "Unfair. That's privileged."

"It's not funny, Mitch. McCann's got the momentum," she shot back. "And these spots show why. He's nailing you where it counts. On TV."

"What about the liberal press? Weren't *they* supposed to be on my side?" he offered with mock innocence, knowing well enough how the *liberal media* had treated him so far.

"I think the leftist media died with Clinton," said Murray.

"It died of *embarrassment*," continued Mitch. The joking only partially eased the anguish of losing his front-runner's edge. He was determined to keep his wounded pride from leading to further bitterness. He was in the race until the end.

"Wanna hear some numbers?" asked Fitz, unsheathing the latest tracking polls.

"I'm starting to feel like a day without numbers is like an airplane ride without those little peanuts," returned Mitch.

"Fun time's over, Mitch. We have to move now if we're going to turn the tide."

"I'll hear the numbers if you all remember one thing." He met every gaze, making sure they were listening. "I wasn't in this thing in the first place. *I was the dark horse.*"

"Grow up," said Rene angrily. "You're the Goddamn front-runner and it's about time you start acting that way. And front-runners are supposed to win!"

He twisted to face her. The tone was unlike Rene. The silk in her voice had turned polyester. "What? You don't think I wanna win this?"

"Sometimes I wonder," she answered, her eyes falling back to her clipboard.

"Is that all?" he asked.

She took in a deep breath. "Sometimes I think your precious high ground was just a place you didn't want to give up in exchange for the seat. That's all."

"That's all?" he mocked. "For your information, I *lost* the high ground a while ago. Her name was Jenny O'Detts, remember?" Mitch spun sideways in his chair. "Now I'll just settle for being able to look myself in the mirror."

Fitz rolled on with the numbers. "Let's go back to July. Just before the O'Detts fuck-up. We were twenty-five points out front with a negative of barely thirty-two. After the fuck-up, we were up twenty-four, but the negative was up into the forty-two, forty-three percent range."

He gave a little look-see over his bifocals to make sure his candidate was listening. He flipped the page. "Okay. Twelve days back we were nineteen points. Not bad. Our negatives were holding under forty-five, with McCann's negatives at just thirty. Still manageable. Nothing to get scared about." And as Fitz flipped to the very last page, he took off his glasses. He didn't need to read these. They were tattooed to his heart.

"As of last night, after just four days of this death-penalty assault, our negatives pushed past the fifty percent mark. And when that happens—"

"Your numbers go south," finished Rene.

"It's a nine-point ball game, Mitch. Overnight, McCann's pulled ten points out of your rectum."

"Ask me if I regret going to New Orleans."

"Hell, no, I won't! Regret's something that happens on November third and you just lost by a single digit!"

"Fine. I'll say it, then. It was my fault!" Mitch held his arms high. Guilty as sin.

"Fuckin' A. So now we're even in the fuck-up department!"

"Fitz!" warned Rene. But Mitch cut her off.

"It was just like in the alley," banged the candidate, standing up and pacing. "Why can't I hear the footsteps? It's like he's been right next to me the whole time. Waiting for me to turn my back for just one second."

"So hit him back!" said Murray, about three months too late with the remark. Fitz shot him a look that said, *Shut the hell up.*

"I hit back, he just hits harder," answered Mitch with shrugged shoulders.

Rene crossed the room and boldly cut into his line of sight. "It's not all bad news. McCann's negatives are up ever since we started slapping him with the 'Who's Shakespeare?' ads."

"He's over forty percent. If we could push it higher, that would kill his momentum and put us dead even," challenged Fitz.

"I thought I was nine points ahead with likely voters."

"We got ten points worth of undecided. That's what makes it a horse race."

"So we hit again with negatives," said Mitch. "But *what* negatives? He's got no record. All he does is preach to the choir."

"We keep hitting with the 'Who's Shakespeare?' stuff. Think of it as feeding a slot machine. Bound to pay off sometime," said Fitz.

Rene slipped back into her sweetest Mississippi tongue. "Then we go to your strong suit. The issues."

"That's what we've been doing. And we're losing, right?"

"Not yet," said Fitz. "Everything from this point on is about timing."

"We make your strong suit his negative," Rene said smiling, "with a series of debates."

"And if he refuses?" Mitch jumped ahead of them. "If he refuses—this is Texas. He'll look like a loser. Afraid to fight."

"And that's what we'll put on TV," said Fitz, relishing the prospect.

"So he can't refuse the challenge," mused Mitch. He was liking the idea. "I get him in the ring and take him apart piece by little piece."

"The first one we sell as just a debate. The second one as the rematch," said Rene. "By the time we get to number three, won't be a local station that won't wanna carry us. *Prime time.*"

Who's Shakespeare McCann?

That was the fish Hollice wanted to land. The question was hanging on the lips of locals. Even those who liked McCann's politics were starting to wonder.

The timing was excellent. When the funeral story hit the newspaper, Hollice wanted to call in his chit. After three days of unreturned calls, the reporter's patience wore so thin that he dialed up a call-in show on Cathedral's TALK 101 where the candidate was guesting. The call screener put the reporter on hold and keystroked his name into the computer.

In the studio, local drive-time talk *meister* Barry Jarret acknowledged the engineer with a nod when Hollice's name showed up on the monitor. But Hollice would have to wait in line. McCann fans were lit up on all lines.

Answering a caller's question about the ever-dominating influence of foreign cars on the local highways, Shakespeare answered with one of his pat isolationist homilies. "You know? I don't get it. When I was just a little boy, I'd get something made in America in my Christmas stocking. That's one way I knew my momma loved me. But if I got something made in Korea, I wasn't so sure. Whaddayou think?"

While Hollice waited his turn in line, they piped the radio show in through his telephone handset. The next caller called himself true, blue, and Texan. A Democrat on the proverbial fence when it came to who he was going to vote for. "Dutton says some good things. He talks like a winner. And isn't that what we need in Washington? A winner?"

"He's still ahead in the polls, yessir," said Shakespeare. "But after this last week, you gotta know that the light he's been seein' at the end of the tunnel is an oncomin' train called Shakespeare McCann."

The caller on line nine was a Hurricane Hammond supporter from way back who couldn't imagine voting for anybody else. Shakespeare asked him, "You a football fan?"

"I am," said the caller.

"Cowboys or Oilers?"

"I like 'em both."

"No harm in that. So do I. But listen to what I'm sayin'," said the candidate. "We understand sports in this country, but we don't understand politics. Now, when we got a losin' football team, we fire the coach, get a new offense, a new quarterback. Follow me?"

"So far."

"Clean it up. Fix the machine. That's what we gotta do in politics. The problem with government today is that it scratches where there's no itch. I aim to *change* that. This country should be about tomorrow. And we can do it if you send your honorable vote my way."

Hollice listened, impressed to hear a different mixture in the usual McCann brew. The homespun wisdom was still the ever-present factor in Shakespeare's politics, but there were some new riffs he'd clearly copped from his opponent, Mitch Dutton. The bold look to the future. The concept of change. The words spun from McCann's mouth as if they were his own.

"Shakespeare McCann?" launched the reporter when his turn came. Forty minutes, he'd waited. He wasn't going to waste his breath. "This is Hollice Waters of the *Cathedral Daily Mirror*. Remember me?"

"Remember you?" laughed Shakespeare. "You're the reason I'm in this horse race. Folks? For my money, this is the only decent political reporter in the entire state. Lemme tell y'all somethin' about this guy. Can I, Hollice? You mind if I toot your horn for a piece?"

In front of tens of thousands of potential listeners, what could Hollice do but agree? "Sure. Be my guest."

"Just days before the news from New Orleans, my campaign office was hipped to my opponent's plans. As y'all know by now, Mitch

Dutton cried over the grave of a first-degree killer, who, I might add, he was trying to get *released* from a Texas prison," fudged Shakespeare over the air. Then he outright lied.

"Now, because of how Shakespeare McCann feels about this death penalty issue, I must've informed just about every reporter worth a plug nickel of what was gonna happen down in New Orleans. Yet Hollice Waters of the *Daily Mirror* was the only writer who thought enough of the public's right to know to pull up stakes and get on down to Louisiana and bring back the story. May I say publicly, Mr. Waters, Shakespeare McCann thanks you. My trusted campaign staff thanks you. And I especially think the voters thank you."

"That's awful kind of you, Mr. McCann," said Hollice. "But like I told you, I just write 'em the way I see 'em."

"You write 'em. The voters read 'em. And I'll ride 'em all the way to D.C. Yeeeha!" whooped Shakespeare, behaving as the preeminent *un*candidate.

"Speaking of writing them, Mr. McCann."

"Call me, Shakes, Hollice."

"How about that interview? I'm sure there's a lot more the public wants to know about you." There. He'd done it. He'd put Shakes on the spot.

"Sure thing. Lemme get back to some more callers and we'll hook up after the show."

Sure enough, after the radio program, Shakespeare called Hollice. Gone was the pitchman candidate at the bully pulpit. Shakes was short and to the point. "Good job on the New Orleans piece. But I didn't see any follow-up articles."

"Paper's on the auction block."

"Really. Who's buyin'?"

"Vidor Kingman."

"That a fact?"

"Solid gold. And my boss wants to play an even hand so he can keep his job," said Hollice. "Now, what about my interview?"

"I'll call later with the time and place." Shakespeare hung up before Hollice could respond.

2

he time and place were set for the evening of September 14. A
Saturday. The address was little more than a rural route number
down in Gilroy, south of town and just about halfway to Mexico.

Hollice, a man encumbered with the world's worst sense of direction, and who sometimes got lost in the *Daily Mirror* offices, followed
the map to Gilroy. From there he had to wait by a Shell station pay
phone until Shakespeare called with the rest of the directions. But
without the aid of street signs or a local map, he found himself stopping barefoot boys and dusty derelicts, asking directions. No help,
though. Hollice showed up nearly an hour late for the interview.

When he finally pulled down the two-and-a-half-mile dirt drive,
the sun had set and twilight was looming beyond the two huge pepper
trees that hung over a three-room ranch house with a twenty-five-
watt bulb for a porch light.

Odd, he thought. Yes, this was *the interview*. But here? It wasn't
even in the congressional district. Gravel crunched under his feet as
he crawled from the car and turned up the stone walk that led to the
front door. There was no doorbell, so he knocked. A voice called
out from inside—Shakespeare's—giving the go-ahead to come on in.
Hollice turned the knob and entered to a dim interior straight out of
some postwar ad in the *Saturday Evening Post*. Furniture. Pictures on

the wall. A woven rag rug. Most everything was covered by a thin layer of dust, the only exception being a Naugahyde sofa and a hoop-backed kitchen chair set nearby. To the side were piled threadbare sheets, which Hollice thought must've been covering this furniture for years upon untouched years.

Shakespeare appeared from the kitchen with a six-pack dripping wet from a Coleman cooler. "Cold one?" He tossed a can to Hollice before hearing an answer. "Fridge's been broke since sixty-four."

"I'm late. I'm sorry," said Hollice. "This is a ways out."

"Come here to think."

"Looks like it's been a while since then."

Shakespeare laughed. "Guess so. Have a seat. Couch is pretty comfy for an old beater." He took his seat in the old hoop chair, his skinny tailbone sliding forward and that sixer of beer dangling from one hand. "So let's get this started. I'm only good for as long as the beer holds out."

"How much beer you got?"

"Well, you were late. I already downed two. The one in your hand makes three. And I'm starting number four," sounded off Shakespeare, looking all too relaxed in a T-shirt and Wrangler blue jeans. "Subtract that from the case in the cooler, that'd leave us just about twenty."

"Sounds like a good start," said Hollice, trying to sound upbeat, but still unnerved by the lousy lighting. "What you got for power out here?"

"Got me a genny in the basement and gas enough to fuel the Indy Five Hundred."

"So why don't we get on with it?"

"This is *your* interview, friend. You got a question?"

Hollice had a question, all right. He had a list compiled from months of notations. Yet he started with what was on his mind.

"Whose house is this? Yours?"

"Yup," said Shakespeare with that single-syllable attitude.

Hollice challenged, "You buy it? How long ago? Feel free to fill in the blanks."

"My mother's house. She left it to me."

"When did she die?"

"Long time ago. Must be twenty years now."

"Did you live here?"

"No. Never even saw the place until after she died. A friend of hers tracked me down and said there was some property I'd inherited.

Turned out to me my mother's. Hadn't seen the woman since I was five years old."

"So you were abandoned?"

"By my mother? Well, I never looked at it that way, but if we were putting it in today's language—sure. She abandoned me *and* him."

"Him?"

"My old man. He's the one that raised me. Never talked about her, though. My whole life, she was just a bad memory." Shakespeare's beer was empty. In a practiced, single-handed move, one can was discarded and another was popped with a carbonated hiss.

"Nineteen," he reminded Hollice.

Hollice remembered he'd forgotten to start his tape recorder. A dead giveaway that the reporter was more nerves than cool. Quickly, from inside his jacket pocket, he withdrew his microcassette recorder and placed it on the arm of the couch, switching it on.

"What's that for?"

"I was going to tape this."

"Let's not."

"My memory is a sieve," said Hollice.

"I thought you was a Luddite. Hated machines."

"It's my only true surrender to technology. Can't do an interview without it."

"Makes me wonder what reporters ever did without tape."

"They wrote shorthand."

"Good enough. But no tape."

"No tape, no interview."

"Suit yourself." Shakespeare crossed his arms. "Don't let the door hit you in the caboose."

"You're kidding me."

"I thought we'd keep this casual."

"You said full disclosure."

"Yup. But I didn't say anything about tape. So you can stay and ask your questions or we can call it a date." Shakespeare waited. "Shame. You drove all the way down here, too."

After sitting on the horns of his dilemma for a good minute, Hollice pocketed the running tape player, replacing it with a pad and pen.

"Where were you born?"

"Texas. Atherton."

"Is there a birth record?"

"Somewhere. Must be," laughed Shakespeare. "I'm here, ain't I? But hell if I can find it."

"And you say your mother left when you were five. Then what?"

"My old man, he didn't like to stay in one place too long. Used to say, if it don't fit in the trunk of your car, you don't own it."

"So you traveled?"

"Here and there. The Midwest. Southeast. Florida some. Wherever there was a mark and his money."

Mark and his money?

Had Hollice heard right? "Your father was a con man?"

"Not just a con man. He was the original Grift Master." Then Shakespeare laughed. "If he hadn't been so addicted to cards and booze, I'da grown up rich."

"So on the record. Your old man *was* a con man."

"Oh, yeah. Kinda poetic, bein' that I'm just now gettin' into politics, don'tcha think?"

"And you're not worried about the voters finding out? Making associations?"

"Why would I? At this point it gives me a colorful upbringing. Tell me, what great Texan didn't have a colorful life? Didn't ol' Hurricane Hammond have a momma who used to whore in the gamblin'-boat days of Cathedral?"

"Yes. But it was something he always denied."

"Well, we're nearing the millennium. Time we all fessed up. Vote ourselves an honest politician. My daddy was a con man. What else you wanna know?"

"Con men are users. Oftentimes they use their kids. Were you involved in some of his schemes?"

"Are you asking if I know the difference between the Jamaican hustle and a common pigeon scheme? Hell yes. Did I ever run 'em myself? Well, I was just a kid. I liked my daddy. Wanted him to love me. Liked to help him out. What kid wouldn't?"

"Did you know what you were doing was wrong?"

"Knew it was the devil's work. But my daddy was a devilish kinda fellah."

Hollice was floored. A thrill shot through his body. He gathered himself, trying hard not to write the story in his head during the interview. He knew he should just keep asking questions and writing answers. Sift and collate later.

"When did your father die?"

"When I was ten. We were in Florida and I had nobody. Didn't know where my mother was. So I got by on the street runnin' a three-card monty table and gettin' chased by the local cops.''

"Ever get caught?"

"Yup."

"How many times?"

"Time enough to get me an education. If it weren't for foster parents and boys' farms, I don't think I'd have gotten any kind of learnin'. Books was always good. Books taught me a lot. But when a kid hits the streets after a turn or two in some kind of institution, he goes back to what he's got. Fifteen-year-old boy can't learn to make a wage in work camp. But if he's got a girl he's sweet on and wants to buy her some flowers, a quick-change artist can buy those flowers and still have money left over for an egg cream.''

"You used to make quick change?"

"What do you think the Fed does? Interests rates go up and down all the time. It's the same game. What we need is a politician that can see through all them Ponzi schemes Uncle Sam plays on us every day.''

"Let's go back. Whatever happened to that girlfriend?"

Without much prodding, the strange man launched into a torrid tale of his first love. A sixteen-year-old named Charlotte from Gainesville, Florida. Without a roof over his head or a dollar in his pocket, he swindled her old man out of pocket change for dates with nothing more than a smile on his face and a borrowed cadet's uniform from the local military academy. The girl's father finally caught on to the scheme, phoned the local PD, and had Shakespeare locked up just to keep the two teenagers apart long enough for their hormones to cool.

"Poor old boy didn't know we'd already done the dirty deed in the back of his pickup truck," recalled Shakespeare.

Hollice put his pencil down. He'd been there nearly an hour, but felt the need for a reality check. "Two beers. That's all you've had?"

"Four. Plus this one. You haven't been listening."

"Get straight with me here. What's your angle with this?"

"Ain't figured it out yet, have ya?" teased Shakespeare, sounding offhanded.

"You realize what my headline is? 'Candidate McCann is Former Con Man.' Dutton could sink you with it."

"I'll make it plain. I'm out to show that politics is *all* one big con. Short cons. Long cons. Dutton's campaign! Now, that's a con. So was Hammond's. Who better to bust open the rotten melon but the farmer who grew it?"

"Sounds like the George Washington cherry tree theory of truth and consequences."

"You can get away with anything as long as you tell someone about it," laughed Shakespeare. "Well, I'm tellin' *you*. What you do with it, well, that's for us to talk about later on."

"How about now?"

"Your interview. My life. What's next?"

"Okay. Fine. So your true campaign game is truth or dare?"

"I'm runnin' up even with Dutton. The voters are now expecting to see a lot of *politics as usual*. Punch, counterpunch. Attack ads. Negative, negative, negative," said Shakespeare. "I'm sayin' this is where the tracks split. So I aim to give the voters the real thing. Turn it all upside down. Be the first candidate to be elected on the truth of the matter. Full disclosure. I'll wear my life like a badge of honor. The public'll love it." Then with a subtle wink, "And I expect, so will you."

"You think so?" challenged Hollice.

"Look around. We both see the same thing. We got us some convicted killers who got higher polling figures than the president himself. Why? Cuz they call it as they see it, with nothing to hide. Everything they got to say is golden. Public is perched on their every word. They're craving *the real deal*. I'm here to fill the bill. And one day you're gonna write about it."

"Try tomorrow."

"Let's stick with today."

Sweat dripped down Hollice's thick legs. He wasn't hearing one story. It was much bigger. In five parts with a Sunday sum-up.

Thank God for the tape.

"You're either crazy or smarter than the rest of us," said Hollice.

"You gotta wait for the end of the movie to find out," reminded Shakespeare.

The empty beer cans were slowly stacked in a neat pyramid next to McCann's chair. And with each dead solider came another story of a scam run by the young Shakespeare McCann. How he'd worked boiler-room operations, selling miracle vitamins or bogus vacation schemes. Summers, he'd work the deep South, hustling personally embossed Bibles. Only the Bibles would never arrive.

"And you can document all of this?" worried Hollice, who'd had a few beers of his own by now.

"I could. But I won't. I'd done all this under so many damned assumed names, Social Security numbers, it'd be near impossible to figure. I don't remember most of 'em myself. Bill Hodges is one. Carlton McGrew was 'nother. My old man used to say, the crazier the name, the more likely a fellah was to believe it."

"How about Shakespeare McCann? Is that your actual name?"

"Good question. Wondered it myself from time to time. My mother's maiden name was Neville. There's a record of that. And she married William McCann. But whether that was my old man's actual name or some phony is a mystery."

"And you say there's no birth certificate?"

"Like I said before. Ain't one. Dare you to find it. I've looked. Tore this house apart once, lookin' for some kind of record."

"There has to be something. School records?"

"Sure there is. But by the time I was in school, we'd moved on and I'd have a new name in every town. I remember I was a Mike Burdsall somewhere in Indiana around the fifth grade. I hated that name. Everybody always called me Birdy on account that I was so skinny." Shakespeare swilled the last of another beer and added the empty to the stack. "'Nother?"

"No, thanks. Let's get back to this birth certificate. I thought the rules to run for office required proof of identity. Including a birth certificate."

"You forget. I was in the print shop business."

"You *forged* your birth certificate?"

"Didn't see any harm in it. *I was born Shakespeare McCann.* That much, I know." Shakespeare spoke this time with undue emphasis. "Should I be denied a chance at public service because my daddy was a con man and my momma a no-good whore?"

"Well, no. I don't think—" stammered Hollice. "It's just that you could be anybody. You could make up any story."

"You think I'm makin' this up?"

"Well, no . . ."

"But you want proof, anyway?"

"It would put it all in a context I might understand better. Without documentation . . ."

Nobody would believe the story.

"If I can't corroborate, I can't print," said Hollice.

"That ain't my problem, is it?"

"Shit! Nobody will believe this!"

"I don't care about anybody else."

"Excuse me?" asked Hollice.

"I only care that *you* believe it."

"What do you care what *I* believe?"

"Scenario one," began Shakespeare. "I get elected. I'm going to need a chief of staff. You're candidate number one."

If Hollice was in the dark, it was all getting blacker. Shakespeare had shifted gears sideways. If that was at all possible. "Are you offering me a job?"

"It's not an offer."

"I can still say no."

"Scenario number two. I get elected. And Vidor Kingman buys your newspaper. I guarantee you, he'll be all over me just like he was all over ol' Hurricane. I ask a favor. You get the shaft. End of story."

"Scenario three. Dutton gets elected."

"He won't get elected," said Shakespeare cryptically.

"So this is a threat," confirmed Hollice.

"It's an opportunity," said Shakespeare, his voice dropping an octave while that patented twang dimished, the tone barely distinguishable from the average Yankee. "Look at you. You've spent your life printing other people's bullshit. Sure, every once in a while maybe you get to tell it the way it is. But deep down, you know that you're nothing more than the local publicity hack, willing to print just about anything the local whosits say just so you can fill in a six-inch column that pays your rent."

How the fuck would you know?

That was the next question. One Hollice dared not ask.

Shakespeare continued, "I bet you've sent your stuff just about everywhere. *Washington Post. New York Times. Chicago Tribune*—"

"And what if I have?"

"Well, you're still here. That says it all, I think."

"Maybe I like it here."

"Chief of staff job. Onetime offer. Washington, D.C. Think of the connections you'll make. It's not too late to win that Pulitzer."

That's when Hollice heard it. *Pulitzer Prize.* And the sudden absence of accent from Shakespeare's tongue. "What happened to your voice?"

The South Texas flavor returned with a smile. "My voice? Nothin', far as I can reckon. Maybe you got a bug in your ear."

"My hearing's fine."

"So what's your answer?"

"I want to think about it."

"What time is it?"

"Nine-fifteen."

"Time's up. It's decision time."

"You can't be serious."

"There's more, you know," teased the candidate. "We ain't even talked about my life as a grown-up."

The reporter's pulse raced. If there was more, his natural instinct wanted to hear it all. But that would mean an answer in the affirmative. Then there was the threat. Vidor Kingman hadn't yet bought the paper. It was only a rumor. Did Shakespeare know better?

Hollice resolved to lie. "Okay. I'm in. Could be fun."

Shakespeare grinned his widest grin ever, popped his next beer, and took a hearty swig before the first gas could escape the can. Next, he pulled up his T-shirt to reveal a small tattoo just above his navel. "Get a good look at that. Good'n close if you have to."

Hollice leaned forward, reading the first letter, *T*, which was crudely drawn in a Gothic script. "What's it say?"

" 'Time waits for me.' "

"What's it mean?"

"To you? Nothin'. But to me? Just about everything. Where I got it's the proof you're lookin for," said Shakespeare with an amused grin. "Taylor State Prison. Just outside of Charlotte, North Carolina."

Bingo. Hollice gulped. "You did time?"

Shakespeare pulled his shirt back down. "So there you have it. Your proof. That ties us up. You and me for the long haul. All the way to Washington."

"How much time?" asked Hollice.

"Twelve years. Best time a man could do. Straightened me out. Set me on the path to reclaim what my daddy took from me."

"And what was that?"

"My name. My destiny."

"Prison taught you to run for office?"

"Prison taught me to stop runnin' and hold my ground. Inside, you see, there's no place to go. You either stand tall or take it up the ass. And I wasn't gonna take it no more, if you get my meaning," said Shakespeare in a sudden and somber voice. "Grifters—like my old man—they were always runnin'. Movin' on before anybody could catch on to their coattails."

"How'd you get pinched?"

"Oh, I'd been runnin' this career scam up and down the Carolinas. Sellin' opportunity overseas. Three-piece suit. Nice haircut. But with a different face." He laughed.

"Country was in recession. I'd place an ad in the newspaper and charge two hundred and fifty dollars for a one-day seminar about jobs in exotic places like the Philippines and Saudi Arabia. Had this telephone set up on a speaker box and we'd call my partner in some godforsaken place and teleconference part of the meeting. Except I wouldn't be calling overseas. I'd set the dialer up on the phone so the furthest it could call was the Ramada Inn a few blocks away. My partner would take calls from the fellahs in the room. Later I'd show some charts and give 'em some bullshit IQ tests to assess whether they're corporate material."

"Lemme guess. They all passed."

"You're right with me. Anyway, I'd shake hands and take their deposits, making sure to close shop by two o'clock so we could make it to the bank and cash the checks before anybody got wind of us. Nightfall, we'd be in the next county."

"But you got caught anyway."

"Yup. My partner dropped a dime and gave me up. Best thing that ever happened to me. If I saw the rat bastard today, I'd probably give him a kiss," mused Shakespeare.

"And this former partner?" said Hollice, hoping for some kind of lead he could run down.

"He's dead. At least I'm pretty sure."

"How would you know?"

"Cuz I know the fellah that killed him. Former cell-mate from Taylor who thought he was doing me a favor. Sent me a letter. It was pretty descriptive," said Shakespeare.

As Hollice's stomach turned, he pressed on. "What about your prison records?"

"A little work and a lotta luck. First dollar I made after I got out went right back into the joint. I paid a trustee to lose my records in the incinerator. Pictures. Prints."

"There's got to be copies."

"Dare you to find 'em. Back then there weren't no national databases for us criminal types. All that was left to destroy were the state and local records. A few dollars here, a favor there—"

"A little blackmail."

"You're catchin' on. Not that hard to erase an alias. And before Taylor, all my arrests were juvenile. *And those fingerprint records are sealed.*"

"What about your face?" dug Hollice. "No pictures."

"Somewhere, I reckon. But they don't look like me."

"Don't tell me. You paid for plastic surgery."

"Didn't pay. Had me a little accident in the pen, so the state paid for the reconstruction. Dumb bastards never got a new picture before I was furloughed."

Wiping his brow, Hollice slumped in his chair. It was all so overwhelming. Unbelievable. A totally tall tale, impossible to document with the exception of the tattoo. And Shakespeare could've gotten that anywhere.

"I know," said Shakespeare. "It's like swallowing a Big Mac in a single bite."

"What am I supposed to do with this information?"

"Cure your curious soul."

"I'm an atheist."

"Of course you are!" Shakespeare slapped his knee. "You're part of the God-forsaking cultural elite. Those that believe that the power of the pen is the only way to the ultimate truth."

"I don't analyze it that way."

"Well, if you ever did, I'm here to tell you it ain't so. Prison shows you that. There's right and wrong, good and evil. And a jail cell is purgatory, where a man is given the choice to go one way or the other. Let's take that Creole boy, Shoop de Jarnot, for example."

"He didn't choose. He died of food poisoning."

"Sure he did. But there's poison food and food that gets poisoned."

"Excuse me? You saying he was murdered?"

"It's a game in there. The guards as well as the cons. And money gets you just about anything you want. Cigarettes. Suicide hangings. Poison foods."

"You *killed* Shoop de Jarnot?"

"I pushed the button. You see, I had this feeling he was gonna win that appeal that Dutton wrote for him. Not a whole lotta political play in that. Best I could do was make Dutton look like a good lawyer who couldn't stomach capital punishment. Buncha intellectual hoo-ha a voter'd never get." Shakespeare sat forward, thrilled at the prospect of sharing his genius. "But get Dutton to show up at a funeral for the murderin' SOB, now, that's a story I can make hay out of. Thanks to you, of course."

Hollice swallowed hard. "But you're confessing to murder here."

"Good idea to know the fellah you'll be serving."

"Who do *you* serve?"

"Ain't but two masters in the Grand Scheme."

A flop sweat broke out on Hollice's forehead, leaking through his thinning hair. His armpits swelled with fluid. How could a man confess to such an act? And where was the obvious flaw in Hollice's character that would lead McCann to believe that he'd go along? Just like that. He'd never demonstrated that Machiavellian kind of ambition. Or had he? He suddenly had a mind to bolt, hit the road running, and stop the first damn cop he passed on the highway. Tell the whole story.

But Shakespeare killed Shoop de Jarnot. He could kill you.

Perspiration had darkened Hollice's pink shirt to magenta. "This is too much. You're pulling my chain."

"Am I?"

"You've had too much to drink. Let's finish this some other time. Sober."

Hollice stood to leave, but found Shakespeare's boot stuck in his chest, shoving him back down into the couch. "Now, that wasn't our deal. We'd talk as long as the beer lasts. Why don't you dry off? Have another cool one and ask me some more questions."

Questions?

Hollice feared another painful boot in the chest. The candidate was worse than a drunk. Alcoholic. The awful kind of drunk who turned sour and bitter at the first sip. A drunk who would lie for affection. It was chemical, hoped the reporter. He'd been late, the candidate had been drinking, and the booze in Shakespeare's brain had left him contemptible, unbalanced, and irrational. Surely he would sleep it off, call Hollice the next day, and apologize.

It was all one big joke.

A benign question surfaced in time to kill the awkward silence. Words caught in Hollice's dry throat, so he softened his larynx with a powerful gulp of the warming brew. "So why politics?" he asked, not giving a crap about the answer. He wanted out.

"Dumb question," answered Shakespeare. "Fool's question."

And with that, the candidate's relaxed posture slowly stiffened, the good ol' smile diminishing to a smirk. *Now, the right question?* thought Shakespeare. It'd been there all along for him to pick out if the idiot had been listening half a whit.

It had been Shakespeare's personal chore to push Hollice to the brink of the man's personal code. Place him square in the middle of the moral crossroads and see which side he'd chose. Ally? Or enemy?

And Hollice had made his choice.

"Why politics?" answered Shakespeare in his best political persona. "Well, it's the ultimate grift, ain't it?"

"You want to put the *con* back in *Congress*," Hollice tried to joke.

"I'll do you one better. Politics is the only con where the mark *wants* to be had."

And nobody puts you in prison.

Hollice followed up quickly, but his voice was faltering, filling with phlegm. "What about . . . You said something about truth. The farmer who broke open his own rotten melons?"

What about him?

"Truth is the greatest con of all," remarked Shakespeare, whose mind flashed back to the books he'd piled in his cell. Books of self-awareness. Self-esteem. Philosophy. Religion. Each one of 'em lamenting about the absolute truth. And not a one of 'em agreed with the other. From Buddha to Nietzsche and every motherfucker in between. Liars all. Betrayed by their own conceited intellects.

"It took me a while, but I finally figured it. Ain't no such thing as absolute truth. Only real truth is the way the other fellah sees it." With his index fingers Shakespeare traced an imaginary frame around himself. "It's like this. You see me. You hear what I say. You don't know if it's true or false. But it scares you. And once I know that you're scared, that's all the truth I need to know. Get me?"

Show me the politician that goes to jail and I'll show you a dog with wings, an old con had told Shakespeare, wise and cement-hardened. *They the ones that build the joints. Ain't a one of 'em ever bent over when he didn't want it.*

"Prison don't teach a man," continued Shakespeare. "It changes him into an animal that don't know nothin' more than four walls and the shiv under his mattress that keeps him safe. That's why they always go runnin' back."

"But not you."

"Not me," said the candidate, popping open another beer and offering it to Hollice.

Half a can later, Hollice finally came up for air.

"Pretty thirsty, huh?"

"Dry out here." But the brew that Hollice thought might calm his nerves made his heart flutter and put a buzz in his head. The reporter's new tack was to keep the candidate talking until the man

262 / DOUG RICHARDSON

was drunk himself. A danger to nobody. Especially Hollice. Afterward the reporter would make a fast exit and be off to make copies of the tape and find himself a lawyer.

"What I don't understand was how you figured to get in the race in the first place. Hammond was unbeatable, and now that I think about it, you didn't beat him. If he hadn't fallen off his horse . . ."

Shakespeare answered the question inside his own head.

I watched the old man. He was like a clock—he'd wake up drinking, work, drink some more, work, then rest. And when Hurricane was done resting, he'd drink himself into a stupor.

Hollice caught the sudden daze in Shakespeare. The faraway look. Hell if the alcohol wasn't finally doing its dirty work. Hollice offered up another beer. "You empty? How about another?"

Those dogs. The old man loved those dogs. Couldn't bear if they ever got away from him. So what I did was cut up two live stew rabbits and drag 'em behind a rented horse. Those hounds, they took to that blood like it was stink on a turnip. I knew it wouldn't be long before that ol' mare got lathered and tossed ol' Hurricane for a loop.

The candidate's gaze was fixed and unwavering. Trancelike. Hollice was certain the booze had finally found the cerebral cortex.

The hard part was the embolism. Couldn't guarantee if the mare threw the old man that he'd die. Tough old fucker, found him up against the tree and breathin' hard. Probably the booze that saved him from a broken neck. Yet all I had to do was act like I was a doctor, and he let me do what I pleased. I found a scuff mark on Hurricane's neck. Good spot to stick a needle. After that, wasn't but a second before I found the vein and fired off a syringe full of air. Then bingo! It was over in a heartbeat.

"Mr. McCann?" asked Hollice, looking for some kind of response.

He was the incumbent. He needed to go.

"Fifteen primary points. That's all Shakes McCann needed to get in the big race. Now look at me."

Oh, Hollice looked. He looked dead-on at Shakespeare and finally saw what was coming, tracing the outline of Shakespeare's dangling left arm. The one that had always held a beer ripe and ready for another swig. Only the beer was gone. Dangling from Shakespeare's hand was a folding Buck Knife, locked open and twisting in his grip.

"I killed Hurricane because I couldn't beat him," whispered Shakespeare.

But I can beat Dutton.

Easing closer, he slipped the knife inside Hollice's coat, pulling away the flap until the pocket and the tape recorder were clearly visible, including that little red light that indicated extended recording mode.

"It hurts being right all the time," said the melancholy candidate.

"Please don't hurt me. I'll do anything—"

"Be quiet."

Hollice obeyed, shuddering a nod. His eyes wide like a stupefied rodent caught in the blaze of oncoming headlights. Shakespeare stood slowly and eased across to the sofa. A warm stain appeared between Hollice's legs as fear released his bladder. Then, speaking with a wispy inflection, he said, "I'm not a fighter."

"I know," whispered back Shakespeare, having sized up his mark long before he ever thought to strike. "Just relax. It'll be over in just a little moment."

Shakespeare straddled Hollice like a lover, his small frame suddenly feminine in the manner it sat astride his victim, his shadow casting a calming darkness.

Hollice never saw the blade again. Shakespeare simply pulled his victim's head to his chest in a warm embrace and slid the knife just underneath the reporter's skullcap. Hollice tensed but felt nothing. His spinal cord severed, all that was left were motor functions. His arms flailed briefly and his pelvis twisted under Shakespeare's bantam weight. But medically speaking, Hollice was already dead.

He'd died knowing the truth.

All excepting that story about the house. It didn't belong to Shakespeare. It was just an old slab and Sheetrock shack he'd known about since his photo-finishing days. He knew that the owner had passed away and the property was in permanent probate. He knew of the small generator in the garage that could power some light in the house. Most important, he knew of the dry well that was fifty paces off the back porch, covered by scrub brush and weathered two-by-sixes. He rolled Hollice's rug-wrapped corpse in a rusted wheelbarrow, then dumped it down the hole. One hundred feet.

To erase the crime, all the house required was a lit cigarette taped to a beer can full of kerosene. The fingerprints were lost in a blaze that lit up the sky for miles around. It would be ashes before fire crews would arrive. By then, Shakespeare had rolled Hollice's car into a nearby reservoir. His own car was parked inconspicuously at an all-night watering hole a mile farther up the highway. Only a fifteen-minute hike.

Heading back toward the Island, he completed his task. Dialing from a cellular phone, he added a message to Hollice's *Daily Mirror* mailbox.

"*Hello. This is Hollice Waters and you've reached my voice mail. Please leave a message.*"

"Hollice, ol' buddy. This is Shakespeare McCann. And the last time I got stood up, she was a helluva lot prettier than you. Guess you got a good reason. Hope she was worth it. Give me a call whenever you want that interview. I'm off to candidate's slumberland. G'night."

Inevitably the Cathedral PD investigators got around to replaying Hollice's messages, finding the mailbox nearly at its electronic capacity. Amongst the cavalcade of usual rumors and tips, Shakespeare's singular call was merely one of many, sandwiched in between the usual political hearsay, a confirmed credit card reservation at a Guadalajara hotel for that very same weekend, and a death threat from an alleged Dutton supporter.

The tangle left the investigators scratching their heads.

3

Mr. Dutton. Along with donations from what might be called your average voters, back in July you were endorsed with a thousand-dollar donation from African-American activist Jamal La Croix. In a time when black role models such as O.J. Simpson, Michael Jackson, and Snoop Doggy Dog are suffering so many indignities in the press and the courts, how do you see yourself filling those shoes?"

Mitch made a smooth turn from the imagined questioner to the TV camera, giving himself a slight moment of thoughtful contemplation before answering. "In a country where we have over twenty-seven million African-Americans, a great many of whom are adults who get up every morning, send their children to school, and go to jobs, we have better than sixty percent of our African-American population living above the poverty level, a significant improvement over twenty years ago when it was forty percent. These good people are the role models of today—"

"Good answer, but listen to *these* numbers," Rene interrupted the mock debate, the lights catching her taupe suit and dangerous hair. "Eight out of ten men have their hands on the remote. They've got small penises and short attention spans."

"Keep my answers shorter," acknowledged Mitch.

The rented TV soundstage sported dual podiums and working

television cameras to help him acquire a better feel for the forum. It was October and they were only one day away from the real debates.

Rene examined Mitch closely, continuing the coaching. "Okay. The makeup seems to be working. You're not sweating yet. But don't be fooled. *Everybody* sweats under these lights. The trick is to get touch-ups during the commercials."

He remembered her telling him of her brief sufferance under the lights as a political TV commentator for some independent channel in Mississippi. She'd had the right looks and the velvet voice to seal some down-home ratings. But she'd hated it.

"Don't face the camera except during your opening and closing remarks."

"I've been thinking about that," he said. He'd remembered Hammond's style of speaking directly to the viewer.

"Talking to the camera is out of vogue," she answered. "Remember. This is a TV show. Folks are tuning in because they're expecting a drama between you and McCann. Direct your answers to whoever asks the question until it engages your opponent. Then go for the jugular. The viewers are gonna want to see some blood."

At the back of the room paced a not-so-calm Fitz, rifling through the latest tracking results. Occasionally he'd glance up to the debate rehearsal, but with nothing to offer. Rene was the pro. She knew all about TV. Seen her work before. Fitz's job was to stay on top of the numbers. And the numbers weren't good.

The tide had clearly turned to McCann's advantage. His TV was hitting hard on the same old point. The death penalty. Not only that, but in the tradition of the great campaign devils, Willie Horton being the heavyweight champ of all time, the deceased Shoop de Jarnot was fast becoming the poster child for capital punishment. Shakespeare McCann gave out Shoop T-shirts on his weekend bus and truck shows around the county. The old school bus, painted red, white, and blue, would appear at shopping malls and parks, followed by a flatbed outfitted with a public address system. After ten minutes of music and the free ice cream that had come to symbolize the McCann campaign, Shakespeare himself would step out onto the stage and give a rip-roaring twenty minutes on the evils of Democrats and Mitch Dutton, lawyer and lover of those who'd take a life. Then he'd hawk those damn Shoop de Jarnot T-shirts for ten bucks a taker and be off to his next stop.

The numbers were bad.

McCann was ten points back in the popular vote. But only four points among the likely voters. If the weather was bad, he'd fair even better. Dead even, figured the paid pollster. The indisputable election fact that bad weather meant bad news for Democrats loomed in the show runner's mind. The Dutton negatives were way up. No thanks to Shoop and Hollice Waters. Fitz cursed himself for ever letting Mitch go to New Orleans. It revealed his weakness. The reason so many candidates under him had lost elections and given him such a losing record in recent years. He let the friggin' candidates run the fuckin' show!

Dead even, thought Fitz. *It's a horse race now.*

While the rehearsal continued, Murray entered from the stage door, stalling a moment to watch Mitch and Rene before angling for Fitz.

"So what do you want—the bad news or the worse news?" offered Murray in a hush.

"Don't tease me! Just tell me!" said Fitz, his voice loud enough to capture the attention of the other two.

"Something we should know about?" asked Mitch.

"Sorry Mitch," said Murray. "It can wait."

"Give it up," pushed Fitz. "Let's hear all of it."

Murray halved the distance between the rehearsal space and Fitz. Then he let loose with the news. "Vidor Kingman is—"

"Is dead?" asked Rene.

"No. He's endorsing McCann," was Fitz's guess.

"Just let him finish," ordered Mitch, who hated guessing games. He simply wanted to know.

"Vidor Kingman," continued Murray, "has endorsed his very own *independent* candidate."

"Independent?" asked Rene in sudden shock. Kingman was the ultimate party player. Both sides of the aisle.

"Independent party?" asked Mitch.

"A new party," answered Murray. "He's found himself the *environmental candidate.*"

The room went silent long enough for all parties to do their own arithmetic. Support from Kingman meant money and press. But even worse, an *environmental candidate* would automatically cut into Dutton's slice of the electorate—the wide-left liberals who'd vote Democrat for lack of anybody else who might hear their call. Mitch had catered to these voters, having mailed extensively on the subject, and

268 / Doug Richardson

he brandished a record of serious environmental credentials. These were his constituency, now taken from him by Kingman in an obvious public relations effort.

"Well, fuck him!" groused Fitz. "He'll probably want his candidate to debate."

"No can do," said Rene. "Format's already set."

"It helps McCann," said Mitch. "He's gonna want to add him to the bill. He got a name?"

Murray went through his pockets until he came up with a note. "Yeah. Peter Garret Dunphy."

"Know him," said Mitch. "Smart guy. He worked with me on settling some corporate stuff."

"Just tell me he's got a terrible case of acne and I'll put him on the show," groused Fitz. "So what's the worse news?"

"The new Hollice Waters rumor."

"You mean the one where he told Kingman that they ought to change the name of the paper to the *Daily Moron*?" said Fitz.

"I thought all trails led to Mexico," said Mitch.

"I got this one off the bulletin board of the McCann Web page."

"Murray. This soundstage is costing us two hundred an hour."

"Okay," continued Murray. "The rumor is that we've got a wealthy contributor with mob ties."

"Of course," said Fitz, "they wouldn't say who."

"It's a conspiracy theory. This business guy wants you in office. Hollice Waters knew about the mob stuff. So they had him rubbed out."

"*Rubbed out?*" laughed Mitch.

"Don't laugh," said Fitz. "I wouldn't put anything past McCann once the cameras light up."

"Can we deal with the issue at hand?" Rene centered herself amid the group. "I think we're going to be asked for a format change by McCann in order to accommodate this new candidate—"

Fitz's cell phone rang from inside his coat pocket. He reached inside and flipped open the receiver. "Hello?"

"*Fitz? It's Marshall.*"

Covering the receiver, he nodded to Rene. "It's Marshall Lambeer. I betcha he's gonna ask us to change the fuckin' format."

"Gimme the phone," asked Mitch with his hand out.

"I got this handled," said Fitz.

"I'm sure you do. Give it to me, anyway." He locked eyes with Fitz, holding out his hand until Fitz submitted. He instantly put the phone up to his ear and said, "Marshall? Mitch Dutton here. Put Shakespeare on, will you?"

All eyes were on Mitch as he peeled away from the group in favor of a darker corner of the stage.

"Marshall? I know he's there," pressed Mitch. "I'll bet you don't send out for lunch unless McCann's standing right over your shoulder. Now, put the SOB on the phone before I come over there and do this in person!"

He gave a wink back toward his team. He was enjoying this.

"This is Shakespeare McCann."

Mitch went right after him. "Listen, you little shit. We're not changin' the format to accommodate a party crasher. And if you dodge this, I swear to God I will take it right to the media. I'm gonna say that Shakespeare McCann would use any excuse whatsoever to avoid confrontation with me on the issues."

"What? You suddenly grow some balls? Wasn't that long ago you caught a lickin' in that back alley."

"I've turned my back on you for the last fuckin' time. I know better. I'm doin' this head-on. Man to man."

"Shake hands and come out fightin'. Just like that?"

"Just like that. So are we gonna get it on? If not, I've got a campaign to win."

"You know, I could go to the media myself. Say we were excluding the all-important environmental candidate. Call you the Democrat that ain't for democracy. Wave the fuckin' flag and say you're not inclusive."

"And I'll call you chickenshit to every newspaper and TV camera that'll have me!" spat Mitch.

"Chickenshit?"

"Those words exactly."

The soundstage was silent. Team Dutton, waiting on pins and needles while Mitch held out for an answer.

"Okay, partner. You want at me? Fine. Let's go a few turns in front of the cameras. And when I get done with you, you're gonna wish you was back behind the Mairzy Doats Café."

Mitch didn't care to respond. He flipped up the receiver on the phone and tossed it back over to Fitz.

"We're on," he said.

As Murray shadowed Mitch out to his car, the daylight outside the studio left the candidate blind, squinting, and fishing for his sunglasses.

"These are from HQ." Murray handed Mitch the stack of pink phone slips. "The one on top's from your father."

"Thanks for the reminder. Anything else?"

The door was open, thought Murray. He'd been waiting for the right chance to hit Mitch up for a staff position come January, should the Democrat win. But he worried a bit too long whether this was his moment.

"Mitch!" called Rene from across the parking lot. "Wait up a second."

Mitch nodded that he'd wait for her. "Something you wanted to say, Murray?"

"Nothing. I'll just see you later."

"Wear your seat belt, hot dog," joked Mitch.

As Murray exited, Rene swiveled her way toward him, serpentining the parked cars and looking far too cool for Indian Summer. Fall had arrived, but in name only. For Mitch it might have been better to think about the weather instead of gazing at Rene, whose legs stretched from underneath her smart suit with every southern step nearer to him. He feared being alone with her.

"What's the hurry?" she asked.

"Got a lunch. Harvey Benton of the Cathedral Business Round Table." There was ice in his voice that was hard to miss.

"Fitz set you up?"

"Of course. I'll pay for lunch, then put a gun to his head and ask him to give the campaign ten thousand dollars."

"Well, I hope you don't say that tomorrow night."

"What do *you* think?"

"I think you're avoiding me."

"Look," he said. "I don't know what I'm going to say tomorrow night." He was still steaming from the phone call. When she looked at his face, he looked cool behind the glasses. But his hands shook when he unlocked his car door.

"I'm not talking about the debate."

He was afraid of that. He was afraid to be cornered by her, alone with her, or too close to her. It was too easy. All he had to do was reach out and touch . . .

"Can we sit in your car?" She was looking around.

"I'm late."

"It won't take a minute."

With a nod, Mitch crawled in, reached over, and opened the passenger door. Rene walked around the car and sat, knees together, her skirt hiked up to midthigh.

"I know I've said I've been here before—"

But I'm in love with you.

"—but when you won't even let me get close enough to whisper," she finished, trying not to crack in front of him. "I've got work to do. You've got to let me do it."

"I wasn't aware I was impeding your work."

And he wasn't. It was just her way into the *real* issue.

"Do you regret it?"

"Regret what?" he said, uncomfortably playing dumb.

"The sex."

No avoiding it now. So he tried to make it about him. Spare her feelings. "I regret falling off the fidelity wagon."

"You would." She nodded a bit too emphatically.

"Look. When it comes to me and Connie . . . I don't know what's going to happen. I know I still love her. I know she doesn't deserve this."

"The campaign?"

"Yes. I promised I wouldn't take her from the Island."

"She may get her wish."

Mitch didn't miss the implication. "So you think I might lose after all."

"I'm sorry. I didn't mean it that way."

"Sure sounded that way to me."

"I've just had some bad . . . *thoughts*. Feelings, you know?"

He waited.

"I *have* been here before, Mitch. And I thought I'd seen all of them. Good ones, bad ones, honest, corrupt."

"But nobody like me," he jested.

"Nobody like *McCann*. No telling what he might pull on TV."

He bravely took her hand in his. "It'll be okay. The worst thing that could happen is that I'll lose."

"To win, you've got to care more than that."

"It's not life or death. It's only politics."

Then came the nonsequitur. "I've been offered a job."

He wondered if he'd heard right.

"They just lost a key consultant and need someone fast. I'd have to start before November."

"Whoa," said Mitch. "Who, what, when, and where?"

"Not why?"

"I'll get to that. Now, let's have it. Who wants to steal *you* from *me*?"

Rene tingled. It was the first proprietary thing he'd ever said about her. "The Com-Atlantic Media Group. It's a senior position, based out of Atlanta. Two hundred thousand to start."

"And?" he prompted.

"And I told them no. Not until I'm finished with my responsibilities here."

"But did you mean it?"

"I don't know," she said deadpan and honest.

"Okay. So here it comes. Why?"

She swallowed before saying it. "Because you're *different*."

Different, thought Mitch, because she *hadn't* been here before. It was a club across his forehead. The one perfect aspect about playing with Rene was the safety net. She didn't care. She could tease him, fuck him, leave him, and never look back.

Them were the rules.

"Look, I said no," she said. "So let's leave it there."

For now.

"What'll it take to keep you?"

"That's not a healthy question."

"How about until Friday?"

"Keep me till Friday?" she asked, curious about the consequences of a deal.

"After that, we can renegotiate."

Her chest rose and fell. She was winded. Mitch could smell her breath. "How about a kiss?"

"A kiss and I get until Friday."

"*A kiss.*"

"I can do that."

A tear rolled down her cheek that she refused to wipe. She let it be, wearing the traces like an open scar. "I guess I'm not so tough after all."

Mitch reached across and wiped the tear. It was the closest thing he could do to show that he loved her. If just a little. But still not enough to risk losing Connie. He held her chin and kissed her once. Sweetly. Long enough to mean it. Then without a further word, Rene slipped from the car.

4

October 23. The day of the debates. Mitch rose after a frightful night of hallucinatory dreams and tried to make as much out of his routine as possible. With the dogs he jogged three extra miles by expanding his running loop to incorporate the lower flats of the Island's westernmost suburb, known paradoxically as Westside Hills. Though Merle was faithfully able to keep with him every step, Pearl was quite literally dogging it at mile six. Mitch slowed for the rest of the run, feeling sorry for the girl and making rest stops so she could catch her breath. Before the campaign she would have made the entire stretch. But he had been forced to cut his runs to barely a third of his usual routine. The dogs' endurance had suffered as much as his.

Then there were the nightmares. They'd been building toward a crescendo over the last week in their intensity, with consistent guest appearances by the opposition candidate, Shakespeare McCann. And last night's had been a head-knotting doozy. Mitch was eating lunch at the Mairzy Doats Café. This time he was with Connie. In the dream she was as beautiful as he could remember, wearing Rene's sleeveless summer dress and sandals. Her hair was slightly unkempt, as if they'd been driving for hours with the top down, and he was braving it by telling her the truth. Not of the beating in the alley. He was telling her of the affair with Rene, and Connie wanted every lurid, sexual detail. Positions. Duration. Discussions. All down to the last exchange of body fluids in weights and measures. During the last leg of Mitchell's morning run, the rest played back in grainy black and white.

Hollice Waters appeared at the Mairzy Doats window, cupping his hands against the glass to retard the glare. Mitch, seeking escape from the reporter, dropped a twenty on the table and ushered Connie to the rear exit and into the back alley where the Mustang was parked just around the corner.

"Your glasses!" she said. "You left your glasses on the table!"

"I'll go back and get them," he said, leaving her alone in the alley. "Wait right here."

Once back inside the café, he couldn't find his glasses. He'd asked the waitress, but she just turned and walked away as if he weren't there.

"Looking for these?" said a familiar voice. Mitch turned to find Hollice Waters seated at a nearby booth. He held Mitchell's glasses, putting them on his face, then taking them off. Putting them on, taking them off. "You know, I could've used a pair of these. I can see a lot better with them on. Now I know why you want 'em back."

"Just cheap ones," said Mitch. "I bought 'em across the street . . ." He pointed over to the five-and-dime. When he looked back, Hollice was gone. Only the glasses remained, left on the table for Mitch to retrieve. He crossed and picked them up, discovering them sticky with semicoagulated blood and strands of Hollice's hair.

As if in no hurry at all, he dipped the glasses in a glass of water and wiped them clean with a napkin. Only then did he remember the alley. Connie was there. Waiting. The dream overwhelmed him with a sense of dread. He pushed through the crowded café to the rear, shouldering his way out the back door and into the alley, where Connie was screaming. He turned to the right, and lying in the exact spot where he'd been so soundly beaten, there was Connie, her dress pulled above her waist with Shakespeare upon her.

Like some animal, he was mauling her, all tongue and claws. His feet scratching at the dirt for traction. Then before Mitch could move, before he could bring himself to cover the short distance that would rescue his wife, a fist caught him from the rear and knocked him to the dirt. He quickly rolled to face his attacker. To see a face that he fully expected. Shakespeare McCann, of course. After all, it was a dream. He knew it was a dream. It was all making some kind of twisted sense. Connie was rescued. And now Shakes was, once again, upon him. Just like before. But the dust cleared and Mitchell's eyes strained to focus without those cheap glasses. A face appeared. A face that owned the hand that struck him to the ground. Not Shakespeare's, though. A face that proved far scarier.

The face belonged to Mitch! Candidate Mitch!

Mitch had tried to scream. He woke with a hacking cough and a burning in his throat. The acid in his stomach had washed up in an ulcerous tidal wave of spit. Connie had merely moaned and rolled to him, gently kissing his back. "You okay?"

"Yeah," he'd said. "I'm fine. Go back to sleep."

"Gonna run?"

"Yeah. Go back to sleep." He'd patted her on the behind and crawled from bed. Thus the routine had commenced. The dogs. The jog.

And the dream? It stuck with him. Like classic movie scenes never to be forgotten, some dreams were meant to linger. But this nightmare. It gripped him by the throat, and strangled his concentration throughout another morning round of debate rehearsals. He appeared tired and unfocused. Badly in need of rest.

Fitz took him aside. "Getting sleep?"

"I'm okay."

"I know you're okay. I was just checking." Then Fitz wrapped his arm over Mitchell's neck in a mock hammerlock. "You're gonna eat his lunch, you know that?"

The studio was small, donated by the local public TV station. Neutral territory, as Fitz had insisted. His negotiations with Marshall Lambeer had been cordial, phone talk. Marshall had an agenda, obviously fed to him by Shakespeare, while Fitz was free to arrange whatever kind of setup he thought would be beneficial to his candidate.

Format? Fitz gave that away. On the issues, Mitch was more than confident. So let the questions fly. What Fitz had worried about was what Rene liked to call the *forum effect*. In holding a televised debate in front of an audience, candidates are forced to play to a crowd. Candidates and their staffs were long known to pack these houses with rabble-rousers, known mostly for heckling the opposition into costly mistakes. It was undignified. And Mitch was the dignified candidate.

Whether it was dignified or not, Rene went ahead and delivered exactly as she'd promised, billing the debate as a *must-see* for potential voters. A civic *battle royale*. In a surprise media rush, she'd plied the day's airwaves with a teasing buy. A blitzkrieg ten seconds of radio and TV that advertised the definitive answer to a voter's choice: *Dutton vs. McCann! The Man or the Sham? Tonight!*

Local TV couldn't resist the tease. By 5:00 P.M. the three other Cathedral stations clamoring for signal tie-in were granted access. Show time was at eight. All players were present. Let the party begin.

"Yeah. This oughta rock," said a cameraman into his headset, the sarcasm dripping thickly as he focused on a two-shot of the stand-ins perched at podiums complete with children's renderings of donkeys and elephants, winners in a contest held amongst Cathedral's competing elementary schools.

"Try not to fall asleep, fellahs," said the director from the booth. "We're about to perform a public service."

"Betcha the shit's gonna flow. We shoulda worn our hip waders," added another cameraman. All the crew were laughing at that one. Those headsets were like being plugged into their own private laugh line. That was until an unfamiliar voice came on from the booth, belonging to the station manager.

"Remember, gentlemen. One of these two men is gonna be your next congressman. And they'll be voting on public TV grants," said the boss over the intercom. "Do your paychecks a favor and make 'em both look good."

Fitz stumbled into Connie on his way to the makeup trailer. She'd been standing behind the sound baffles, waiting for someone she recognized. Instead, it seemed everyone had been looking at her. Red dress. Just enough leg to make a young man look, but distant enough for only a mature man to brave. Or a campaign manager. Fitz was quick to ease her with a warm smile. "Been a while, Connie. You look ravishing. Maybe we should put *you* on tonight. Give Mitch a break."

"I'm sorry I haven't been around much," she said. "I've been spending too much of the campaign at home."

"Too exciting for you. I understand," he said, trying hard not to sound patronizing. "Bet you're looking for Mitch."

"Actually, I was just wondering where I should sit."

"Front row. Right behind the panel." He offered his arm and escorted her up past the cameras to a small, fold-out chair set four feet behind the press box with her name tagged on it. He'd handpicked that very seat, just so that every time the director cut to a question from the panel, Connie would be right there in the immediate background. "How's this?"

"Fine, thanks. When does it start?"

He checked his watch. "Nine minutes now. Fasten your seat belt." Then he was gone.

Connie watched him leave. She hadn't wanted to come. That afternoon in a soft voice she'd asked Mitch if he'd mind if she watched the debate on TV. Mitch hadn't heard her. And she hadn't brought it up again, afraid she might choke on the words. She was surprised to discover her fear of telling Mitch about the rape was a far greater fear than seeing Shakespeare again.

The makeup room was a permanent trailer parked on cinder-block pilings outside the TV stage. A security guard stood post at the bottom step, smoking a cigarette.

"How's it goin'?" asked Fitz as he started into the trailer.

"Looks like we got us a storm on the way." The guard nodded toward the sky.

From the top step Fitz took a moment to check the sky. Sure enough. The usual southern twilight was obscured by encroaching cloud cover, boiling up from the Gulf. "Just as long as the roof doesn't leak," he said as he ducked into the trailer. Inside, the final touches of pancake makeup were being applied to the evening's panel, Margot Wallace of the local National Public Radio station, and a print journalist from the *Evening Breeze* named Kevin McWorter—an eleventh-hour replacement for the media MIA, Hollice Waters.

The third chair was filled by Mitch. His conservative suit from Barney's New York was bibbed to save it from messy makeup. And Rene was at her candidate's ear, giving a last-minute pitch.

"Keep your knees bent and breathe," she whispered. "Stay in the moment. You're *good* in the moment. We both know that. Remember to listen, don't leap. Say 'thank you' after you're asked a question."

"What if I sweat like Nixon?" he joked.

"Don't sweat," she said simply. He looked at her in the mirror. She was cool. All business. Yesterday, a memory.

He turned to his interrogators. "You guys get a copy of those easy questions I wanted you to ask me?"

Margot laughed. "You mean the ones with the single-syllable words?"

"So you got 'em. Great. Use those on McCann," he quipped. Even the makeup artist laughed.

Fitz appeared in Mitch's mirror view. "Where's bachelor number two?"

"Somebody said he's got his own makeup man and a rented Winnebago somewhere hereabouts," said Rene.

"He must be nervous," figured Fitz.

"No," said Mitch. "He's saving the handshake for the cameras."

Shake hands and come out fighting.

Mitch started coughing, as if he'd inhaled a lungful of dust from behind the Mairzy Doats Café.

"You okay?" asked the makeup girl.

"Fine," he coughed and then turned to Rene. "Water."

She was already on the case, quickly filling a Dixie cup from the water cooler. She handed it to him. "Relax, sweetie. Calm."

"I bet it was the hair spray," offered the makeup girl.

"Five minutes," said the director over the intercom speaker.

Fitz leaned down close to Mitch. "You ready, son?"

Mitch drained the Dixie cup, cleared his throat, then checked his look in the mirror.

"Lemme at him."

5

The studio lights burned. Thousands of watts poured onto the simple set, erasing any natural shadows except for those that would be underneath the candidates' feet. For cleaner sound, the director in the booth ordered the air conditioning to be turned off. The room immediately began to cook. Ties were loosened and women in panty hose began to wonder why they'd worn them at all. It was sweltering, destined to be a contest as to who would melt first. Mitch or McCann?

The red light on camera two flashed on while a taped announcement played over the air:

"The League of Women Voters and the Cathedral Chamber of Commerce are proud to present this special debate forum. Tonight, candidates for the open seat in the House of Representatives' Thirty-first Congressional District of Texas."

At the tape's end, the director called over his headset, "Cue the candidates."

A stage manager cued Mitch to step out onto the stage while opposite him entered Shakespeare McCann, all smiles and hubris. The man's hand outstretched in a gesture of friendship and fair play.

Shake hands and come out fighting.

In the glare of the lights, Mitch smiled and clasped Shakespeare's hand, fully expecting a sort of schoolyard squeeze. Boys with vise grips. Instead, Shakespeare gave Mitch a sweaty palm and a grip like a wet rag. *He's nervous,* said Mitch to himself, smelling blood in the water.

"Good evening, gentlemen," spoke Kevin McWorter, already impaneled next to Margot Wallace. "Would you please take your podiums."

Mitch eased over to his assigned space, grasping the podium as he'd rehearsed and facing his interviewers with his chin up. A glance over to Shakespeare revealed a mirror image of professional coaching.

Kevin McWorter continued, "Our format this evening consists of an opening statement from each of the candidates of two minutes apiece, followed by an open forum of questions and answers, finishing with two minutes apiece for closing statements. A coin toss has decided that the Republican candidate, Mr. Shakespeare McCann, shall go first. Mr. McCann."

"Thank you. But I cordially yield to let Mr. Dutton speak his piece first."

Yield? What is this? thought Mitch. Some kind of tactic. Or did McCann look as unprepared as his handshake might've revealed?

"Mr. Dutton?" asked Kevin McWorter.

On cue, and without much forethought, he simply turned to the camera with the red flashing light and began his opening statement. "Ladies and gentlemen. My name is Mitch Dutton. And I'm here not only as a candidate, but also as a concerned citizen who sees the great state of Texas straining at its limitations while ignoring its greatest assets. You. The people of Texas."

As he continued, the cameras relaxed briefly and swiveled away from Shakespeare, who shuffled his colored three-by-five note cards into no apparent sort of order. Shakespeare scanned the room, then tossed friendly smiles over toward the panel, whom he'd not yet had an opportunity to meet. From them he got scant nods of acknowledgment. Then, in the semishadow behind them, he caught sight of the red dress. Connie. Dutifully watching her husband. Legs crossed. Arms crossed. Avoiding Shakespeare's gaze.

Mitch went on. "More so than any other state, Texas is saddled with an immigration problem that the federal government has turned a blind eye toward with ineffective policies and an understaffed INS . . ."

But Shakespeare. Once his eyes had settled upon Connie, they would not release. He stared, flat and even. Dead on her as if from that twenty-five-foot distance he could reach across and prod her. Slap the bitch's face.

I gave you a message for Mitch. Did you tell him? Bet you didn't. Naw. I know you didn't! Maybe I didn't fuck you hard enough. Was that it? Maybe I shoulda left you black and blue. Left bruises for you to explain. Bet that woulda done the trick.

"As taxpayers, you are overburdened. As property owners, you are undervalued. As businesspeople, you are underwhelmed. And as teachers and health care providers, you are overwhelmed and in grave need of relief."

Look at me, you cunt! You think you're tough? You think you can keep a secret? Look at me!

Connie knew he was glaring at her. But prayed she was wrong as, with the slightest turn of her neck, she peeked Shakespeare's way.

That's right. honeypie. It's me. Your handsome boogeyman. Look at me and tell me why.

Somehow, she was being drawn merely to see if it was really *him.* Really the same man who'd charmed her, drugged her, and crawled into her bed and so violated her. Dressed in a neat suit, hair combed, madeup, and ready to go on TV and charm the rest of the foolish county.

That's it. It's me. You remember, don't you? How could you forget?

He was smiling at her now. That sick, twisted grin the cameras never seemed to catch. She shuddered, gathering herself up tighter within her arms. She tried once again to focus on Mitch.

"We need new ideas for better schools, a stronger economy, a safer community where you can rest your head and raise your children, with waste-free water and fresh air and a future filled with hope," continued Mitch, tactfully addressing the camera, unaware of the game Shakespeare was playing with his wife.

When it's my turn, bitch, will you listen to me? What would I have to do for you to look at me the way you look at him? Get a law degree? Make a pile of money to keep you in that big old house?

Connie snuck a look back at Shakespeare, whose gaze hadn't wavered. He was sending her a message. What it was, she hadn't a glimmer. She didn't *want* to know. The best she could muster was a simply mouthed *Fuck you.*

You already did, honey. And you liked it!

"To the good people of South County, I'm not just asking for your vote tonight. I'm asking for your eyes, your ears, and a reasonable place in your heart to do what's necessary to raise our own limits of possibility. You can do that on November third. I know you can. Thank you.''

"Mr. McCann?" cued Kevin McWorter.

The cameras swiveled, and with the simplest of expressions, Shakespeare dropped his evil gaze from Connie and turned to face the viewing audience with a look of wonder.

"Rich lawyers," he said. "You can love 'em. You can elect 'em. But you can't trust 'em." He turned to face Mitch, already on the attack. "Counselor, I applaud your opening ditty. You're awful slick, but so is that pigpen called Washington. You know how many lawyers they got there? Thousands, by my count. And I say to the good people out there in TV land, who think handsome is as handsome does. I say lawyer is as lawyer does. And one wrong vote . . ." He let the implication hang for a slow moment. He smiled broadly at Mitch, then looked at his watch. "Now, if my watch is correct, according to the rules, I got me a minute and a half more of opening statement. Tell you what, Counselor. I'll concede the entire debate in exchange for an answer to a simple question."

McCann twisted like a defensive back waiting to tackle. "I want Mr. Dutton to tell us how much the average working mother should expect to pay for a dozen large eggs."

Mitch froze at the trick question. It'd been years since he'd done the shopping. It was Connie's domain. And when she couldn't, he had his assistant pick up groceries.

"Is that your approach to the issues?" he deflected. "A dozen eggs?"

"You think it's a silly question?"

"I do, yes."

"I'm sure the voters who scrape every week to feed their families don't think so."

Mitch looked to Margot Wallace.

"Mr. Dutton. The format does not require you to answer the question," she said.

"No," he said. "I'll answer."

"So let's hear it," said Shakespeare, arms crossed and waiting.

"The Republican candidate will forgive me. I live in a traditional household. And my wife buys the groceries. But I would expect a dozen eggs would run about a dollar twenty-five."

"Try two and a quarter," said Shakespeare. "In my opinion, that makes you, the rich lawyer, nearly eighty-five percent out of touch with the average American family." He swerved to face the camera.

"Good and fair people of Cathedral, my name is Shakespeare McCann and I'm seeking office in the U.S. House of Commons. That means *House* of the *common* man. My opponent just proved that he is anything *but* common. But what should we expect? He's a *lawyer*.

"Me?" he continued. "I'm just your *common* South County businessman. And where I create jobs for this community, what does a lawyer do but steal a piece of the action? He creates *nothing*. He produces *nothing*. He's antimorality. He's antifamily. And he and his big-business supporters want to send more of your manufacturing jobs overseas or south of the border, leaving y'all with barely a minimum wage to pay your mortgage and feed your children."

"Thank you, Mr. McCann," interrupted Margot Wallace.

"One last thing," he rolled on. "Y'all have no job security, health security, or Social Security. When we stop letting government in our lives, the better off we'll all be."

"Thank you—"

"America's economy is like a patient with walking pneumonia. He's out of bed, but he ain't doin' so good."

"Time's up, Mr. McCann. Now can we please start?" pressed Margot.

"Just gettin' warmed up, ma'am."

Mitch, who'd patiently been waiting for the smoke to clear, stepped up to his mike. "Since *Dr.* McCann's informed us all as to the state of our poor and lacking health, it might prove helpful if he'd show us his medical diplomas before recommending surgery."

"All right, gentlemen," said an exasperated Margot Wallace. "Our first question is for Mr. McCann. Let's go to your opening statement. You just referred to Washington as a pigpen. Lobby reform has long been an issue that Capitol Hill has refused to engage. If elected, how would you vote on lobby reform if it affected, let's say, the liquor industry? And how would you balance that against a congressman's power to induce a corporation to build its newest brewery in your district, thus creating a thousand new jobs?"

"Well, that would depend on the brand of beer they were cookin'," quipped Shakespeare, eliciting a room full of laughter. "Margot, let me first say that I don't drink. Those days are long over, though I don't deny anybody's legal right to the occasional nip as long as they're not driving a car or running for high office." More laughs.

He turned serious. "As for your question about dirty, sneaking lobbyists out to corrupt our once fair government? I say throw the scalawags out of Washington and make 'em go get real jobs. We got jobs enough to go around down here if we just gave the Immigration Department a good kick in the behind. None of which excludes the liquor companies from building a plant down here, anyway. If it's good for Cathedral, bring 'em on. Who needs a lobbyist for that? Our primary problem as a community is how to create *taxpayers*. And you create taxpayers by building strong companies with *American* workers."

"Mr. Dutton?" asked Margot. "Would you like to respond?"

Mitch, having recovered from the lousy start, turned to face Shakespeare, waiting for his peripheral vision to catch the cue from the camera's red light. "You know, it's awful hard to win an argument when your opponent is utterly unencumbered with the facts." Then he smiled. "But I'll try anyway. Mr. McCann? You ever hear of Arkansas?"

"Sure I have."

"Well, what Ms. Wallace is referring to is Budweiser and the plant they wanted to build in Cathedral City, only to lose out to Little Rock when they were able to offer greater tax incentives and postpone sewer levies for a period of time until the plant was in profit." Mitch made a professional acknowledgment to the camera, then finished his answer looking straight across at Margot Wallace.

He went on to explain what he thought was wrong with lobbyists, then turned, looked back over to Shakespeare, and dropped his patented camera-ready style in exchange for a slight down-home kind of Texas twang. "In other words, when you're up to your behind in alligators, it's hard to remember that your original plan was to drain the swamp."

There it was, a folksy little salvo fired right up into McCann territory. A torpedo shot that, when the TV director called for a two-shot, seemed to catch Shakespeare by surprise. The homilies were McCann's domain. Slick and substance were for the other guy. Mitch Dutton. The Democrat went on with his rebuttal. "We live in a free market. Business should be free to promote itself to a government free of corruption. Instead, we are governed by a Congress that will *not* govern itself. For example, that's why I've cut from the national Democratic platform and endorsed term limits. The professionals in Washington are no longer the businessmen. They're the members of Congress themselves. I'm advocating that politics return as a moral and spiritual awakening to public service. That's my plan."

"Would you go as far as setting your own term limits as a congressman?" asked Margot in a follow-up.

"I would. I plan to spend no more than eight years in office. I have a life here in Cathedral," answered Mitch, nodding toward Connie. "I don't want to grow old on a farm in Virginia."

"May I say something?" interjected Shakespeare.

"You have one minute to respond, Mr. McCann," answered Kevin McWorter.

"That was a nice speech, Counselor. But who says once you're in office, you're gonna get a free ride for eight years? Congress, if I remember the rule book, is a two-year deal that a fellah makes with Mr. and Mrs. John Q. Public. That means, if you ain't pullin' the freight, the voters out there can pull your meal ticket just about anytime they darn well think it's a good idea. And that's the way it should be!"

In the green room, Rene and Fitz were fixed on the studio feed monitor. "You can see the coaching," she said. "Just watch McCann. He's about to go iambic."

Sure enough. Shakespeare started punching at the air with his index finger, like a conductor counting the beats of a verbal symphony.

"If elected, all *I* can do is *promise* to make some *waves* in the name of *God, Cathedral,* and the *Great* State of *Texas*. And if the *good* people who *put* me there don't see *me* makin' *headway* in the first *two* years, they got the *God-given right* and privilege to hand me my *walkin'* papers and *send* me *packin'*!"

"He looks like a forehead artery stuffed into a gray suit," dissed Fitz before diving into his breast pocket for the cell phone. He flipped it open and dialed Murray to see what the focus group was thinking.

Miles away, in a meeting room at the Cathedral City Holiday Inn, Murray had corralled fifteen undecided voters who knew nothing of Murray or his affiliation with the Dutton camp. For the promise of free pizza and twenty dollars, the focus group agreed to watch and score the debate in three-minute segments.

"Time," he would call out, and each of the participants would pass to the right a preprinted card that read either "Dutton" or "McCann." Murray would score the rounds like a professional boxing match.

Afterwards, a discussion, the free pizza, and doling out those twenty-dollar bills. Murray's phone rang. He picked up, knowing it could only be Fitz. "How's it goin'?"

"So far so good," answered Murray.

"Scores?"

"Opening statements were six to nine, McCann. The next two were eight to seven, Mitch. Then the last was eight to seven, McCann."

"Bullshit! Except for that hattrick at the gun, Mitch is cleaning the little bastard's clock! Did you score that term-limits question?"

"I'm just reading you what I got."

"I'll call back." Fitz flipped the phone back up and pocketed it, switching his attention back to the green room monitor where Mitch was giving a practiced answer to a question from Kevin McWorter.

"You know, Kevin," said Mitch, calling up the same catalogued answer from the studio rehearsal, "when I think of African-American or minority role models of any kind, I think of the better than seventy percent of those minority men and women who get up every day, pack lunches for their children, and head off to a job that pays a mortgage or a babysitter. Those are the role models of today. To offer up the likes of some fallen sports or music personality is an insult to all those good people who earn their keep day in and day out."

Kevin McWorter turned to Shakespeare. "Mr. McCann. You have two minutes to respond."

"You know what? I'll yield my two minutes in exchange for some straight answers from my opponent," fired Shakespeare in a not-so-generous-sounding gibe. "I wanna know who's a role model? Last July you cashed a thousand-dollar check from Jamal La Croix. A man who we all remember led a mob of black hoodlums that tore a hole right through the center of our precious tourist industry. Now, my question is, who wants to be the role model? Sounds like you do, Counselor. In Congress. On Capitol Hill. Consorting with the desperate likes of Jesse Jackson and Louie Farrakhan."

"It *sounds* like you're *doggin'* me, Mr. McCann."

"Call it what you want, Mr. Dutton."

Again Mitch flavored his response with some tangy Texas barbecue. "Well, let me first say that my daddy taught me never to stand between a dog and a fire hydrant."

Back in the green room, Fitz howled. Nobody had seen that coming. Only Mitch, who'd saved the line, set it up, and let go with it at the opportune moment. The candidate knew the TV cameras had him in close-up, so he took a moment to return to his classic pose before moving on to the meat of his answer.

Mitch continued, "Secondly, from your characterization, one would *infer* that I *invited* Jamal La Croix to endorse my campaign. Whereas the answer to that question is, obviously, no."

Shakespeare mocked. "*Whereas* and *infer.*"

But Mitch continued, "I did not invite the endorsement, nor did I ever give it credence and acknowledge it. We returned the money. Still, if your characterization was correct, I might *infer* that you *invited* the Ku Klux Klan, The American Nazi Party, and other white supremacist organizations, all of whom have publicly committed to your campaign, to endorse you."

Shakespeare wheeled to face the camera, waiting for the cue of the red light. "I have never been a member or accepted money from any racist groups. And I resent that you might imply otherwise, *Counselor!* My question was legitimate and pertained to the man who led the riot which ravaged *our* city. Good, innocent people were either injured or murdered. And the best you can manage is a smug 'I returned the money.' "

With that, he swung Mitch an accusatory look. That's when Mitch saw it. The sweat. Upper-lip sweat. Nerve sweat, bleeding through the thick makeup that was there to protect against such occurrences. Sweat creased Shakespeare's eyebrows, leaked from his temples. A deadly giveaway the TV cameras would not be able to hide.

Shakespeare's jugular was exposed. All Mitch needed was the blade to cut it. And then the words came. "Role model," he said. "If that is the heart of your question, then yes. I would like to be a role model. I've lived and worked in this community my entire life. I am a property owner. I am a taxpayer. I am a loving husband. I serve on the boards of numerous charitable organizations. And during this campaign, I have stood by my convictions to my own detriment. In other words, I'm an open book. Yet opposite me, we have a man who stands only on what he says. Not on what he does. Who he is or where he's been. He's more like a mystery novel. Turn another page and there's a new twist. Another tale. And when he talks, all we know for sure is that his mouth is moving."

"Now, that's just a damned lie," said Shakespeare in a sparked response.

"In the case of Mr. Shakespeare McCann," hammered Mitch, "the only thing to scratch is the surface."

Shakespeare tried to save himself. "With all respect to your party's mascot, Mr. Dutton, any ol' jackass knows how to kick down a barn. But only a carpenter can build one. Jesus, I might add, *was* just the kind of carpenter I was thinking of—"

Margot Wallace interrupted the verbal brawl. "Mr. McCann. We would like your response to the next question."

"But I want to respond to this slander. We're on TV," he shot.

"I'd have to say no," she said. "The format requires questions and response."

"Forget the format. Voters don't care about format. They care about action and words. Ain't that right?" Shakespeare was reeling. Pumped up, poking his fingers in the air. "Now, in front of all the good people out there, this man has questioned my character. When, in actual fact, I know that just moments ago, he lied to y'all."

"Can we please have another question?" asked Mitch.

"Just hold your horses, Counselor. You got somethin' to answer to here. Just moments ago I heard you call yourself a loving husband. Am I correct?"

Mitch didn't respond. He saw what was coming and held against the impulse to look at Connie.

But in the green room, Rene bit her lip. "Oh shit." Shakespeare knew about her and Mitch. And he was about to tell the entire fucking viewing audience.

"He wouldn't dare," countered Fitz. He wasn't sure about Rene and Mitch. But he *knew* about her. And had been suspect for months.

"Oh yes he would," she said, stepping closer to the monitor. For the first time in years, she found herself praying.

On the TV screen they watched Shakespeare, in a wide two-shot, look at the camera while pointing a finger at Mitch. "When I know for a fact that my opponent's employed women on his campaign staff for the express purpose of—"

The studio power failed. Lights out. The cameras off. Five full seconds passed before the stand-by generators kicked in and washed the soundstage in the white harshness of thousand-watt safety lights.

Outside, the brewing storm had enveloped the TV station. The squall pushed through the streets and alleyways, bending phone and power lines.

Fitz and Rene broke from the green room for the soundstage, where crew and technicians were rushing about trying to retrieve some power and signal. Entering from the rear, they caught Mitch and Shakespeare circling each other, the distance between them dwindling. "Ding ding. Saved by the bell. Huh, Counselor?"

"Better have proof of the stones you cast," warned Mitch.

Shakespeare got hissing close to Mitch. "He who attacks need only to *vanquish*. He who *defends* can do nothing more than merely survive." Then he pointed at Mitch. "I don't need any proof. All I gotta do is look at you and I *know!*"

"You don't know anything."

"What? You gonna sue me? We both know libel and slander laws don't apply to politics. So I'll say what I will. It won't matter a whit after November third."

Shakespeare was blotting his wet face with a piece of white cotton cloth, smiling as if to ease the sudden tension. "Got in some good shots. I'll give you that. Looks to me like you worked yourself a good sweat."

When Shakespeare reached out to dab Mitch's face for him, Mitch swatted his hand away. The bunched cloth unfurled, falling to the floor at Mitch's feet.

Panties.

Shakespeare kneeled and picked them up, once again offering them to Mitch. "I thought I might return these."

"What?"

"The panties. They belong to your missus."

"Fuck you, asshole."

"Oh, wouldn't that be somethin' for the newspapers. I fuck her. Then you fuck me."

Mitch reached out and snatched the panties. At first inspection they were only women's underwear smudged with flesh-colored makeup. They could've been anybody's.

Shakespeare moved closer. "I've been there. In your house. Upstairs and to the right. Double doors. Green curtains. View of the backyard."

Mitch threw the panties back at him. It was a sick game and he wanted none of it.

"Fine. Don't believe me." Shakespeare fired a subtle nod toward Connie's seat. "Just look at her. She'll tell you everything. All you have to do is ask."

"Get out of my face—" Mitch shoved him "—you sociopathic sonofabitch."

"You screw around on her. She screws around on you. I mean, fair's fair, am I right? Shouldn't hurt none."

"That's right. It doesn't hurt. That's because it's bullshit."

"A woman's truth is in the eyes. So look at her. I dare you."

Oh, Mitch wanted to. But even more, he didn't want to turn his back on Shakespeare. Didn't want to give him the satisfaction. A battle of instincts raged within Mitch that left him paralyzed.

A bell sounded and the studio lights ignited in a blazing flood. The frozen moment melted as quickly as it had begun. As if awaking from a dream, there was Shakespeare standing only two feet away, looking over Mitch's shoulder toward the panel's seats. The sweat had vanished. Control had returned along with that twisted smile.

"Going back to air," shouted the stage manager after getting instructions from the booth. "Ten seconds. Candidates to their podiums."

Shakespeare gave Mitch a friendly wink and headed back to his place. But Mitch didn't move a muscle. The stage manager appeared at Mitch's side. "Mr. Dutton. Five seconds to air."

He walked Mitch back to his mark. Bunched in Mitch's hand, those panties. He was afraid to look at Connie. What would be in her eyes? Truth? Hate? Goddammit, Mitch was confused.

"Three, two, one," called the stage manager, and they were back on signal, broadcasting to thousands of interested homes.

Kevin McWorter didn't miss a beat. "Our apologies to our viewers and candidates. I guess Mother Nature feels she has a vote in this election, too. To resume our debate format, Margot Wallace had a question concerning the issue of the candidates' campaigns."

"Thank you, Kevin," started Margot. "Mr. McCann. Your campaign has been criticized by your opponent as largely negative and without any social merit. How then would *you* define your campaign?"

"Glad you asked, Margot," said Shakespeare. "Ya see, I'm the dark-horse candidate. And that means I'm the little fellah who never had a snowball's chance in hell of bein' up in front of y'all tonight except for the good graces of some hardworkin' folks who saw a need for an alternative voice. We call it the new, populist conservatism of the heart."

He droned on, comparing his life to some unseen Norman Rockwell painting, and leaving Mitch off-camera to brave a look at Connie. Right over Margot Wallace's shoulder, Connie sat in the space between stage light and studio shadows. Red dress. Dark hair. Tear stained makeup running down her face. Lower lip quivering as she mouthed to Mitch a simple, *I'm sorry.*

For God's sake, was it true?

Mitchell's eyes narrowed upon her. Not in anger, but in a soulful need of clarity. And there, before his eyes, she was crumbling, the secret she'd kept for those two miserable months leaking in a chain reaction of shakes and silent sobs. Changing colors in Mitchell's mind.

Shakespeare continued. "All along, I've been doin' nothing more than callin' 'em the way I see 'em. If the front-runner is misleading ya'll, I'm gonna say just that. A fellah that starts at the back of the pack can't afford to be a nice guy and let the other candidate make a doormat out of him."

Mitch burned. The anger inside him came from somewhere south of hell, cutting loose in a tidal wave of heat. He felt the surge of a bullied animal, pushed to the wall and cornered. Within an inch of life.

"Now, the counselor here. Can I help if he thinks he should get a free ride to Congress? He thinks he can do whatever he likes because, one, he's good-looking. He's got good name ID. Speaks well in public. Then there's number two. He's the front-runner. Or at least has been, until he took advantage of the people's mandate. Flaunting public opinion and showing his elitist face at a funeral for a convicted murderer. Cryin' over the body of a killer who a Texas judge and jury decided should be put to death."

He swung a pointed finger at Mitch, prompting the director in the booth to call for a wide two-shot that included both candidates.

"This man," accused Shakespeare, "this man, I tell you, was cryin' tears over an avowed agent of evil. We all saw the pictures. There he was. Dressed in the black mourning attire of somebody who cared about the devil himself!"

Mitch never even heard a syllable of it. He was in a fugue state, fueled by rage. The colors of his brain skewed to monochrome while his body moved involuntarily.

Fitz saw it, too. From the back of the studio, he knew something bad was about to happen. Something disastrous. His stomach told him as it churned in acid. Then Rene nudged him.

"What's with him?" she whispered. "Why the hell doesn't he respond?"

But Mitch did respond. His lips clamped shut and his jaw went rigid. His right fist tightened around those panties into a bludgeon that, when he finally strode across the stage, closing those short ten feet between himself and McCann, clubbed Shakespeare across the ear. The studio mikes picked up the sound of crunching bone as Mitch's right hand shattered against Shakespeare's skull.

And Shakespeare never saw it coming.

One moment he was playing to the camera, swollen with his own menace and commanding the medium. The next, Mitch was upon him with flying fists and teeth gritted with spit and a seething wail. "You sonofabitch! You motherfucking sonofabitch! I'll kill you!" Shakespeare was pinned. Mitch's weight was on his chest. He couldn't guard himself from the balled right fist that jackhammered time and time again into his face. Cartilage cracked. Blood sprayed across his face as his nose bled and lips split apart.

Stagehands leapt into the fray as the cameras realigned to capture the slugfest. Mitch was peeled away, instantly shrugging off Shakespeare's saviors and shoving right past Rene and Fitz, who'd come rushing to the fore.

"Mitch!" called out Rene.

Suffering from an aural myopia, Mitch didn't hear a word. His tunnel vision was aimed at Connie, finding her right where he'd last seen her, frozen stiff and fetal in that same chair just one row back from the on-camera panel. She was scared to death of what he might do.

"I'm sorry," she wailed. "Please, Mitch. I'm sorry."

"Ssshhh," he calmed her. "Just be quiet. Now, where's your car?" His tone was surprisingly soft and careful. She caught her wits, nodded, stood, and led him out the side exit where she'd first entered. Past silent and stunned onlookers. Nobody tried to stop them. If anything, people got out of the way.

6

Gina Sweet watched the entire debacle. In the comfort of her darkened guest house, she'd curled up to watch the main event from a down-feathered bed that was more pillows and stuffed animals than mattress. The quaint little cottage had been hers since high school, opportunely buffered by an alley with her own private garage and entrance. Convenient for a woman who didn't want to be bothered by her benefactors, parents or not.

Since her motel tête-à-tête with Shakespeare, her resolve had been to run. To get out of that motel room alive, she'd made too many promises. Love. Devotion. And dirt on Mitch Dutton. Real dirt. Facts. All promises, deep down, she knew she couldn't deliver. The best she could offer were more lies, empty promises, and some humiliating sexual acrobatics at the harsh hands of her tormentor. Just to get out of that fucking motel room.

Then run, she did. To Europe mostly. And, as was her custom, she'd returned with more bags than she'd left with. Unpacked luggage surrounded her. If it weren't for her damned parents' fiftieth anniversary party—an event at which she'd promised to play the part of hostess—she'd have stayed clear of Cathedral until well after the election.

With a pint of Häagen-Dazs to boost her spirits and a bottle of cognac lifted from her old man's private reserve, Gina settled in for a night of channel-surfing. That's how she tripped over the debate. Her first instinct was to switch stations. She didn't care to hear word one from either of those assholes. But a fascination took over. The prefight warm up made Mitch Dutton and Shakespeare McCann out to be political gladiators, movie stars on the rise. Stars whom she knew far better than the average viewer. So she stayed tuned. And watched.

Ten minutes more of talk, followed by twenty-two minutes of debate that ended like no other in modern history, destined to be a story that would go national. Certain to air again and again and again. Rerun, analyzed, and covered to death.

And when it was over? Gina wanted to vomit. Her emotions had swelled into a potent mixture of contempt and fear. She quizzed herself as to which man she hated more. Mitch or Shakespeare. She couldn't choose. There was a moment she recalled when the camera had briefly cut to Connie, seated stoically in the studio audience. It was catalyst enough to curdle all the ice cream in her stomach.

Then as quick as she'd thought she'd puke, Gina leapt for the phone. She had to call Connie and tell her. Everything. All about Shakespeare McCann.

As Mitch and Connie drove home, both observed a kind of silence that only those whose souls had connected in marriage could understand. The thunderstorm had passed like so many before it, quickly, leaving a clean smell coming off the roadway. He cracked a window and inhaled all he could. Each breath slowed his pulse and brought healing blood to his mangled right hand. It was beginning to throb with each heartbeat. He let it lie in his lap while Connie shifted gears.

But his mind raced. He knew nothing of his wife and Shakespeare McCann. Wherever or whenever or whatever had taken place. He knew about evil, though. He'd gone toe to toe with it. Live on TV. If he'd touched Connie. Hurt her. Or if she'd touched him . . .

Curious, he thought. The instinct to forgive her was as powerful as his instinct to ball his fist and beat the daylights out of his opponent. To slug the sonofabitch into breathless submission so that he might never rise again to harass, stalk, or tell another lie. Fair was fair. Justice, though, would surely command a high price. Mitch knew that would come, too. By morning it would be over. After that, there would be only Mitch and Connie.

Entering the house, the couple bypassed the answering machine that was quickly eating tape with each and every plaintive call. Mitch disconnected the telephone so it wouldn't ring and disturb his strange peace. Connie took care of Merle and Pearl, letting them outside then wrapping a tray of ice cubes in a dish towel for Mitch's swelling hand.

"You wanna tell me about it?" he asked.

She first crossed the bedroom, kneeled at his feet and carefully packed his hand in ice. "Leave it there for a while," she said as she stood up and turned her back to him. "Help me with my dress?" With his left hand, he unzipped her. Afterward she walked three steps from him and sat on the edge of the bed, the dress falling off her shoulders.

"I wanted to hurt you," said Connie. Her words were clipped and succinct. "Instead, he hurt me."

"Did he touch you?"

She had thought about her answer since the dreadful night it happened. But she hadn't ever come to sort out what she would say. "Gina—" she began, and stalled. She wanted to be articulate. She wanted it to make sense in as few words as humanly possible. "You were gone to Washington."

"The day I told you about Jennifer O'Detts."

"Yes," she went on. "I called Gina. I guess I told her how mad I was at you. Resented you. I mean, I was mad *before* the newspaper article. I was just—madder." She began to cry softly, though she quickly recovered, as if talking would mitigate the pain. "I worked a long day for the charity. I came home. I started drinking. Gina showed up . . . with *him*."

"And you let him in."

"Yes. They brought some grass. We smoked it." Connie was shaking her head. "Then I went to bed. I left him with Gina. Mitch, I'd come to dislike him so much that night. He was nothing like I'd remembered him from the yacht. He was perverse and disgusting."

"Go on." Mitch tried keeping an even tone. Still, he left her alone on the bed. That's the way she liked to do these kinds of things. Alone. If she had something to say, she didn't like to be prompted with care and kisses. That would make her melt. And neither wanted that.

"I was sleeping." She took a deep breath. Exhaled. "When I woke up, he was on top of me. He made me take some kind of pill. But before that, he did it."

"Raped you," confirmed Mitch. The hellish rage inside him once again began to boil.

Not now, Mitch. Don't lose it now. She needs calm. She needs to tell. Most of all, she needs you present.

He cranked open the window, breathing in some of the cool air. He wanted to cry.

"It wasn't anything. It didn't hurt as much as it was so violating. I was drunk. It was like a bad dream. And I knew I could handle bad dreams."

"Why didn't you tell me?" he braved, swallowing hard on the words.

Anger rose in Connie's voice. "Because that's what he *wanted*. For me to tell *you*. He told me, 'You tell him what I done to you or I'll come back and kill him.' " Her voice struck eerily close to Shakespeare's, confirming any possible doubt that Mitch might've harbored up to that point.

"So I didn't tell you. Not just because I didn't want to hurt you. But because I didn't want to give him the satisfaction!" Her voice finally broke. She was at the edge. One more nudge and she'd be over. She looked at him. She needed to hear his words.

"You don't need my forgiveness," he said, walking to her, kneeling at her feet as she began to crumple. "That's because what you did doesn't need forgiveness."

"I let him in."

"That's okay."

"I didn't believe in you," she said under a waterfall of tears.

"*I* didn't believe in me!" underscored Mitch. "Don't you see? You just saw through all the talk. You almost always could. Connie, it's all bullshit!"

"But I want you to win. I want you to get what you want!"

What I want? What I want?

He was shaking his head. In his mind everything was all turned around. He didn't want to think about the campaign. The debate. None of it. Just her. Only her. Protecting her! That's something he understood. That's something he could do!

"I don't know what I want."

"You want to be a congressman," said Connie, wiping her tears, relieved to be talking about something other than herself.

Mitch stood, putting his arms around her and pulling her head to his chest. He inhaled, exhaled, seeking a piece of realistic thought. "Doesn't matter, anyway. If I wanted it or not," he said, his voice barely a monotone. "It's over. After tonight. What I did. Christ Almighty. I've become a joke."

"It can't be that bad," she lied.

"It's worse than bad. It's the end. And right now I don't really care. I feel relieved."

"Because it's over, or because you punched his lights out?" laughed Connie through her tears. A real tension reliever.

"I don't know," he said, searching for something concrete. "I know that I've been wanting to hit him for months. Really hurt him. And now I finally did."

"Something a political wife can be proud of," she joked. He laughed, too. In the face of it, some sense of humor seemed intact. And then, for just a while, they held each other. Kissed. Mitch wiping her tears with his cuff. She was crying again. He cupped her head in his hands, looking her straight on until she looked into his eyes.

"There's something else," she said.

"What?" he asked without condition. He was there for her. That much he knew. In the cyclone of confusion that was his brain, *she* was his clarity. "You can tell me anything."

"I know."

"Then go ahead."

"M-M-Mitch—" said Connie, tripping over his name, even.

"Let it go."

"I'm pregnant."

Mitch's hands, still cupping her face, began to tremble. Violently. The synapses in his head making the connections at lightning speed. The consequences instantly becoming all too overwhelming. "Tell me it's mine."

"I can't."

"No!" he raged.

"The doctor. We've tried. It's too close to know!" she screamed. "I wanted to have an abortion. Have it out of me if it's his!"

"But it might not be," he finished.

"Yes. And if it's yours, we might not be able to have another."

"Jesus, Jesus, Jesus," he ranted.

"I love you, Mitch. I'll do whatever you want!"

Whatever I want? I don't know what I fucking want! Christ!

"How many weeks?"

"Eight weeks. I'm due the end of May, God willing."

God willing, yes!

It was all Mitch could do to throw himself at her feet, clutching her. Kissing her. Thanking God for her. And pray, he did. For the first time since he was a boy, he prayed aloud. Asking Christ for guidance, forgiveness, and a direction.

There was a chance, he prayed. A chance the baby inside Connie was his and not some evil, inbred Son of Satan. Instead, a child made of love and second chances in a marriage that had once gone so very wrong. For that, Mitch could pray. For that, Mitch would give up everything.

7

Fitz needed to escape. After the fracas, his first inclination was to face the media and spin like the devil. And the sooner, the better. *But with what?* he thought. His candidate had just, without sufficient provocation, mercilessly beaten the crap out of McCann and then bolted from the scene. Would charges be pressed? A good spin was only as good as the result. If counterspin was required, it might be like trying to reverse the direction of a speeding tank. No. He had to get out of there. Sort it out.

So he dumped it on Rene.

"Don't spin. Just stand there. Listen. Take it all in and promise to have each and every question answered as soon as you're able."

"What's it matter, Fitz?" she moaned. "It's over."

The two were back in the green room with the door locked.

"Bullshit!" he snapped. "We got a week and a half to turn this around."

"How? Mitch just *assaulted* McCann. What if he presses charges? They'll have video of Mitch in handcuffs!"

"They had video of McCann in cuffs and he rebounded."

There was a knocking at the door and the sound of a crowd gathering. Marshall Lambeer at the fore, probably leading a throng of media. "Kolatch? Are you in there?" The knocking quickly turned to pounding. "Goddammit, I want some answers and I want them tonight!"

Fitz turned to Rene. "Don't spin. We don't know Mitchell's state of mind. Without it, we're stuck. Hold 'em until we talk to our candidate."

Throwing open the door, he gave a broad smile to Marshall. "Call me." Then he shoved past the growing crowd, leaving Rene to wave them all in.

"Okay. Come on in. Let's get this over with," she said, putting on her sweetest southern smile. "We can *all* talk. Just one question at a time."

To Fitz, *sorting it out* equaled booze and the time to drink it. The crushing inconclusiveness of his circumstance led the show runner to a mom-and-pop convenience market just off the Interstate. Buying a fifth of bourbon, he was going to park in front of some public beachfront, suck back some Jim Beam, and let the liquor do the thinking.

His far-from-stellar career as a campaign strategist might be ending. What would be next? Consultant? Lobbyist? A long stretch of unemployment and a retired life viewed through the bottom end of a bottle?

The cashier, a 7-Eleven reject who was probably not in the mom-'n'-pop family, was seated on a stool at the register with a small black-and-white TV switched on. When Fitz came up to the counter to pay for the bottle of booze, the cashier proved surprisingly articulate and on-point. "Can you believe this shit?" he said, gesturing to the TV.

"What shit?" asked Fitz, politely tuning out and certain the clerk would be just another clueless slacker.

"Took the guy right out," said the cashier. "I mean, a Democrat. A fuckin' wuss of a Democrat. I thought they was all flower sniffers and antiviolence, know what I mean?"

Fitz gave a sideways glance to the TV. Nervous about the confrontation. Did he smell of Mitch Dutton? "I'm sorry. I don't know."

"Mitch Dutton. The debate with Shakespeare McCann. Did you see it?"

"No," he lied.

"It was *awesome.*"

"You must be a Republican," grumbled Fitz, shucking a twenty-dollar bill from his wallet and laying it on the counter.

"I don't vote. But my parents. They're, like, right-wing. They said this Dutton guy was a fag-lover, too."

"Bottle of Jim Beam and a Dixie cup," reminded Fitz.

"Hey. Check it out." The cashier ignored him, turning up the volume. On the screen, a reporter was already conducting the man-on-the-street-style interviews. The subject? The debate that ended in assault. The microphone was stuck in the face of an older gentleman wearing a white Stetson.

"I dunno. I think he had it comin'. Maybe that Dutton guy had just had enough. Sometimes, I know, I've had enough."

The interviewer cued a tape with more interviews, edited into snippets. A random sampling of South County sexes and colors.

"Didn't see it. What happened?"

"Candidate for Congress Mitch Dutton ended a televised debate by hitting the other candidate, Shakespeare McCann."

"Did he deserve it?"

Then another snippet. Fitz found himself riveted.

"I saw it. Best debate ever. That Dutton boy's got a temper. But if it was me in that spot. Hot lights. Some fellah pointin' fingers. Who knows?"

And another.

"I was definitely on the fence until tonight. And I must admit, I thought Dutton was just your regular weak-kneed politician. But he showed me something of himself. He's a fighter. And I liked it. Gotta say, I liked it a lot. Maybe he'll go back to Washington and kick some congressional tail."

"But how would you feel if McCann pressed charges?"

"What for? Looked to me like he had it coming."

One interview after the next. Fitz couldn't believe what he was hearing, seeing. Where was the negative? Dutton had clearly *assaulted* McCann. Yet the viewing audience, at least those interviewed, were seeing something completely different. They were seeing Mitch as a fighter. Mitch Dutton?

"Change the channel," barked Fitz.

"But this is good," returned the cashier.

"Just the other news. Channel Nine!" Fitz didn't wait for an answer, he simply reached across and switched channels himself.

On Channel 9 was more of the same. Anchors and political pundits remarking on the surprise ending to the debate in mostly positives. None quite so frank as to endorse Mitch or his actions, but all finding it difficult to hide their glee at the outcome of the event. Words and phrases were used like *"surprised"* and *"I didn't think he had it in him."*

The focus group! thought Fitz. If there were positives, Murray would've called. He dove into his coat pocket for his cell phone, only to find the battery dead. "Where's a pay phone?"

"Just around the corner." The cashier pointed.

Fitz headed for the door in a hurry, leaving the bottle of Beam, the Dixie cup, and the twenty-dollar bill on the counter. He was around the corner, feeding the pay phone with a quick quarter and dialing Murray's cell phone. At the other end, Fitz didn't hear the phone even ring. He just heard Murray's voice saying, "Fitz!"

"Sorry. My phone died."

"I've been dialing for over an hour now."

"Just gimme the grislies," said Fitz in his usual low timbre.

"I can't explain it," said Murray. "I mean, it sparked a discussion like I'd never seen."

"Bottom line?"

"Bottom line? They're hooked. I mean, I thought we were dead. When Mitch hit him. Hell if I didn't think I'd be typing my resume tomorrow."

"They liked him?"

"*Loved him!*" said Murray. "I mean, it wasn't a hundred percent. I had one lady who turned in her cards and left the hotel. But most, I'd say, they thought Mitch showed some real chutzpah," finished Murray, breathless and relieved to pass on the news.

"Did you remind the focus group that Mitch had just committed a crime? That he'd assaulted McCann?"

"This is Texas, Fitz. It's all about whether a fellah had it comin' or not. And I guess they thought McCann was out of line pressing the Shoop de Jarnot thing."

"They thought it was about Shoop?"

"Wasn't it? Looked to me that he was pushing Mitch right to the edge with it."

"What were the scores?"

"Well, it's pretty unscientific. But we started with fifteen undecided voters and scored it eleven to three, Dutton."

"It's not too late," figured Fitz in wonder. "We could start a new track tonight. Finish by morning. Who knows? We might have a whole new ball game."

A whole new ball game?

Shakespeare McCann never played sports. As a boy, he was always small, always the new kid in the school, and rarely picked for the team. Sports was for bullies and buttholes. And hustling was for off the court.

"I know. I should see the other guy, am I right?" said the young resident, already expert in the art of repairing faces after fisticuffs. "Now, I want you to hold still. Just a little prick of lidocaine."

After Mitch had vanished from the debate scene and before Rene took on the pressing media, Shakespeare was whisked away by one of his volunteers to a county emergency room, dropped at the entrance, and left to walk in under the assumed name of Alan Funt.

"Mr. Funt," asked the Nicaraguan-born nurse, "I jus' need a signature. This say you are indigent and uninsured. And initial here, please?"

Underneath Shakespeare's silence and pain, his mind was clicking through the options. To press charges? To feign greater injury for the sympathy vote?

No!

And though he knew the police would be looking for him to see if he wished to file a complaint . . .

Tit for tat, considering the Jennifer O'Detts arrest!

. . . placing the shoe on the other man's foot might work as a ball and chain, leaving Dutton stuck somewhere between the final stretch and the finish line. Something, though, made Shakespeare think otherwise. A boiling in his gut that told him that Mitch Dutton had, with one flash of a fist, clutched his campaign into overdrive and would see nothing but blue skies between himself and November third.

"Okay, Mr. Funt. Nod when it's numb," said the resident.

Shakespeare nodded. And silently, without so much as a whimper, he endured the hook stitches that sewed his split lower lip back in place. The doctor worked, paying no mind to anything other than his task. The swelling in Shakespeare's face was so bruised and awful that the young emergency room doctor didn't even recognize the dark-horse candidate who had become so popular, let alone the satirical alias.

"Funt," said the resident. "Have I heard that name before?"

Shakespeare mumbled, "Not 'less you hang out at soup kitchens."

"Your nose is busted. But looks like it wasn't the first time."

Shakespeare nodded and waited for the procedure to end. Leaving the sympathy option open, he agreed to be admitted overnight for observation. An orderly wheeled him into a seven-bed ward room. Three beds were occupied. The curtains were drawn. Away from the office and his home phone, it would give him time to think. To plot. To plan his next move. For the moment, it would serve him to be anonymous.

But instead of helping him look forward, the smell of the room reeled him backward.

Taylor State Prison near Eugeneville, North Carolina. Day three. Inmate number TSP18360G, Campbell Delacourt—a.k.a. Steven Bidwell, Lester McCann, or Franklin C. Harmon—assigned to duties in the prison infirmary, known amongst the other cons as the No Tell Motel. This was where those perceived as the inmate population's small and weak were first assigned. Where doctors were few and the nurses, trustees. This was where bitches were born, initiated, and later assigned to cellblocks and passed around as whores for the studs who ran things. Once he was a bitch, even cigarette cartons, the currency of prisons worldwide, couldn't buy a man a new name or ID. A bitch would always be a bitch, forever incarcerated to receive the worst side of man's sexual impulses. Rape.

Campbell Delacourt, a man who could con old ladies out of their Social Security checks and husbands out of their Friday gambling dough, didn't know the angles. Didn't understand that con was short for convict. And negotiations took place only after the violation.

To that very day, Shakespeare remembered the bloodied sheets of the infirmary bed where he lay long after he'd been tied up and penetrated by the hardware of Taylor State's three most trusted inmates. Trustees. Another code word. And trust had nothin' to do with it.

And then it came to him. With no place to run, no new state to escape to with a new name and a new scam, he had to turn it around. Make them understand they'd fucked the wrong man. That he was nobody's bitch. Options, he thought. Count 'em. Slim and none. Action? Soon. And if he failed? Well, he'd rather die trying.

Remembering a formula from some high school chemistry pranksters, he lifted some isopropyl alcohol and ammonia crystals from the infirmary. Then, shortly thereafter, extended an invitation to a trustee who was all too quick to drop his drawers at the promise of some good head. Pretending the chemical solution was a mouthwash, he took a mouthful and dropped to his knees. A match was quickly lit and brought near his lips. From there, Delacourt blew fire onto the trustee's genitals, igniting them in a wet spew of flame, but burning his own face in the process. The screaming of the trustee. An involuntary action brought his knee up to smash Delacourt's jaw in six places.

Talk of the depraved act was quickly passed along through the penitentiary, and by the time he emerged from twenty-seven hours of plastic reconstruction and six months' recovery in the prison hospital, a certain respect had been cultivated simply through word of mouth. Prisoner to prisoner. Guard to guard. Campbell Delacourt had entered the hospital a bitch, but had returned a man worth reckoning.

Prisons are like hospitals, thought Shakespeare. They all smell the same. He rose from his hospital bed and crossed to the mirror, finding a stool to lean on. Even with the lousy light, the darkened man could see enough of his features to accurately assess the damage. Of course, he'd seen worse. He'd been burned over sixty percent of his face. And that was nothing compared to the afteraffects of orthopedic surgery.

It took eight external steel screws to set the new jaw. For five and a half months Campbell Delacourt drank meals through a straw, passed time with a TV, and spent hours upon hours with the state-appointed psychologist.

Dutton had used the word tonight.

Sociopath. The shrink wasn't dumb enough to use it in the presence of the patient. She just wasn't smart enough—didn't know that Campbell Delacourt could read upside down.

The patient calculated the time upon his face. Two days to lose the swelling. Another four for the bruises to subside enough that makeup would, once again, render him camera-ready. The lower lip, though. It would be weeks until it was fully healed. The stitches hideously started at his chin and traversed the thick part of his lower lip like train tracks.

It was no longer a public face for a public figure. The shelling he'd given Dutton in the alley had at least left his opponent with time to recover. Now there was no time left. Shakespeare had already flipped through the newscasts while alone in his infirm state. All with their own frame-by-frame replays of the assault, followed by commentary ad infinitum.

Smile. You're on "Candid Camera."

Just as his stomach had tried to tell him earlier, Patient Funt saw the coming consensus. Dutton was back on top with that all-important *momentum* on his side.

You must turn the tide back. Turn it back now!

Gathering his clothes and losing the hospital johnny in the nearest waste bin, Shakespeare checked Alan Funt out of the hospital by traveling the three floors down to the A-side emergency exit and calling a cab.

         *   *   *

Connie rolled over in bed to find the clock reading 8:44 A.M. "Shit!"

She bolted from bed, afraid of the expected. Mitch was usually out the door by eight-thirty and on the way to the campaign office. She was drawing her robe around her as she rushed down the stairs, tying it when she hit the bottom step and rounding the corner into the kitchen, where much to her surprise, Mitch sat in his running clothes at the table.

"You didn't run?" she said, noting he was dry as a desert breeze.

He lifted his hand up onto the table. It was even more swollen than the night before, dripping wet from a bucket of ice water he held between his legs. "Thought I could, but it hurts too damn much."

"You should get it X-rayed."

"I'll go see old Doc Dominguez. Even though he'll probably want to talk about my old man."

She poured a cup of coffee and sat down across from him. "Did you sleep at all?"

"Some," he said, his voice lowering with his eyes to the newspaper in front of him. "And just when I'd decided to hang it all up . . ." He twisted the front page around so she could read it. "Looks like I'm back in it."

Connie scanned the front page. Above a grainy, video-transferred image from the debate capturing Mitch frozen in the act of throwing that first punch, the headline read:

DUTTON FIGHTS BACK!!!

"I talked to Fitz. He says the numbers are crazy," he continued. "Says the overnight tracking puts me back ahead by eight points. That in one swift swing I've removed the wimp factor from my public persona." He tried not to seem insulted. "I didn't even know I *had* a wimp factor."

She looked glum at the news. The fact was, she didn't know what to think. "Does this mean you're going to win?"

"If I stay in the race, I'd say the probability is up there. But I'd have to be a candidate."

"But you *are* a candidate."

"Not if I withdraw. I mean, it's too late to take my name off the ballot, but—"

"But is it what you want?" Connie was genuine. She didn't want him to give up because of her.

Mitch stood and stepped over to the sink, where he emptied the ice bucket and wrapped his nearly numbed hand in a dish towel. "I had a long time to think last night," he started, searching for the right words. "At this point, the only reason to stay in it—other than pride—is because I don't want to see that sonofabitch in office." Then he heaved and leaned against the kitchen counter in a slump-shouldered, defeated posture. "There's also a strong voice. And it sounds like my father's."

"What's it say?"

"That the public gets the government that they deserve."

"You can't be serious."

"They *want* to be lied to. They *want* only for me to tell them what they want to hear. That everything's just hunky-dory. Nothing's wrong with the country. Nothing needs fixing." He was shaking his head.

"But a lot of them want you." She pushed the paper toward him. "Says right here, in black and white."

"Correction. Black and blue."

"You're ahead. The majority will probably vote for you."

"Not for *me*. Just the bullshit *I've* told them," said Mitch. "Politics is simply about whose bullshit sells the most tickets."

"You don't believe that."

"I didn't. But I do now."

"I think you should think about it."

He shook his head. He didn't want to think about it anymore. He wanted off the ride. That's when Connie got up from the table and walked over to him, undoing her robe so that when she put her arms around him, her naked skin would press against him. She knew he liked that. "You want to go back to bed? Fool around? Afterward, maybe, you can get up on the right side of the bed."

But Mitch was still shaking his head. "You don't get it, do you?" He kneeled to the floor, pressing his face into her not-yet-protruding stomach. "I've found new hope. In you. In the baby."

"Mitch!"

He rose up to look her in the eye and press an index finger gently to her lips. "I'm going upstairs. I'm going to shower. Then, carefully, I'm going to drive to the doctor and have my hand X-rayed."

"Don't make any rash—"

"I promise you. Today I'll only think about it. I won't do a thing without talking to you first." He removed his finger. "Happy?"

"Only if you are." Connie was emphatic. He was trying to get away with making a snap decision, something about him that always galled her. He'd gotten into the race in the same way.

"Are you sure?" she would ask. "Is this what you want?"

And he would say, "What's it matter, sweetie? I'm never going to win against Hammond. This is just my way of stirring the pot. Getting folks to do some thinking."

While he showered, she quickly tired of the newspaper and her coffee. Morning sickness hadn't quite turned her into a porcelain goddess, but she found that eating was playing second fiddle to mindless chores. Connie decided to do Mitch a favor and clear the telephone machine of messages from the night before. A couple of calls were perfunctory. And even more were congratulatory. Then there were the two calls from Fitz. One at nine and another closer to ten, urging him to call at the soonest possible moment.

Second to last on the answering machine was another call from Gina. That jack rabbit voice of hers eating tape with one contrite sound bite after the other. Apologizing for not calling. Apologizing for not being around. Apologizing for being afraid to call. But then begging for Connie to meet her. They had to talk. Lunch. Anywhere. Just please, call back!

"Okay, Gina. Enough!" It had been too long since the best friends had spoken, and the last time had ended so poorly. There was plenty to talk about.

Connie made a mental note to call back and then played the last message. The electronic voice stamp began with the time. "One forty-six A.M." Afterward, a muddied voice crept out, as if mumbling a tune through swollen lips:

"Rock-a-bye-baby, on the treetop. When the wind blows, the cradle will rock. When the bough breaks, the cradle will fall. And down will come baby, cradle and all."

When the tape ended, she sat and clutched her stomach. *How did he know?* she wondered. How could he? Or was it just coincidence? A wild guess? She rocked herself in the chair, praying silently. Yes. She knew the child was hers. But whose seed had worked its way into the egg? She prayed it was Mitch's. If God loved her, it was Mitch's. If he was a compassionate, caring God . . .

Connie stood and hit the erase function on the answering machine. Quickly the tape rewound and rubbed out any record that Shakespeare or anybody else had called the night before. In doing so, she forgot about Gina. Not until later that day would she remember.

8

"See there? Fractures there, there, and a little hairline fellah right there, just above the first knuckle. See it?" Dr. Dominguez pointed out to Mitch the damage to his right hand, aided by an X ray that the old doctor held up to the fluorescent light overhead. Not that he didn't have a view box. This was just the way he'd been checking out his X rays since the Korean War. What jet black hair the doctor had left was cut to spiky military specs. "By what I saw on the TV, looks like the other fellah got the short end of the stick, though. So be happy."

"Are you going to have to cast it?" Mitch hated casts. As a kid, he'd had four.

"Think I'm just gonna wrap it up good 'n' tight." The doctor gave him a stern eye. "That's only if you promise to stay away from shaking hands for three weeks or so. Which, in your chosen profession, might be a hardship." Dr. Dominguez changed his mind. "What say we go for the plaster?"

"Why don't we wrap it?" suggested Mitch. "Shaking hands is the last of my concerns." He left it there. He wasn't bowing out just yet.

"Yeah. I guess you won't need much handshaking. Just about everybody figures you got the seat wrapped up. Last night was the icing on the cake."

"Ever hear of the fat lady?"

"How's this for you?" offered the old war doctor. "Close only counts in horseshoes and hand grenades."

"Heard it, stole it, and wore it out," chuckled Mitch.

"You know? I talked to your old man last week."

"Well, you got one on me."

"He called for a consult on his tendonitis," said Dr. Dominguez. "But then we got talkin'. He wanted to know *everything.* How many points you were up. If this guy McCann was any kind of challenger. Sounded real interested in your prospects."

"So what'd you tell him?" asked Mitch, covering up his surprise with a question.

"I told him you were gonna kick McCann's butt!" The old doctor was sharp on this point. "You know? I never did trust him from the minute he started up with the ice cream deal."

Mitch gave an appreciative laugh. "So what do I do about the pain? And please don't say Tylenol."

"Nope. I'm a believer in the old-fashioned pharmacology. Morphine when you got the stomach for it. And lesser degrees when you don't." Dr. Dominguez scrawled out onto his prescription pad three days worth of Percocet with the relevant instructions. Two tablets to be taken with a meal. Do not drive. Do not operate heavy machinery.

The directions were fine by Mitch. With a quick call from his car phone, he informed Fitz that he was celebrating his sudden lead in the polls with a day off at his law office. There his partners would leave him alone, and between signing papers and perusing legal briefs, he could have time to think.

As he expected, Fitz put up a fight. "You think McCann's taking the day off?"

"Well, I don't think he'll be doing any public appearances," said Mitch, "unless it's with the county sheriff to swear out a complaint."

Fitz countered with facts and figures from the late-morning tracks to show the lead was significant, but could still swing back the other way. Rene was busy plying the media, but sooner or later they'd demand to see the candidate.

"For every action, there's a reaction," continued Fitz. "Politics is no different. We gotta bottle this antiwimp vaccine and get out there and sell it!"

Mitch was intractable. "My hand hurts so bad, it's giving me headaches. And hell if I know what this medication's gonna do. I might have an allergic reaction. I might say things in public *you'll* regret."

They'd all make do without him, he thought. Fitz, Rene. Hell, the whole staff was so damn capable, he told him, he could probably spend the next week in Bermuda and he'd still come out a congressman. And although Fitz knew bullshit when he heard it, it was bullshit sweet enough to cut Mitch enough slack to spend the rest of the day in legal peace.

"Okay. We'll leave you be," Fitz relented. "But you gotta check in every couple of hours."

"That's a deal."

Then after they hung up, and unbeknownst to his candidate, Fitz gave Rene the go-ahead to schedule a Sunday morning press brunch at the Marriott. He'd have plenty of time to sell Mitch on the prospect later in the day when he'd mellowed from overmedication. On short notice, Kevin Cronyn and Brad Pustin from the National Committee had agreed to partake in the event, flying in from Washington that afternoon.

Yes. The planets had lined up for Mitch to finally slam-dunk the election. Fitz was going to leave nothing else to chance.

All day Mitch kept himself inside those smoked-glass windows of his fourth-floor office on the West Strand, ordering lunch in and washing back the first two of those Percocet capsules. And though the pain never seemed to dull enough to where he found himself comfortable within his own thoughts, the peace from the solitude and his legal readings calmed him. For the first time in months he was able to look at his surroundings and appreciate them. His office. A legal practice that did more good than bad. His life represented in the photographs that were scattered about. Comfortable, he thought. Solid. Why would any man give it all up for a daily assault that was all that a seat in the House could truly guarantee?

He decided he would attend church the following day, inviting Connie to wear something cheerfully flowered. They would hold hands during the service and pray for a healthy baby. Afterward he would meet with all relevant parties and make his announcement. Mitch Dutton was going to withdraw from the race. It was the only way to save himself. The voters would have to fend for themselves.

The fiftieth anniversary bash for Gina's parents was, as expected by their daughter, Dullsville, populated by the Geritol brigade. They'd arrived in their designer best from another decade. The old men in tuxedos, and their ancient wives hobbled by the heft of their best jewelry. And as much as Gina tried her level best to play the practiced role of the only child and adoring daughter, the chitchat swirled. She could hear the drunken ladies yammer their condolences about the Sweets's unmarried little girl.

"Isn't she thirty-seven?"

"Why isn't she married?"

"And what about grandchildren?"

It was enough to make her sick.

She'd kept up her best smiles for the toast. Held her drink high, yet held her tongue when it came to saying what was on her mind.

Screw you and the high-assed horses you rode in on. At dawn tomorrow, I'm gone. Back to Europe. Paris. Milan. Topless beaches. With a truckload of condoms. Maybe later ya'll can help me pack?

The cliffside house rested on stilts and rocks that rimmed the eastern end of the harbor. It made for some special sunsets, just the way Gina's father had designed. But darkness had already descended as she made her way out onto the deck. From inside her bra she came up with a rolled joint, ready to smoke. Only she'd forgotten the matches.

"Shit."

She knew there were plenty of old men inside who, just for a peek down her dress, would be more than willing to come up with a match to light her joint. Big mistake, she decided. Her trust money was still in Daddy-o's back pocket, so she circled around the pool and ducked into her guest cottage. Once inside, she quickly blazed up the joint, sucked in some of that precious *sinsamilla*, then thought to check her machine.

Number of messages—zero.

"Little Miss Popular."

It vexed Gina that Connie hadn't called back. If she'd thought about it, she could make excuses. After the debate, it must've been as if the roof had caved in on their Flower Hill manor. Connie wouldn't have time. Then, combined with their last words to each other . . . Gina tried to understand. But she was impatient and scared. Europe was calling for her return. A place far from—

"You were gonna help me."

She spun around so fast, the ashes from the joint spilled down her cleavage and stung. Shakespeare was seated on that comfy bed of pillows and stuffed toys. His pummeled face obscured by shadows.

"What are you doing here?" was all she could think to ask.

"Could ask you the same question," he said, kicking over one of her suitcases. "You comin' or goin'?"

"I was gone . . . I just got back."

"Liar, liar, pants on fire."

Gina sucked in some air, recalling where she was. Safe on her parents' property with three hundred party guests scattered about the main house. So she huffed, "I'm going. Okay?"

"But you were gonna help me," said Shakespeare. He stood and approached.

"I can't help you. I'm sorry."

"But you can."

"No I can't—"

Shakespeare's fist broke her nose and dropped her. Before she could scream, he had a handful of hair and a hand over her mouth.

"Yes you can," he hissed.

9

The underground parking at 315 West Strand, typical for most high-rises, was concrete, pillared, and darker than the average tenant would like. It felt unsafe. For years women in the building had lobbied for the building manager to install better lighting. But all they'd gotten were promises and no action.

When Mitch stepped from the elevator at nearly eight o'clock, he remembered the complaint. Monday, he said to himself, he'd make that his first order of business. Get the landlord to fix the lights. That single idea made him feel more productive than he'd felt in all the months of the campaign. He smiled to himself. He was back.

Ignoring the warning from the pharmacist, he was going to drive home. Ten minutes from the office to *Casa de Dutton*. Saturday night, traffic light. Plus, he felt just fine. His right hand was medically numbed and his head felt clearer than it had in ages. As he keyed the door lock on the Volvo and sat inside, closing the door behind him, the first thing he noticed was the stink. Had he stepped in something between the elevator and his car? He turned over the engine and rolled down the window. It was only a ten-minute drive. The dark garage was giving him chills.

Wimp factor, thought Mitch. *Maybe the pollsters are on to something.*

He put the Swedish sedan into gear and checked his rearview mirror. He jumped at what he saw.

"Evening, Counselor," mumbled Shakespeare from the backseat. "You forgot your seat belt."

And before Mitch could think of reaching for the door handle, Shakespeare roped a nylon cord around his neck, pulling it tight and knotting it behind the headrest in a solid square knot. Mitch struggled against it, trying to slip his fingers between the rope and his neck.

"Now, now. It's just a safety precaution. Don't go makin' things worse. We're strapped in. The sooner you drive, the sooner I cut you loose." Shakespeare revealed a blade, the same one he'd used to kill Hollice, right next to Mitch's cheek. He let the cold blade touch skin, letting it slide around to the base of the skull where he dug it in just a bit. Mitch flinched.

"Easy, now. This is right where I stuck Hollice Waters. Right in the little soft spot." Shakespeare leaned closer and into a small shaft of light so Mitch could see a face nearly swollen beyond recognition. "You get where I'm comin' from, Counselor?"

"Yeah," was all Mitch could choke out.

"Drive slow and legal. We're gonna have us a little talk, you 'n' me."

"Now?"

"Now."

Mitch let his foot off the brake, and the car rolled backward out of the assigned spot. Then, somewhere between the fear and the Percocet, he stood too hard on the brake. The car jolted to a stop as the knife dug into his neck. He howled. "Sonofabitch!"

"Careful, Counselor!" said Shakespeare, withdrawing the blade a notch. "Now, let's try this again. Slow and easy."

Shifting into drive, Mitch wheeled out of the garage, circling three stories upward to the exit, out onto the Strand, and into a light rain. The streets were wet and traffic was that Saturday Night Lite.

"Wipers," reminded Shakespeare.

Oh, yeah, realized Mitch. He reached forward and, switching on the wiper blades, asked, "Now where?"

"Just keep it the way you're headed. This won't take long," began Shakespeare, removing the knife and leaning back into the rear seat. "First off. Congratulations. I made a mistake. I underestimated you. I didn't think you had it in you to take a swing at me on TV."

"I apologize. Is that what you want?"

"Don't need none of that shit from you. It was the right move. Put you back up on top. Gave you the momentum."

"What do you want then?"

Shakespeare laughed. "I want to win!"

"Then I'll withdraw," offered Mitch a bit too soon. He didn't know it was a negotiation. "There's a press conference tomorrow."

"Well, wouldn't that be easy?"

"I've already written my statement. I'm getting out of the race. I don't like what this race has become."

"A dogfight? Is that what you're sayin'?"

"I'm not saying anything," said Mitch, cautiously braking into a red light, then looking back at Shakespeare in the rearview mirror.

"Like what you see?"

"I'm saying that I'm out."

"Too late. Can't take your name off the ballot. And I can't take that kind of chance."

"So what's left, killing me?" said Mitch, emboldened by the narcotic. It was a patent conclusion considering the circumstances.

"Thought of it. But this late in the game? No, sir. Too suspect," answered Shakespeare. "Hammond was killin' enough. You. I gotta beat at the ballot box."

Goose bumps broke out on Mitch's skin, stopping at his numbed right hand. *Hammond killed?* A prime piece to the puzzle had found its place.

"Not that killin' you's entirely out of the question. Now, what I need is a dark side street."

"What you need is a shrink."

"Seen 'em. Psychologists, psychiatrists, psychotherapists. Know what they said?"

" 'Sociopath'?"

"Betcha don't even know what the word means."

"Oh, I got a good idea."

"Clinically, it simply means a person with antisocial tendencies."

"I gather that would include stark raving madness?"

"If there's a *method,* there's ain't no *madness.* Turn left when it goes green."

The light had switched. Mitch waited for an oncoming car to pass through the intersection before wheeling the Volvo left and up a darkened side street.

"Stop up here on the right. Away from the streetlight."

Mitch performed as instructed, sliding the car into an unlit portion of the block. Behind them, traffic continued to pass along the Strand, but no cars followed up the street. "So what's your next trick?" he prompted, his patience growing thinner from the drugs. And his hand was starting to ache.

"I'm about to up your negative into the political freaking stratosphere. A vote for Dutton'll be a vote that nobody with an ounce of human decency would ever permit."

Shakespeare opened the rear passenger door. The overhead lamp switched on, giving Mitch one last look at the damage he'd done.

"This'll take only a second," said Shakespeare, slipping around behind the car, and with a twisting wrist, he punctured the right rear tire. As the car slowly sagged into the curb, Shakespeare threw open the passenger door opposite Mitch.

"For the record, I shoulda killed your wife." Shakespeare winked. "I don't think you would have survived it. I don't think you would've had the will to fight."

"Another mistake." Mitch boiled and lurched against the rope. It burned his neck. Then Shakespeare dropped the knife on the seat and walked back toward the Strand. Mitch watched McCann through the rearview mirror until he was out of sight. A cold sweat broke out on his face. And his mind reeled.

Up my negatives? But I'm quitting the Goddamn race!

He reached for the cell phone and dialed 911. His first time ever. Shock that it was to the candidate, the phone rang a total of twenty-two times before an emergency operator answered. But before she did, his mind continued flying off the handle.

Nine-one-one. What's that, Mr. Dutton? Your opposition just tied a rope around your neck, threatened you with a knife, cut your tire, said he should've killed your wife, then walked? You sure it wasn't just somebody who said he was McCann?

"Emergency operator," answered the passionless voice.

Then there's the knife, thought Mitch. *The one Shakespeare used to kill Hollice Waters? Jesus, I didn't even know Hollice was dead! If McCann wanted me out of the race, why didn't he just kill me?*

"Emergency operator . . . Hello?"

And Hammond. Shakespeare said he'd killed him, too. More threats. More intimidation. Truth or fiction? The line with McCann was a constant blur.

Blood swelled in Mitchell's head. His vision shook. Then his ears finally picked up the voice between the throbbings in his brain. "Emergency operator. Is anybody there?"

He pressed the end button on the cell phone. He had to think. He reached across to the passenger seat and picked up the knife, slipping the blade under the rope. The sharpness of the instrument was frightening. The rope slid away and he was free. The blood instantly drained. He rubbed his neck. It stung.

Now what?

Mitch dialed Fitz. He was good at this. He'd have a clear perspective. Fitz's line rang once before his machine picked up. So Mitch dialed the campaign office and got a teenage volunteer who knew absolutely nothing about anything, let alone the whereabouts of Mr. Kolatch or Ms. Craven.

He was hyperventilating. He had to get out of the car. Get air. He pushed open the door and stepped out into the misting rain, circling back around to the sidewalk. There he saw the flat tire and realized, that much, he could do.

That much, he could fix!

The flat tire. It was punctured just inside the first row of tread. And there was the obstacle of Mitch's broken hand. His next inclination was to call the auto club from the car phone. They'd surely answer and come fix the damn thing. It'd been years since he'd changed a tire. Hell, he wasn't even sure there was a spare in the trunk. Had he ever even looked, for God's sake?

Back inside the car, he dialed information to get the auto club's number. South Texas Mobile Express put him right through. Only then did he catch a dim look at himself in the rearview mirror. The reflection revealed a red rope burn that traced his neckline just above the collar. And when he shifted his focus to the car seat, he noticed blood from the prick at the base of his neck, smeared all over the gray leather.

That and his hand was throbbing. The medication was wearing off.

The car was a mess. So was he.

"Auto club," answered the voice.

He hung up again, briefly pausing before diving into the glove box for the owner's manual, written for luckless morons who had bought the fine Swedish car, but knew not a singular iota about the difference between a lug nut and a tire jack. With the manual in hand, he chose to suffer the rain and change the damn tire himself. He'd think better at home once he'd knocked back another Percocet with a shot of Absolut.

In the dimness of that side street, Mitch would've had to feel around for the trunk lock had it not been for a lost load of tourists in a rental car that turned up the street. He hurried, fumbling with the keys to try and open the lock. Then, there in the wash of headlights, he saw the first traces of blood smeared upon the lid. Red on silver. He froze and the car passed without stopping.

My blood from my hands. Mitch, get a fuckin' grip!

He inserted the key into the lock and popped the lid. The springs unloaded. The trunk yawned and ignited with two panel lights placed right and left. Mitch gulped back the rise of sour acid his stomach fired upward.

Jesus, Gina . . .

Twisted, bloody, and horribly dead. Gina Sweet's eyes were fixed and screaming, just as they'd been when Shakespeare drew the knife across her soft neck. Her mouth, gaping and wide as she had tried to make a shriek, only to gag on her own blood.

He felt his knees weaken before an autonomic electrical shock coursed through his body. He tumbled into the rain-filled gutter, crawling backward to the curb.

Jesus, God . . .

His eyes bugged and kept to the trunk, half expecting to see Gina come crawling out, laughing it up in some sick Halloween joke she'd cooked up with Shakespeare McCann.

She never crawled out. She was oh so dead in the car's trunk, lid up, the rain washing away at the sticky, dried blood.

Another piece in the puzzle dropped into position. The colossal negative from which Mitch would never recover. His wife's best friend. His car. The knife. A flat tire. What was next? It had to be the police.

His mind raced ahead through all the culminations, combinations, ramifications. A domino effect of calamity. The media would crucify him before trial. The police would leak the evidence. The exposure would demand a first-degree prosecution. The evidence would compel a jury.

Mitch Dutton had motive.

Mitch Dutton had access.

Mitch Dutton had his fingerprints on the murder weapon.

Most important, Mitch Dutton was *violent*, as witnessed by the thousands who'd seen the debate, only twenty-four hours earlier.

Think, Mitch! Think!

Nothing came. He didn't move. He wanted a way out. He wanted to call the police. None of it jibed, though. None of it spelled *s-o-l-u-t-i-o-n*. It all spelled disaster.

Time's wasting, dummy!

That's what he was doing. *Wasting time.* Sitting on his hands and waiting for the police to take him away in handcuffs. Mitch would never recall how long he sat on the curb, staring back at the open trunk in utter and confused shock. One minute. Two, three, four. Five minutes. The rain soaking him. He was in his own head. Moving from conclusion to resolution to prosecution, and back again.

I am truly alone now. Nobody can help me. Not Fitz. Not Connie. Not the police. And unless I do something now, something quick, I'll lose Connie. I'll be dead or in prison! Now, Mitch! Now! Do something now!

He had to get off his ass and change the fucking tire, is what he had to do. He had to change it fast and get off that fucking side street. That meant moving Gina's body. Suddenly he found himself back on his feet and rushing to the car. His legs were wobbly. His hand throbbed. And the damn drugs weren't helping the matter.

Don't operate heavy equipment, it said on the bottle. *Don't drive or change tires or move dead, stinking bodies.*

At the trunk, Mitch whirled two quick three-sixties. Just to see if anybody was watching, if cars were coming. After that, he stood over the body, his chest heaving once, then twice.

Just change the damn tire!

"One-eight-one?" chirped the radio.

"One-eight-one," responded Officer Mark Alan Lucas of the Cathedral PD. He was alone in his radio unit, eastbound on the Strand. It was 8:39 P.M.

"Got a cell-phone call from a Mr. Samuel Torres. Says he spotted Mitch Dutton trying to change a flat tire off on Howard Street."

It was a slow night. Rain had a tendency to drive away potential crime-doers. And Officer Mark Alan Lucas, after the enthralling debate the night before, welcomed the opportunity to shake the candidate's hand. Even if it meant he'd have to get his hands dirty changing a tire.

"One-eight-one en route to help with that flat tire up on Howard. ETA less than one minute."

The dispatcher crackled back, "While you're kissing the fellah's ass, see how he feels about wage hikes."

"That's a ten-four," shot back Officer Lucas.

Any excuse to switch on the lights atop the car was excuse enough for Officer Lucas. The stoplights went faster that way. He'd only have to slow, then roll on through. Code two, they called it. The police handbook specifically designated code twos as *urgencies*. Not to be confused with *emergencies*. That would've been a code three. Sirens would then be in order.

One block up and to the left was Howard Street. The officer swung the car wide right before making the turn. This way he wouldn't have to switch on the flood lamp fixed next to his driver's-side window. As he cranked the wheel to the left, the police cruiser's headlight beams swept up the short hill that was Howard Street. Officer Lucas braked midway up.

"Dispatch, this is one-eight-one."

"Go ahead."

"Parked up here on Howard. And I don't see a damn thing. No car. No flat tire. Can you check the address again?"

"Checking," responded the dispatcher. "Howard Street. One block north of the Strand."

"I'm on Howard. And I'm one block north. All I got around here is dark."

Dark. That was it. A dark street. A dark sidewalk with rain running down the gutter. Parked in the middle of the street with his headlights pointed north, Officer Lucas was surely disappointed. There was no Volvo with a flat tire. No candidate Dutton in need of help. Zip. There went his story for the wife. There went his handshake.

Backing his cruiser out onto the Strand, Officer Lucas didn't see the prima facie evidence. He was only looking for a car with a flat tire. And clearly there was none. If he'd made a closer inspection, gotten off his wide ass and out of his unit and run a flashlight up the sidewalk, he might've seen the tire jack the candidate had left behind. Or the blood smears on the walkway, slowly diluting and spilling into the gutter with every drop of rain. Mitch had caught his first break.

10

*K*eep thinking, Mitch. Just keep thinking.

Crossing the bridge to the mainland, he chanted his new mantra as he carefully held to the speed limit. Now, if the tire would just hold for another twenty miles. He swallowed another two pills.

Thinking, thinking, thinking.

Back on Howard Street, he had almost lost the game, attempting to pull the spare tire loose from underneath Gina's stiffened body. With only one good arm, it proved impossible unless he could find some way to lift the body clear from the trunk. That begged two stupid questions. What if someone drove by and saw the body? And if that didn't happen, how the hell would he get the body back in the trunk? So he risked his right hand, successfully sliding the jack from underneath her dead weight and frozen muscles. But the tire, it wouldn't budge. That's when he looked her right in those dead eyes of hers and cursed. "You fucking bitch!"

Then he saw the aerosol canister.

It was wedged underneath her head. Fix-a-Flat was the brand. One of Connie's Price Club "impulse buys." She'd bought a canister for each car, tossing them into the trunk for emergencies. Forever forgotten. Until Mitch needed it.

Wonder product or rip-off? he thought.

He was about to find out. He shook the can and spun himself around to the right rear tire, unscrewed the cap on the flat's stem, and connected the can. Miraculously, the tire inflated.

Sonofabitch! The damn stuff works!

In mere seconds he was back behind the wheel, ignition engaged and flooring it. The tires slipped against the wet pavement, caught some traction, and lurched up the hill. The headlights were an afterthought. Had he switched them on before making the right-hand turn onto Ocean View Avenue, Officer Lucas might've caught a glimpse of the silver Volvo when he'd turned his radio car onto Howard.

It was *that* close. And Mitch would never know.

The Span touched the mainland and split. The Gulf route to the east. The Interstate to the north. Mitch swerved left onto the Interstate for the second part of a plan that was still forming in his head. He *must* get rid of the body. McCann'd surely called the police with some anonymous report. Candidate with a flat tire needs help and votes. It was brilliant, with Mitch in de facto possession of a dead body.

Route 64B, otherwise called Owens Road. It was Cathedral City's gateway to a remote landscape made up of gravel roads and dry gulches that flooded in the slightest rain. The geography was a legendary boneyard for transients, rape victims, and failed kidnappings. And the guilty, well, they clearly knew where to go when there was dirty laundry to be washed. The Old Boneyard off Owens Road.

Mitch picked his turn off the highway. The drugs had kicked in once again, but all they did was fog his vision. His hand still hurt like hell. Headlights off, he rolled down the window so he could hear the gravel underneath his tires. An old trick his father had taught him during duck hunts. That way a hunter'd know he was on the road without spooking the fowl. Quentin Dutton never knew that driving with the headlights off spooked *Mitch.*

The smell hit him harder the second time. When the odometer clicked at the quarter-mile mark, he stopped and popped the trunk. Death. It had a warm goo to it that stuck inside his sinuses like spoiled milk. He wanted to puke. But after stepping away to suck back a lungful of clean air, the candidate rallied and, reaching into the trunk with his left hand, tried hard to forget that he was grabbing hold of Gina Sweet. He bit his lip, grasped the body by its sleeve, and tugged. Her shoulder cleared the trunk first. Then he went for the right leg. It swung free, but the left leg was hyperextended, stiff and wedged into the corner.

Gina's bloodied party dress was pulled all the way to her neck.

And when Mitch grasped a bundled hold of satin to lift the body out, the fabric simply ripped away. Her bra was all that was left for a handle. An underwire contraption that was designed to show more breast than lace. He slipped his only good hand under the strap, praying it would hold the deadweight. With that, he'd touched her skin. It was cool and felt like smooth rubber. Inhuman. With a three-count in his head, followed by a mighty tug, he lifted, the wedged limb swung free, and the body tumbled from the trunk to the gravel. With his feet he finished the job by rolling Gina into the ditch.

The retch he'd been holding back surfaced, and he was on his knees, puking.

She's dead, Mitch. And there's not a Goddamn thing you can do about it but save your own ass. Get onto part three and save your prayers. You're gonna need 'em.

As he hurried through the darkness, on his way to his next destination, the candidate's mind wandered briefly to a faraway place he'd once called the *high ground*, a vision as distant as the Himalayas.

Romantically speaking, Mitch was a dead issue. And with only days left in the campaign, the best Rene could muster was some hard work between the hurt and the hangovers. So she tasked her way through her daily duties of turning him into a congressman. That required hours upon hours of late nights, churning out media-friendly copy, spinning the day's events to match the candidate's platform, and pimping media relationships into positive propaganda. And lately when she needed a break from all of it, she'd begun drinking French champagne while packing boxes in her loft above the Strand Bicycle Shop. A week and a half until November third. On November fourth, Rene wanted to be history.

After early cocktails and dinner with Kevin Cronyn, Brad Pustin, and Fitz, she'd settled in front of her PowerBook with a flute of bubbly and a plan to e-mail her revised resume.

The phone rang.

"Hello," she answered on the half ring. Whoever it was, she wanted to get the caller off as quickly as possible. She had but one line. And tonight it was dedicated to her modem. That was until she recognized the voice and the crackle of a cell phone.

"Mitch?"

"I have something I want you to do. And I want you to do it right now. No questions asked," Mitch said over the dubious Route 64B connection. If he'd had any kind of time, he'd have stopped and used a hard line. But the risk of recognition was more dangerous than a bad cell connection wherein some unwitting caller might hear his conversation.

"Listen, Mitch. Unless it relates to the campaign, I'm off the clock tonight and—"

"Do you love me?"

The query caught her between the eyes. "Mitch, I . . ."

"If you do, you'll help."

"And if I don't?"

"Then God help me."

He was asking her to give a piece of herself that she knew he wouldn't give back. Hadn't she given enough already?

"What do you need?"

"I need your promise to follow my instructions to the absolute letter."

"Okay," she said flatly. "Do I need to write this down?"

"I want you to drive to my house. I want you to tell Connie that, *on my instructions,* she's to pack a bag and fly to San Francisco. It's for her own safety. And I promise you, she'll understand."

"Mitch. What's this about?"

"No questions, Rene. Just do it. Do it now," he urged. "Promise, Goddammit, you'll do it now!"

"I have to ask, Mitch. Why not Fitz or Murray?"

"Because I'm asking you."

"You trust me with your wife."

"My wife *and* our baby."

Baby?

"That's as much as I can say. The less you know, the better for you. But I need you to do this now! Just go. Hang up and go!"

Rene found herself saying okay and doing just as Mitch asked. She hung up the phone, but didn't leave right away. She was still trying to make some kind of sense out of it.

Hang up and go?

Go to Connie? Was Mitch mad? He was talking about the wife. He hadn't said she was pregnant. And why didn't he call Connie and have her go to the airport herself? Was the phone off the hook? She picked up the phone and dialed Mitch's number. Two rings. And Connie picked up. "Hello?"

Hang up and go!

Rene hung up. This time she stopped figuring and started moving.

Connie was frightened by the last hang-up. The day had been chock-full of strange and eerie circumstances. The urgent calls the night before from Gina. Followed by Connie's unreturned calls to her. Then there were the hang-ups. The phone would ring. She would race for it, hoping it was Mitch, only to hear the caller hanging up. Just like the last one.

When Mitch finally reached her by eight, he'd promised no stops or delays. And now the dinner she'd cooked was gelling into a tasteless lump in the oven. It seemed obvious that Mitch was roped back into the campaign despite his clear and heartfelt resolve that very morning.

All that and she was pregnant.

A smooth glass of Chardonnay would've been a tonic while she waited. She couldn't turn on the TV or radio without being overrun with political attack ads. So she was stuck with nonalcoholic beer, *People* magazine, and a hopeful prayer that Mitch knew what he was doing. It was raining. There was always that fateful, awful chance . . .

Headlights washed across the downstairs windows. Connie sighed, tossed the magazine, and went to the kitchen to see if she could rescue the meal. But instead of keys in the door, she heard the bell. The dogs started barking. She squeezed her eyes shut. "Shit."

Bad news. It's gotta be bad news.

She shut the dogs in the kitchen and flipped on the outdoor light to see who it was.

Rene Craven?

Swinging open the door, Connie wanted to say a simple "hello." But the worry in her stomach could only shovel up something less friendly. "Listen, he's not here. He's supposed to be, but . . ."

Rene was waiting for her to stop talking.

"Mitch called me. He asked me a favor. He said you'd understand."

"Understand what?"

Rene struggled. "That you . . . Something . . ."

"Excuse me?" asked Connie.

"He said it's not safe."

"Where was he?"

"He wouldn't say. He just said to hang up and go."

"But he was calling from the car?"

"I think so. I don't know where from. You want to tell me what's going on?"

"Did Mitch say I would?"

"He said the less I knew, the better."

Behind the wheel of her Nissan Maxima, Rene wouldn't bother telling her the rest. The part where Mitch asked her if she loved him. She'd rather forget that part, anyway.

"Mitch says your whole family's in politics," Connie said.

"Pretty much the whole clan," answered Rene, wondering how much Mitch had told Connie about her. Especially when he'd told Rene hardly a damn thing about his wife.

"Must make for interesting table talk," said Connie, trying to make polite conversation.

"It would. If we could ever get us all in one place."

As they drove to the airport, the polite talk faded into a worried silence, leaving an icy trench between the women. The conversation had begun cordially back at the house, where Rene had diplomatically chosen to wait downstairs while Connie packed, pacing all the while, and killing those long twenty minutes with numerous checks of her own answering machine. When she thought they were finally prepared to go, Connie kept returning to the house to turn off a light or the gas or something else of minor importance. The last effort was to leave the dogs at a neighbor's. By ten-thirty they were on the road. At eleven-forty, they were at the airport.

As instructed, Rene was to drop Connie at the airport and drive off unnoticed. Instead, when they pulled up to the curb, Connie stayed put in the passenger seat, staring dead ahead.

"You gotta go," said Rene. "Mitch didn't want anybody to see us."

"I know," said Connie, her eyes fixed on nothing.

"Do you want me to get a skycap?"

"I want you to please take care of Mitch."

Jesus. Does she know? After all this time, does she know everything?

"Sure I will," said Rene, hoping it would end there.

Connie nodded. "I know you love him. And right now, I suspect, he's in a lot of trouble. He's going to need someone he trusts." She finally brought herself to look at Rene. She *was* awfully beautiful. Hard to resist. "Can he trust you?"

"I think he can," answered Rene, trying not to show signs of nerves. She felt naked in front of Connie. Undressed to her soul.

"Okay," finished Connie, opening the car door. "You better go then." She wheeled a single piece of carry-on luggage behind her and never looked back.

Instinct. Wives can smell it on a man.

That's what Rene's momma used to say about her father when

he'd come home from an afternoon of sport fucking. Wives just knew, that's all. And Connie knew. Just like Rene's momma. Never saying a word to anybody about it. Especially her man. Wouldn't give 'em the satisfaction of knowing that they were ever hurt.

Traffic was backed up along the airport route—strange for that time of night. Both southbound lanes were awash in the glow of red brake lights. Rene checked the inset clock in the dash: 12:18 A.M. Quickly she thought back to Connie. *Did she know where she was going? Was there a plan in place wherein Mitch simply used Rene as a key? What was any of it about?*

A mile ahead, she could see dark smoke reflected in hundreds of stalled headlight beams. Ahead there was an overpass and the faint glow of a gasoline fire. Rain, she thought. Slick roads. People die. Tens of thousands in traffic accidents every year. Thousands in Texas alone. Drunks who thought speed was something ol' boys did on Saturday nights in their souped-up muscle cars and big-wheeled trucks.

At 12:32 a fire truck rolled by, hugging the soggy shoulder. Shortly thereafter followed Texas state troopers who quickly coned off north-bound traffic into one lane and then began siphoning off the stalled southbound cars. Rene dropped her car into gear and followed the taillights.

As she neared the accident, she tried not to look. She feared traffic accidents. Had nightmares about them. But she looked anyway, drawn like all rubberneckers to face the grisly reality of human road kill. All she could see was the glow of a car ablaze in an empty irrigation canal. Flashing lights. Paramedic crews. No dead bodies. At least none she could see.

"Move it, move it, move it!" A flashlight blasted at her windshield, waved ahead by a state trooper. Beyond Rene was a clear highway. She'd slowed to a near stop, trying to get a good look at the wreck. And now the trooper wanted her moving. "Let's go, lady!"

She hit the accelerator and left the scene behind her for the open road ahead. Taillights moved far ahead as traffic spread out along the slick asphalt. She found herself hugging the right lane and driving slowly. She was chilled. Her spine tingled in a sudden, unexplained terror. And for another three hours, she wouldn't know why.

At four in the morning, Murray would call with horrible news. Mitch had been in a terrible car accident. McCann supporters were behind it. And the candidate's car had been totally destroyed in a fire.

Mitch hadn't had the time to feel bad about manipulating Rene. He knew she was in love with him. There was nothing he could do about it. He had been too busy devising the last part of his plan.

The easiest move to plot, proved the hardest to execute. All the instructions were in Mitch's memory. Ten years old, at least. From a time way back when Mitch was assigned as a co-litigator for an insurance carrier plagued by auto accident fraud. The plaintiffs were a cagey bunch of scam artists that would lease expensive cars, insure them for serious cash, and stage accidents in which the car and incriminating evidence were always consumed in a fuel fire. The carrier was forced to settle with the criminals and pass along the cost of doing business to its overburdened clients.

Mitch never forgot the simplicity of the swindle. All he needed was a deserted highway and a steep turn on a rise, often found over a concrete flood channel. Fortunately for Mitch, this was a scenario easily duplicated on Airport Route 15.

For three hours now, he'd gone from plot to conclusion over a hundred times in his head. He'd eventually settled on executing the final act of his play on the southbound route from Houston to fit the story he would later tell in sketchy detail. Simply told, the candidate had just dropped his wife at the airport, and the accident had occurred on the rain-slicked highway on his return trip to the Island.

All Mitch had to do was work the scam.

One. He picked the accident scene—a stretch of empty highway—looking it over before any state trooper or good Samaritan had the opportunity to stop, help, or ask directions.

Two. He circled back northbound on the highway to an exit ramp where he stopped the car and, with a tire iron, smashed the windshield as if it had been struck by a thrown object.

Three. He opened the gas cap to the car, took off his bloodied shirt, and, inch by inch, made a wick by twisting it into the gas receptacle.

That was it.

He climbed back in the car, once again waiting for a gap in traffic where he couldn't see headlights for miles behind him. Then he rolled the Volvo back into the southbound lane and raced the mile or so up to the predetermined accident scene. In the candidate's mind, it was all so painfully simple. Easy.

Stay calm, Mitch. Execute. And wait for help.

At the turn in the highway, he rolled his car onto the soft shoulder and set the parking brake. Heart pounding in his throat, he opened his door, stepped out, and checked the highway once again. Not a car in sight. All he had to do was light the wick and release the brake.

Light the wick? But with what?

A sudden panic set in. A flaw in the plan. He didn't smoke. Didn't keep matches in his car because Fitz would always want to smoke, and that damned lingering smell was enough to make Mitch sick. There was the cigarette lighter, but he had pulled the plug on that when he bought the car. Had he thrown it out? Or just left it in the glove box?

He dove back into the car. First, digging into the console between the two front seats, he dumped everything out. No lighter, though. Next he went for the glove compartment and madly rummaged. He tossed everything out. Owner's manual. Audiotapes. Tissues. And no damn lighter!

Lights appeared. Far in the distance, two tiny headlights made the grade. He began tearing at the car, reaching under seats and between cushions. In moments the car would be upon him. A witness. A good Samaritan. And Mitch, caught with both doors open. Wick shoved into the gas tank.

Shut the doors! Crawl inside! Hope the car passes!

He stretched across the driver's seat to the passenger door, reaching to swing it shut, when suddenly he remembered the whereabouts of the lighter. It was in the passenger door compartment. *That's* where he'd put it. Slipping his fingers into the compartment, he fished around and came up with the lighter. Fast as he could, he jammed it into the receptacle and, while waiting for it to pop back up, peered through the rain-spattered back window to check the oncoming car.

The lights brightened. High beams, he thought. Maybe a mile out and closing. He rechecked the lighter. It had already popped up. He pulled out the plug and crawled from the car to the rear. He grabbed at the bloody shirt. He didn't know if it would ignite. All he could do was try. So this was it. He stuck the lighter to the wick and prayed.

God, let this work. Please, God . . .

The wick flamed and seared his right hand, catching fire to the bandage. He screamed as he stumbled backward, only to see those headlights fast approaching. He had to scramble. It was now or never. He leapt back into the sedan and released the parking brake. Instantly the heavy car began to roll, and Mitch with it, his injured arm suddenly tangled in the damn seat belt. The car picked up speed. Mitch running along with it, trying to pull free. Jesus Christ! It was going to drag him down the hill and into the channel! He was going to die!

And the rest was a blur.

He recalled stumbling, the seat belt caught around his arm and hauling him down the embankment with the car. Then there was the left rear wheel. If he didn't go over the concrete wall and into the canal, he thought the seat belt might give way and the wheel would roll over him, smashing his skull.

As the car plunged toward the flood channel, the seat belt finally gave way and, miraculously, the left rear tire skipped over Mitch as the car tumbled headlong into the canal, striking the concrete floor and erupting into flames. The last thing he remembered was the fireball. The sky alight, reflecting in the light rain. The fireball and the smell of his singed hair, curling from the heat.

Lila Gonzales, the driver of the oncoming car, saw the explosion and nearly lost control of her car. Unmarried and middle-aged, she was returning to the Coast from a Texas State Social Workers' Conference in Houston. In her experienced opinion, the event had gone far too late into the evening. She was tired, frightened by the slippery road, and deathly afraid she'd fall asleep at the wheel and end up a double statistic. Unmarried *and* dead. Lucky for Mitch and his bungled plan, she was driving well under the speed limit.

The explosion rocked her vision, lighting the whole sky. Out of reflex she stomped on her brakes, sending her little Ford Fiesta into a four-wheel spin that nearly put her into the center guardrail.

Jésus Mío, thank Saint Christopher, there were no other cars, she later told the news cameras.

When she recovered control of her vehicle, Lila sped toward the wreckage ahead of her, crossing her heart and blurting a string of Hail Marys until she was out of the car and stumbling down the steep bank toward the fire. She found Mitch unconscious, shredded, and stranded at the edge of the canal. He looked as good as dead. Battered, bloodied, but alive.

A horn boomed. She screeched, nearly falling into the trench from fright. A southbound trucker had pulled over, his tractor-trailer rig stretching across the horizon of the overpass. He leaned his meaty body out the window and belted out, "You called for help yet?"

In the ambulance, Mitch regained partial consciousness. A paramedic came into focus. And Mitch thought he heard him say, "You're gonna be okay, buddy." Trying to talk, he gagged and could only cough into the oxygen cone. Leaning closer, the paramedic calmed him. "Just relax. We got ten more minutes drivin' until you see a doctor."

But he couldn't relax. The aching from his right hand surged all the way up to his shoulder. "My hand," he mumbled from underneath his mask.

"What's that, buddy?" asked the paramedic, turning his ear to the cone.

With consciousness came unfinished business. Mitch hadn't finished the play. The plotting wouldn't work unless he laid that last piece of pipe. He shoved aside the oxygen cone and choked out a single word. "McCann."

The paramedic stuck the oxygen mask back onto his face. "I said *relax!* Don't try to move. You might have some broken ribs. You talk, you could puncture a lung."

The other paramedic moved into his obscured periphery. She wore a sweet face that reminded him of Gina. Round and cherubic.

"What'd he say?" she asked.

"I think he said 'McCann.' "

Then she recognized him. "Oh my God. You're him. You're that guy."

Mitch was done, the curtain falling on his performance in three acts, each folding together into an accident that pointed the finger at Shakespeare McCann. The other pieces, he thought, were buried or burned or dumped in a stump-filled graveyard some sixty miles from the scene of the accident. Gina was dead. He couldn't fix that. Connie was safe and on her way to San Francisco.

And he was alive.

The pain swarmed him, his consciousness fading. He lost sight of the paramedics. It was 2:18 in the morning. Mitch wouldn't wake again until six.

Fitz heard about the accident closer to four when he got a call from Murray. He was still up, worrying. Ahead of Fitz lay November third and a potential slam-dunk. A win for Mitch and for the spin meister's sagging career. Numbed by more alcohol, Fitz was on an emotional roller coaster he could no longer control. And when it was all over, what then? Another campaign? No way, he'd decided. It was time to move on. Win or lose, it was time for a career change.

From the moment Mitch had uttered "McCann," word was passed ahead to the dispatcher that candidate Mitch Dutton was on his way to the Blessed Virgin Hospital at Cathedral City's north end. When his home phone number turned up unlisted, the hospital called the campaign office, where they got a service. Service calls were forwarded to Murray. Murray called Fitz.

"Something about McCann."

"Who said?" asked Fitz.

"I just got off the phone with the dispatcher," said Murray from the hospital. "The paramedics said something about McCann. That's all I got."

Murray was first to arrive at the hospital, though all the EMT crew from the accident were still finding excuses to hang around. He did his best to eavesdrop. It turned out they were all waiting for the TV cameras to arrive and interview *them.*

"What's it like down there?" asked Fitz.

"Well, the PD's squared off against the state troopers in a jurisdictional squabble. And the woman who found him . . ." Murray referred to his notes. "Name's Lila Gonzales. She's here too."

Poor Lila, she was still seated in the waiting room, hoping someone would take a statement so she could go home and get some sleep. She didn't care much. She didn't know Mitch Dutton from Shakespeare McCann. Didn't vote.

"Anybody seen him?"

"Family and that's it."

"Connie there?"

"Nobody can find her. No answer at the house. So I sent my roommate over. I hope Mitch doesn't kick my ass for waking up his wife."

"Don't worry about it. I'll cover you," said Fitz. "Just sit tight. Don't make any statements. And I'll be there in a half hour."

"Yes," answered Shakespeare.

"He's in the hospital. Car accident. But he's alive, from what I hear."

"Anything else?"

"There was a fire. His car was toast."

"Any other bodies?"

"What do you mean?"

"Was there anybody else in the car? Like some woman?"

"Woman? I didn't hear anything about a woman."

12

The scheduled Sunday press brunch was abruptly moved to the Blessed Virgin. Rene was in charge of disturbing the South County media chorus's early morning peace, clueing them in to the news of the accident and the unexpected change of venue. All on two hours' sleep.

In a black DKNY suit, she hit the campaign office and Power-Booked her way through the list. No, brunch would not be served at the hospital. They would try and have coffee and maybe some doughnuts. But this was politics, where sudden turns of events were expected. The campaign's position?

We're just glad he's alive. Aren't you?

She left the task of redialing the unanswered numbers to an ardent volunteer before she piled in her car and started for the hospital. In the quiet, she fused it all together. The call from Mitch. The warning. The drive to the airport. The fire on the highway.

God, Mitch. What've you done?

The concrete statue of the Blessed Virgin fixed atop the old teaching hospital had oxidized to such a degree that it bore a rusted patina, resembling dried blood. The locals fittingly called the hospital Bloody Mary's. Appropriate, considering it boasted the busiest trauma room in all of South County. More car accidents were rolled through the Blessed Virgin's doors in a month than through most other hospitals in a year.

The press conference was set up in one of the residents' small amphitheater classrooms, crammed with cameras on tripods, battery packs, monitors, and hundreds of yards of cable that snaked to each of the stations' news vans. The crews either complained about the cold coffee and stale doughnuts, or speculated about the fate of Hollice Waters, now missing well over a month, and wondered over their radios if the local stations would actually preempt football in exchange for the live microwave feed. Ten o'clock came and went. The natives were getting restless.

"Let's get this over with," was shouted from the back of the room, to much agreement.

"Just hold your water," cautioned Fitz, uncertain himself as to when Mitch would appear. Then he read off the scratch Rene handed to him. "We've got ER chief Dr. Ally Schwartz here to give you the medical update."

"We're just completing a few tests," she said, offering little more. "All I can say is that, considering the description of the accident scene by the paramedics, it's a miracle that Mr. Dutton is still alive."

While the doctor fielded questions, Rene stood to the side and fanned herself with Xeroxed copies of the prepared statement she'd so meticulously written. Those halfsecrets she was holding so tight strained at her insides, proving far more powerful than any infidelity. The secrets smelled like death. Sweat beaded through her fine makeup. She had questions that Mitch would have to answer.

"Where's the eggs Benedict?" joked Mitch as he was wheeled into the press conference.

He wore a borrowed robe, a fresh plaster cast for his broken hand, and a Houston Oilers baseball cap to cover his bandaged scalp and singed hair. At his request, he'd forgone the expected pain drugs in exchange for a lucid tongue. And as he waited for the room to hush, he floated Rene an encouraging smile.

Just listen, was the telepathic message he was sending her.

"Today we'll see what's more important to Texans," continued Mitch. "Politics or football."

The line barely lightened the room. A fusillade of questions followed, overwhelming him. His head ached.

Fitz stepped in to hold up his hands until all were hushed. "The candidate has a statement."

Mitch cleared his throat and leaned closer to the banded microphones. "Thank you for coming. I know it's Sunday and most of you have families waiting for you. So I'll make this brief." Through heavy-lidded, bloodshot eyes, he made an effort to connect with the faces before filling his lungs with air and speaking forcefully from the wheelchair.

"Early yesterday evening, my wife received a call from her great-aunt in Eureka, California. She is recovering from a stroke. She'd missed the last flight out of Cathedral, so I drove her to Houston and kissed her good-bye," he began without even a sideways glance at Rene. He wanted this to sound real and matter-of-fact. Then he unwound the tale.

"Sometime after midnight, upon my return to the Island, a pickup truck followed me and pulled alongside my car. I could not identify the occupants even though I know there were at least two. They were shouting from an open window. And though I don't recollect everything they said, I recall abusive language and something about, and I quote, 'campaigning for McCann.' A moment later, they pulled ahead of me, and one of them in turn threw an object which smashed my front windshield, causing me to lose control of the car.

"I've already given complete statements to authorities from the South County Sheriff's Department and Texas State Highway Patrol, copies of which will be made available. I thank God for my survival. I thank Ms. Lila Gonzales and Chuck Bonnerz for coming to my aid. And I thank the efficient emergency technicians along with the doctors and nurses of the Blessed Virgin Hospital for my care through the last ten or so hours."

At what looked like the end of the statement, the media crush became alive with questions, reporters muscling to get theirs in first. But Mitch held up his cast-covered right hand to halt the onslaught.

"In answer to the obvious question, I must first say that after Friday night's debate, I am embarrassed at my behavior and I humbly apologize to my opponent. Violence is never an answer to a problem, and especially has no place in politics."

"However . . ." He then switched hands, lowering his right and raising his left index finger as if to draw a punctuation point in the air. "Let me add that where I sought only to throw a single punch at the man called Shakespeare McCann, retribution like this will not stand. If my opponent, or any supporters of my opponent, seek my untimely demise before or after election day, then let me offer this one caveat. I will not run. I will not hide . . ."

And then, as if to direct the message right through the cameras to Shakespeare McCann himself, he let slip with his own subtle impression. "Y'all know where to find me."

With a nod to a nurse, Mitch was quickly wheeled from the room. Representatives from the Highway Patrol moved in to take the podium and block the wave of insatiable media that crushed after the candidate. Dr. Schwartz squeezed in to address the horde. "I'll be taking questions on the condition of the candidate if you'll please just relax!"

On the outskirts of Meyers stood an aging, gated community built upon a bulldozed plateau, called Villas Las Lomas. The one-story homes were once pricey, boasting private security and one of the few views afforded in the pancake-flat real estate that was South County. But the glory days were gone. The homes were well tended, but reasonable and middle-class.

As for the homeowners, they hadn't a single complaint about their most famous neighbor, other than they never really saw him. Shakespeare's old-model Caddy would usually be spied easing into the automated garage around midnight, only to be gone by daylight the next morning. The curtains were always drawn. The gardeners would come and go. The same went for the pool man. When local Republicans thought to stop by one weekend and give Shakespeare a neighborly high-five, they found a note next to the doorbell reading:

Please don't disturb. Candidate sleeping.

The rental house had come furnished. Shakespeare's only additions were the TV. The easy chair. And the computer. The rest was the landlord's flea-market leftovers. Easily abused. The motel-quality paintings were stacked behind the couch, replaced by thousands of those colored three-by-five cards. Each scrawled upon and pinned into the drywall, floor to ceiling.

Scattered on the tabletops were piles of Internet printouts and downloaded speeches. *Reagan, Buchanan, Kennedy, Goldwater, LBJ, Nixon, Gingrich, Clinton, Perot.* And loaded like ammo on top of the big-screen TV were hard-core videotapes mixed with sound-bite rewinds of "Larry King," "CNN Inside Politics," "Washington Week in Review," and "Meet the Press."

This was the McCann bunker. But that particular Sunday, it was church. In the semidarkness, where the black density of night bled into daylight, Shakespeare sat in that big easy chair, drinking mescal from his chalice, a Rush Limbaugh gift mug.

Mitch Dutton was on the big screen.

"Why doesn't somebody ask him where's the fuckin' body?" bitched Shakespeare to the worm, scratching his temple with the muzzle of a revolver registered to Hollice Waters. He'd pinched the weapon from the dead writer's glove compartment before he'd sunk the car in the reservoir, briefly amused that, when it came down to it, for all his aspirations, Hollice was like every other Bubba in Texas. Gun in the glove box. Six-pack in the trunk.

But Shakespeare was no longer amused. He was deadly drunk and thinking of the possibilities. Suicide was always an option. Swallow the barrel and pull the trigger. Bring it all to a peaceful ending. The cold muzzle felt good against his skin. It smelled of cleaning oils, and the cylinder spun like grease.

I killed Hurricane. I killed Hollice. I killed that rich little bitch. Must I now kill Dutton?

The worm wouldn't answer, so he sucked it back into his throat and washed it away whole with the rest of the booze. The bottle was drop-kicked into some dark corner to join the other empties.

He opened the revolver's cylinder and dumped out all six .357 rounds onto the carpet. Dropping to his knees, he retrieved three cartridges and randomly reloaded them into the gun, snapping the cylinder shut and giving it a hard twirl. "Speak to me!" demanded Shakespeare, screaming out against the recessed corners of the tract house.

There were no answers. At least, not from the worm. All he could hear was the TV talking at him from Bloody Mary's Hospital of the Damned.

It's me or him. One of us will die. One of us will win.

A fifty-fifty chance. That's what he gave himself to beat the revolver. He spun the cylinder once more, drew back the hammer, and took the muzzle into his mouth. His thumb slipped easily inside the trigger guard and rested.

Fate is my teacher, said the worm from inside Shakespeare's hollow gut.

He pulled the trigger and the hammer fell with a resounding, metallic thud. The empty cylinder echoed. The lot was drawn.

As he turned his attention to the TV screen, the fog lifted and he was renewed. He celebrated fate's decision by leveling the revolver and unleashing a single shot. The gun bucked and the TV summarily imploded in a display of sparks and crinkling glass. The tube smoked and sizzled in the bullet's wake. In Shakespeare's universe, Fate had just chosen sides.

13

Mitch wasn't certain what he'd say once he was faced with Rene. She'd done him the favor of a lifetime, a chore dutifully performed with no questions asked. In exchange, she'd surely expect an explanation. Some form of truth.

Barely an hour after the press conference, after all the media had folded up their equipment and gone back to what was left of their weekends, he found himself alone with his onetime lover. She'd done her best with the rabid press. Based on little more than what Mitch himself had fed them in his brief statement, she had played it all over for them as simply as he had implied. Politics had gotten dirty. Criminally so.

They'd been left by the autograph-seeking doctors and nurses to some peace and quiet, the only person within earshot, the deputy sheriff stationed outside the door. Rene found a comfortable chair next to the window, staring out. The day outside had started warm, but was quickly turning overcast as was the custom with Gulf skies. There could be a storm brewing. Or the next day could be fit for a bluebird. This was the South Coast and them was the rules.

"I could tell you everything," began Mitch from his hospital bed. "I trust you that much. But with the truth would also come a burden. Crimes have been committed. A little knowledge could be dangerous."

She kept her arms folded. She lowered her head. "I think that's a decision for me to make."

"Accessory after the fact. Potential for perjury. I don't think so. If I tell you, it's conspiracy. I keep it to myself, I stand a chance of getting out of this clean."

"Does Connie know?"

"She knows some. But she's in danger. And you will be, too, if you stay too close."

"In danger from who?" she asked sharply. It was all so Goddamn mysterious. "You? Or Shakespeare McCann?"

"I want you to take that job."

"I said I turned them down."

"If they wanted you last week, the offer'll still be good."

"I said no."

"Then you're fired."

Rene swiveled a look at Mitch.

"Don't look at me like you didn't hear what I said."

"I heard you. It's what you're not saying—"

"The less you know, the better! Just pack your bags and get the fuck outta Dodge!"

"Before what?"

"Before you get hurt."

With a knock at the door they were interrupted by the appearance of the one and only Warren Redden, Cathedral's ever-so-politic police chief. He stood in the doorway, literally with hat in hand. He gave a gentleman's nod to Rene, then turned to Mitch. "Is this a bad time, Mitch?"

Mitch paused. What did Redden know? Anything? Mitch had to guess he didn't. The hulking chief wouldn't have been standing in the doorway looking so lost had he suspected a damn thing. Mitch took in a deep breath, choosing to let the painkillers steady his voice. "It's okay. Come on in, Warren."

"I had something to speak to you about," said the chief. "In private."

"I guess that means it won't be a *public* endorsement."

"Aw, Mitch. I told you before. I'm not political."

"Well, I'm a candidate for office, and this is as private as it gets. Anything you have to say, you can say it in front of Ms. Craven." Then he winked at her. "She can keep a secret."

The chief stepped over to the bed, pulling up a chair. He was a big man, and the chair proved rather small. He sat at the edge of it, leaning close to Mitch. "I know," started the chief, "that I've steered kinda clear of the endorsement thing. I wanted to remain . . ." The chief was searching for the words, so Mitch helped him.

"Unbiased?"

"Unbiased. Yeah. That's it," said the chief. "You know, I'm not good at the diplomatics."

"Nobody said you were," jabbed Mitch. He was in control, certain now that the chief didn't know a damn thing.

"A month or so back, I'm afraid to admit I might've voted for that Shakespeare fellah. Republicans, you know, are better with the crime stuff."

"That's the rumor. But you know I aim to change that," said Mitch, smelling the endorsement coming. A little late. But not unwelcome. Relieved the chief apparently had no other motive for the chat, he offered his hand. "Never too late to climb aboard. Welcome to the party."

But he was wrong. The chief recoiled. "Mitch. I said this ain't no endorsement."

Rene sat up in her seat, suddenly frightened. Had Mitch played him all wrong? Then into Mitchell's waiting hand the chief slipped a short pistol, rubbed clean down to the serial numbers scratched from the frame. A .380 semiautomatic. "That episode last night. After your debate, I shoulda seen that comin'," said the chief. "Anyhow, I figure a lefty like you wouldn't want a gun around. This one belongs to nobody. You use it to protect yourself, you say you got it from a friend. Not the chief of police. I never seen it."

With that, the chief stood and addressed Rene. "I know you, missy. You're the one that whips up those news boys into all that free advertising for Mr. Dutton here. Now, I'm not gonna be reading anything about what you seen here, am I?"

She simply nodded to Mitch. "He's the boss. What he says goes."

The chief turned back to him. "Don't go lookin' at this as some kind of . . ."

"Endorsement?"

"My job's just seein' that nobody gets hurt," said the chief, though he gestured to the gun. "Least nobody that don't deserve what's comin'."

Donning his police cap, he left. Rene waited for the door to close behind him. "For a minute there, I thought he was going to arrest you."

"For what?" asked Mitch, letting the pain mask his nerves.

"For punching the opposition on TV."

As far as he was concerned, the conversation was over. "I want you to take me home."

"I thought I was fired."

"You are. Just look at it as your last assignment."

Despite the doctors' requests that he stay another night for observation, he bundled himself into a borrowed sweatshirt, pocketed the gifted pistol along with handfuls of free prescription samples, and made it out the back way of Bloody Mary's. Rene was waiting in her Maxima.

The thirty-five-minute drive to Flower Hill went by wordlessly. It hurt for Mitch to breathe, let alone talk. And Rene, she was planning her speedy withdrawal from the campaign, Cathedral, and Texas.

At the house she left the engine running, not even bothering to take the car out of gear. He got out of the backseat and circled around to her open window. He looked pathetic, hobbled and hunched over.

"I'm gonna miss you," he said, trying to leave things on some kind of sentimental note.

"I hope you do," she said, staring dead ahead. She wouldn't even look at him.

"Well, I will—"

Rene booted the accelerator and the Maxima kicked up leaves as it hurried back down the drive.

You had it comin', Mitch.

After a minute standing there, he resolved he wasn't in the mental shape to assess his entire relationship with Rene at the very moment when she'd left him in the dust of his own driveway. Walking around to the back of the house, he took the spare key from a small magnetic key holder attached to the back side of an electrical subpanel.

Key in the back door, he entered the house, disturbed not to be met by the dogs. He worried a moment before remembering Connie would have arranged for a neighbor to care for them. But the canines' absence added to the strange darkness that enveloped the old house. Without Connie or the dogs, it felt empty and ominous.

Mitch locked the door behind him, then checked the answering machine, bypassing all the incoming calls until he found the expected message from Connie. It was short, almost tragic-sounding.

"Mitch, it's Connie. I hope you get this. I hope . . . I hope you're okay. I'm at area code 415-555-8372. It's Sunday morning. I love you and I miss you."

He scribbled down the number, then summarily erased all unheard messages from the machine. Pocketing the slip of paper, he poured himself a glass of water and, pillaging the refrigerator, shoved two cold hot dogs in his mouth. His head was throbbing along with his casted right hand, which with every pounding pain felt as if the swelling alone would crack the plaster. He needed to swallow the prescriptions with food. Then he needed to call Connie. It was 4:20 P.M.

The armload of goodies was dumped on the desk in his study. Prescription drugs, cordless telephone, the pistol. Mitch swallowed the prescriptions without so much as glancing at the dosages, then dialed the number Connie had left for him. The pills kicked in quickly. And soon after, he was sleeping. Or so he thought. The stoned apparitions were more memory than fiction. A haze of pain and distortion.

Mitch talked to Connie. She was well but worried. What happened? Where was Gina? Was the campaign over?

Somewhere between sleep and more pills, he showered, changed into a pair of jogging sweats, switched on the TV. Live 9 News recapped the press conference, followed by an investigative follow-up on the ongoing Hollice Waters mystery. There were no clues. The Mexican National Police were assisting the Cathedral PD, the South County Sheriff's Department, and the FBI. Not a solid lead had turned up in over five weeks. But rumors abounded, thanks to the McCann campaign camp. Sandy Mullin was the newest suspect, with alleged ties to organized crime and the Mexican Mafia. The story ended with the new, Vidor Kingman–owned *Cathedral Daily Mirror* offering a twenty-five-thousand-dollar reward for information leading to the arrest of the killer.

That was if Hollice Waters turned up dead.

The 11:35 P.M. Sunday Sports Final followed. Football scores sandwiched in between paid political advertisements. Commercials for county supervisor. For state Senate. For Congress.

FACT: *Mitch Dutton is a rich corporate attorney.*

FACT: *Mitch Dutton once represented a Houston chemical company convicted of dumping thousands of gallons of toxic waste into our precious Gulf waters.*

FACT: *If elected for Congress, it's clear that Mitch Dutton would fall victim to rich corporations that would spoil our environment for profit.*

QUESTION: Can we trust rich corporations and their lawyers to know OUR business?

Paid for by Citizens for a Clean Environment.

Pro-McCann ads. Pro-Dutton ads. Anti-Dutton, Anti-McCann ads. Mitch remembered thinking, *What kind of person could vote and know they'd chosen wisely?* It was a battle of two evils. The devil you know versus the devil's advocate. Kingman's third party candidate was the invisible man.

The clock read 1:00 A.M. Time for more pain medication. He washed it back with a glass of scotch. He remembered staring at the Weather Channel. A storm was swirling up the Gulf. The newsman was calling it Tropical Storm Les. Mitch wondered who made up those storm names. Would there one day be a storm named Mitch? Or Connie? Or Shakespeare?

Then memory crashed into dream.

Yes, he'd showered. That much was real. He pictured it. Remembered it. But all of a sudden there was so much blood! Gina's blood! It was dried and wouldn't scrub off. On his hands and his face. The TV viewers must've seen it! How couldn't they? The doctors too. Did they think it was Mitchell's? Had someone scraped a sample from him to keep for DNA tests? Jesus, that would be as good as fingerprints!

Mitch jolted awake, sucking air into his lungs, his eyes wide and dilated—then at once, relieved that it had all been a dream. The TV. The news.

Or was it?

He was still in darkness, parked in his chair with the TV beaming at him from its appointed shelf. Surrounding him, though, was the aftermath of his own medicated unconscious. A nearly empty bottle of scotch, four fully consumed frozen meals on the couch, dirty cereal bowls. Pillows and blankets strewn. A thinly scattered *Daily Mirror.* And not a Goddamn lick of it remembered.

My God, he thought. *And it's still dark? It can't be any later than 5:00 A.M.*

To make matters more confusing, there was the television program. He didn't recognize it. He watched so little TV as it was. But he knew enough to know the program he was watching was some prime-time sitcom. And they didn't rerun primetime shows just before dawn. He aimed his focus to the desk clock. His eyes were still fuzzy in the dimness, so he switched on the lamp. The light blazed and his eyes squeezed shut. Yet he'd seen the clock, and the image remained latent against his eyelids.

8:36 P.M.!

Couldn't be. Mitch waited for his eyes to readjust before he looked again, just in time to see the digital numbers switch to 8:37. He dove for the newspaper, automatically looking at the upper right-hand corner for the day and date.

Tuesday, October 27.

Slowly it began to come together. The meals. The empty bottle of booze. The TV. Mostly, the two prescription bottles left open, colorful capsules spilled across his desktop. All of it lost without a single recollection.

My God. Two full days? Lost?

Crossing his study, he opened the door to a dark living room and a chilling breeze. The front door yawned, unlocked and swinging wide open. Leaves were blowing about with each gust. Then, at the top of the stairs, the door to the master suite slammed shut! He jumped, his heart in his throat and throbbing at warp speed. Was this his house? And who the hell was upstairs?

"Connie?!" shouted Mitch from his subconscious. But she was in California. Safe and sound. At least, that's what he thought.

Fear got the better of him. He rushed back to the study and the phone, punched up 911, but found no dial tone. The lines were dead. He grabbed the pistol and his spare set of keys and ran out the front door to Connie's Mustang. The wind and leaves swirled.

"Fuck!" he shouted. The spares belonged to the Volvo. The Mustang keys were always in Connie's purse. She carried both sets in case she ever locked a pair inside. Reeling, Mitch took a look back up at the big old house with its darkened windows and steeply pitched roof. It scared him. Anybody could be inside. A medicated delirium. *Sure*, he thought. But to hell with the house. And feeling no compulsion to return, he backed down the driveway, eventually pulling the hood of his sweatshirt up over his head and breaking into a slow, painful run. His back ached. His ribs were sore and swollen. The cast on his arm, heavy like a handful of lead.

Push it, Mitch. Push, push, push.

After he'd put a solid half mile between himself and the house, the runner's engine warmed, the knotted muscles loosened, and for the first time in days, his mind seemed clear and conscious. Faster, he ran. Harder, begging his endorphins to ease the pain.

14

"*McCann of the People Campaign Committee.*"

"I need to speak with Shakespeare McCann."

"*The campaign office is closed. This is the service. Do you want to leave a message?*"

"Maybe you didn't hear me. I said I *must* talk to Shakespeare."

"*I said this is the service, sir. We only take messages.*"

"Do you know where I can find him?"

"*'Fraid not. Now, if there's a message—*"

"It's important. He *must* get this."

"*And the message is, sir?*"

"I'm thinking."

"*I'm waiting.*"

"Okay. The message is from Ron. It says, 'Deandra is having both parties for cocktails.' "

"*Deandra is having a party.*"

"No! I said, 'Deandra is having *both* parties for cocktails.' Tonight, nine o'clock."

"*How do you spell Deandra?*"

"Fuck if I know."

"*Excuse me, sir?*"

"Just read back the message."

"Deandra is having both parties for cocktails. Tonight at nine o'clock."
"Thank you. And I'm sorry for my language."
"You should be."

Tropical Storm Les was formed in a barometric crush off the north coast of South America and whipped its way up the east coast of Mexico and back out into the Gulf. Farther south, another disturbance stirred in the same low-pressure vortex. The crashing of the two turned Les into a full-blown hurricane that threatened to lick the boots of South Texas if the normal trough of Arctic-cooled jet stream flattened and failed to blow the SOB back out to sea. Cathedral was used to such threats. Most storms evaporated into nothing more than harsh winds and rain, speculation by the locals, even a hurricane lottery. But not all.

As with most locals, had Mitch known of the hurricane warning, he wouldn't have given it a second thought other than, maybe, to spur fond political memories of the late, great George Hammond. The gusts of wind weren't enough yet to knock him off his feet, and the rain was insufficient to soak him to the point of discomfort. He was running. And when those endorphins kicked in, they killed *all* the pain. He was feeling strong in body, crystal in clarity, and lucky. The sloped harbor road was leading him to safety and the arms of his ol' Uncle J.

The Harbor Motor Inn was a former Motel Six he'd rescued from bankruptcy when Jasper Hargroves retired from a life of shrimping and roughnecking on offshore oil rigs. The deal was sweet, put together by his lawyer nephew. Jasper had the cash from the sale of his three-boat fleet, and Mitch knew the owner of the motel in question. The twenty-room dump overlooked the harbor that Jasper'd known his entire life. Mitch helped make sure his ol' Uncle J would never have to trade in the sea air for a mainland retirement plan.

He made the downhill turn onto Salisbury Street, nearly a straight shot down to the harbor. A car passed on the left as memories came and went. He remembered the old sailor had been fond of giving the boy Dutch rubs on his crew-cut scalp. A sign of affection, surely. But Mitch never let on that he hated those moments and that Uncle J's nasty, raspy voice scared the bejesus outta him. Yet a bond had formed aboard those summer shrimpers. Uncle J and Mitch, allies in the war against the old man, Quentin Dutton. Lousy boss and lousy father. They'd bitch and moan, swap stories, and Jasper'd teach Mitch a thing or two about life. It was, indeed, a sweet deal.

Young Mitchy was going to ask Uncle J for a room, no questions asked. J would keep the secret. In exchange, though, he would surely give Mitch a ration for not returning his calls during the campaign. That much, Mitch could handle. The trade-off was cheap by recent comparisons.

Nearing the harbor, he twisted onto Lefcourt Place, otherwise known as the Loop, a quarter-mile stretch of two-lane connecting back onto the main drag whether a driver was headed east or west. He cut safely across Beach Road and onto the Loop, switching back to the oncoming lane as the street swept sharply toward the waterfront. There, at the bottommost portion of the turn, the motel was saddled against the hill, neatly tucked below the main road. Its yellow fluorescent sign surely blazing until dawn. The neon beacon, calling out *Vacancy* to lonely fishermen skunked from spending too much time in any one of the many hard-luck harbor bars, blinked at Mitch as if to signal him that all was clear. Cross the road and enter.

But he stopped to catch his breath. He needed to find a smile for old Uncle J before pushing through the motel office doors. And that's when the cramps set in, locking up his thighs and practically hobbling him dead center in the street, right at the bottom of the Loop. *Dammit*, he thought. He hadn't stretched before the run as was the habit of most experienced runners.

From the south came headlights, roaring down the blacktop and straddling the center line. Dead on and bearing down at Mitch. With his left foot he tried to shove off, but his leg wouldn't respond. It shut down. The muscles were bound, bent, and left him crashing to the pavement, the gravel stinging his palms.

He crawled a single arm's length before he looked up for the last time to see the car rushing headlong down the center path. He tucked a shoulder underneath himself and rolled away from the swerving car. He felt a rush of wind as it roared past, its wheels set on a track that led away from the motel. Aiming not at Mitch. But at some other unknown destination.

Then came the image. A picture tattooed crisply in his memory as if the car were still rushing at him, twenty feet away and prepared to expel him of his last breath. It was a license plate.

ISPIN4U.

Mitch twisted upon the pavement, dialing his vision back up the Loop to the receding car. The brake lights flashed and turned off the Loop down toward the harbor, giving him a brief yet distinctive profile of a BMW 540 . . . Fitz's leased BMW.

ISPIN4U.

Once again balancing on his feet, he stumbled back to the edge of the road opposite the motel to get a good look down into the harbor. Through the misting rain it wasn't hard to pick up the BMW's lights. He followed them all the way down to a nearly empty parking lot along one of the docks reserved for recreational boats. In the distance he could make out Fitz's rotund figure, hustling from the car out onto the dock. All the way to the end where a launch idled, waiting to pick him up. Fitz awkwardly crawled aboard and the boat quickly pulled away.

"Gawd, ding it!" bitched Jasper at the sound of the door buzzer. Rail-thin, bald to his empty follicles, feet up in his La-Z-Boy lounger, TV remote in one hand and a fifth of low-budget bourbon in the other. But drunk, he wasn't. He liked to lick at the bottle more than guzzle it. If he drank too much, he'd get sleepy and miss the news. The remote control allowed him to jump back and forth between broadcasts to catch each and every weather report. See if all them weather boys were in sync with his own predictions.

The office buzzer rang again.

"Customers," grumbled the old man. He was in the customer business. He just wished the customers would all check in before ten. Because that's when the first newscast would begin, and he didn't want to miss the damn weather.

A curtained partition and a storage closet were all that separated J's apartment from the front office. And when Jasper saw the hooded man standing outside the glass door, he thought to retreat and pocket a pistol. He was a cautious man. He hadn't been robbed . . . *yet!*

The stranger knocked at the glass as Jasper turned back toward the rear. He gave him one more look in time to see Mitch pull the hood down. "Uncle J! It's me. Mitch!"

"Well I'll be a sonofabitch."

Jasper reached underneath the counter and buzzed him in. Mitch shoved through the door with the ultimate non sequitur for a candidate only days away from November third. "Jasper, do you still watch the boats?"

"Is that any way to say hello to your ol' Uncle J?"

Mitch walked around the desk and pushed to the rear. "You old sea snake. You gotta have a telescope!"

"Sure I got a scope," said Jasper, who was caught off guard, following Mitch back into his own apartment. "You know, you never called me back! That musta been months ago!"

There it was, not five feet behind Uncle J's La-Z-Boy, a telescope on a tripod, pointed out through a big, curtained window and aimed toward the harbor. Mitch threw the curtains open and stepped behind the scope. He put his eye to the viewfinder, but saw nothing but pure blackness. "Why can't I see anything?"

"You okay, sonny boy?" This was a Mitch Uncle J didn't remember. The boy was never this urgent. Always polite. Well behaved. In control. A *natural* politician. "How about some bourbon? Settle your ass down some."

Mitch fiddled with the focus ring. All he could see was black. "Just help me, Uncle J."

Jasper reluctantly crossed over to the scope and simply removed the lens cover. "Keeps the fuzzies from the carpet off the lens."

Relieved, Mitch aimed and focused. He started at the dock where the launch had picked up Fitz, then panned back and forth while tilting toward the horizon.

"Whatcha lookin' for? Maybe Uncle J can be good for *somethin'*."

"A launch. It was headed out of the small boat docks . . ." Mitch steadied the scope. In his viewfinder appeared the cigarette boat. Only it was tethered to a large yacht anchored midway in the harbor. With the powerful scope it wasn't hard to make out the name. *Deandra*. Vidor Kingman's summer retreat was parked again in Cathedral's waters. Only now it was fall and there was a hurricane brewing a hundred miles offshore.

"Find what you're lookin' for?"

"Yes, sir," said Mitch, his tone turning polite and thoughtful. "Give it a look, Jasper. Tell me what you think."

Mitch stepped away from the telescope and made room for him. He stuck his face down onto the eyepiece. "Yup. That's a big boat. Kingman's. Why's he parked out there when they say we got a first-class hurry on the way?"

"He bought the paper. He's probably living on it."

"Which one? The *Mirror* or the *Breeze*? I sure hope he didn't buy the *Breeze*."

"The *Mirror*," answered Mitch. "You think the hurricane's gonna hit?"

"Fifty-fifty. If I were a bettin' man, which I am, I'd say no. High pressure's still hangin' on to the Coast. My guess is it gets pushed over to Louisiana and heads south. Takes a good piece of Florida real estate before she's done.''

"It's called Les.''

"Les, Leslie. Who the crap cares? All hurricanes are bitches. Don't matter what name they give 'em. Now, tell me, sonny. Why didn't you return my telephone calls back in *June?*''

Mitch had his eye back to the scope's viewfinder. He was following Fitz along the gangway to the upper deck. Once there, the rotund show runner was greeted with a hearty handshake from a smiling Vidor Kingman.

So Kingman's finally come on board, thought Mitch, briefly forgetting the last couple of days and Kingman's eleventh-hour endorsement of the environmentalist candidate, Peter Dunphy. The political animal that had grown inside him calculated the timing of the handshake. Kingman's the pragmatist. Like most businessmen, he wants to be on the side of the elected office. The events of the past week, the turn in the polls, had paved the way for the moment when Kingman would come aboard and acknowledge the future congressman with some flashy display of unconditional support. Clearly Fitz was still on the job.

Goose bumps rose on his neck as another man came into view. Stepping from the shadows with all smiles for Fitz was none other than Marshall Lambeer, reluctant proxy for the McCann platform. He shook Fitz's hand with the relish of a car salesman about to make a deal.

What's this? Some kind of political powwow? In whose honor?

All of a sudden Mitch was boxed. He was there to ask Uncle J for a room. A quiet, safe place. Where he could think things out. Then, just when he felt he had enough information to make a cogent new plot for those final campaign days—to leave the fog and reenter the race with his life intact—Fitz Kolatch nearly ran him down on his way to make a private date with Vidor Kingman and Marshall Lambeer. Common sense turned, once again, into gobbledygook.

His broken hand was aching again. Probably swollen from the run. But fearing another blackout, he wanted to ask Jasper for nothing stronger than an aspirin.

"Do you still have a boat?'' he found himself asking.

"A little outboard. Gets me around when it's warm and I wanna drop a line of stink bait.''

"Take me out to that boat?''

"Now I know you got something loose," sparred Uncle J. "Got a hurricane comin'. Or weren't we just talkin' about it?"

"You said it wasn't gonna happen."

"Puttin' up ten dollars is one thing. Puttin' up half a brain and a boat is another."

"All I want is a ride out there. I'll get back okay. I got friends on that boat."

"That's what you come here for? To get a ride?"

Mitch didn't want to argue. He was already on a short rope with ol' Jasper. He had to deal. "You give me a ride, I'll have that drink with you. But later. We'll piss on my old man. How's that?"

"You promised to call me back, sonny boy."

"I didn't. And I'm truly sorry."

"When you make it to Congress, you call me back then?"

The irony was thick. Congress? Mitch wasn't thinking past the next hour. Congress may as well have been a million miles away.

And better left there, thought Mitch.

"Okay. I'll call you back."

"From Washington."

"Talk about whatever you want."

Jasper grabbed his keys. "Okay, then. Let's get wet."

15

Stepping from the launch and climbing *Deandra*'s gangway, Fitz was hoping *not* to get wet. The gusts were getting stronger and everything was slippery. At least when it came to handshakes, nobody would notice the sweaty palms. At this point, nerves didn't matter. Only action.

Marshall was swell enough, thought Fitz, offering up some flattering words as they followed Vidor downstairs and into a carpeted smoking cabin. Carved teak ceiling, red leather swivel loungers bolted to the floor, wet bar, oil paintings.

"You ran a good one, Fitz," said Marshall. "Looks like you got yourself a winner."

Platitudes aside, Fitz wasn't there for concessions or early congratulations. He was there to hear the offer.

So let's get to it before I get seasick and retch.

"How about a drink?" offered Vidor with that deep, mellifluous voice. "We're smoking Cuban. Rafael Gonzales. On a night like this they'll go swell with some Irish single-malt."

The rolling of the boat was about as much as Fitz could take. His stomach was already knotted. He declined and found a comfortable seat with a window overlooking the muted city lights. A horizon was what he needed. Something to help keep his balance.

"Marshall's right. You ran a good campaign," complimented Vidor.

"Thanks," said Fitz. "I have a stellar candidate."

"So you do," Vidor rolled along. "Too bad I picked the dark horse."

"The environmental candidate?" asked Fitz, certain his question was leading enough to get the real answer: McCann.

"Oh, I'm sure y'all saw through that ol' card trick," said Vidor. "My environmental campaign, a thinly veiled effort to cut into some core Dutton votes."

"So you've been behind McCann from the start?"

"Marshall and I go back a ways."

"Back then we were both sweet on the same girl," chimed Marshall.

"But *you* married her," added Vidor.

Fitz understood. Marshall was a respected campaign man. Dyed-in-the-wool Republican. The matchup between him and McCann had never made sense.

"And I thought you did it for the money," said Fitz.

"Loyalty had *somethin'* to do with it," answered Marshall. "But when it comes down to it, I'm as mercenary as the next show runner. That's why you're here."

That's why Fitz was there, all right.

Palms sweating again, he rubbed them along his pants legs. "Changed my mind. I'll have some of that single-malt."

Vidor gladly poured. "Winning campaigns is about success," he started. "Now, somebody say I'm right."

"You're right," cued Marshall. "Now, don't treat Fitz like he's a dumb-ass. Just get to it."

He would. But nobody told Vidor what to say or how to say it. Vidor had a speech planned and he wanted to hear himself deliver it. "You win a campaign, your price goes up. The next candidate pays more. Show runner, spin meister, whatever you call yourself, it's about money. Market price." He brought the drink over to Fitz. "Now, tell me I'm right."

"Your stock goes up if you win."

"And down if you lose," continued Vidor. "Dutton musta gotten you for a rock-bottom deal."

"Going up against Hurricane Hammond?" reminded Fitz. "He wasn't supposed to win. The campaign was just supposed to be a showpiece."

"For you or the candidate?" asked Vidor.

"Both. Mitch Dutton wanted to put himself out there. See if anybody would bite."

"And you?" asked Vidor.

"I wanted to show what kind of bite we could take out of a Republican stronghold."

"In essence—if you lost, you'd actually won."

"Yes," answered Fitz.

"Turning losing into winning."

Marshall capped it again. "You didn't expect to win?"

"No." Then Fitz shrugged and smiled as he let the whiskey slide back over his tongue. "But here we are."

Vidor stood dead center in the cabin as it slowly rocked back and forth. His long legs expertly cushioning the roll of the water, keeping his head still as he spoke. "George Hammond died tragically. You were instantly on the side of the front-runner, caught up in a dogfight with some pip-squeak challenger nobody ever heard of. Then nearly lost the race, had it not been for a fluke punch in a televised debate."

"He had the momentum. We didn't," admitted Fitz. "The debate turned it around."

"If you win, you won't get the credit," offered Marshall.

"I'll get some. And that's enough. Don't forget, I picked a winner."

"Perception, yes. That's important. Not necessarily credit where it's due. But perception," mused Vidor, who hadn't yet moved from the middle of the cabin. The boom was about to be lowered from on high. Vidor wanted Fitz to know who had ahold of the mainsheet.

"I'm listening," said Fitz.

"I picked McCann to win this race. And I've got only a week to make it happen. I'm asking for your help," said Vidor in his lowest octave.

"In exchange for . . ." pressed Fitz, though he couldn't believe he'd said it. Maybe because he knew he could always retract any agreement. Why not hear the offer? He was in the driver's seat. He was sitting on top of a winner. Entertain the deal. That's why he was there, for Christ's sake!

"King Media is about to merge with a yet-undisclosed West Coast syndicator. The company is public and I expect the stock will double in price. Part of my deal is thirty million in preferred stock already at two-thirds the market value. You follow me so far?"

"Go on," choked Fitz.

"Dutton loses. You're out of a job. Nobody will hire you with the exception of Vidor Kingman, who sees value in Fitz Kolatch and engages him to run his new Southern California enterprise. As part of the deal he receives options on, say, half a million dollars of some of that aforementioned stock. Late the next year, with the syndication deal closed, Fitz Kolatch is the Golden State's newest millionaire. All for losing a campaign."

Marshall joined in. "Remember. You weren't supposed to win in the first place."

Fitz's head was spinning. It was one hell of an offer. More money than he could ever imagine from hustling one campaign after another. A retirement package. Yet it was just talk. Words floating on air. A hypothetical result without a plan.

Not to mention the Goddamn ethics of it all! Fitz, are you out of your mind? It could never—Mitch would never—

He backpedaled. "I'm sorry. I thought you asked me out here so you could buy in to the Dutton campaign."

"That's horseshit and you know it!" sounded Vidor.

"He's just negotiating," managed Marshall.

"You say? And what about that prick-tease of a media consultant, Rene Craven?" groused Vidor. "I thought *she* was *negotiating*. You know what I went through to get that cunt a honey-pot position at Com-Atlantic? She's still raking those eastern boys over the coals for a job that was s'posed to get her off the Dutton hump."

Knocking back the rest of his liquor, Fitz wiped his brow and entertained the pair with some facts. "We've got the momentum back. And losing the campaign at this point would require involving the candidate in his own political demise. That's not Mitch Dutton."

"Don't you think I know that?" boomed Vidor. "Why do you think I backed McCann? Because I liked his damn politics?"

"Mitch has his own ideas."

"That's a lotta crap, too. Dutton's as corruptible as the next guy. Get him on the Hill, you watch him learn which hand washes the money and which one picks up the check. My problem is that he *thinks* he's an idealist. He *thinks* he's got all the answers." Kingman finally sat. "And at my ripe old age I don't have the patience for it. I need somebody I can work with. And if it's McCann, it's McCann. End of subject."

The cabin fell silent around Vidor. He let his words hang out there for a while until there came a knock on the door. "What do you want?"

The ship's captain entered. He looked pallid and tired from days at Vidor's beck and call. Yet he nodded with deference to his boss. "Harbor Patrol thinks we oughta tie up somewhere near the commercial docks."

Vidor waved him off. "Fine, fine. Now, leave us alone."

"Yes, sir," said the captain. "Just thought I'd tell you the tide's way up, so it could be bumpy crossing the second breakwater."

Vidor nodded, followed the captain to the door, and, as soon as the captain was gone, locked it. No more interruptions. Marshall took the cue and withdrew a large leather suitcase from underneath a seat cushion. He drew closer to Fitz as he opened the lid and tilted the case to reveal what was inside. The obvious. Cash. Money. But it wasn't for Fitz.

It was street money. The dirty little secret of campaign politics.

Instantly Fitz saw the plan and was shaking his head. "It won't work."

"What won't work?" offered Vidor. "You pay for votes. Buy off some of them partisan poor. Spread the money around, and don't be shy about it."

"And then what?" asked Fitz.

Vidor stood again and drew close to Fitz, punctuating his plan with his finger in his chest. "Then *my* newspaper will raise holy hell about you all trying to buy votes."

"In this campaign? After all that's come and gone?" said Fitz with a laugh. "It's a pimple on a gnat's ass."

"It could turn the tide back in our direction," said Marshall, sounding not entirely convinced himself.

"A week before the election?" scoffed Fitz. "At this point? The only thing that's gonna sink Mitch Dutton would be pictures of him humping some farm animal."

Fitz crossed over to the bar. The boat rocked wildly. But he made it to the bar and poured himself another. "You don't mind, do you?"

Vidor moved in behind him. Close. Towering. "I'm asking for your help, Mr. Kolatch. And I'm offering you a pot full of gold in return."

Fitz poured his drink and knocked back a lick of it, still keeping his gaze out the window toward the ever-dimming lights of Cathedral Island. A shadow crossed his view, though he thought nothing of it. It was just a deckhand. No. Fitz was looking out the window, trying only to see his future.

"You want to turn the tide?" he asked. "Well, it's going to take some kind of personal testimony from somebody close to him. Somebody who is willing to lie. Someone who is willing to say that Mitch Dutton is unfit to serve in Congress. That he lies. Is unstable. Psychotic, even.''

Vidor smiled and spoke softly. Fitz was playing ball. ''And who might that be?''

Fitz tossed back the rest of his drink. ''It might be me. But I'll need *more* than what's on the table—a helluva lot more.''

A quick smile flashed from Vidor to Marshall, who looked away in disgust. He was there to aid in the breaking down of Fitz Kolatch. Marshall had half hoped for failure. Hoped that Fitz would stand tall, and by his candidate. Dutton wouldn't make that bad of a congressman. Kingman would still be a *gazillionaire*. And Marshall would be happy in his retirement.

Marshall said to himself, ''I gotta get out of this business.''

From the motel window the water hadn't looked that rough. After all, it was *harbor water,* protected from the madness of the ocean beyond by the double breakwater. Then there was Jasper's theory of how to drive rough seas in a twelve-foot outboard. Rear of the boat, full throttle, bouncing off the peaks, staying out of the valleys. The hull slammed crest after crest. Mitch stayed low, tucking his casted right hand away from the rain in the pocket of the borrowed seaman's jacket.

''Bet it hurts like a sonofabitch,'' shouted Jasper over the motor and wind and slapping rain.

''What?'' Mitch shouted back.

''Yer hand.'' Uncle J held up his own right, balled into a familiar-looking fist. ''Yup. I saw it. Live on the TV. Reminded me of the time I whacked your old man. Right across the ol' forehead. Broke three knuckles.''

''Why?'' Mitch had to ask.

''I was drunk and he was being himself.''

''So what happened?''

''He kicked the shit outta me,'' howled Jasper. ''Like father, like son.''

Mitch let the subject drop. He looked ahead to the yacht. They were close. Barely a hundred yards to the gangway. Jasper throttled back and eased the outboard closer, noting that nobody was there to greet Mitch. ''Expected, are ya?''

''Not exactly. But I'll get a ride back to shore if that's what you're asking.''

"Actually, I was hoping for an invite. Supposed to be some kinda beauty inside."

"I'm crashing, Uncle J. And two's a crowd. Sorry."

"Best you board 'er from the bow."

Mitch crawled forward, balanced in a crouch, then readied himself with a foot up on the rail. When the water underneath the bow swelled and the gap between the two vessels closed, he flashed back to when he was a boy.

He'd let the rush of water pushing up the bow catapult him from the shrimp boat to the dock. Sometimes twenty feet into the air. He'd tuck and roll when he'd land, smile on his face, dusting himself off. Maybe a splinter or two, but otherwise okay. All boy. Mitch would look back to the boat to see if his Uncle J had watched the stunt.

He braced for the next swell and pushed off early to avoid the catapulting effect. He was no longer a boy and didn't want to come crashing down on the metal gangway. Instead, he landed steady on his feet, catching hold of the *Deandra*'s railing. The gifted pistol, though, it tumbled from his pocket, clattering off the gangway and slipping into the black water.

"Give 'em hell, sonny boy!" Jasper gave a hearty good-luck wave before shifting into forward and charging back toward shore.

With no captain or deckhand there to greet Mitch, he hung tight to the gangway and felt the rumble of idling engines. And the shifting air brought wafts of diesel to his nostrils.

Memories. *Diesel. Shrimp boats. Churning water.*

He cleared his mind, resolving to climb, crash the meeting, and let *them* do the explaining. He prayed for clarity. Hoped for some answers. If anything, he seemed guaranteed brief asylum from the madness he'd left onshore. There was safety in the harbor, despite the wind, rain, and a threat from the bitch hurricane.

The vessel rocked underneath a large swell and the gutters ran dark. Mitch balanced and aimed for the lights glowing from the cabins below deck. There was movement, shadows cast across the deck. Life. People. The meeting to which he was not invited. Silently, he cursed all of politics and its defiant secrecy against the public trust. The pricks! To his right was a downward stairwell and the door to the smoking cabin. To the left, a lit porthole.

Eavesdrop, Mitch. Get your bearings before shocking them.

He couldn't hear the screams. His ears were buffeted by gusts and his eyes were fixed on the dancing shadows cast from the porthole across the deck. Images, moving quickly. A shadow movie. He didn't want to be seen or discovered just yet. He only wanted to see . . .

. . . and see it, he did.

At first it was all red. A still life of blood and hacked bodies strewn across the cabin. There was Vidor Kingman. His distinctive frame lying facedown on the floor, arms trapped underneath his body.

Then there was Fitz. Poor Fitz. His bloodied, twisted head came hurtling toward Mitch, slamming against the porthole at which he was staring in awestruck horror. He fell backward, screaming, his howls for help falling deaf on the ears of a hurricane wind.

Where's Marshall?

At the porthole appeared Shakespeare McCann, spattered in feral blood and peering through the smeared glass. Could he see Mitch? Mitch couldn't tell, let alone move. He sat there, butt solid and frozen to the deck, back against the rail. Scared even to pull his feet into the safety of the shadow where he was fixed. Motionless. Agonizing. Watching in close-up as Shakespeare McCann scratched his stubbled beard and plotted his next move.

And then . . .

With the wonder of a child and his first canvas of finger paints, McCann took his index finger and marked the bloodied porthole with a message, the letters spelled backward to Mitch:

McCann for Congress.

Taking his cue, Mitch pulled away from the horror show, sliding from his perch and finding his feet. With wobbly legs and shaken vision and balance, he climbed. *Up,* he thought. *Go up.* His instincts were giving the instructions now, drawing him to the top deck and through the swinging, open door of the wheelhouse. Once there, he knew why. The radios. He had to call out a Mayday. Ship in distress. *Deandra* needed help.

God . . . Mitch needed help!

Upon reaching for the radio, he saw the damage. The dials had already been smashed. The handsets ripped from their sockets. "That's right," he said.

He'd have taken care of that. He'd have cut the communications before the kill. The kill! Jesus! It made no sense.

Yet his instincts broke through the confusion. He knew there was always another radio. On large boats, even three or four.

The pilot bridge.

He pulled down the spring-loaded ladder, kneeling to lock it in place.

"Help me . . ."

Mitch screamed, "JESUS CHRIST!"

Marshall was fetal, tucked up underneath the console and bleeding from a blow to the head. Knees to his chest. Beacon-white and convulsing so badly, he couldn't buckle his life preserver.

"I can't . . ."

"Marshall. I thought you were . . ."

"He thinks I'm dead."

"The captain. Where's the captain?"

"All dead." Marshall helplessly held out the buckle toward Mitch. "I can't swim."

Mitch had but one good hand. With Marshall's help, he had two.

No endorphins this time, Mitch. It's pure adrenaline from here on.

With the buckles clasped on Marshall's vest, he nodded upward and asked, "Is there another radio on the pilot bridge?"

"Hurry . . ."

"Say again," said Mitch, easing closer on his hands and knees. "Did you say 'hurry'?"

"Hurry-cane."

He followed Marshall's wide eyes, grabbing hold of the wheel and pulling himself upright. He scanned the high-tech display until his eyes rested on the Doppler, a tracking device keyed in to a satellite-fed weather map. Green crystals blinked in his face, forming a swirl off the Cathedral coast and closing fast. Uncle J was wrong. The hurricane *was* coming in. Dead on for Cathedral.

He dropped back down to Marshall. He had but one more question. After which would come the clarity that he so awfully craved. A renewed sense of purpose. And a plan so final, it was . . .

A final act of public service.

"After you, is there anybody left but him—and me?" asked Mitch.

The old campaign dog shook his head ever so slightly. Mitch grabbed Marshall by the vest and lifted him to his feet. "Can you walk?" Nods. "Can you keep your head above water?" Nods. "Then let's go."

Mitch slung on his own vest and hauled Marshall out the door, down two decks, over the rail to the edge of the churning water.

"The tide'll carry you back to shore. Just keep your head up! Breathe at the crests."

"I'll hold on to you!"

"No. You won't."

"But you're strong!"

"I'm not comin'."

Mitch gave Marshall a shove and the old man was overboard, splashing down between swells and bobbing away from the boat.

The engine room was warm and steamed. Shakespeare, naked to his Wranglers, tacked ahead with his plot, spilling fluid from the spare diesel cylinders as he prepared to start a fire that would consume the boat and the evidence of the retribution he'd exacted. He thought them all disbelievers. Judas goats! Plotting against him. Turning tail. Preparing to endorse the front-runner and probable winner, Mitch Dutton.

If he only knew.

Madness choked the killer into mental asphyxia. Truth was contaminated. Fact was flipped. Turned over like a pancake. The men he'd killed were his last and only allies, having just put the finishing touches on the deal that would've put Shakespeare McCann firmly in the seat of Congress.

Betraying Shakespeare McCann!

The rumble of the idling engines was steady, governed by efficient fuel computers. They could run all night at that speed. Shakespeare wouldn't need that long. Only another ten minutes. Then he'd set the fire and wait for Harbor Patrol to rescue him. They'd find him stranded, clinging to a life raft and ready to tell the tragic tale of a meeting fouled by fire and a surprise explosion.

But the engines revved and engaged. Shakespeare felt the propeller turn as the yacht suddenly surged against the rising surf.

Somebody was driving the boat!

With tools found underneath the helmsman's bunk, Mitch barred both doors to the bridge, port and starboard. And when it came to the life vest, the best he could do was to forget the buckle and tie the damn thing with a simple, one-handed square knot. Engaging the engine prop, he began slogging the boat forward. It was all coming back. And quickly. The harbor. Wheeling the old shrimp boats toward the first break into the Shoot. From there he could cross the second break over to the commercial side of the harbor along with the other fishing boats, oil tankers, and freighters. All of it navigated by memory and city lights. Landmarks picked off hillsides and structures.

Fearing he'd flood the engine with a full-throttle thrust, he eased ahead. If he killed the motor, he was sure he wouldn't be able to get it started again. There were all kinds of safeties aboard such boats.

He pinched two more notches out of the throttle and egged the vessel on. The sharp V of the hull sliced into the growing tide. Cresting and crashing well beyond the safe harbor speed limit. Yet there would be no patrol boats to sound horns and pull alongside the ship. They were all tied down for safekeeping against the coming onslaught. Jasper's wise voice called to him.

Sailors in the shit, son. They're on their own.

The wheelhouse window began to fog, and Mitch had no clue where the defrost switch was. The only switch he knew that wouldn't kill the engine was the one marked "autopilot." And he was saving that one for the end. He just kept wiping the window with his shirt-sleeve to keep his bearings. The first break was two hundred yards ahead. The water in the channel would be rough. It would try to throw the vessel sideways if he entered on too wide a trajectory. He had to cut it close and at an angle. Risking the rocks before making what looked like a thirty-degree final turn.

Fogged again, he worked his shirtsleeve, keeping a close eye on the outcropping. Then he increased the throttle two more notches. The gauge in front of him topped out at thirty knots, twice the projected speed of the oncoming hurricane. In his head Mitch did the math, adjusted his watch, then went to wipe the window again.

He didn't see Shakespeare right away. His focus was beyond. To the outcropping of the first break and the channel. His angle was good. Once he hit the channel, he'd only have to turn that projected thirty degrees south and leave the rest to the ship's computer. From a flash of lightning directly overhead, the bow turned bright white, and with it, Shakespeare. He stood poised with a ten-foot gaff, which he thrust through the window once he found his aim. The glass exploded inward, followed by a rush of wind and pelting rain.

The gaff caught Mitch right at his heart, a deadly stab guaranteed to kill. But for the life vest. That blessed vest stalled the iron hook millimeters from total penetration, and instead, he was simply thrown against the wall by the force. Another flash of lightning and Shakespeare stood crouching in the window frame like a mountain cat ready to pounce. And he was grinning. "Counselor? I'm not surprised to see you!"

"No?" said Mitch, pushing aside the gaff.

"Hell no! God brought me to the Judas goats who were about to betray me," shouted Shakespeare with a paranoid flair. "And then you to me so I could finally fulfill my Destiny."

Mitch returned to the helm as if to face down Shakespeare in a debate of words. As if to engage him.

"And just what the hell is your destiny?" he shouted to the shorter man, all the while looking beyond into the wind and rain. With a nudge to the helm, he was taking dead aim.

"My Destiny?" Shakespeare smirked. "That's between me and the devil."

Mitch throttled the boat fully and twisted the wheel to the right before bracing for the crash. Before impact, his eyes locked with McCann's.

And the clarity returned. A rare moment of sense and purpose. It was singular and without conflict. It simply . . . was.

The rocky outcropping of the breakwater was just off the starboard side. Shakespeare turned to look, but saw nothing but night and blackened water. He couldn't see what was beneath the water—what Mitch *knew* was there. The hull and the jagged break were about to connect. Then it happened, gouging a four-foot chunk from the *Deandra*'s underbelly. The impact threw Shakespeare clear from his window perch. Disappearing. Gone.

Washed overboard, Mitch prayed. *McCann was gone. Drowned. Dead.*

Mitch lurched forward and pounded his plaster-casted fist on the autopilot button. The red light blinked as the ship's computer took over. All he had left to do was to right the boat into the center of the channel until the compass read due south. The rough waters of the incoming tide rocked the boat as it crested and crashed on wave after wave. He kept a grip on the wheel and married the compass with the loran directional. There. That was it! He was now heading dead into the hurricane. From then on there would be no turning back. Five hundred more yards and the *Deandra* would clear the channel and be in open seas on its due-south heading with destiny.

With a one-handed twist of a pipe wrench, he unhitched the wheel. The bolt spun off easily, freeing the wheel in his hands. From there he tossed it through the open window, shoved the wrench into his pants, and climbed, crawling up the ladder affixed to the helmsman's bunk and pushing through a hatch that led to the pilot's bridge. Water dumped over him and the wind howled in his ears. He couldn't hear a thing . . .

But he felt the animal grab hold of his leg!

From the opening below, the little man clawed and ripped at his pants, pulling him back down through the hatch. Mitch kicked at him and tried to pull himself through the opening. But Shakespeare kept his grip, making it to Mitchell's belt and hoisting himself up. In Mitch's groin, he found another handhold. Mitch screamed in pain, his howls lost against the wind. He wanted to let go. He wanted it all to end. But he found the strength in his left arm to keep his grip outside the hatch, and swung that hard-plastered right hand downward. Mitch couldn't see a thing. Couldn't aim. All he could do was pound away at what he thought was Shakespeare's head.

The first blows landed hard, but the wet cast quickly softened with each connection with Shakespeare's skull. The pain of it shot all the way up to his shoulder. His arm felt like it would explode as he kept hammering until the evil clutch loosened. Shakespeare fell away, leaving Mitch free to climb through the hatch with a dangling right arm and stumble up the stairs that followed.

The pilot bridge was dark, and because of its height on the boat, it swayed with greater momentum with every crushing wave. Mitch huddled by the wheel to catch his balance, wits, his breath.

His purpose.

The right arm was useless, a hanging limb that barely felt attached. So by feel alone, he reached out to connect with the only other wheel on the vessel. The nut felt the same size as the one below. *Lucky*, he thought. With the wrench, he fit the jaws around the nut. Only this one was tight. He had to stand and drop a knee to the wrench. Finally the bolt gave way, as did the wheel. Once he tossed that overboard, there would be no turning her around. It was head-on into the bitch hurricane. Over and out. The rest would be up to Mother Nature and the incoming tide.

Mitch burst from the pilot's bridge, and when he threw the wheel overboard, was nearly cast over with it, clear into the churning water and the thrust of a huge swell. And where was Shakespeare? He didn't much care. He didn't want to know. Dead? Unconscious? It didn't matter. Soon enough it would be over. He only had to reach the stern and throw himself into the channel. The life vest would keep him afloat. The tide would either suck him back into the harbor or crush him onto the rocky break. Either way. It would be over. That was the clarity. The purpose inside him. To live or die no longer mattered. It was simply a matter of doing what needed to be done.

Kill the evil bastard.

The rubber on the third step had peeled away, and with the ship yawing wide to the starboard side, his foot slipped through and he fell, tossed upside down, hanging in the rung, with the back of his head cracking hard against the stairwell. Once again his vision blanked, faded, and slowly returned, only to find the twisted and gashed face of Shakespeare inches from his own. The lips moved. Yet Mitch likened it to a movie out of sync. The words didn't match, though they rang clear.

"There can only be one," Shakespeare borrowed from himself.

The synapses in Mitch's brain found a strange new path, relating the fucked-up campaign trail to a mythical trial fit more for Greeks than modern, civilized men.

But who said politics was civilized?

"You fought like a man," continued Shakespeare. "But you done lost." He began tearing at Mitch's life vest, trying to wrest it from his upturned body.

And Mitch didn't fight. He let the evil man struggle with the buckle, forgetting even that he'd tied it. It was dark and Shakespeare's hands must have been cold and numb. Not even knowing they were fighting a simple square knot. Yet Mitch didn't struggle. He simply focused. His head hanging near the belly of his opponent and his eyes trying to fix on the bloodied blade that rested, sheathed, inside Shakespeare's belt.

Frustrated by the unwilling life vest, Shakespeare reached for the knife. He was going to cut the vest from Mitch, slip it on, and throw himself clear of the doomed ship. When he reached to his belt, the sheath was empty, the button unsnapped. The knife gone, yet not so far.

Mitch closed his eyes and plunged the knife deep into Shakespeare McCann. The sharp blade, sinking into the devil's flesh, twisted easily until it found an artery. Mitch felt a gush of warmth as the blood spilled over him in the frigid, numbing rain. A massive swell rose up underneath the vessel and the *Deandra* heaved heavily to the port side, taking on a wall of water, rinsing Mitchell's act clean with a stinging spray of sea foam and salt. When he opened his eyes, all that was left was the knife in his hands and the sweet relief of a purpose fulfilled.

16

The rest would forever be a source of true wonder. What was memory and what was imagination? To have Uncle J tell the story, it was a daring rescue—an old seaman's last hurrah. Plucked from retirement on the night Hurricane Les blew a messy kiss at the Cathedral shores before it curled back to the sea from which it was born. No sooner had Jasper gone back to his motel when he gave one more look-see though his telescope, only to see that the *Deandra* was not heading across the second breakwater to the safety of the commercial side, but striking a path out of the channel and into the open arms of the hurricane.

His uncle, knowing that not even Harbor Patrol would brave the weather, returned to his outboard and set out to chase down the vessel, secretly praying all along that his adopted nephew had an old sailor's smarts and jumped ship before the *Deandra* cleared the channel and broke loose in the upheaval of the open sea.

And the story grew hazier with each recollection.

Jasper recalled finding Mitch unconscious and bobbing midchannel, with the tide carrying him dangerously close to the rocks. He gaffed him with a boat hook and dragged him onto the outboard, pumping the water out of his lungs until Mitch gagged.

Mitch only remembered drinking the hot rum and eucalyptus.

Jasper served up the sailor's brew only after he'd capitulated on his plan to take Mitch to the local ER. A bed at the motel served hospice enough for the surviving candidate—in exchange for the promise of a full explanation of the events leading up to the rescue. At least those remembered. Mitch owed him that. And days later he eventually disclosed the entire whale-tale to his Dutch uncle over a bottle of good bourbon, knowing J's promise to keep it all to himself was golden as long as Mitch returned his phone calls in a timely fashion.

After that, Mitch connected with Marshall Lambeer.

"How's the weather up there?" asked Mitch over a motel hard line. He'd found Marshall at the show runner's summer house in Maine.

"Fine. How are you?"

"Healing up okay. Gotta look my best for the big night."

"Four days. You must be excited."

"It's been a long road."

"You know, I was sorry to leave the campaign. But my wife, she was sick. Needed to get away."

"I hope she's better."

"Much so. Thank you, Mitch. And good luck Tuesday."

"Marshall?"

"Yeah."

"Whose party was it?"

Mitch could hear the static as Marshall weighed his answer.

"It was our party. We just forgot to invite the guest of honor."

"And he thought it was about me."

"Gotta go, Mitch."

To his death, Marshall kept his secret. After four hours of spitting up the foul harbor water, he had crawled from the stormy waters near the pleasure docks, rested, found a phone booth, called a cab, his wife, then hopped on the first plane out of Houston. Distance was key. His wife's health, his alibi. Retirement had come a week earlier than scheduled.

For Mitch, the dreams of the hurricane were indistinguishable from the true recollections. Had he pulled himself free from the stairwell? Crawled aft and jumped? Or had another wave simply washed him over the side and into the arms of the churning waters that eventually sucked him back into the harbor? Only a vague image remained—from the point of view of a man being tossed from crest to valley amongst the waves in the frenzied channel.

The pleasure vessel, slugging away at the heavy surf, vanishing, then appearing, peak to valley, high water to low, holding a ghostly course into a deadly cauldron of wind and rain.

The *Deandra* vanished never to be heard from again. Her passengers only remembered. Sometimes fondly. Always foolishly. Players in just another political battle that ended with a whimper only days after their tragic disappearance. November third, there would be no curtain calls for Fitz Kolatch and Vidor Kingman.

Or Shakespeare McCann.

Officially, the front-runner was no help when it came to information about that night and its strange events. According to police records, he'd spent the hurricane with his old Uncle J, drowning his fears in booze and talking hurricanes. When the Cathedral PD tracked him down after the storm had been rebuffed by Uncle J's all-but-certain high-pressure system, they sadly informed him that his precious Flower Hill home had been torched. The suspects were McCann supporters. Mitch showed true shock and retired to his motel room to inform his wife Connie of the horrible news.

17

Election Tuesday arrived with no fuss and little fanfare. One storm front after another followed in the wake of Hurricane Les, soaking the first Tuesday in November with three inches of nonstop rain. The voters stayed home, and coupled with the fact that it was a nonpresidential election year, the turnout at the polls was a record low twenty-three percent.

By nine o'clock, broadcasters projected Mitch Dutton the winner.

Mitch sat alone in the same Hilton hotel room at the edge of the same stiff bed, remote control in hand, flipping between stations. It was on all the channels. Mitch Dutton. The winner. Each projection was followed by some vague commentary about the parade of mysteries still dogging the campaign. Beginning with the strange disappearance of Hollice Waters, followed by the tragic boating deaths of Vidor Kingman and campaign manager Fitz Kolatch, rumored to have been cutting a deal on Vidor Kingman's luxury yacht when they had mistakenly braved the hurricane in search of friendlier ports of call.

Then there was the opposition candidate. Nobody had seen him since the debate.

Even stranger were the numbers. Mitch couldn't help but think that had Fitz survived to see the finish line, he'd still be crunching figures just so he might understand the actual outcome. Presumed either dead or having left the county in total disgrace after that ill-fated debate, Shakespeare McCann had still garnered a clean forty-eight percent of the vote to Mitch Dutton's fifty-two. No doubt a closer call because of the damned weather. It was just like Mother Nature to have a say in the outcome.

Connie emerged from the bathroom, dressed and ready for the victory gala that would take place three floors below. The open bathroom door threw a spotlight onto Mitch that was uncomfortable. He asked her kindly to close the door or turn out the light.

"It's not like you to sit in the dark. Since you're the one seeking the bright lights," she joked. He gave her a strained smile and switched channels. Once again they were announcing the victory. "Looks like you're a congressman."

"Looks like it."

Sitting next to him, she laid her head on his shoulder. He liked that. It felt right that she was there with him to share the underwhelming win. Since her return from California, they'd hardly been apart. In pieces, he'd been giving her the real story of his victory, for that's all she could take and as much as he could give. Pieces. Eventually she would know everything. But for now, it scared her so. And with the baby on the way, neither was taking chances. Tender loving care was the order of the day. It would be so for a while.

With her makeup left to complete, she left his side with a soft kiss and returned to the bathroom. He leaned back on an elbow, forgoing the channel-surfing for a more pensive pose.

Congressman.

The TV coverage switched to a live remote at the Dutton gala, where Mitch was rumored to be giving a victory speech any moment now. *If they only knew,* he thought, *how far from victory he actually felt.*

The cameras zoomed in on Rene Craven, looking lively and spinning for the home team and Congressman-elect Dutton. The day before, she'd tendered her resignation from the campaign in a letter to Mitch. It was a professional correspondence, to the point and matter-of-fact, but read between the lines, it was a sorrowful good-bye. The campaign had crushed her. She'd lost a friend to it, and a lover. Also, in the end, no answers had been provided. No explanations to the carnage the campaign had left in its wake. And she knew enough not to ask. Mitch would never tell, plainly for her own protection.

Despite his warnings, though, she'd stuck it out. He owed her. One day he'd pay her back.

In her letter Rene described her new job. She was leaving campaign politics for commentary, accepting an offer with a Memphis television station as an on-camera political reporter. *It was her*, he thought. As he watched her spin for him on the hotel-room TV, she looked like a million bucks. With her silky drawl and attractive looks, the networks were sure to make offers, luring her to New York, Chicago, Los Angeles, or, God help him, Washington, D.C.

When he'd finished reading her letter, impressed with her stately ability to turn a phrase, leaving out any hint of longing or the brief affair, he thought he'd caught a bare whiff of her perfume in the envelope. He'd put his nose to it again, but only smelled the glue from the envelope flap. There wasn't even a smudge of lipstick to be found. She'd licked it clean before sealing the letter inside. That was her way.

A knock came on the door. From the other side Murray's familiar voice was calling for him. "It's getting about that time, Congressman." Mitch could hear Murray's chuckle at the very end of "Congressman."

"Soon enough, Murray. Thanks."

"Okay. But the animals are restless!" Murray had already hit Mitch up for a job in the D.C. office. Mitch had promised to give it some thought.

When the TV cameras panned the crowd of hard workers and well-wishers, he tried his best to recognize the faces. Some he knew. But not a name would come to him. All those people who'd worked so diligently to get him elected. All for naught. If they only had a Goddamn clue as to what it had actually taken to win the race and the numbness it had left in the candidate's soul. The only thing he could say for certain was that he loved Connie. That when he looked at her, there was true feeling. And the rest was just pretend. Later, when giving his acceptance speech, he would pretend to be victorious, humble, thrilled, in control, and deserving.

Congressman Mitchell Dutton.

Connie called out from the bathroom. "Was that Murray?"

"Yes," answered Mitch.

"Is it time?"

"Whenever you're ready, sweetheart."

He was in no hurry. He was watching the TV show that had become his biography. They were back to the bubbleheaded anchors who were waxing brilliantly about rising campaign costs and the rumor that the Dutton/McCann fracas had topped Cathedral's all-time spending record for a local congressional race.

No shit.

Oh, yes. The costs were high. Shoop. Hollice. Gina. Fitz. Vidor. All of them dead. A chill slipped along Mitch's spine.

What about George "Hurricane" Hammond? Had Shakespeare really had a hand in that? Why not? Was it a setup from the very beginning?

The thought terrified Mitch, who'd tried desperately not to be terrified again since Uncle J had pulled him from the channel. He was shaking, and across the screen, images flashed that were not made for the airwaves. He was flashing back to the horrors he'd witnessed, the hell he'd crawled from to emerge victorious. And he couldn't seem to control himself. His breathing quickened. He couldn't seem to catch his breath. "Connie—" he wheezed. "Connie!"

In a flash she was there at his side, sliding onto the bed with him and whispering in his ear as she held him tight. "Ssshhh. It's okay. It's okay, darling. I'm here. It's over."

Moments passed and he emerged from his horrible fugue. His pulse returned to double digits, but the sweat stuck to his skin. His shirt was stained and his hands were clammy.

"What was it?" she asked.

"I don't know," said Mitch, his voice barely a whisper. "Some kind of panic. I saw—I saw death on the TV."

"It's over. He's dead."

"I'm covered in blood."

"You're sweating. That's all."

"I lost the house. It burned."

"We can rebuild. As a family."

"Where are the dogs?"

"They're fine. They're at the Wrights'."

Mitch nodded. The reality check was over. She was there. And she was all he'd ever need. "I love you."

"And I love you," said Connie. "Now let's dry that shirt. I'll get the blow dryer."

The telephone rang. He thought it might be Rene wondering when he'd take the podium. Between rings he picked it up, bringing the receiver to his ear.

"Yeah, it's Mitch."

"Yeah. And it's your old man."

He was caught speechless. Six months of trading calls with the codger, machine to machine, message to message, without a whit of contact.

"Surprised, ya. Didn't I?" said Quentin Dutton.

"You could say that. How'd you get the number?"

"Called Doc Dominguez. He said you'd be gettin' on the TV any minute now."

"It can wait," said Mitch.

There was a long silence. Two men, father and son, each waiting for the other to make a move.

"Congressman, huh?"

"Looks like it."

"Well, I'm not surprised."

"You're supposed to say you're proud."

"Well, if you'd let me get around to it."

"I won't hold my breath."

"Good idea."

Another long silence. Then it was Mitch's turn.

"So you ready?" asked Mitch.

"Ready for what?"

"To be a grandfather?"

"No kiddin'."

"No kiddin', Pop."

"Well, I'll be . . ."

Was it his father, Uncle J, or some nameless schoolteacher? Mitch didn't remember. But somewhere along the line he'd been told that history was written by the winners. The Greeks did it that way. As did the Romans, Napoleon, Stalin, Mao, Kennedy, et al. The same went for Mitchell Dutton. He was the winner in his own dangerous contest. And how he got there would be told solely by Mitch. It was his story to tell. After all, who was left to dispute it?

As the weeks turned to months, he practiced the story in his mind. Sharpening his whereabouts, his recollections, replacing the facts with his own historical fiction. Doing so eased his soul, and eventually the nightmares began to recede.

Sadly, though, nobody seemed to care. Nobody ever asked if he was anything but the duly elected Gentleman from Texas. All anybody ever wanted to do was shake Mitch Dutton's hand and offer certain congratulations for winning a tough race. It was over. The news machine no longer seemed to work on conspiracies, only on what was next. For South County that was a series of corporate takeovers and plant closings. The only absolute remaining was that Mitch was the winner. How he'd gotten there was no longer relevant.

The legacy of Shakespeare McCann seemed to vanish as quickly as he'd appeared. The loser was rarely recalled—only in the brief recognition of a peeling bumper sticker on the back of a southbound pickup truck. His epitaph was written as the polls closed, and talk of him watered down to mere gossip. As for his populist message, that was washed away with the endless November rains.

Duck hunters found Gina's body during the first week of December. The November rains had left the plains between Cathedral City and Houston afloat in casual water with no place to run off. Waterfowl had flocked to Mother Nature's newest waterway while odd-shaped hunters, decked out in uniforms of camouflage and safety orange, braved the subfreezing mornings to bag their legal limits.

A father-and-son pair, the boy carrying a single-shot 410-gauge he'd just gotten for his tenth birthday, discovered poor Gina's remains while floating decoys in the short darkness before dawn. At the shock of the awful sight, the boy dropped his new gun into the shallow water and lost it forever. After a twenty-minute hike back to the father's four-wheel-drive, the Cathedral City Police were raised on the CB radio. The funeral was four days later.

It would be five years before Hollice Waters's body was discovered. And though identification was difficult, an autopsy eventually revealed that foul play and a sharp knife were the causes of death. But without a suspect, the story barely made page three of the corporate-owned *Cathedral Daily Mirror,* Hollice's life proving as disposable as the paper he'd written for.

There was one front-page story the newspaper was keen on, appearing only six months into Congressman Mitch Dutton's freshman term. It was a fluffy Sunday piece on the birth of Mitch and Connie's first child. A boy they'd named George Jasper Dutton.

Privately Mitch had declined the blood test that would prove he'd fathered the child. Neither he nor Connie cared to know the truth. They loved the child as their own and planned to buy him a pony.

Last heard from in June, Mitch was negotiating with the Hammond estate to buy ol' Hurricane's Virginia horse farm. The family was said to be giving the new congressman one helluva deal.